Rosh Hashonah
5768

To Danny Benants

Best Wishes for a happy, healthy Jewish year!

Rabbi McVicker

DEEP BLUE

Meir Uri Gottesman

A TARGUM PRESS Book

First published 2007
Copyright © 2007 by Meir Uri Gottesman
ISBN 978-1-56871-434-9

All rights reserved

No part of this publication may be translated, reproduced, stored in a retrieval system, or transmitted in any form or by any means, electronic, mechanical, photocopying, recording, or otherwise, without prior permission in writing from both the copyright holder and the publisher.

Published by:
TARGUM PRESS, INC.
22700 W. Eleven Mile Rd.
Southfield, MI 48034
E-mail: targum@targum.com
Fax: 888-298-9992
www.targum.com

Distributed by:
FELDHEIM PUBLISHERS
208 Airport Executive Park
Nanuet, NY 10954

Printing plates by Frank, Jerusalem
Printed in Israel by Chish

I dedicate *Deep Blue* to the
memory of my three holy ancestors
named Uri:

Reb Uri of Strelisk
yahrtzeit 23 Elul 5586 (1826)

Reb Uri of Rhotin-Stretin
yahrtzeit Lag Ba'Omer 5649 (1889)

Reb Uri of Podolsk
yahrtzeit 3 Tishrei 5677 (1916)

*May their holy memory
bring a blessing for Israel.*

Amen!

Acknowledgments

With gratitude to the Almighty.

Special thanks to my dear wife, Susan, for being a wonderful *eishes chayil* and partner.

Thank you to the Targum staff, particularly Miriam Zakon, Diane Liff, Avigail Sharer, and Bracha David.

I wish to acknowledge the memory of the late Rabbi Moshe Dombey, *z"l*, whose tireless efforts contributed so much to the greatness of Targum Press.

PART ONE

THE WILL

ONE

"Ladies and gentleman, please be seated. Mr. Bookman will be in shortly."

The small group gathered in the boardroom of Bookman and Bookman, one of Toronto's most prestigious law firms, self-consciously seated themselves around the huge, polished mahogany table. Although they were family, brothers and sisters-in-law, they spoke in hushed, respectful tones. The tall, book-lined walls, the stern faces that gazed down at them from richly framed portraits, the dark maroon curtains; all reeked wealth and power, all elicited a reverence bordering on awe.

There was tension in the room. The brothers smiled nervously at each other, the wives tried to make whispered conversation, but their attempts were stiff and stilted. Their grandfather's will was about to be read, and the next few minutes would affect the rest of their lives. How had Zeideh — Captain Elijah — distributed his fortune? With Zeideh, no one knew — no one ever knew what Zeideh did or why. Alexander, Solomon, and Uri glanced at each other and shifted in their seats, waiting, waiting.

They were kept for about ten minutes before the large oak door at the far end opened abruptly, and Edwin Bookman strode briskly into the room, flanked by two juniors. Uri began rising respectfully, but when he saw that everyone else remained seated, he fell self-consciously back into his chair. He did not see the smirks that flitted over his brothers' faces.

Mr. Bookman did not look up. He opened the thin file that lay before him on the table and lifted a sheet of paper. Finally, he looked up, peered over his glasses, and nodded curtly.

"Let it be noted for the record who is in attendance. Please introduce yourselves."

"Alexander Schiffman."

"Ruby Schiffman."

"Solomon Schiffman."

"Zahava Schiffman."

"Uri Schiffman."

"Chaya Schiffman."

Mr. Bookman peered round at the faces. "So who is Eerie Schiffman?"

A low laugh rippled through the room. Uri lifted his hand like a schoolboy.

"That's me. My grandfather called me Eerie instead of Uri — a bit like Johnny instead of John."

Mr. Bookman could not contain a chuckle.

"Couldn't the Captain find a better designation than Eerie? You're not eerie, are you?"

Again, Alexander and Solomon snickered, a bit louder this time, and their wives could not suppress a smile.

Uri tried to ignore them. *Eerie eerie shir dabeiri...*

Bookman lifted the will and addressed the group.

"As you know, your grandfather, Elijah Schiffman — the Captain — was my good friend for many years. You also know that he passed away four months ago. As executor of his estate, it is my responsibility to represent him now that he is not here himself, and read out to you the disposition of his estate."

Bookman paused and carefully wiped his glasses. No one breathed. Bookman smiled inwardly — no one ever breathed at this moment. He replaced his glasses and began reading the legal preliminaries in a drone-like mumble. Finally he came to the heart of the will. It was Zeideh's own words:

"I was deeply saddened when my only son, your father, Leo, died at an early age. He was a good son, with a good heart — but he was not blessed with years. But it is not for us to question G-d's will. You, my grandsons, have given me great comfort. You are all good men, you have all found excellent wives, and you are raising decent families. I am glad that I have been able to leave you some of what I acquired to help you go through life."

Edwin cleared his throat momentously.

"To my eldest grandson, Alexander, and his wife, Ruby.

"I bestow the family mansion at 412 The Riding Path, the house, the servants' quarters, the garage and its contents, all the furniture and paintings. They will be the exclusive possession of Alexander and Ruby Schiffman."

Alexander Schiffman's cheeks flushed red, and he gasped. Ruby wept with joy. The mansion was theirs — theirs!

"*Mazel tov*," Uri said to his oldest brother, "*Mazel tov*, Ruby —"

Solomon sat silent and pale, hardly breathing. Zahava sat immobile — waiting.

"To my grandson, Solomon, and his wife, Zahava.

"I bestow my beloved boat, the *Swift Current* — with the dock and marina facilities, the restaurant, and all its accumulated revenues since my passing. Solomon Schiffman will be its sole owner, proprietor, and manage it as he sees fit."

Solomon couldn't contain himself. He jumped out of his seat and jabbed two thumbs up.

"Yes! Yes! Yes! We got the boat!"

Zahava began clapping excitedly.

Mr. Bookman took off his glasses, sighed, and gave them a patient look.

"Please, Mr. Schiffman, let me complete the reading of your grandfather's will with proper dignity."

Solomon finally contained himself and sat down. "*Mazel tov*, Solomon," Uri said.

"Finally, to my youngest grandson, Eerie, and his wife, Chaya.

"You have given me great pleasure with your desire to dedicate yourself to Torah study. I know that you are very sincere, and I have felt much pride. To help in the way you have dedicated yourself, I bequeath to you my personal collection of the Talmud, which I know you will put to good use.

"To help you materially, I bestow upon you ownership of ten thousand shares of Gortel stocks. I hope they will assist you in supporting your fine family.

"There is one other item to be disposed of, but I have given instructions to my executor, Mr. Edwin Bookman, and he will deal with it at the proper time.

"May you all be blessed, and may you use your inheritance wisely, carefully, and in good health."

Bookman looked up. "The letter is signed and witnessed:

Your loving Zeideh,
Captain Elijah Schiffman."

A profound silence descended on the room. Uri looked at Chaya and smiled. Her cheeks had colored.

Ten thousand shares of Gortel stock — ten thousand! Not to mention Zeideh's own *Shas*! Uri knew about it, but had never really seen it. Zeideh kept it in his private, locked office in the great mansion. Uri searched out his brothers to share their joy, but they had an odd look on their faces and seemed to avoid his gaze.

Edwin Bookman coughed significantly and lifted a second sheet of paper.

"It is customary to have all assets appraised before we execute the actual transfer of ownership, in case there are any questions or objections. I had all of Captain Elijah Schiffman's assets appraised by

Leoncorp, a well-established and respected appraisal firm. I am able to give you the following figures.

"Alexander and Ruby Schiffman:

"The property known as 412 The Riding Path has a current appraised value of —"

Bookman cleared his throat and Alexander and Ruby balanced on the very edge of their seats.

" — A value of two million, three hundred and fifty thousand dollars."

"Whoo, whoo!" Solomon shouted joyously. "Alexander, you hit it big!"

Alexander could not contain himself. He jumped out of his chair and started clapping his hands deliriously. His wife's face shone with excitement.

"Ahem," coughed Edwin Bookman impatiently. "Ladies and gentlemen, I really would appreciate it if you would control yourselves for just a few minutes, so I can read these figures in a dignified manner. Please!"

Alexander took a deep breath and forced himself to be seated. He beamed from ear to ear; his face dripped with jubilant perspiration.

Edwin Bookman next turned to Solomon, who waited eagerly.

"It was much more involved to get a clear appraisal of *Swift Current*, as there are only a few boats in its class in Canada, and no other boat with its...shall we say, unique embellishments."

Even Bookman had to smile, and a snicker rolled through the room.

"But the appraisers did extensive research in the States and even Australia of similar operations, and made projections of anticipated income over the next few years, and matters of that nature. In short, they came up with a pretty fair estimate. *Swift Current* itself has a market value of approximately one and a quarter million dollars, and the total attached assets, including restaurant, marina, parking lot, have an approximate market value of two and a half million dollars."

Bookman peered up at Solomon. "Congratulations, Mr. Schiffman."

Solomon jumped up and shouted excitedly.

"Zahava, we're rich, we're rich! We're rich, Zahava! We never have to worry again!"

In his enthusiasm, he high-fived his brother, Alexander, who shared his excitement.

"*Mazel tov*," Uri cried out to his brothers. "*Mazel tov*, Alexander! *Mazel tov*, Solomon!"

Bookman rapped his glasses sharply against the table, and a veneer of calm returned to the room. Having watched the jubilation with poker-faced dignity, Edwin Bookman lifted his paper again. He looked at the paper, then at Uri, and imperceptibly, his head shook. He seemed hesitant to continue. Finally, Bookman turned to Uri.

"Rabbi Schiffman, you understand that Captain Elijah left you ten thousand shares of Gortel. Now, when he wrote this will, Gortel was worth more than a hundred fifty dollars a share. It was the darling of the tech stocks. But you know what happened to the tech stocks. Gortel stock finished last night at ninety-eight a share —"

"Ninety-eight dollars?" asked Uri.

"No, ninety-eight cents! Where have you been, Rabbi Schiffman? Don't you know what happened to Gortel? It's been on the front pages of the financial papers for the past year."

"I don't read financial papers," Uri answered apologetically. When his brothers broke out in an audible chuckle, Bookman gave them a hard look.

Bookman shook his head.

"I'm sorry you don't read the financial news, Rabbi. Maybe you should. Gortel stocks melted like ice in July. Anyway, as of this morning, the total value of the Gortel stocks that your grandfather left you is...nine thousand, eight hundred and sixty-two dollars."

A shocked, funereal silence descended on the room. Finally, Uri managed to choke out, "Is that it, Mr. Bookman? Alexander received a house worth two million, Solomon was given the boat and land worth two million — and my wife and I receive less than ten thousand..."

Bookman looked down at the table. "Plus the Talmud and assorted notebooks —"

"Mr. Bookman, it doesn't seem fair!" Uri cried, near tears.

Bookman looked at him sympathetically.

"Listen, Rabbi Schiffman. These things happen! When your grandfather composed his will, Gortel was a rising star — the shares were worth over a million! But it collapsed like a busted balloon! Real estate could have burst its bubble, the tourist business gone sour...but, unfortunately, it was Gortel and the tech stocks. I'm sorry, but that's life!"

Uri looked over to Chaya. Her face was white. Uri turned to his brothers, trying to find some sympathy. Alexander looked up at the ceiling. Solomon studied his nails. No one looked at him, except his wife.

Chaya smiled at him bravely. "Uri, it's still ten thousand more than we had before," she said.

Uri took a deep breath, collected himself, and turned to his brothers.

"Alexander, Solomon...Ruby, Zahava... *Mazel tov* to you! *Mazel tov!*"

His brothers looked up at him guiltily and nodded their thanks.

Edwin Bookman rose. "Ladies and gentlemen, the reading of Captain Elijah Schiffman's will is over!"

⛵ ⛵ ⛵

Uri and Chaya drove home from the meeting in silence.

Uri was deep in thought. It was a bitter pill. Alexander, who made a comfortable living in sales, was given the two million-dollar mansion, plus two cars. Solomon, who was a smart financial advisor, inherited *Swift Current* and all that went with it: the dock, the beautiful restaurant, and the waterfront land. Uri, who studied half the day in a *kollel* and supported himself by tutoring students in Gemara was left with...nine thousand, eight hundred, and sixty-two dollars.

What kind of trick had Zeideh Elijah played on him? Zeideh always did things strangely, but this was...shocking! Hadn't Zeideh known that Gortel stock had shrunk to almost nothing? Zeideh passed away just four months ago, and Bookman said that they had begun melting almost a year ago. Did Zeideh forget?

Uri sniffled under his breath.

Chaya watched him through the rear view mirror.

"Uri, are you crying?" she asked.

"I'm not crying!"

She didn't answer immediately, letting him dry his face. Uri stared determinedly ahead, embarrassed.

"What are you thinking, Uri?" Chaya asked.

"I am thinking what a nice day it is outside," he answered glumly.

"What are you thinking, Uri?"

"I am thinking how Zeideh was such a wonderful grandfather, and he loved me so much — at least, I think he did! How could this happen?"

"Uri," Chaya answered. "Don't be angry. This is what Hashem wanted. You heard Mr. Bookman, these things happen in stocks — they go up, they go down."

"I'm not angry!" Uri yelled. "I'm not angry! I'm perfectly calm. But...but it's like studying a piece of *gemara* and there is an obvious, big question — and there is no answer! Alexander and Solomon have plenty already, and now they got more. We're struggling to pay our kids' tuition, and we get...nine thousand, eight hundred and sixty-two dollars!"

Chaya nodded. "Maybe you should discuss it with Reb Klonimos. He was so close with Zeideh, maybe he can explain what happened."

"But what can he do about it now?" asked Uri.

"He's a tzaddik, Uri. Maybe he can give you some encouragement."

It was not an easy matter to visit Reb Klonimos Kalman. He was a *mohel* and a *shochet*, and many people turned to him for blessings and advice. Zeideh Elijah had been his most loyal chassid. Even after the Great Race, when Zeideh became almost a recluse, conducting his affairs from the house and rarely showing himself, he still slipped away three, four times a week to study with Reb Klonimos. If anyone knew Captain Zeideh, it was Klonimos. Maybe he could explain what had happened.

It was not until a few nights later that Uri managed to wrangle an appointment with Reb Klonimos. He knocked nervously at the door of the large house that stood sheltered behind a row of tall hedges. The *mohel* himself opened the door and greeted him warmly, a sweet smile on his face. He led Uri to his small, book-lined study and gave him a seat across a narrow desk piled high with *sefarim*. The only illumination was a green teller's lamp. Uri gazed around the dim room where Zeideh had spent so much of his time, and felt his grandfather's presence hovering about the walls.

Klonimos read Uri's thoughts.

"I really miss your Zeideh, the Captain," he said. "We spent many good hours here, learning and talking. You must miss him very much."

"He was a Zeideh and a father all wrapped up in one. He was the only one who cared about me through my childhood and as I was growing up."

Klonimos nodded and smiled reflectively. "An exceptional Yid."

He looked at Uri, waiting.

Finally, Uri broke down. He shook his head, and his eyes grew moist. "Reb Klonimos! You were my Zeideh's friend – his Rebbe! Maybe you'll understand. Maybe you'll help me understand...what Zeideh did to me!"

Klonimos's face darkened with surprise at Uri's outburst. He leaned forward, staring into Uri's troubled face.

"What happened, Reb Uri?"

Uri told the tzaddik about Zeideh's will. "My brothers, who already make a good living, received millions – literally. And me – with my five children and barely getting by – I received almost nothing."

"How much?"

"Ten thousand dollars – and who knows if it's even worth that now."

"And there was no mistake? That was your grandfather's wish?"

"Absolutely. Zeideh's lawyer read the will."

Klonimos's brows knitted, he shook his head and smiled sympathetically. "*Gam zu l'tovah.*"

Uri raised his hands in anguish. "Reb Klonimos, I know *gam zu l'tovah*. But I have come to you for understanding. You knew my Zeideh better than anyone. The Captain loved you –"

Klonimos shook his head modestly.

"Yes, he did! He hung onto your every word! Reb Klonimos, why did he do this?"

"Perhaps it was a mistake?"

"Zeideh Elijah didn't make million dollar mistakes, Reb Klonimos! Tell me...what did he have in mind? Do you know?"

Reb Klonimos shrugged and looked down at his desk.

"Who can know? Who can know what was in his mind — or what Hashem has in mind?"

"But what shall I do? It's so unfair! Should I contest the will? Bring it to a *din Torah*?"

Reb Klonimos looked at Uri sternly. He shook his head. "And what, Reb Uri, start a terrible *machlokes*? Create such bitterness for yourself and your family? Do you think there will be a *berachah* in such money, even if you get it? No," he said firmly, "that is not the way. That is not the way!"

"Then what?"

"How much did you receive?"

"Ten thousand dollars."

"Then enjoy the ten thousand! Let the ten thousand dollars grow, *yeish mi'yeish*! Enjoy the ten thousand dollars that you did not have before! Thank Hashem for what you received!"

He sounds just like Chaya, thought Uri.

Reb Klonimos grew silent.

"And is that it, Reb Klonimos?" asked Uri "There is nothing more for me to do?"

The tzaddik rose, walked around the desk, and clasped Uri's hands in his.

"Reb Uri! May you have great *nachas* from your beautiful children. May Hashem grant you blessings from deep, deep wellsprings whose bounty you cannot even imagine! May you always be *samei'ach b'chelko*, happy with your lot. Amen!"

"Amen," answered Uri quickly, not quite sure what Reb Klonimos meant.

He escorted Uri to the front door.

"*Berachah v'hatzlachah,*" he said, and then showed him out.

Uri stood for a moment outside Klonimos's house, and contemplated the tzaddik's words. There was no answer for what Zeideh had done — except to have *bitachon*. He shrugged, and smiled to himself. *And that's all, folks!*

But ten thousand dollars was still ten thousand dollars. Uri called Bookman's secretary and made an appointment to sign the necessary legal papers.

"When is Mr. Bookman available?" he asked.

The secretary seemed rushed.

"To sign papers for the receipt of your estate? It doesn't really matter if Mr. Bookman is present — it is a very simple matter. One of Mr. Bookman's junior associates can handle it, or even Gladys, his personal secretary. Any time is fine."

Uri made an appointment for the next week. The shock of his meager inheritance had worn off. He and Chaya had lived modestly up to now — Zeideh was always closefisted — and now they would not have much more than before. He wished Alexander and Solomon well; they could enjoy their bounty with his blessings. The Almighty had sent him a test, and he must not transgress "Thou shalt not covet!"

A week later, Uri swung open the heavy glass doors of Bookman and Bookman, and presented himself at the receptionist's desk. It was early afternoon, after morning *kollel*, but before he began teaching his students.

The young woman dialed someone inside. She appeared surprised by the response. She hung up, rose respectfully, and smiled at Uri.

"Rabbi Schiffman, Mr. Bookman himself is going to handle your papers. He doesn't do that very often; it is actually very irregular. Please follow me."

She led him deep into the recesses of Bookman and Bookman, through a thickly carpeted hallway lined with beautiful artwork, to the elegant, private boardroom where the will had been read.

"Please wait here," she said. "Mr. Bookman will be in shortly."

She closed the door behind him, and Uri sat down to wait. The room smelled of wealth, of power, of momentous decisions.

Uri took out a small, paperback Mishnayos and started learning. This was probably the first Mishnayos ever learned in the boardroom of Bookman and Bookman. Uri was learning Torah where it never existed before, and he studied with special fervor, lifting his voice discreetly in a singsong, and swaying as he chanted the holy words. He was so intent that he didn't notice Mr. Bookman pause at the doorway for a few moments, watching him absorbed in his studies. Finally, Mr. Bookman coughed, and Uri looked up. He rose respectfully.

Mr. Bookman was an elderly man, perhaps the same age as his grandfather. This time he was alone, without any assistants or secretaries. He greeted Uri, sat down at the head of the board table, and motioned Uri to be seated. He set down a thick file on the table.

"Thank you for taking the time to see me personally," Uri said. "I understand that what I have to sign could be handled by your assistants."

Bookman did not answer. He studied Uri intensely. The elderly lawyer cut a very impressive figure. Every stitch of his clothing was perfect, from the matching deep blue tie and lapel-pocket handkerchief, the engraved gold monogrammed ring on his finger, and even the old-fashioned gold watch that hung from his vest.

"You know your grandfather, Captain Elijah, was a good friend of mine. He was not just a client, Rabbi Schiffman, he was an intimate. He talked to me for hours about himself, and the *Swift Current*, and his family — and about you."

"About me?"

"Yes, especially about you! He was very proud that you had decided to go your own way, different from your brothers or even himself. You know — there were no two Captain Elijahs — no one was like him! He did own his thing, and that's why he was so loved. Of course, later...things changed."

"After the race —"

"Yes, of course, after the race. Things changed after that. But before the race — he was the toast of Toronto! Do you remember those days? Free turkey days! Captain Elijah's Birthday Cruise for a penny! The whole city celebrated his birthday!"

Uri smiled. "Sure I remember, I'm not that young. Those were fun times. Tell me, Mr. Bookman, did you see my grandfather much after he —"

"Disappeared?"

Bookman nodded. "Oh, yes! We had a lot to talk about, both personal and business — but always very private, at the house."

Bookman opened the thick file.

"Your grandfather had a special fondness for you. When I saw what he had left you of his estate, I felt very sorry for you."

The embers of Uri's frustration suddenly flamed alive again. He leaned forward.

"Mr. Bookman, didn't my grandfather know what the Gortel stocks were worth? Didn't he know that they had melted down, and I would received so little?"

Bookman frowned heavily, uneasy at the question.

"Who knows what he knew, Rabbi? Maybe he did, maybe he didn't. Maybe he didn't want you be rich like your brothers — he didn't want to spoil you."

"You mean he did it on purpose?" Uri asked, incredulous.

Bookman leaned towards Uri and spoke so low it was almost a whisper. "Who knows?"

Bookman's whisper was like another man's shout. The dignified lawyer pulled himself up stiffly and assumed a more professional manner. He took out a few of the papers.

"Rabbi Schiffman, you can just sign these papers, and your portion of the inheritance will be transferred to your account. But for the sake of my long friendship with the Captain, and what I see of your own sincerity, I would like to do more. I would like to offer my firm's professional counsel to you pro bono — at no cost to you — so that we can manage your portion of the inheritance and invest it profitably."

"How much is my portion worth now?"

"As of this morning, Gortel recovered slightly. It's up to a dollar ten, and your portfolio is worth approximately eleven thousand dollars."

Uri's brow creased as he considered Bookman's generous offer.

The lawyer leaned over and placed his hand on Uri's arm.

"Rabbi Schiffman, let me manage your stock for you. We can trade it and reinvest it profitably. Let it grow! Who knows, in a few years, it could be worth a significant sum."

Uri smiled, but shook his head.

"Mr. Bookman, thank you. But I have five children in day school. It is costing me a fortune, even with a lowered tuition rate. I am behind in my payments. I need the money now, just to catch up."

"Perhaps you can leave half with us — something to invest."

Uri ran his finger across the polished tabletop. "I am so behind, Mr. Bookman. Can I make a counter proposal?"

"Certainly. What do you have in mind?"

"I plan to give ten percent of what I inherit to charity. I need the rest of the money for my family. But we have a principle: *yeish mei'yeish*. We always leave something on the table so that new blessing can grow from it. Would it be too much trouble if I put ten percent into your hands?"

The lawyer looked at him and smiled tightly. "Ten percent — that's only about a thousand dollars —"

"I can't afford more right now," Uri insisted.

Bookman shrugged. "Well, if it's ten percent, it's ten percent. It's better than nothing."

The lawyer took out a swath of papers and laid them in front of Uri.

"Before I hand over your estate you have to sign these waivers. Lot of papers to sign for a modest estate."

He handed Uri a pen and began passing papers in triplicate for him to sign. For a moment, Uri felt like a wealthy man. But it was more papers than money.

"I'm sorry not to agree to your generous offer," Uri mumbled as he signed. "I just can't afford it."

"I understand," the lawyer answered quietly.

Uri finally finished signing and handed the pen back to Bookman. He slipped it into his pocket, and, in its place, extracted a magnificent gold-plated pen.

"Rabbi," Bookman said, "I really feel badly that you received the short end of the stick — but that's life. I would like to present you with a personal gift. Please accept this pen…"

Uri had never seen such a fine instrument in his life.

"Mr. Bookman," he said, "I can't accept such a gift. That pen is worth more than my inheritance."

Bookman chuckled. "Not quite, but it is a thing of real beauty. You know who gave it to me?"

"No."

"Your grandfather, the Captain. Just like that! You know the Captain — he just did things on the spur of the moment. He once used the pen to write something down at a meeting, and then he just handed it to me."

"It's worth a fortune," Uri said, admiring its gold frame.

"It is and it isn't," said Bookman. "It's more a showpiece. I haven't used it in years. It's probably dry as a bone. But it meant a lot to me because your grandfather gave it to me, and I would be extremely happy to see it in your hands. Please —"

Uri stared intently at Bookman. The first time he saw him, Uri had thought he was a reserved, detached, and completely professional man. He was wrong. Uri realized that Bookman sincerely wanted him to have Zeideh's pen; it would be wrong to refuse. No wonder Zeideh had trusted him so.

"Thank you," he said.

Bookman smiled, and placed the pen ceremoniously in Uri's hand.

"Your grandfather would have been very pleased," he murmured.

He placed the signed papers neatly into the file. "I will arrange to have your funds transferred to you by tomorrow noon, less the ten per cent we discussed."

"Thank you."

"Now, one more matter. As was mentioned at the reading of the will, beside the Gortel stocks, your grandfather left you his personal set of Talmuds. I wish to begin transferring the volumes to you today."

Uri lifted his hand. "Mr. Bookman, you have put yourself out too much for me already. You offered to manage my stocks, you gave me my grandfather's gold pen. I really appreciate it! But a set of *Shas* is very heavy! Please, just let one of your assistants handle the cartons, it'll be too much for you —"

Bookman smiled at Uri. "Rabbi, I may be getting old, but I'm not frail — not yet."

He reached into his pocket and extracted a deep blue yarmulke that matched his tie. "Just remain seated."

Bookman rose and strode to a side table. For the first time, Uri realized that the embroidered cloth had been hiding a large Gemara underneath. Bookman removed the cloth and returned to the table with the volume. He sat down, clutching the large Gemara in his hands like an award.

"Rabbi Schiffman, it is my honor to present you with the first volume of your grandfather's Talmud."

He passed the Gemara ceremoniously to Uri. Uri accepted it with equal formality, and laid it heavily down on the table in front of him. It was a huge volume.

"But I thought my grandfather left me a whole set of the Talmud?" he asked.

"He did, indeed. But in his legal instructions, Captain Elijah directed me to give you just the first volume, for now."

"What about the rest? There should be twenty volumes altogether."

Bookman shook his head firmly. "I am sorry, Rabbi Schiffman. Those are your grandfather's instructions. One volume now — the rest, later."

"Later? When?" asked Uri.

"You will know yourself — when the time comes."

Bookman stood up abruptly and put out his hand.

"Good luck, Rabbi Schiffman," he intoned. "I look forward to our future meetings."

He slipped off his yarmulke, turned, and quickly left the room.

Deep Blue

Uri stood at the *shtender* of his study. His Zeideh's beautiful Gemara rested on its sloping wood top. Uri was very tired — it had been a long, emotional day, especially his meeting with Bookman. He had come back and told Chaya about the expected money, and she was busy calculating out which bills to pay off first — mostly the tuition for the schools.

He had davened *ma'ariv*, put the twins to bed, and now he gazed down on the magnificent leather-bound volume, embossed with glistening gold letters: *Talmud Bavli*.

Who could afford such a *Shas* except his grandfather?

He touched the fine leather. It felt like skin, like he was again feeling Zeideh's hand.

Zeideh, we were such good friends, he thought. *I was closer to you than my brothers! What happened with the will?*

Uri inspected the volume carefully. It was perfect! He turned the Gemara on its side and admired the gilded paper, the seamless binding without a scratch or bruise. The Gemara looked like a museum piece, so different from his own torn, coffee-stained volumes, whose learning could be measured by the finger marks on the bottom of each page.

He opened the Gemara reverentially.

Berachos.

The embossed gold letters shone. They were as perfect as the day they were stamped. Uri sighed. What a pity: so beautiful, and so unused. The Gemara was so clean that Uri was reluctant to turn to the first *daf* and learn. He argued with himself — should he use Zeideh's Gemara, or keep it as an heirloom in his breakfront?

He opened to the first *daf*. An envelope was set carefully in its crease. Surprised by the unexpected discovery, Uri lifted the envelope and studied it.

On the outside was inscribed:

To my grandson, Eerie Schiffman

Uri stared at the envelope. Something in him whispered, *Don't open it!*
Why not?
What is Zeideh up to now?
But how could he not open his grandfather's final letter to him? Uri reached into his desk drawer and drew out a small letter opener. Carefully, he opened the flap. The letter was written on two sheets of fine white vellum. Captain Elijah did everything with style. Uri dropped the envelope on his desk and unfolded the letter carefully over his *shtender*. It was written in Zeideh's beautiful, European-style script.

> *My dear grandson, Eerie:*
>
> *If my guess is right, you will be reading this letters a few months after I have passed from this world.*
>
> *Knowing you, you probably miss me the most of anyone, and I will miss you the most also. I will look down over you from wherever they have taken me.*
>
> *I have tried to make your lot a little easier with the Gortel shares I left, so that you can continue your Torah study and raise your beautiful children with an easier mind.*
>
> *Someday, with G-d's help, things will work out well for you, of that I am certain.*
>
> *You know that I acquired a set of Talmud that was very precious to me, especially in these last years. Now this set is yours, and it is a sign of my deep love for you.*
>
> *But, in turn, I must ask a profound favor from you, Eerie! These Gemaras were mine, and yet, although I looked at them from time to time, I started on my journey of learning much too late. There were many pages that I did not learn at all, and even what I studied, I cannot say that I mastered – by far.*
>
> *So, here we are, my beloved grandson! Probably a half-year has gone by since I have passed on.*

Uri paused, and calculated. Zeideh was off by only three weeks!

So now, how long would it take to complete the whole Talmud if you studied one page a day? Seven years, plus some.

Here is the favor that I ask of you: Dear Eerie! Please help me in this Next World that I have been sent to! You know that I tried my best for you, and for many others! But who knows how my soul will be judged? Mitzvahs are public, but transgressions are kept well hidden! But if you, my most beloved, pious grandson, will learn the whole Talmud for the sake of my neshamah and complete it for my eighth yahrtzeit – what an incredible kindness you will be doing for my poor soul!

I know, Eerie, that you are busy with many other family matters and other Torah study, but, this special learning, this daf yomi that will finish on my eighth yahrtzeit, will be an incredible deed! That is why I instructed Edwin Bookman to give you just the first volume for now. I wish you to acquire each volume, one by one. As you finish one Gemara, then Edwin will present you with the next.

Eerie, please understand! This is a favor I ask you, it is not a command! I cannot order you to undertake such a great obligation! If it is too difficult, then contact Mr. Bookman and say that you cannot fulfill your grandfather's last request. He will know what to do then.

But if you do undertake this mitzvah for my soul, I shall bless you with all my heart and soul – you and your children and your children's children!

With love,
Zeideh Elijah

Uri gazed at the letter and ran his fingers over the beautiful handwriting. Even after all these months, the letters glinted as though Zeideh had just written them. But what a request! Complete the whole *Shas* for Zeideh's eighth *yahrtzeit* — and then climb Mount Everest!

Uri carefully folded the letter, placed it in its envelope, and slipped it deep into a back page of the Gemara. He tugged at his beard, reflectively. He didn't know if he could do it. He didn't even know if he should do it!

He did not want to trouble Chaya with his startling discovery — she had her hands full already. When he saw the joy on her face as she prepared to pay off some bills, he kept silent.

He went to bed, read a little, and fell asleep briefly. Soon he was awake again. He tossed this way and that, tried to relax, but finally, he gave up. It was one o'clock, and Chaya was fast asleep. He pulled on his robe and padded discreetly out of the room.

Entering his study, Uri turned on the tall corner lamp and placed his own battered Gemara on the *shtender*. He was learning *Bava Basra*. He loved *Bava Basra*. He understood it, he loved learning the Rashbam's lengthy commentary. When he studied *Bava Basra*, he felt he was walking on the ground of Eretz Yisrael, buying a house, selling a field, digging a pit, drilling a well, planting a vineyard... He was erecting a stone fence somewhere in the Jezreel Valley, not on Grant Street.

But what was Zeideh asking of him? To learn the whole of *Shas*, and to learn it on schedule, without pause, to understand clearly — and using Zeideh's own *Shas*! Uri knew himself. He wasn't stupid, but he wasn't the Vilna Gaon either. Everything came hard for him. Every new line was like breaking rocky ground. He loved *Bava Basra* because he knew *Bava Basra*. He came back, over and over, to the same *machlokes*, the same questions and answers, the same *Tosafos* that he had struggled through.

But to undertake to learn the whole *Shas* for the soul of his grandfather — that was something else! He couldn't just start and stop. If he undertook a great mitzvah, he undertook it, and it was a sacred obligation! Yet, his Zeideh had begged him to do it! How could he say no?

But Zeideh...what happened?

Alexander got the house, Solomon got the boat — and Uri gets the mitzvah and a few Gortel stocks? Where is the fairness?

But that was small thinking. Zeideh had asked him to learn for his *neshamah*! Gortel was Hashem's will — not Zeideh's.

Uri leaned over his beloved Gemara, but he stared across the *shtender* to Zeideh's beautiful, untouched volume that lay on the desk.

"Uri, why are you up?"

Chaya entered the study noiselessly. She always sensed when he was awake, noise or no noise. He rose and made room for her at his desk chair.

"I have a real dilemma."

"Are you still crying about the will?" Chaya asked. "I thought we were over that!"

"No, it does not have to with money. Here —"

He had shown her Zeideh's Gemara earlier in the day, but now he reached over, stood it on its side, and slipped out the envelope he had hidden in its pages. He gave the envelope to Chaya.

"Read what's inside."

She looked at Uri in bewilderment, unfolded the letter and began reading. Even as she read, Uri knew what she was thinking. She nodded, frowned, shook her head in astonishment. Finally, she handed it back to him.

"What a beautiful, beautiful letter," she said. "Zeideh had such a beautiful *neshamah*."

"But look what he wants from me!" Uri responded. "To learn the whole Talmud in time for his eighth *yahrtzeit*!"

"But how can you say no?" she asked. "He was your Zeideh."

Uri shook his head. "I don't know if I can do it! I have so much on my plate already: my students, morning *kollel*, learning with the children. If I start learning the whole *Shas*, I can't stop midway — it's worse than not starting at all!"

They sat there silently. Finally, Chaya broke the silence.

"Uri, speak to the tzaddik, Klonimos Kalman. He'll tell you what to do!"

"You think so? It's a big decision."

"A tzaddik knows, Uri, a tzaddik knows."

⛵ ⛵ ⛵

Klonimos was easier to reach this time — as though he were expecting Uri's call.

The next night, Uri sat across from the tzaddik in his darkened study. The hour was late, but it had only taken a day to see Reb Klonimos, not weeks. His very room radiated peace and holiness, and Uri felt a new calmness. Klonimos looked at him, smiled pleasantly, but said nothing.

"Thank you for seeing me so quickly," Uri began. "These have been a difficult few days."

"Your Zeideh was my *chavrusa*," he answered modestly, as though he were Zeideh's friend, not his rebbe. "I owe him that much to see his grandson when he wants. What is the matter?" he asked. "Are you still bothered by your small inheritance?"

Uri waved his hand deprecatingly.

"I forgot about the money! I took your advice — and my wife's. Whatever we received, we received from Hashem, not the Captain. That was what we were supposed to get, no more. But now there is something else. Zeideh has given me a new obligation, and it's too much."

Uri quickly described Zeideh's gift of a beautiful set of Gemaras, to be collected, volume by volume, and Zeideh's final request: that he learn the whole *Shas* in time for his eighth *yahrtzeit*. It was a huge, difficult assignment that would take seven years, day after day, without fail. It was not Uri's way of learning, and it would be terribly difficult. Uri was afraid to begin.

Klonimos listened, swayed back and forth, squeezing his fist open and closed meditatively over his chest, like a beating heart. He was deciding Uri's next seven years for him! Finally, with a solemn face, he looked Uri straight in the eye.

"Reb Uri! It is not such a terrible request, is it? Many people learn *daf yomi*! So, you will just have a different schedule. What does it matter? Tell me, have you finished *Shas* yet?"

Uri shook his head. "Not even close, Reb Klonimos. But ask me on Grandmother *Basra*!"

Klonimos smiled for an instant, and then shook his head impatiently. "Listen, Talmud is more than *Bava Basra*. Don't you see that your Zeideh is doing you a great favor — he's making you learn *Shas*! Maybe that was his real motive and the *yahrtzeit* is just an excuse?"

But what was so easy for Reb Klonimos to say meant seven years of bitter toil for Uri.

"Reb Klonimos…am I obligated to fulfill my Zeideh's request?" he asked.

Reb Klonimos shrugged non-committally. "Obligated? That, I don't know. I can't say."

Uri was left perplexed.

"Reb Klonimos, please, tell what to do! It's a seven-year *achrayus*, day after day! I don't have the world's best head, and my grandfather wants me to learn from his own Gemaras — without notes! He wants me to struggle on my own. It'll be very hard!"

Klonimos pulled himself straight and faced Uri sternly. His voice rose.

"Reb Uri, listen! Torah must be hard or it is not Torah! Your Zeideh — the Captain — was an unusual person. He had a golden heart. When your father died and your mother was not capable of taking care of you and your brothers, he raised you like his own children! He helped hundreds of people in the city! He was a walking *kiddush Hashem*. Tell me, are you still angry at him for not leaving you enough money — is that it?"

"No!" answered Uri angrily.

"No? Good! But tell me: if he left you a million-dollar boat or the big house, would you be asking me now whether to follow his request?"

Uri looked down. He did not answer.

Klonimos, seeing Uri's obvious disappointment, spoke with quiet compassion.

"Reb Uri, Reb Uri, what is the question? Captain Elijah raised you like a father! So…you are really angry with him that he did not leave you as much as you wanted – or deserved. But still, he is begging you to do a great mitzvah for his *neshamah*. How can you refuse? And it will be good for you, too! What *ben Torah* doesn't know all *Shas*? What should you do, Reb Uri? You know what to do!"

Uri nodded. He lifted his head and smiled shamefacedly.

"You make it sound so easy, Reb Klonimos…"

The tzaddik smiled and shook his head. "Easy? Buy a *HaModia* – that's easy. Torah is *yegiah, yegiah, yegiah*! You are a *talmid chacham* – do I have to tell you?"

Klonimos suddenly rose, and Uri stood also.

"Reb Klonimos," he said. "Before I go, give me a *berachah* that I can finish the *Shas* in time!"

"I give you a *berachah* that you complete *Shas* on your Zeideh's eighth *yahrtzeit*, and that I should be there to see it!"

Uri stood outside the tzaddik's house. The February snow banks were just beginning to melt. So that was it…he was going to begin *Shas*.

Outside it was cold, but inside, Uri felt warm.

He knew he was doing the right thing!

TWO

The house was blessedly quiet; Chaya and the children were still asleep. Although it was not yet five, the first morning light seeped through Uri's tall, narrow study window. It was Uri's birthday, and this was his present to himself — the day to start learning *Shas*. At forty-five, it was time. He reached to the very top of a bookshelf and brought down Zeideh's Gemara from where he had safely hidden it. He had let the children have one quick, admiring glance at the beautiful volume and then placed it out of their reach.

He lay the huge Gemara on his *shtender*. It was almost too big for the *shtender* top, but rested firmly against the raised bottom ledge. He ran his hands over the soft leather cover. It felt warm, like embers burned inside.

He opened to the first *daf*, closed his eyes, and recited:

"*L'sheim yichud Kudsha B'rich Hu u'Shechintei...* Behold, I wish to study Your holy Talmud so that it will guide me to fulfill Your commandments, lead me to righteous conduct, to deep understanding of Your Torah!"

Uri opened his eyes and gazed heavenwards.

"Hashem," he prayed, "it's such a long way I have to go! My understanding is so limited! Please — stay with me!"

Uri looked down at the page. It was so absolutely clean!

I must keep it from looking like my own, disheveled Gemaras!

He stood stiffly at attention, checked his hands, and held the Gemara by its edges. Holding the Gemara at arm's length, he whispered the first holy word:

"*Mei'eimasai —*"

The volume slipped from his hands and snapped closed. The binding was so tight that the Gemara would not stay open unless he held it down strongly. He would almost have to bend back the leather spine to make it lie flat.

Again he opened the Gemara, holding it firmly by its sides. He stood rigidly, and again began:

"*Mei'eimasei —*"

The covers fought back. Uri sighed. He couldn't learn like this. He couldn't stand over this Gemara like a guard, hands stretched out rigidly. His whole body had to lean into the Gemara, his hands, his elbows, his head. But if he did that, this volume would soon look like his own Gemaras — battered and smudged.

He tugged at his salt-and-pepper beard and pondered. He had to find a way to tame the cover, lean normally into the page, yet not dirty it. He looked about the room and saw a solution — a solution from Zeideh himself!

On one of the shelves rested two small, heavy paperweights shaped like boats. Zeideh had given them away during one of his *Swift Current* One-Penny Birthday Cruises. He took one down, opened the Gemara, and laid the paperweight on the resisting right side. The cover tried to rise up, but the weight was too heavy. It fell back and lay quiet. Uri smiled.

He leaned into the Gemara, laid his finger on the *mishnah*, but then pulled back abruptly. When Uri learned, his finger was like an anchor. He dropped it firmly on the line he was studying, and then his eyes would roam across the page — to *Rashi*, to *Tosafos*, to the back of the Gemara, to another *sefer* — but his finger stayed glued to the page. That was how he learned, and his finger smudges marked every page. He could measure how long he worked on a *sugyah* from how smudged the page was! But this was Zeideh's Gemara.

He needed a pointer — clean, dry, trustworthy. All his ballpoint pens leaked, and his pencils left streaks. Again, he tugged on his beard, tugged, tugged, and then chuckled to himself.

He had a perfect pointer! He reached high behind a set of *sefarim* and extracted the gold-plated pen that Bookman had given him. He had kept it hidden, high up on the shelf and disguised, for fear that his unstoppable twins, Dovid'l and Yisroel, would find it. He juggled it in his hand and delighted in its rich heft. The pen was beautiful, it was impeccable. It was Zeideh's.

So now, he was ready. The Gemara lay patiently, waiting. He pressed the pen to the first line and, *b'kol d'mamah dakah*, with a still, small voice, he began:

"*Mei'eimasai!*"

Outside, a little bird chirped joyously and beckoned to the blue dawn with a flutter of its little crimson wings.

His long journey had begun.

It took some adjustment. When Uri learned before, he was all over the Gemara. He wrote notes, underlined, erased, wrote new notes. He always had a drink nearby, taking reflective sips, spilling some, as he tried to understand a passage. He was *heimish* with his Gemara, it was a part of him.

Not so with Zeideh's immaculate volume. Uri approached it with reverence, and, although he leaned in closely, he never touched the page with his fingers, but used the gold pen as a pointer. After a few days, the Gemara loosened up and it lay flat without a paperweight.

He studied early each morning, before the children woke. But sometimes he snagged on a question, and the morning hour was not enough, so he continued at night. He shut his door tight and kept the children out. Children and Zeideh's spotless Gemara did not mix — especially when the children were his seven-year-old twins, Dovid'l and Yisroel.

By the second week, their interest was fully aroused. Uri stood over his *shtender* one evening, studying intensely, when he heard a rustling behind him. He turned — but saw no one. But the door was opened just a crack, and then he heard some giggling. Two little faces peered at him, one atop the other. Seeing they were discovered, the twins threw open the door and raced in boisterously.

"Abba, where did you get that gold pen?" they demanded.

Their shouts were like screaming cannon shots in Uri's tranquil study.

Uri grabbed the pen and slipped it out of sight under the Gemara. The twins saw his move and began scaling his chair onto the *shtender*, nearly toppling the Gemara.

"Out!" he ordered frantically. "Out!"

"Can't we see the pen?"

"Out!"

Intimidated, the seven-year-olds retreated to the floor, ran to the door, and slammed it behind them. Uri smiled slyly and turned back to the Gemara. He retrieved the pen and anchored it back on the page. He counted to ten, and then he twirled swiftly towards the door — the boys were staring at him through an open crack.

"Out! Out! Out!" he bellowed in his meanest, deepest voice. "To bed with you! Go read a book! Say Shema! Anything, just go!"

There was an appreciative giggle at his performance, and the twins finally shut the door. For good measure, Uri turned the lock. He shook his head. They were the world's sweetest, most unstoppable twins, and they now knew that there was forbidden treasure hidden in his study! He would have to hide everything high up, out of reach: the pen, the Gemara.

Baruch Hashem for such problems!

By the third week, Uri had grown accustomed to his new life. He had never learned a *daf* a day before, one great folio after another, no pauses, no excuses. He knew that he could find plenty of help – *shiurim*, tapes, discs, e-mails, *chavrusas*, rebbes, speakerphones. The world was full of Torah! Yes, and yet, he had to learn his way. He had grown older, grayer – but a child still lived in him.

Since childhood, Uri's only companion had been his own aloneness. His father had died, his mother was ill, Zeideh was busy with *Swift Current*, and his brothers, uncaring. He grew accustomed to loneliness and aloneness; they became his companions and comrades, even in learning. He was his own favorite *chavrusa*. He could teach many students, teach with all the heart and love that was his nature, but when it came to mastering a difficult *gemara*, he had to unravel it by himself, line by line. What he did not have in brilliance, he had in determination – to sit, to stand, to *shuckel*, to sing, to pull at his beard, to break the wings of each line so that it would not fly off, so that it remained clear – that was how Uri learned.

So, this *daf yomi* was a different sort of learning than he was used to. This was Zeideh's learning, from Zeideh's set of Gemaras, and Uri walked it alone and happy. These clean, white pages were like newly fallen country snow, and Uri made a track where no one had walked before. Certainly, Zeideh had not learned from these pages – they were too clean. Who knows if he had even opened this volume, except to slip in his famous final letter.

Uri did not spill his coffee, he did not let the page get dirty, he treated this Gemara with new reverence – and so the learning itself took on great *kedushah* in his eyes. Each morning he stood joyfully over Zeideh's Gemara, studying the new lines, while a little bird sung out its heart outside his window, greeting the new day. The pages added up faster than he expected. It was a struggle, true, but he thought about Zeideh and what it meant to him. Zeideh had drawn him on a wonderful journey.

Uri had made peace with his lot, even if he still did not quite understand. How was it that Zeideh left the least to the grandson who needed the most? The grandson with the most children, the least *parnasah*, the most learning, the most love... He let the sweetness of his learning drive out the bitterness of his small inheritance, and he pressed on.

And then...a discovery!

Uri completed the first side of page thirty-three. He turned the *daf*, and there, in the crease of the Gemara, lay a thin, newly minted, hundred-dollar bill. Uri looked at it in shock, wondering whether it was a mirage. *Hashavas aveidah, I must return it*, was his first thought. But, to whom? This money wasn't misplaced! The bill had been carefully laid into the fold of the Gemara with a glue so fine that when Uri lifted the bill, it did not leave the slightest mark on the page.

Whose is this?

It's mine!

Uri stared at the bill, and his face grew warm. A gift from Zeideh!

The discovery sent Uri into deep thought.

Up to now, Uri was certain that Zeideh had never opened this Gemara or turned these pages. He was the first to study these holy words, and he was on a lonely march. But he was wrong! Zeideh had been here before! And he had left the money for Uri, just at the midpoint of Gemara *Berachos*!

There were no two Captain Elijahs. Zeideh did things his way — even after he was gone! What other surprises did Zeideh have hidden for him? And...was there more money hidden in Zeideh's *Shas*?

There is learning and there is learning. It is a different learning when you know that a hundred-dollar bill might be stuck in the next page. It was the same beautiful *Berachos*, but it was a different Uri. For each new *daf* he learned, a little chime went off in his head: *Maybe there's money on the next page?*

But what kind of learning *lishmah* was that? No! He had to learn for the mitzvah, not for Zeideh's money. But it was so hard sometimes — he really could use some more money: for food, for clothing, for tuition. Of course! No one was watching. He could flip quickly ahead through the pages — *bedikas cash*! But that was...cheating. It wasn't right. If more money turned up, so be it, but to go looking for it? Was that what a Gemara was for?

Each morning he learned the new *daf*, wishing, hoping for another surprise. Learning went fast when you hoped to find another hundred dollars. Fifty *dapim*, sixty *dapim*. It was good learning — but no money. On the morning he completed *Berachos*, he couldn't hold back any longer. He leafed through the back pages of the Gemara, hoping the holy Maharsha would know if there were any more hundred-dollar bills. But there was nothing.

Uri closed the Gemara and gazed out the window at the beautiful summer day. This had to stop! Was this Torah *lishmah*, this searching for reward? He was letting a hundred-dollar bill spoil everything! Maybe Zeideh was testing him, setting out cheese for a mouse? Maybe the money was left there by accident?

There was only one person he could ask.

⚓ ⚓ ⚓

Uri managed to salvage a few pieces of cake for Chaya and the children from the *siyum* he made after *shacharis*. He had already placed the call to Bookman's office. The secretary was very respectful; she almost sounded like she expected him. Uri worried that it would take days to see the lawyer and he would miss learning the first few *dapim* from Zeideh's own volume. But he was given an appointment for the very next afternoon.

That afternoon, Uri was ushered deferentially into the exclusive boardroom, and sat waiting for Bookman amidst the hushed, elegant surroundings. This was the third time that Uri had visited the boardroom, and he was no longer overawed. He quickly took out his Mishnah and began learning, swaying over its worn pages, chanting the words quietly. Bookman entered silently and watched him from the door, the great volume clasped in his arms. He waited for Uri to notice him, but Uri was involved in his learning and did not look up for several minutes. Bookman smiled inwardly — no wonder the Captain spoke about this grandson above all others.

Finally Uri looked up, startled to see Bookman watching him. He rose respectfully.

"I didn't see you standing there," he apologized.

Bookman entered without answering and waved Uri to a seat. He sat formally at the head of the table, and gazed at the heavy volume before him.

"Thank you for making the time to see me," Uri said, breaking the silence. "You didn't have to trouble yourself to give me the Gemara personally. I could have picked it up from your secretary at the front desk."

Bookman shook his head.

"I had an understanding with the Captain," he explained. "No one was to give you these Talmuds except I — as long as I'm around. The books passed from him, to me, to you — hand to hand. I hope to keep my word."

With great formality, he passed over *maseches Shabbos* to Uri. Uri leaned forward and accepted the heavy volume with equal seriousness. He ran his hand over the rich leather cover and stared at the embossed gold lettering. The volume was magnificent.

Bookman watched him, and smiled. "It is beautiful," he said.

"What's inside is even more beautiful," Uri answered.

"Is it?" Bookman asked, and then nodded.

Embarrassed at his naive happiness, Uri set the Gemara on the highly polished table. He took a deep breath and prepared to speak. There was a puzzle that only Bookman could explain. Uri cleared his throat nervously.

"Mr. Bookman, did my grandfather ever mention that he left something for me inside the first volume you gave me?"

Bookman shook his head. "No."

"Do you know what was in there?"

Bookman seemed perplexed by Uri's question.

He shrugged. "Just the Talmud."

"But he never told you anything else — that he hid something inside?"

Bookman stared at Uri squarely. "No."

"Mr. Bookman, do you want to know what I found hidden in those pages?"

But Uri's question had a strange effect. Bookman's whole demeanor changed abruptly. He raised his hands in agitation and turned his head away.

"No!" he said emphatically, "I don't want to hear anything!"

He regained control of himself and turned back to Uri. He spoke quietly. "Rabbi Schiffman, your grandfather was one of my closest friends. He told me everything — that is, everything he wanted me to know. If he didn't tell me that he hid something in those pages, then it was meant for you, not for me. He simply didn't want me to know! I don't want to know now, or I would be violating his wish for privacy."

He looked at the clock, his fingers drumming nervously on the table. He was clearly uneasy and wanted to end the meeting.

But Uri persisted. "I apologize, Mr. Bookman. I know you are busy. But may I ask you just two questions? Something I need to know."

Bookman looked warily at Uri and then nodded. "Yes?"

"I found cash in my Gemara — a hundred-dollar bill. Did you put it there?"

Bookman's face tightened. "Absolutely not."

Uri gazed at Bookman's face and believed him.

He lowered his voice apologetically for one last question. "The last time we met, you gave me a gift of a gold pen. You told me my grandfather gave it to you —"

"Yes, he did."

"But... Was it your own idea to give it to me, or did my grandfather ask you to give it to me when I received the first volume of his Talmud?"

Bookman hesitated, then smiled ever so slightly. He lifted one finger off the table and pointed it at Uri.

"You would have made a good lawyer, Rabbi Schiffman. Who told you?"

Uri tapped the Gemara in front of him. "My Zeideh's Gemaras are not simple books, Mr. Bookman! They have a soul, and the pen also has a soul. They told me! They are all linked: the Gemaras, the pen, Zeideh — and you."

Edwin Bookman stared down at the table for a moment, lifted his head, and stared at Uri.

"Your Zeideh always said you were special — now I know why."

⛵ ⛵ ⛵

Forget the money!

Uri stood at his *shtender*, the Gemara *Shabbos* open before him. He was glad that he did not have to miss even one day from learning from Zeideh's own *Shas*. Forget the money! After that one time, there was no more money to be found, anyway! Maybe it was just an accident — maybe Zeideh had hidden the bill in the Gemara before Shabbos. It did not matter. He had to learn for the sake of the mitzvah: "*Hareini rotzeh lilmod Torah lishmah* — I wish to study Torah for its own holy sake" ...not to find a reward.

Almost subliminally, Uri knew this volume was different. Unlike *Berachos*, which had felt so stiff and untouched, this Gemara had a normal flexibility. When he opened the Gemara, the cover lay open. Yes, it still had a snowy whiteness, unmarred by smudges. It was clear, though, that someone had been through these pages before. But who? Zeideh?

Uri laid his pen on the first *mishnah*:

"*Yetzios haShabbos shtayim she'hein arba...*"

It was sweet, sweet learning. Uri hadn't studied *Shabbos* in ten years, but the laws were familiar and he had learned it well the last time. Some Gemara learning is like a rough storm, but this was an idyllic cruise across the sacred pages. Instinctively, he was more at ease with this volume than with *Berachos*. The Gemara had been studied before and, although the pages were spotless, the volume had a *heimish* feeling.

On day three — *daf dalet, amud beis* — Uri turned the page and stopped like he had been struck. There, for the first time, he saw proof that someone had indeed studied from this Gemara! On the edge, along the border of the long *Tosafos*, "*Be'ilan*," was etched a large...question mark. What did it mean? Did the person have a question on the *Tosafos*? Did he not understand the *Tosafos*? Was it a question not at all related to *Tosafos*? Who could tell? Just a question mark. But what seized Uri's imagination was the color of the ink with which the question mark had been drawn. It was deep magnetic blue, a blend of sea and sky, so hypnotic that it drew one's eye down into its depths.

Who wrote this?

The delicate shape of the one large question mark, the beauty of its cerulean hue all pointed to…Zeideh! Uri was not thinking about money now, but of the great love he felt for his grandfather, will or no will. He turned a few more pages until he found another mark. This time, it was not a blank question mark, but a note written in tiny, fine script:

Ta'anis. Must look up.

Uri recognized the handwriting immediately — it was Zeideh's. His grandfather must have learned this Gemara with Klonimos Kalman and written this note to himself. Uri beat rhythmically on Zeideh's note with the end of his pen. He flipped more pages: another question mark. Another page: another notation, another question. He turned to the back pages of the Gemara, and saw that Zeideh's notes became more frequent. Uri smiled. Zeideh had really gotten into the learning!

So this Gemara was not just a museum piece, after all. Zeideh really learned. Uri turned back to *daf dalet* and traced the end of his closed pen along the curved line of the question mark, like a child following a path. Uri's face suddenly flushed red with excitement.

Carefully, he unscrewed the pen's gold top, exposing its razor-sharp point. The point was bone dry from years of disuse, and someone had wiped it spotlessly clean. Uri removed his glasses and carefully studied the point. At this distance, without glasses, his eyes were like a magnifying glass. He smiled. Despite someone's best effort, a few dried crystals of blue ink were discernable — the same magnetic blue of Zeideh's notes.

Uri screwed back on the case. He stared at the pen in his hand. It was all here, it was all his! Zeideh's Gemara, Zeideh's notes, Zeideh's pen — Zeideh's *neshamah*! Overcome, he gave the pen a quick kiss. Maybe Zeideh had really evened out the inheritance. How much were these Gemaras worth? How much was it worth to be so close to Zeideh, to the hours he spent studying, to his own beautiful, pithy notes? Zeideh's soul hovered over these pages, these notes, the very pen he grasped!

So...learn, Uri, learn!

Each morning Uri opened the Gemara with a *simchah*, cruising swiftly from page to page, sometimes covering even more than a *daf* a day, so that he had time to dwell deeply on a *Tosafos*, look up the *Shulchan Aruch*. The pages flowed like a *Swift Current: Bameh Madlikin, Kirah, Bameh Ishah*... Each small note left behind by Zeideh was like a little flag, a wave...

And then, on the sixty-seventh *daf* – bingo!

There, lying patiently for him at the start of *perek Klal Gadol* were two hundred-dollar bills! They lay there coyly, two freshly minted bills, laying in ambush for him. Uri picked up the bills like a man plucking flowers. This time, he was not shocked, not floored. In his heart of hearts he had expected this money. Zeideh was playing a game with him, just like he had when Uri was a child. It was Zeideh's favorite game of hide-and-seek, but Uri knew Zeideh was really always there and would show himself when he was ready! Zeideh had hidden away the big inheritance from him, but he was slipping cash – when he was ready – into his Gemaras. He gave him the almost worthless Gortel stock, but he had left him with a precious final letter. He left him a spotless, snowy white set of Shas, but they were filled with his private notes.

Uri held the money in one hand, the precious pen in the other, and Zeideh's Gemara lay obediently open in front of him. Now he realized: Zeideh was playing a game with him – a long, seven-year game!

Uri smiled. *So, Zeideh, let's play!*

THREE

Even Uri's study door could not keep out the sounds of life that rang through the house. The oldest twins, Tova and Dina, filled the house with their Bais Yaakov friends. If it was not a project, then it was a convention or a birthday party. The girls were very good-natured, and they often invited newly arrived Russian girls to spend Shabbos. Dovid'l and Yisroel were unstoppable, irrepressible, and the rooms resounded to their laughs and escapades. It was the music of children and life, and Uri loved it. But now, as Uri struggled determinedly towards the end of *Eiruvin*, a new sound flowed through his door, and it was beautiful.

His middle child, Yirmiyahu, was cut from a different cloth than either set of twins. He was much more to himself, serious and determined, rarely without a *sefer* or a book in hand. Yirmiyahu had begun his bar mitzvah lessons, and Uri could hear his boyish soprano singing his haftorah from the living room. Yirmiyahu was his quietest child, and it was a pleasant surprise to hear his voice ring out strongly and on key. From time to time, Uri stopped learning and listened. Yirmiyahu's bar mitzvah was still half a year away, but he already had the haftorah down beautifully. Next came the Torah reading, and maybe even *shacharis*. A few times, Uri came and sat down next to his son just to listen to him sing, but Yirmiyahu begged him not to listen – so he didn't.

One evening, Uri came from *ma'ariv* and was met with a surprise. Yirmiyahu, usually so intense and standoffish, was actually waiting for him. He stood outside Uri's study, *Tikkun* in hand. Uri saw him and hid his astonishment.

"Hello, Yirmiyahu, what's up?" he greeted him.

"Abba," he answered. "Do you want me to say the haftorah? I think I know it now."

Uri studied Yirmiyahu. *What's got into him?* But, a son is a son, and Yirmiyahu was an excellent boy. Uri played it cool.

"I'd love to hear you," he said. "Just let me get something to drink."

Uri made himself a tea and came into his study. Yirmiyahu was standing at his *shtender*, the *Tikkun* open. Uri shook his head.

"No, no," he said. "You sit at the desk and I will stand at the *shtender*."

Yirmiyahu demurred. "But Abba, it's not proper that I sit and you stand!"

Uri smiled at his seriousness. "I'm *mochel*," he answered. "Anyway, I sat too much today, teaching."

He took down his Chumash from a shelf and laid it on the *shtender*. Yirmiyahu sat at the desk, bent over his *Tikkun*.

"Yirmiyahu, sit up straight when you sing. Otherwise your voice won't project."

Yirmiyahu immediately bolted upright. Uri shook his head imperceptibly. *He's too serious*, Uri thought. The haftorah was from *Parashas Behar*, from the Prophet Jeremiah.

"Start!" ordered Uri.

Yirmiyahu began singing. His perfectly pitched, pure soprano filled the room with such beautiful sound that Uri could hardly contain himself. Was this really his child? Uri listened with his heart in his throat. There was a beauty not just of Yirmiyahu's voice, but of his whole heart. Uri sneaked a look at his son's face, so intent, so sincere – so Yirmiyahu!

Yirmiyahu finished the haftorah with a flourish, and the room fell suddenly silent. Yirmiyahu closed his *Tikkun*.

"Wow, Yirmiyahu!" Uri exclaimed.

Yirmiyahu did not smile. His serious demeanor did not leave him. Something was on his mind, Uri knew.

Yirmiyahu turned to his father. "Abba," he began, "can I ask you something?"

"After such a haftorah — anything!" Uri answered.

"What kind of tefillin are you going to buy me?"

Uri was surprised at the question. He hadn't thought about it yet. "I don't know. I was going to speak to Reb Velvel, the *sofer*. Why?"

"Abba, Pinny Hoffman's bar mitzvah is a month ahead of mine. His father is getting him a special pair of tefillin from Yerushalayim, written by a *sofer* who is a great tzaddik."

"Oh, who is that?"

"Reb Zelig Schreiber, of Meah Shearim —"

"Oh! Reb Zelig! I've heard of him."

"Abba, Reb Zelig writes only three sets of parashiyos a year, and he does it with all the special *kavanos* and *chumros*! Can I get a pair from him also?"

So that was the reason for the special performance!

"Do you have any idea how much they cost?"

Yirmiyahu paused. "Thirteen hundred dollars, American."

Uri's eyebrows went sky high. "Thirteen hundred dollars American...almost two thousand dollars Canadian! Yirmiyahu, we can't afford that!"

"Abba, they are so, so special! Can't we find the money?"

Uri dropped to his chair, so that his face almost touched his son's. He gazed at Yirimyahu. His son had the deepest, bluest eyes he had ever seen on a boy, so deep you could swim in them. He sighed.

"Listen, Yirmiyahu! Pinny Hoffman's father is a billionaire, do you understand? Not a millionaire — a billionaire! He can afford whatever he wants...but we can't. We can get a beautiful, *mehudar* pair of *gassos* for seven or eight hundred dollars Canadian — and even then I'm going to have to find the money somewhere! But tefillin from Reb Zelig Schreiber...it's out of the question!"

"Abba, I have some money, I can help!"

Uri placed his hand on Yirmiyahu's. His son looked like he was going to cry. He was such a beautiful child.

Uri spoke quietly. "Yirmiyahu, we just can't afford it! Do you understand?"

Yirmiyahu's face fell. He stared down at his knees. *Is he crying?* Uri wondered. Finally, Yirmiyahu nodded assent.

"Go to sleep now, Yirmiyahu," Uri murmured. "You sang the haftorah beautifully. I'm very proud of you. Now it's getting late."

Yirmiyahu collected his *Tikkun*, rose, and, still hiding his face from Uri, quickly left the study.

Uri watched his son leave the room. He picked up the pen and twiddled it with his fingers, staring blankly at the page in front of him. He didn't want to hurt his son. But wasn't it better to cut off his hopes from the start, clearly, sharply, and finally?

⛵ ⛵ ⛵

A month passed. It was well into December, and Uri had started *Eiruvin*. The days were short, and when Uri rose to learn, it was still night. Outside, it was dark and cold; inside, the house was still. Uri opened his Gemara, cherishing the peace and silence. He began the day's *daf* and had just read a few lines, when he heard a faint knocking at the door. It was so tentative and soft, he thought it was his imagination, but it persisted.

Who was up so early? He went worriedly to the door and opened it. Yirmiyahu was standing in the doorway, a paper clasped in his hand.

"Yirmiyahu, what are you doing up?" Uri asked. "It's just gone five."

"Abba, I wanted to show you something," Yirmiyahu answered. "I didn't want anyone else to see."

Uri grew alarmed. "Oh?"

He ushered Yirmiyahu into his study, carefully tucking the gold pen out of sight.

"What is it?"

Yirmiyahu handed him the sheet. Uri quickly scanned the page. It was a test that Yirmiyahu had received back from his rebbe.

"Where's the mark?" Uri asked, confused.

"The rebbe put it on the back of the page – with a note."

Uri gave his oldest son a quick, worried look, and turned to the back. On the bottom, the mark was drawn in bold, red ink: 110%. Underneath, in small, deliberate script, the rebbe had written a note in Yiddish:

Yirmiyahu vagst ah gadol b'Yisroel! Shept nachas!

Uri looked up at his son standing there in the dim light. Little tears welled up in Uri's eyes.

"I'm very proud of you," he said.

But why had he brought him this paper now, at five o'clock in the morning?

Yirmiyahu looked imploringly at his father. "Abba," he asked, "can't I please get those Zelig Schreiber tefillin that I want?"

Uri looked at his son, who was setting such a standard of excellence for the family. Yet, Yirmiyahu was also in a way an enigma, a son whom he could not quite fathom. *How can I afford almost two thousand dollars for his tefillin?* Uri asked himself. *There is no way!* And yet, how could he refuse such a treasure?

Uri sat there, gazing at his son.

"Yirmiyahu, I want you to be truthful with me. Do you want these tefillin because they are so holy – or because Pinny Hoffman is getting a pair? Be honest!"

His son stared straight back, unflinching.

"Abba, I want it because of their *kedushah* – and because Pinny Hoffman is getting them."

Uri shook his head in astonishment. "What? You admit you're jealous?"

But Yirmiyahu was unrepentant.

"Abba, I want the tefillin because they will give me great *kedushah*.

And I also want them because if Pinny Hoffman can have them, I also want them."

"What? You are allowed to be jealous of Pinny Hoffman?"

"Yes, Abba! My rebbe said I am allowed to be! *BaShamayim mima'al* — when it comes to *Shamayim* things, you're allowed to look at someone who is holding higher than you and try to copy him!"

Uri wagged a scolding finger at Yirmiyahu. "Your rebbe didn't tell you that, Yirmiyahu. I taught that to you!"

"Right, Abba, I know you did!" Yirmiyahu answered with lightning speed. "I didn't say which rebbe said it! You're also my rebbe, aren't you? You said it, Abba, yourself! You said to look up when it comes to mitzvos! So, you'll let me get those tefillin?"

Uri glanced at the clock. It was five fifteen in the morning, and outside it was still night. Uri couldn't believe he was sitting here, being out-*mussared* by his son!

Uri didn't know whether to laugh or cry. Sitting in front of him was a son who was half man, half boy, but in him were the seeds of greatness, *gadlus* in Torah and *yirah*.

How am I allowed to say no? he asked himself.

Uri looked at his son. "If I say yes, will you go back to bed now?"

Yirmiyahu's face suddenly lit up with joy.

"So I can have the Yerushalayim tefillin?"

Uri took a deep breath. *Hashem help me.*

"Yes!"

Yirmiyahu jumped out of his chair and did a little-excited jig. Uri had never seen his intense son like this before — so completely happy and excited. Just to see his reaction was worth all the money!

Yirmiyahu finally left, and Uri went back to his Gemara. Meanwhile, the money wasn't there...and Uri had promised.

Uri sighed. Where would he find the money? He lay his pen back on the *daf*.

First learn: worry later.

For he knew where the answer lay, although he dreaded it.

After all, Yirmiyahu did not only have a father and mother. He had two uncles, uncles who had won the inheritance lottery and who were now very rich. Was it not right that they take some responsibility for their nephew's bar mitzvah? There had to be some fairness in the world!

Since that fateful meeting when Captain Elijah's inheritance had been distributed, Uri had not seen his oldest brother, Alexander. In truth, they barely spoke, except to wish each other a *shanah tovah* — and Uri always placed that call. Otherwise, nothing. They had never been close, and now, now they had veered off into different worlds. Alexander had Zeideh's mansion, the land and servants' quarters, the two cars. And that was that.

⛵ ⛵ ⛵

Uri stood at the great wooden doors of what was once Zeideh's mansion and rang the bell. A maid ushered Uri inside. It had rained earlier, and she firmly requested that he remove his shoes, brother or no brother. She gave him a pair of furry slippers, and he flip-flopped his way through the house. Uri gazed at the rooms admiringly, trying hard not to transgress "Thou shalt not covet." There was a lot to covet. Ruby had done major renovations since Zeideh's time. Zeideh had left the large house simply furnished, but now it was like a palace.

"Is Ruby home?" he asked the maid politely.

"No, she had to go out to a school meeting," the maid answered. "But she told me to make you lunch if you are hungry."

Uri shook his head self-consciously. "No, no, tell her I wasn't hungry. Where's Alexander?"

"Follow me, he's in the den."

Uri had not been in Zeideh's house for almost two years, and it seemed even larger than he remembered. He passed through one elegant room after another, with great, two-story high windows dramatically framed by French drapes, until they finally reached the great, oaken doors of Alexander's den. The maid rapped softly, opened the door for Uri, and there, poring over some papers, sat Alexander.

Alexander saw his brother and rose grandly. "*Eerie eerie shir dabeiri!*" he greeted cheerily. "*Shalom Aleichem.* Why are you standing there at the door like some *meshulach?* Come in!"

Alexander's welcome was hearty and loud, but Uri felt...like a *meshulach*. He flip-flopped into the den, and the two brothers shook hands.

"Sit down, Eerie," Alexander waved to a chair in front of his desk. "Please, sit down."

"Alexander," pleaded Uri, "Uri, not Eerie. You know I don't use that name. Uri, Uri, I am called Uri!"

Alexander lifted his finger. "But Zeideh called you Eerie, right?"

Uri sighed. It was true, Zeideh had always called him Eerie.

"But my name is Uri, Alexander! I call myself Uri! I am called to the Torah by the name Uri!"

Alexander chuckled, having gotten a little rise out of his brother.

"Okay, Uri, don't get excited. It's Uri, okay? So, tell me, how are you, how are your beautiful children, and how is Chaya?"

Uri sat down across the desk. "*Baruch Hashem*, fine, everyone is fine. And with you, Ruby, the children?"

"No complaints! Who would listen to my complaints, in any case, right?"

There was an awkward silence.

"So, how are you?" Alexander asked, just to break the silence. "And the kids, they're all in school?"

"Yes, *Baruch Hashem*. And yours?"

"No complaints."

Alexander gave a little nervous cough. They were running out of conversation.

Uri coughed back nervously. "Alexander, I need a favor from you."

Alexander looked down at his desk and toyed with his little calculator. He looked up cautiously. "What favor, Uri?"

"My oldest son, Yirmiyahu, is becoming bar mitzvah in a few months. He is an excellent boy, very dedicated. He has his heart set on a very fine set of tefillin, and I can't afford to buy them for him."

"How much are they?"

"Thirteen hundred dollars — American."

Alexander whistled in amazement. He bolted upright in his chair. "Thirteen hundred dollars? When my son was bar-mitzvahed I bought him an excellent pair for five hundred dollars, a beautiful set. Why the hefty price tag?"

Uri leaned forward earnestly. "These tefillin are very special, Alexander! There is a scribe in Yerushalayim, Reb Zelig Schreiber, he's a great tzaddik! He writes only a few sets of tefillin *parashiyos* a year. He does everything himself: prepares the *klaf*, shapes the *batim*... He meditates on every holy *kavanah* when he writes G-d's name. It's a pair of tefillin for a lifetime —"

Alexander sat up, looked down on his desk, and shook his head.

"It sounds very nice, but Uri, I really can't help you."

Uri could not contain his frustration.

"Alexander! You know that when the inheritance was distributed, I was left with almost nothing! You got the house and cars, Solomon got the boat and dock — and I got almost worthless Gortel! But I didn't complain. I accepted G-d's will! And now, can't you please help with this...just to make things a little fairer?"

Alexander looked at his brother with a patronizing smile, and he shook his head again.

"Uri, you are a great Torah scholar, but you don't know much about money. Do you think Zeideh did me any favors? Yes, he left me the house. But do you know how much I had to pay to bring it up to par? The house was falling apart! And to decorate it properly? After grandmother died, Zeideh neglected the house for years — he didn't buy anything! Do you know what I paid just to fix the roof? And the taxes and the utilities? Uri, you're lucky you didn't inherit this house, believe me! I don't have an extra penny."

Uri swept his arm over the richly furnished den. "But Alexander, this house is worth millions!"

Alexander lifted his hands impatiently, like he was speaking to a child. He shook his head.

"Listen, Uri, you have to understand. I can't let the equity of this house just sit there, not making money. Whatever equity it has, I've invested it on down payments for fifteen condominiums. They haven't even been built yet, and they're already worth thirty percent more than I paid! That's how you handle money, Uri, you don't leave it in a bank account. But money? Cash? I hardly have enough for my own expenses."

"But Alexander, Yirmiyahu's your nephew!"

Alexander continued swiveling back and forth on his executive chair like it was on a timer. He looked Uri straight in the eye and spoke hardly above a whisper.

He mouthed his words slowly and carefully.

"Uri, read my lips. I – just – can't – help – you!"

⚓ ⚓ ⚓

Uri hadn't been on Zeideh's ship, *Swift Current*, for many years. When he was a child and Zeideh waxed strong, he used to visit almost every week. Even later, when he was in yeshivah, he would visit during *bein hazemanim*, sneaking down to the waterfront and hopping aboard. Sometimes he took a Gemara and hid up in the pilothouse with Zeideh at the wheel and watched the Toronto skyline fall away even as he learned.

But that was ancient history. Zeideh changed, he changed, and now he felt like a stranger as he crossed the gangplank to see his brother. Solomon was in the special cabin that Zeideh had built on the upper deck, complete with a desk, cabinets, and a comfortable bunk. Uri had come straight from *shacharis*, but already the boat was busy with workmen chipping ice off the handrails, cleaning away winter grime, and readying the boat for the first spring cruises. The bitter wind off the lake chilled Uri to the bone.

He walked up the stairs to the upper deck and knocked on the cabin door. No maids this time. Solomon himself came to welcome him, flinging open the door into the warm cabin. He had a wide smile on his face.

"Look what the wind blew in! *Eerie eerie shir dabeiri* – how are you doing little brother?"

Uri sighed, glad to be in from the cold.

"Hello, Solomon. But please, Uri, not Eerie. My name is Uri."

"Eerie, Uri, what's the difference? Come on, you're on Zeideh's boat now. You know what he used to call you!"

"But Solomon, when I'm called to the Torah it's Uri, not Eerie. Boy, it's nice and warm in here."

Solomon motioned Uri to be seated on a wooden folding chair, and pulled another chair next to his. Only two years separated the two brothers, but Solomon had advanced far in life. Besides Zeideh's inheritance, he was a shrewd financial planner with many wealthy clients.

Uri looked around the cabin and out the two large portholes. He smiled gratefully at Solomon. "You haven't changed anything, Solomon. Just like when Zeideh was here."

Solomon lifted his finger for emphasis.

"Nothing is changed, Uri! This was Zeideh's castle in his heyday, right? Do you know, there are still the nicks on the desk from when he used to sharpen pencils with a penknife. Eerie — I'm sorry, I mean Uri — I feel Zeideh's presence whenever I work here. I try to come down at least once a week, to watch over things. I even call my clients from this cabin. Zeideh's spirit is here on board, just like the good old days, before..." his voice trailed off. "Well, you know —"

A gloomy silence suddenly fell on the cabin, as memories flooded in.

Uri nodded to his brother. "Zeideh really changed those last ten years, didn't he?"

Solomon laid his big hand on Uri's arm. "Do you want to see something? You won't believe this!"

Without waiting for an answer, Solomon leapt out of his chair and lead Uri to the porthole windows. Uri followed him and looked out to the harbor. Great white chunks of ice bobbed up and down in the gray waters.

"Look," he pointed, "there she still is, just like all those years ago."

Uri looked out to a cruise ship that laid tied to port, just a few docks away. There was no mistaking its identity. It lay deep in the water, white sails furled closed, its artistically painted blue walls still breathtaking despite the heavy skies. On its side, in unmistakable indigo letters, was etched its name: *Deep Blue*.

"Does she still sail regularly?" asked Uri. "I haven't kept track of the lake."

Solomon shook his head ruefully. "It sails, Uri, it sails, believe me! It's doing great business — just like we are. You know, we're booked into next year already! Zeideh's boat is like a license to print money!"

Uri caught his breath. For a moment he was so caught up in the memories of Zeideh that he forgot why he had come. The two brothers stood shoulder to shoulder looking out at the harbor, summoning memories. True, Solomon and he had gone in different directions, but now memories of Zeideh brought them close.

"Solomon," he began quietly, still looking out at *Deep Blue*, "I need a favor."

"Oh. What, Uri?"

"You know, my oldest son Yirmiyahu is going to be bar mitzvah in a few months."

"Oh, I didn't know. *Mazel tov*! I didn't even ask you how your family is. They're okay?"

"They're fine. But I want to get a special pair of tefillin for Yirmiyahu. He is a wonderful boy, and will be a great *talmid chacham* some day. But I can't afford them —"

"How much are they?"

"Thirteen hundred dollars, American."

Solomon gave out a whistle. "What are they, golden boxes?"

"No golden boxes, Solomon. Golden *kavanos*, golden *neshamah*! Reb Zelig Schreiber, the man who writes them in Yerushalayim, is a great tzaddik. His *parashiyos* are very special."

There was a moment's silence and Uri whispered a prayer to Hashem. Then Solomon spoke.

"You are my kid brother, Uri, and I'm going to help you."

Uri breathed with relief. Solomon wrapped his arm around Uri's shoulder and led him back to the chair. "Sit down," he said, "let's talk."

Uri sat down across from his brother. Solomon leaned forward.

"How much are you short for the tefillin?"

"I need...at least fifteen hundred Canadian."

"The money's yours."

Uri smiled with gratitude. "Thank you, Solomon," he murmured.

Solomon suddenly stood up. "But not the way you mean, Uri! You think I'm going to write you out a check?"

"What then?" asked Uri. "Cash?"

"No, Uri, better!"

"Credit card?"

"No, Uri, I'm not to going to give you a penny of money – I'm going to give you a job!"

"A job?"

"Yes, Uri. I'm going to let you break out of the poverty cycle you got yourself into! I'm going to give you your dignity, your respect! I need a bookkeeper here on the boat. Someone I can trust, who can handle the cash. I even have an ad in the paper. But here you are."

"I am not a bookkeeper, Solomon."

"I'll teach you."

"I don't want to be a bookkeeper, Solomon! I spend my days learning and teaching Torah! That's my life! My life is Torah. I don't want to spend my time counting nickels and dimes —"

Solomon grew angry. "So then what do you want from me, Uri? I give you a chance to earn a livelihood and you turn it down?"

Solomon grew hot under the collar, and his voice rose. Uri saw that he was upset, and deliberately lowered his voice, in an attempt to calm his brother.

"Solomon, I appreciate your offer. I really do! But I will not change now, not at my age! I have spent my whole life in Torah, and I'm going to throw it away now? Do you know how precious every moment of Torah learning is to me? I finish a whole *masechta* each year just waiting on line at the bank or the cleaners! And now you want me to become a bookkeeper, counting tens and twenties."

Solomon looked at his brother coldly. "Look, Uri, it's your life, your wife, your kids! But if you come to me – that's my offer."

Uri looked at his brother pleadingly. "Solomon...I thought...I thought that since you have the boat and the dock and all your investments, and you say *Swift Current* is making so much money...and all I got was Gortel –"

At the mention of Gortel, Solomon snorted derisively.

"I received so little, and you and Alexander got so much... I thought that maybe you could help me."

Solomon shook his head – just as Alexander had. Solomon was a great mimic, and he now imitated a comic-book character. " 'That's...that's...that's all folks!' " he stammered with a high-pitched drawl. "Everything is in G-d's hands, right?"

"Right!"

"G-d wanted Alexander to get the house, me to get the boat and you to get..." here Solomon couldn't repress his snigger, "ha, ha, ha – Gortel. I offered you an honorable, decent paying job, Uri! Take it, or leave it."

"Solomon, you know I can't take it!"

Solomon looked up at his brother and raised his hands helplessly. "I'm sorry, Uri, but I can't help you."

Uri rose and sighed deeply. He gave his brother long, imploring look. Solomon didn't notice. Uri gazed around at his Zeideh's cabin, and turned to leave. He paused at the porthole by the door and gazed out. There lay *Deep Blue*. Uri was a gentle man, a generous man, but he could not help but stare at the inanimate ship with...hatred. No! He was not allowed to hate, even an inanimate object like a boat. But he was angry. *You ruined my Zeideh's life – you and whomever you belong to!* For that was the boat that had ruined Zeideh, humiliated him in the Great Race, and changed him from a fun-loving sea captain whom the whole city loved to a...cheerless recluse.

He turned. Solomon was standing next to him, shoulder to shoulder.

"Brings back memories, doesn't it?" Solomon said.

Uri nodded. Solomon put his arm apologetically around his younger brother.

"Look, Uri, don't be angry that I didn't give you the money. I mean it for your best – and your family. The job offer is always open. But, hey…I can't leave you without something –"

Solomon reached inside his jacket and extracted a little golden toothpick. On its top waved a little golden flag, with a dollar sign etched in its center.

"Look, Uri, take this for good luck."

"What is it?"

"It's a little flagpole made out of eighteen carat gold. That's what I'm telling all my clients: put your money in gold. Oil is going to go up, then down. The Canadian dollar is going to go up. China is the next big economy. Gold will shoot up like a rocket! Uri, I believe in gold! So here, for whatever it's worth, take this little flag and put it where you won't lose it –"

He opened Uri's jacket and pinned it to the lining, over his inside pocket. "Let this be your little gold nest egg, from me to you."

Uri looked at his brother. Solomon was worth millions, and he was giving him a…toothpick?

"*Yasher koach*," Uri mumbled. "Thank you, Solomon…"

And he left.

⛵ ⛵ ⛵

There is only so much a person can take, only so much frustration, so much…unfairness. If Uri were made of stone, he could have endured it all easily: strong, confident, joyous. But Uri had a soft heart, a generous *neshamah*, a soul that wept at injustice. It was too much, too much even to understand. He needed to speak to the tzaddik, Reb Klonimos – for understanding.

It was not so easy to see him. More and more people recognized his greatness, and Uri had to wait almost a week, and then late into the night, to meet him privately. But it was worth the wait. He had not seen the young tzaddik up close for many months, just from across the shul, or to greet him with a "*gut voch*." His face had grown even more purified, and he radiated *kedushah* like a glowing hearth. And yet, he had no airs about him. He greeted Uri warmly, casually.

"So, how is it going, Reb Uri?" he asked. "Are you keeping up with your Zeideh's learning schedule?"

Uri was surprised that Reb Klonimos remembered his undertaking.

"It's not easy," he answered. "But I'm trying. I'm into *Pesachim*."

Reb Klonimos nodded and smiled. "Good, good! Your Zeideh was my good friend! It is a great *zechus* for his *neshamah*."

"Amen."

There was an awkward silence. Uri didn't know how to start. Reb Klonimos looked down at a closed *sefer* in front of him, waiting patiently.

Finally, Uri heaved a heart-breaking sigh and poured out his heart.

"Reb Klonimos, I'm having a terrible time understanding Hashem's ways! My learning is not bad, but I am struggling so hard for *parnasah*! I loved my Zeideh, and he loved me — I know he did! Yet he left all his fortune to my brothers and I was left with nothing except a few stocks, and a set of *Shas*! And I don't think it was a mistake. It was some sort of joke he played on me, like a game. Reb Klonimos, I've found money in the Gemaras that I have learned, cash that my Zeideh placed there for me! He knew I would need the money, so he left me a few extra dollars —"

At the mention of the money, Reb Klonimos's heavy brows rose in surprise. Then he looked down, listening.

"Now I need money for my son Yirmiyahu's tefillin. He's a boy with a special *neshamah* — and a *gaonishe* head! He is begging me to get tefillin from Reb Zelig Schreiber of Meah Shearim —"

"They're excellent!" interjected Reb Klonimos.

"Yes, excellent," said Uri hotly, "but they cost a fortune — money that I don't have —"

"May Hashem send you all the money you need for them," said Reb Klonimos.

"Amen," answered Uri. "But Reb Klonimos, all of this I can understand. We received almost nothing from my Zeideh's inheritance because my stock went down — that was Hashem's will. But I can't take..."

Uri paused abruptly. He battled with himself whether to speak or not...but he had to.

Reb Klonimos waited. Uri finally poured out his bitterness.

"I can't take how selfish some people are! I went to my brothers who both inherited fortunes to ask them to help with the tefillin — and they wouldn't give me a penny!"

Uri reached into his lapel and pulled out the golden toothpick with a little flag on top. He passed it to the tzaddik.

"Here, this is what I received — one gold toothpick! How can people act this way...brothers! Brothers who have so much, and share so little —"

Uri's sensitive face became so sad, so sad that he had to share these words with Reb Klonimos.

But Klonimos stayed very calm. He studied the little gold toothpick and its flag, twirling it around in his fingers.

"What's this little "s" on top?" he asked.

" 'S' is 'Solomon' — my brother believes in gold."

Klonimos chuckled and returned the toothpick.

"You're right, Reb Uri," he said, "money is funny, isn't it?"

Uri raised his hands in frustration. "Reb Klonimos, it's not funny, it's crazy! Why do some people who have so much not want to part with a penny! And they are driven to make more and more? It's like a...sickness!"

Klonimos suddenly stopped smiling and looked hard at Uri.

"Reb Uri, I know the reason. It's a very, very sad reason. Do you really want to hear it?"

"Yes, please! It's all so crazy, the whole world is so crazy!"

Reb Klonimos shut his eyes, and began swaying. When he finally spoke, it was in a low song, a *niggun*.

"The *pasuk* says in *perek pei-dalet* of *Tehillim* —"

He stopped swaying and opened his eyes. "Do you ever read *Tehillim*, Reb Uri?"

"Yes." Uri responded like a child and subconsciously began swaying in time with the tzaddik.

"The *pasuk* says: 'Nichsefah v'gam kalsah nafshi l'chatzros Hashem, libi uv'sari yeranenu el Keil chai — My soul yearns, it pines, for the courtyards of Hashem! My heart and my flesh pray fervently to the Living G-d.'

"Reb Uri, listen! A Jewish *neshamah* is *nichsefah*, it longs for Hashem... It longs for Hashem like a drowning man longs to rise up into the air, to breathe. The *neshamah* longs for its holy *shoresh* like our lungs seek air every second! There is nothing we seek more than our next breath, and there is nothing that our *neshamahs* long for than their *chiyus* in Hashem! What a love, what a yearning!

"But, Reb Uri —" The tzaddik suddenly fell silent, and his face contorted with burning intensity. He *shuckel*ed furiously, and Uri quickened his own swaying.

"But, Reb Uri, instead of *nichsefah* for Hashem, the *nichsefah* fell into *klippos*, into impure shells! *Nichsefah* was turned into — *kesef*. *Nichsefah* and *kesef* are two mighty kings: one soars Upwards, and one is trapped Below. The *sitra achra* pulls the love of Hashem down into the shells and turns it into a love of —"

Suddenly Reb Klonimos's eyes opened wide and darted wildly around the room. He had such an utter look of ugly contempt on his face that Uri barely recognized him.

"Money! *Kesef*!" he shouted. "The *kesufim* that our *neshamah*s have for their holy *shoresh*, has fallen into lifeless shells! Money!"

Reb Klonimos said the word money with such disgust, his face was so twisted with anger, that Uri grew frightened. The tzaddik was losing control! But it passed quickly, like a summer storm, and his usual beautiful, holy countenance returned.

Reb Klonimus opened his eyes and spoke more calmly.

"Reb Uri, money is just a tool, that's all, like a hammer or shovel. It is a tool to serve the *neshamah*, to serve Hashem. But your brothers, *nebuch*, they have been trapped in the *klippos*, snared by the *sitra achra*."

"But what can I do to change them?" asked Uri. "It's so hard...I have so many bills, and now the tefillin! And they have so much..."

Klonimos laughed sadly. "You? What can you do? You can't force them to do anything, Reb Uri! Money is in Hashem's hands, don't you know? It is a *galgal*, a big wheel. One day it rolls to me, the next it bounces to you — this is Hashem's way!"

Uri finally smiled. "Reb Klonimos, I need a *berachah*! Maybe you can get the wheel to roll a little bit in my direction — just so I can get the special tefillin for my son —"

Klonimos smiled, but then he leaned forward with great earnestness. He reached across his desk and lay his hand over Uri's anxiously clasped hands. His face shone in the glow of the lamp, and his eyes flashed fire.

"*Bitachon*, Reb Uri! You must stay the course! Help will come, I am sure — help that you can't even imagine! Don't despair and don't be bitter! Push on with your holy learning, rejoice in your son's bar mitzvah, and the money you need will fall at your doorstep just like the manna fell for the Yidden in the desert."

Uri could not remain silent anymore. "Reb Klonimos, please — manna doesn't fall anymore," he said, too boldly.

Reb Klonimos sat up like he had been struck. He looked hard at Uri. "What? Is this my Reb Uri speaking so? You are wrong, Reb Uri! It falls, it falls! But it's hidden in the *tzintzenes,* in the jar!"

Uri looked at Klonimos, puzzled.

Reb Klonimos leaned forward and shared a secret, speaking barely above a whisper.

"When the manna fell, Aharon was commanded to hide a portion in a *tzintzenes,* a jar. Do you know why? It was a sign: manna would never stop falling from *Shamayim* — never! But it is hidden, hidden in a salary check, hidden in an inheritance, in a lottery ticket, in an investment that suddenly shoots! But it is not a salary check — it is manna from *Shamayim,* cloaked in a check. It is not an inheritance, not a stock that brings money — it is all manna hidden in a *tzintzenes*! It falls for me, it falls for you, Reb Uri! But, *bitachon*! Be joyous! *Simchah*! Not bitter! Not angry! You hear?"

Uri looked at Reb Klonimos's holy countenance and nodded. If Reb Klonimos had told him at that moment that day was night, and water was wine — he also would have nodded.

Klonimos abruptly grew silent, smiled, and nodded. Uri knew that others were waiting. He rose and Reb Klonimos walked Uri to the door, arm on his shoulder.

For a few minutes, Uri stood alone outside the tzaddik's house. There was a scent of spring in the air and the sound of migrant birds chattering in the dark branches. He glanced up at the thin moon for an instant, pulled himself up straight, and began walking home.

⛵ ⛵ ⛵

Reb Klonimos's confident words sustained Uri for the next days. He cast all doubt aside, all concern about raising money. It would come. He learned with a *bren*, like a yeshivah *bachur* who has no worries except when his parents' next allowance check will come. His mind was focused; the golden pen sailed joyously over the *daf*, and he even searched out the Rif and Maharsha.

But the calendar moved on, days turned into weeks and Yirmiyahu grew more anxious. He knocked each morning at Uri's study door, and politely but insistently inquired:

"Abba, when will we go for the tefillin?"

Always the same answer from Uri: "Soon, Yirmiyahu, I'll have the money soon."

But the days grew shorter. It was almost two months to Yirmiyahu's bar mitzvah. And there was a danger. The *sofer* had promised to hold the beautiful pair of Zelig Schreiber tefillin for Uri — but not forever. There were half a dozen other fathers who were willing to pay the *sofer* even more than he had asked to grab this very pair of holy tefillin! The *sofer* was kind and patient, but there was a limit. Uri had to buy them soon — or give them up. Meanwhile, he did not have the money.

One morning, even before he began learning, Uri made a list he dreaded. It was a list of ten very wealthy men, fine men, whom he could approach for a loan. He gazed at the list of names and phone numbers, and hid it carefully in the cover of his Gemara, so Yirmiyahu should never see it. Each morning he opened his Gemara, glanced at the list, studied the names, and then set it back inside.

I'll call later, he promised himself. But Uri never called, day after day. He hated asking others for help. He knew they would even offer to give him the money — charity! But he didn't want a loan. He didn't want charity. He always relied on his own resources, big or small. Even asking his brothers was terrible — and what a strikeout!

Klonimos's brave words faded, and Uri was left with a terrible dilemma. He learned, but no longer like a carefree yeshivah *bachur*; part of his brain brooded on the names in his cover. They seemed to grow bigger and bigger, demanding action: why didn't he call?

And then each morning, the dreaded knock at his door: "Abba, when are you going to get my tefillin?"

Just one last ray of hope shone for Uri.

In the last *masechta* that he had learned, *Eiruvin*, Zeideh had planted three one-hundred-dollar bills throughout the pages. In the Gemara *Shabbos* before that, Zeideh had had fun... He sprinkled little patches of bills, sometimes a twenty, sometimes two twenties, even a one hundred-dollar bill, randomly here and there for extra surprise. Zeideh must have had a good time! Uri imagined Zeideh sitting at his desk, sticking in money here and there, laughing to himself —

"I'm going to surprise Eerie here! He's going to find money just there!"

Even in his old age, when he lived so somber a life, Zeideh didn't lose his love of games. And what a game — a game that Uri counted on for his life! With each bill that Uri plucked out of the page, he saw Zeideh slipping in the money. Hide and seek!

But...he could not learn Torah for money. He had to learn Torah *lishmah* — otherwise, what *kedushah* did it have? His *bitachon* had to be in Hashem, not in Zeideh! So he had made a rule: if there was money, *Baruch Hashem*, but he would not go looking for it!

So he had done up to now. But who knew what Zeideh had planted in his present Gemara, *Pesachim*? Uri already had accumulated five hundred dollars for the tefillin. He had hidden away all Zeideh's cash that he had discovered in the Gemaras, but he still needed another thirteen hundred.

Uri lifted his Gemara *Pesachim* as though he was weighing it. There were one hundred and twenty *dapim* in *Pesachim*. He had learned ninety, and there were thirty more to the finish. So far, there had not been even one hidden dollar! Did Zeideh forget? Zeideh never forgot! It was all part of Zeideh's Gemara game — hide and seek!

Zeideh was hiding money somewhere, but where?

Uri struggled with himself.

Bitachon, Uri!

But I need the money — now!

A knock at the door. It was Yirmiyahu.

"Abba, can we go for the tefillin today? I'm afraid the *sofer* will sell them to someone else!"

Thirty more pages to go in *Pesachim*: almost six weeks. Who knew what fortune lay inside those thirty pages, what hundred dollar bills?

One morning, Uri walked determinedly into his study and laid the Gemara on his desk. He had made up his mind.

"Hashem," he whispered, "please forgive me — but I need the money!"

He turned to the page he was up to — ninety-four — and began turning page after page. He perspired with guilt, but he kept to it, "*Arvei Pesachim*"...one hundred pages...one hundred ten, carefully searching for the money, checking his desk to see if any bills dropped out. Finally, he reached the last *daf*. There was nothing. Zeideh had skipped *Pesachim*.

"*Baruch Hashem*," he whispered to himself, "it serves me right!"

I cheated — and I struck out!

And yet...Hashem forgave Uri his little indiscretion, for his salvation suddenly appeared from none other than his unstoppable twins, Dovid'l and Yisroel!

It happened one afternoon a few days later. A student had cancelled and Uri came home unexpectedly from tutoring. Chaya was in the kitchen, davening *minchah*. The twins should have been home from cheder, but the house was strangely quiet. Uri heaved a sigh of relief at the calm, hung his jacket on a dining-room chair, and opened the door to his study.

He stood there in a state of shock.

"What is going on here?" he demanded. He couldn't believe his eyes. Dovid'l stood on a chair alongside his tall bookcase. Yisroel had somehow climbed onto his shoulders and was clinging with his fingertips to the top of the bookshelf, searching for something. He was an inch from falling and toppling the heavy bookcase on both of them.

They sprung around together like acrobats and turned in Uri's direction. Yisroel barely held on to the top of the bookcase with two fingers of one hand.

"Hi, Abba!" they greeted him cheerfully.

"Never mind 'Hi, Abba!' " Uri yelled. "What are you doing in my study, and why are you up there? The whole bookcase could come down on your heads!"

It began to dawn on them that they were in serious trouble.

"We're looking for something," Dovid'l explained.

"What do you mean 'we're looking for something,' " Uri yelled even louder. "You – are – not – supposed – to – be – in – this – room! Get down from there!"

Dovid'l, who held Yisroel's legs in his hands, suddenly leaned forward, throwing Yisroel down to the floor with a crash. Some of the *sefarim* tumbled out of the top shelves behind him onto the floor.

Uri raced to the fallen books in horror. He quickly lifted them, gave them each a brief kiss, and stacked them on his desk.

"Look what you've done, you nutty professors! What are you doing in here?"

Dovid'l finally jumped down from his chair, and the twins stood trapped against the back window. They were both...giggling. Uri stared at them, and then started laughing. They were impossible, and he loved it!

His voice returned to normal.

"What are you doing here – tell me the truth!"

The twins looked at each other, and Dovid'l, who was always bolder, explained: "We were looking for your gold pen."

"My gold pen? How do you know about my gold pen?"

"We once saw you use it! It's so...gold! We asked Mommy to see it, and she told us you hid it, so we were looking for it."

At that moment, Chaya, who had heard the crash in the middle of her *Shemoneh Esrei*, ran into the study. She saw the *sefarim* strewn over on Uri's desk and the overturned chair.

"Uri, what happened?" she asked.

"It's your troublemakers," Uri said, rolling his eyes, "your twins. They broke into my study looking for my gold pen."

"Oh. Did they find it?"

"Where I hid it, no one can find it — not even the twins!"

Suddenly, Chaya switched allegiance to the twins. She stood next to them protectively.

"Well, Uri, we would actually all like to see your famous pen! You know, this study is a big mystery to us. You lock yourself in here every day, and we would like to see the special pen you use."

Uri looked around helplessly. The twins beamed triumphantly. Chaya gave him The Look. He was cornered — and outnumbered.

He smiled at his wife, but whispered in her ear so that only she heard: "Benedict Arnold."

He faced down the mob. "All right, I'll show you the pen. But everyone has to turn around. No looking when I get it!"

Chaya and the ever-giggling twins obediently faced the door, while Uri backed discreetly towards the wall and extracted the pen from its hiding place behind an innocent row of *Mishnah Berurahs*. He deliberately made a lot of unnecessary noise at another corner to confuse them.

He returned to the desk.

"Okay," he announced, "here it is!"

The twins turned and ran to the pen. Uri held it near to the desk, so they could get a good look.

"Can we hold it?" Yisroel asked.

Uri passed him the pen. "Be careful."

Yisroel took the pen in his hands and gently turned it. Soon Dovid'l was trying to grab it from him.

"Easy!" Uri watched, delighted, as the twins fingered the precious pen, turning it about and upside down. He glanced at Chaya, glad that she had intervened for them.

"Does it write?" asked Dovid'l.

"No," said Uri. "It's all dried up. Look —"

The twins had never seen a fountain pen before. Uri unscrewed the cover, exposing the sharp silver point. Very gingerly, he touched the tip of the point.

"You see, this is where the ink comes out. But the pen is all dry because it hasn't been used for so long. If you are very, very careful, I'll let you feel the point with your fingers. One finger each."

They each offered a finger and nervously felt the point.

"It's so sharp," Dovid'l cried, jerking back his finger.

"You see, boys," Uri said. "I told you! It's all dried up, and it's very sharp. That's why I hid it from you — for your own sakes!"

"So, Abba, how do you use it?" asked Dovid'l.

"I don't use it as a pen. But if you absolutely promise not to touch anything, I will show you what I do."

"Whoo hoo!" they screamed.

"Never mind 'whoo hoo'! Let me see your hands." Uri checked their fingers for chocolate and other dirt. They were strangely clean.

"Okay, stand on the chair."

He stood them together on the chair next to his *shtender*. Uri went to the bookshelf, and he carefully extracted his Gemara *Pesachim*. He lay the Gemara on the *shtender* and opened up to the first *daf*.

"You see, this pen was my Zeideh's and this was his Gemara. See how he kept it so clean! When I learn, I use his gold pen as my pointer. See —"

Swaying slightly, Uri swept down a few lines with his pen, reciting the words.

Finally, he stopped. "So, boys! That's the whole mystery of Abba's gold pen. Are you happy now?"

"Abba," said Dovid'l, "I saw a picture of your pen!"

"Oh," asked Uri, "where?"

"It came in yesterday's paper, in one of the flyers!"

Uri and Chaya exchanged glances. Chaya shrugged and shook her head. Dovid'l was off in a flash. In a minute he raced back, grasping one of the innumerable flyers that came with the local newspaper that was dropped free at their step.

"Here, Abba!" he exclaimed, "look, it's just like your pen!"

Uri took the paper: It was a Father's Day flyer from Kirk's, the exclusive jewelry shop. There was a display of beautiful pens for fathers, all the way up to a thousand dollars.

Dovid'l was very sharp. "Look, Abba, here's your pen!"

Uri studied the sheet. Indeed, it looked like his pen, but not as nice. It was called "The Brooke Executive."

"It does look a lot like your pen," said Chaya. "Uri, is yours a Brooke?"

"I don't know," said Uri. "I never noticed."

He lifted Zeideh's pen and studied it closely. For the first time he noticed the tiny stamp that surrounded the little glass adornment at the bottom of the case. He smiled. "Sure enough, it is! I never heard of Brooke before."

"Very exclusive," said Chaya. "It's made in Switzerland. Happy Father's Day!"

So, Uri didn't know that he had been using a Brooke pen — whatever that meant. And it was worth over a thousand dollars new!

The little scandal blew over, and peace was made between all sides. It was impossible to be angry with the twins, they were just too cute, too innocent, and too smiley.

The family left, and Uri was held holding the pen: a thousand-dollar pen.

That night, after *ma'ariv*, Uri approached one of the men who was in the jewelry and fine gift business.

Uri showed him Zeideh's pen.

"Nachman, could you tell me what this pen would be worth if I wanted to sell it?"

Nachman took the pen, removed his glasses, and studied it in the harsh hallway light. He turned it around and around, ran his fingers carefully over its tapered grooves, and inspected the Brooke insignia. Then he lifted it up and down, like he was weighing gold. He returned the pen to Uri and put back on his glasses.

"Reb Uri, where did you get a Brooke? You must be doing good in the *chavrusa* business. This pen is top of the line, especially with the diamond!"

"Diamond?" asked Uri, "what diamond?"

Nachman retrieved the pen. He pointed to the little gem near the trademark. "There, look!"

Uri looked at the tiny crystal. "I thought it was glass."

Nachman sighed. "Oh, Reb Uri, Reb Uri! Can't you see — it's a diamond!"

"It is?" He peered at the crystal again. It still looked like glass. A diamond! "If I sold the pen, how much could I get for it?" he asked.

Nachman glanced at the pen again, and made a quick calculation in his head. "I would say…fifteen hundred, easy!"

Uri was overwhelmed. "Really? Really…fifteen hundred?"

Nachman made a this and that face. "Maybe, maybe even more."

"And could you sell it for me if I asked you?"

"Sell it for you? Reb Uri, why would you want to sell such a beautiful pen? I'm telling you, it's a Brooke exclusive, an heirloom! Keep it for your kids, even for the *einiklech*!"

Uri pulled Nachman to the corner of the hallway, out of earshot of passersby, and lowered his voice.

"Nachman, I need the money now — for my son's tefillin. If I gave it to you, could you sell the pen for me?"

"Are you kidding? A Brooke Executive? I'd have a customer for it in a day."

"And I want you to take a percentage, as commission," said Uri.

Nachman waved his hand impatiently. "Don't bother me, Reb Uri! Percentage? For what? There's no work — two phone calls and it's done."

Uri almost started crying for joy. Nachman looked at him impatiently.

"Now what's the matter?"

"Reb Nachman, where can we find people like you in the world?"

Nachman made a sour face, and waved his hand.

"Leave me alone, Schiffman! If you decide to sell it, give me a call, no problem. I'll handle everything."

He ran off, fearing he would hear more thanks from Uri.

A great weight suddenly lifted off Uri's shoulders. What Zeideh had not left him in money, he left him in the beautiful gold pen. The next morning he woke eagerly, ran to his study, and extracted Zeideh's pen from its hiding place. He fell into learning like a young man, for he had been rescued from begging for help. He ceremoniously took out the list of ten wealthy men, ripped it to shreds, and threw it into the waste bin. Later that morning he called the *sofer* and made a definite date to buy the tefillin.

Later, when Yirmiyahu knocked at his door, he had a clear answer. "Right after I finish *Pesachim*, we'll go together to buy the tefillin."

Yirmiyahu was happy and stopped knocking at Uri's door each morning.

Uri told Chaya about Nachman's appraisal.

"Uri, are you really sure you want to sell your Zeideh's pen?" she asked.

"Chaya, Yirmiyahu's tefillin are more important than any pen," he answered resolutely. "It's the only way we can afford the Schreiber *parshiyos* without begging for help!"

Chaya was pleased to see the joy and peace on her husband's face. It was Uri's pen, and Uri's decision. Everyone was happy — and Chaya sighed with relief.

And yet...the next morning, and the mornings after, when Uri took out his pen and stood over the Gemara, all he could think of was — Zeideh's pen in his hand. Every line he learned, every Rashi he studied, he felt the pen in his hand stroking him. From time to time he lifted the pen and stared at it. It was so beautiful, with its tiny diamond and the Brooke mark...and it had been Zeideh's. No one saw him, so when he finished learning the *daf* that morning, Uri gave the pen a little kiss before hiding it.

The next morning, Uri again extracted the pen and began learning. The pen seemed to hold onto his fingers, like a baby grasps a father's hand, following him anywhere, trusting completely. The pen held on to

Uri's hand like it did not want him to go away.

One morning, the feeling was so strong that Uri lifted the pen and scolded it:

"Listen, you are just a pen! Leave me alone!"

And yet, the feeling did bother Uri, greatly. The closer he came to finishing *Pesachim* and making the *siyum* — after which he would sell the pen — his preoccupation with Zeideh's pen grew stronger and stronger. All day, wherever he went, with whomever he learned, he saw the pen. It was like a cloud that hung over his head, larger than life, and heavier. He had to sell the pen, but it was Zeideh's pen! It was Zeideh's gift, through Bookman. He felt he was selling...Zeideh! But the tefillin that Yirmiyahu longed for were even more important, holier.

Even as the *simchah* and excitement of the bar mitzvah grew in the Schiffman household, Uri felt trapped. He dreamed about the pen at night, and his hand trembled even as he held it.

A week before Uri was to complete *Pesachim*, Nachman called him.

"Reb Uri, good news! I have a definite buyer for your pen. He is a collector, and your pen is almost unavailable anywhere. You may even get two thousand! Two thousand — you hear? When can we arrange things?"

Uri did not answer.

"Reb Uri...Rabbi Schiffman, are you there?"

"I'm here, Nachman."

"Just one second —"

Uri put down the phone. He closed his eyes. This nonsense must end! Yirmiyahu needs the tefillin! *Hashem, give me the strength!*

He picked up the phone, and his voice was firm.

"Good, Nachman. Here's the story. I am finishing *maseches Pesachim* in another week. I feel I should hold on to my Zeideh's pen until then, because I started learning the Gemara with it as a pointer. I'll call you right after that and we can work out the details. Is that all right?"

"Whatever's good for you, Reb Uri!" said Nachman, "Just let me know!"

For the first time in weeks, Uri felt at peace. He had made a decision, a wise decision, a decision that made Yirmiyahu happy, and where he did not have to ask others for help. Zeideh himself would have approved!

The final pages of *Pesachim* moved quickly, and one bright Monday morning, Uri stood in the shul surrounded by his *chevrah* and made a *siyum* on *Pesachim*. There were *l'chayim*s and *mazel tov*s, but no one was more excited than Yirmiyahu, because he knew that in a few days he would finally receive his longed-for tefillin.

⛵ ⛵ ⛵

It was a beautiful spring morning. Uri entered his study before five and rolled open his study window. A fresh, sweet breeze flowed through the room, and outside a lonely bird twittered and sang to its mate.

It was a bittersweet morning for Uri. He was pleased that he had completed *Pesachim* after four months of hard learning. But this was his last day with Zeideh's pen. He had an appointment to meet Nachman that evening. He would hand over the pen and have his money in a day.

He lay the *Pesachim* volume on his *shtender*. He had to finish off a few pages of *Shekalim* at the back, and then he would collect the next volume from Bookman. He went to the bookshelf, pulled back two volumes of *Mishnah Berurah*, and retrieved his pen.

Uri stood at the *shtender* and inspected Zeideh's pen. He turned it slowly in his fingers, flicking off a drop of dust that had collected overnight. It was a work of such beauty! Every groove was etched perfectly, and the pen itself was shaped was like a long, thin tear-drop. He turned it over and admired the tiny stone that served as the foundation for its beautiful form, and the trademark Brooke, engraved in tiny, perfect letters.

He was sad, very sad to part with the pen, and yet, because it was so hard, he was doing a tremendous mitzvah. *Beharimchem es chelbo mei'imanu* — he was offering his fattest lamb, his most beloved possession to Hashem! True, the pen would be gone, but the holy *sheimos* that Reb Zelig imbued into the tefillin would lie on Yirmiyahu's head and across from his heart!

The pen felt soft, not hard, and warm like a hand. Zeideh's hand had rested just where his hand now rested, and he felt Zeideh's hand in his...but that would be soon gone. *Where will the pen go next?* he wondered. *To a collector's shelf? Or will some wealthy businessman use it to sign big checks and finalize contracts?*

Uri silently said goodbye to the pen. *Golden pen, I am offering you up as a korban to Hashem! In your gold and your little diamond, you contain a spark of kedushas tefillin! I am raising you from a simple pen to the holiness of tefillin! Be joyous, Zeideh's pen, for you are having an aliyah! Wherever you will be, I, and Zeideh, and Yirmiyahu's tefillin – we will be with you!*

Uri glanced at the clock, it was already well past five. He was late. He quickly turned past the pages of *Pesachim*, and opened to *Shekalim*, a small *masechta* nestling in the back of the Gemara. He laid the pen down on the first *mishnah* and began reading:

"*B'echad b'Adar mashmi'im al hashekalim...*"

It was an easy Gemara, and Uri learned quickly. But he soon had a problem. The pen bounced up and down on the page like a car that has driven onto a railroad track. He tried to ignore the bumps, but the pen rode up and down, distracting him. The paper seemed warped and bent, probably from disuse. He needed to force the pages flat and even.

He turned over the *daf* to find the problem. He froze – and stared. Under the page lay a long, green row of hundred-dollar bills tucked into the fold. The bills were neatly folded, origami style, and looked like leaves on a tree. Uri took a deep breath. *Zeideh, Zeideh...* He lay down his pen, and plucked out the green bills, like leaves from a branch...

There were exactly thirteen one-hundred-dollar bills, and something more. Under the bills, Zeideh had pasted a little yellow note. Uri unfolded it.

It was written in Zeideh's tiny, fine script:

Dear Eerie,

If my reckoning is correct, you should be nearing Yirmiyahu's thirteenth birthday. If it's not too late, use this money to buy him the best pair of tefillin.

Zeideh

Uri stared at the note, and at the money piled on the desk. He did not want to unfold the money and make a neat stack. The folding itself was a work of art — no, a work of love — Zeideh's love! He saw Zeideh a few months before he died, an old, lonely, sad man, sitting patiently in his study and folding this money into little green leaves of cash just to surprise his grandson!

What joy he must have had — and what a sad secret.

Uri's first instinct was to run to Chaya and show her the money. It was a miracle! The very same day he was going to sell Zeideh's pen, and now, all was cancelled!

Uri lifted the pen and spoke to it:

"Pen! You are not going anywhere! You are staying right here, understand?"

Uri was beside himself with excitement. What should he do first?

Call up Nachman right now and cancel the sale — at five thirty in the morning?

Run to Chaya and Yirmiyahu and announce to them the good news, the miracle news, of the thirteen bills?

He pulled himself together. *Uri: stick to your mitzvah!*

He let the bills lay in a pile on the desk, quickly recited *Mizmor L'Sodah* to thank Hashem, and, with unbelievable *simchah*, returned to learning *Shekalim*!

He was so stupid! Of course! Whoever thought of *Shekalim*? Where else would Zeideh hide the money but in the Gemara about *shekalim*, money! Why hadn't he thought about it, looked through *Shekalim*?

All those months of unnecessary worry — what a reproof for never thinking enough about poor, neglected Gemara *Shekalim*!

Controlling his excitement. Uri finished the *daf*. He even learned past his usual time. It did not matter — today was a *yom tov*! Finally, he closed the Gemara. He quickly gathered up the folded money and carefully placed it in an envelope so Chaya could see how much love and labor Zeideh had put into his gift. He kissed the Gemara, quickly hid the pen back in its hiding place, and ran out joyously to tell the family the wonderful news!

Deep in its dark hiding place, Zeideh's pen stirred with holy desire. Uri had gazed upon it with such profound sanctity he had ignited the holy *nitzotzim* it contained. Uri's holy *machshavos* lifted it to new heights — and it did not want to fall back down again!

Inside its long, thin, golden sheath, a tiny pool of deep blue liquid stirred and quickened, bubbling up like a miniature sea, with stormy swells and roiling waves. And it lifted its inky head and cried: "I also want to serve Hashem!"

FOUR

The bar mitzvah went beautifully.

Yirmiyahu read the *parashah* and haftorah, davened *shacharis* and *mussaf*, and delivered a *pshetl* that he wrote almost completely by himself. His rebbi was right: Yirmiyahu was an exceptional child: serious and absolutely determined. Uri prayed that he should stay that way, and not lose his fervor.

Now, Uri could finally settle back to his teaching – and learning Zeideh's *daf*.

Zeideh had established an elaborate game, and Uri was caught inside. Zeideh had enticed him into learning a daily *daf*, but on his terms, and on his schedule. Each day he studied, Zeideh was still alive, running things. Before he had become a recluse, Zeideh loved playing games. Now he had gone back to his old tricks: he was playing hide-and-seek with Uri. Zeideh's Gemaras looked untouched, but it was just a front. They had been touched, alright, touched and learned and filled with Zeideh's comments.

Uri suspected Zeideh meant these notes for him. On a particularly difficult piece of Gemara, he scribbled in: "Tough going, these lines, eh?" When Rashi and *Tosafos* argued, he would mark in carefully: "I see there's a real fight here."

Zeideh could hardly read without the *nekudos*, so he must have had a lot of help from Reb Klonimos. But what Zeideh didn't know in learning, he knew in how to draw in Uri deeper and deeper, so that he was tied to his game. Like a child getting candy for reciting Alef-Beis, Uri never knew where his payoff would come. Zeideh had salted his pages with his comments — and with money. Uri never knew when, or how much, or why. Sometimes it was a crisp twenty-dollar bill, sometimes just two fives, then sometimes he turned the page and there, pressed into the margin, was a hundred-dollar bill. Occasionally, Zeideh stuck in a tiny yellow note, telling him the money was for *yom tov* or Shabbos. Zeideh was always on the mark, all was worked out. Uri loved the game. He was a child again, and it was the old, fun Zeideh, and he was alive — alive just for Uri!

Uri knew he could leaf through the pages as soon as he received a new volume from Mr. Bookman, but that was cheating. Such money had no *ta'am*, no joy. This game of hide-and-seek was Zeideh's way of cleaving to him — even in death. So he learned *daf* by *daf*, played the game, and when Zeideh was ready, Uri received his reward.

There were no two Captain Elijah Schiffmans. Zeideh always did things his way — even when he sometimes, unwittingly, caused Uri pain. There was the matter of Uri's name. His parents had given him and his brothers noble names: Alexander, Solomon, Uri. But Zeideh would not leave his name alone. After his father died and Zeideh took them into his home, he gave each grandson's name a new spin. Alexander was Alexander the Great. Solomon became Solomon the Wise. And Uri became...Eerie, like his great grandfather had been called in Galicia. It was irresistible for Alexander and Solomon. Uri's new name became a torment. When his brothers surrounded him in the kitchen, they would sing in a mocking whisper: "*Hey, Eerie Eerie Shir Dabeiri!*"

Zeideh meant no harm. Uri had begged him a few times: "Zeideh, my name is Uri, not Eerie!" But it didn't help. Zeideh persisted in calling him, Eerie. Finally, Uri gave up and learned to live with his grandfather's quirks.

⛵ ⛵ ⛵

After the drama of Yirmiyahu's bar mitzvah, Uri's life settled into a calm cruise. The children were all doing excellently in school. Tova and Dina were growing into beautiful young women – sincere, caring, self-confident. Yirmiyahu was learning in the best yeshivah in the city, so intensely that Uri hardly saw him from Shabbos to Shabbos – and then only during meals. Dovid'l and Yisroel were full of spunk, jumping upstream like salmon, from Siddur to Chumash and Mishnah, and then to Gemara and Rashi. Chaya was happy tutoring and with her morning job of preparing breakfasts for the cheder minyan.

Uri's only sadness was Alexander and Solomon. They all lived in one big city, but his brothers were now in a different social class, like planes flying at different altitudes. Uri always phoned them before Rosh HaShanah and the holidays, but that was that. They now lived in an elegant, urbane world – and he in a very modest one.

Money, money, money… Uri fretted about money every day. The money Zeideh's planted in the Gemaras was just enough to sweeten his learning, but the family always needed more.

But the tzaddik, Reb Klonimos, had been right. Manna drifted down each day anew, disguised in all sorts of *tzintzenes* jugs. And suddenly, Uri's manna fell in rich measure – disguised as Edwin Bookman!

The first time Uri met Edwin Bookman, he was afraid of him. He was one of Toronto's oldest, wealthiest, most distinguished lawyers. He had even received the Order of Canada for his good work. But as they met every few months to receive a new volume of Gemara, Uri's awe turned to respect, and then to devotion.

Bookman's appearance commanded respect. He was always impeccably dressed: with his balding, snowy white hair cropped close, his perfectly tailored suit, and trademark blue tie. He never lifted his voice. Although he knew Uri's limited financial circumstances, he was always respectful — even fatherly. In the last year, he had always worn a yarmulke in Uri's presence.

Almost three years had passed since Uri began Zeideh's *Shas*, and he was about to start *Seder Nashim*. As usual, Bookman arranged to hand Uri the volume personally. Uri sat in the private inner boardroom, reserved for the most distinguished clients. Bookman entered the room briskly, clasping the Gemara. Uri rose respectfully, and he waited for Bookman to be seated. The lawyer smiled, looking unusually relaxed and cheerful.

"Tell me, Rabbi Schiffman, who taught you such good manners?"

"What good manners?" asked Uri, surprised.

"I don't know. Just your whole way. The way you conduct yourself, the respect you show —"

Uri flushed in embarrassment.

"What is so special? You are an older, distinguished person. You take the time to see me personally. I know you are busy and your time is valuable. How can I not show respect?"

"Not everyone appreciates my time."

Bookman seated himself and nodded Uri to sit across from him.

"How are your studies going?"

Uri shrugged.

"So far, not badly. It's a lot of pressure to keep up to the daily schedule. I have to struggle to really understand what I'm learning, not just read words. Now, I'm beginning the section called *Nashim*. It is very difficult, dealing with the laws of marriages, vows, Nazirites — you name it. Very hard! I will have to work very hard."

"Tell me, Rabbi. Do you enjoy this study, or are you just doing it to fulfill your grandfather's wishes?"

Uri smiled, and tried to understand why Bookman was asking him this curious question.

"It's a good question. I started studying this *daf yomi* because my Zeideh — Captain Elijah — asked me to, out of respect. But now it has become part of me, and I wouldn't abandon it for anything."

Bookman gave him a long, thoughtful look. He lifted a pencil off the table and fingered it reflectively. Uri waited, something was on his mind.

"You know, your grandfather and I were friends for many years —"

"I know."

"I was not just his attorney — we were real friends. I knew every little secret about him, more than you, more than anyone."

Uri nodded. Bookman had never been so personal or intimate with him before.

"Rabbi Schiffman, I am going to ask you a favor...between us. In his last years, your grandfather scolded me every time we met for not studying Torah — he said my head was made for Talmud. Regrettably, I didn't quite appreciate what he meant... I was younger then. But he is gone now, and I deeply regret I didn't take up his offer. I feel that if I study with you, it will be like I am studying with the Captain himself. You know, you were the apple of his eye!"

Uri's face grew red.

"Rabbi, I see you are a true Torah scholar. Tell me, would you study with me?"

Uri's eyes widened with surprise. He laughed.

"Tell me, Mr. Bookman, does a wolf have to be coaxed to eat a lamb chop? My whole life is dedicated to studying with people. Of course! I would be honored to teach you what I can."

Bookman stared down at his pencil, then looked up at Uri.

"But...it's not just for your grandfather, you know. There is a tradition in my family that way back, there were great rabbis and scholars in our family. We abandoned much of that...but when I see your ardor, your love of learning, I am inspired to reconnect with my own past."

"*Achsanyah*," murmured Uri under his breath.

"What did you say?" Bookman asked.

"I'm sorry, I was mumbling to myself... I said '*achsanyah*.' Achsanyah means an innkeeper who welcomes guests into his home. The Prophet Isaiah prophesied: '*V'ani zos brisi...* — And as for Me, this is my covenant with them, said Hashem. My spirit that is upon you and My words that I have placed in your mouth shall not be withdrawn from your mouth, nor from the mouth of your offspring, nor from the mouth of your offspring's offspring, said Hashem, from this moment and forever...'

"The Talmud teaches that when Torah has been established for three generations in a family, *Torah machzeres el achsanyah shelah,* the Torah comes knocking at its host's door: let me back in!

"The Torah is knocking at your door, Mr. Bookman. She wants back in!"

Bookman stared hard at Uri, but Uri met his gaze earnestly, head on.

Bookman shifted agitatedly in his chair. "Well, the Torah is certainly knocking now. But I hope the Torah realizes that I am a very busy lawyer. Could you arrange your schedule to come down here once a week, let's say for an hour?"

"Of course, I would be honored. How much do I have to pay you for your...for the privilege?"

Bookman laughed. "Never mind paying me. How much do you charge for your lessons?"

Uri hesitated, embarrassed. "It will take me a bit of extra time to drive downtown, find parking. Is fifty dollars reasonable?"

Bookman dropped his pencil and stared at Uri in astonishment. "Fifty dollars? An hour?"

Uri was surprised at Bookman's outburst.

"After all," he explained, "it does take time to get down here."

Bookman leaned forward with emotion.

"Rabbi, do you know how much people pay me an hour for listening to them and arranging a few contracts? My fee is six hundred dollars an hour! And you want fifty dollars? That's ridiculous! Your grandfather would have swallowed his cap if he heard you. I will pay you four hundred dollars an hour — and that's it!"

Uri looked at Bookman in shock. "Mr. Bookman, no one gets paid four hundred dollars an hour for teaching Gemara!"

"You will!"

"No! How can I take so much money?"

"Yes, you will! You agreed to teach me and I set the fees. I loved your grandfather, and now I can help his grandson and study Torah — wouldn't he want that? Rabbi Schiffman, wouldn't your grandfather want that?"

"Captain Zeideh?"

"Yes! He would be very pleased — at both of us! You will take the money, settled!"

Uri grew flustered. He was excited and overwhelmed and embarrassed at the same time. Was it payment, or charity? He raised his hand feebly.

"Okay," he mumbled. "I will accept. But on one condition."

"What?"

"You will pay me for a full lesson, not for an hour. We can't watch the clock. If we will need to, we will go on longer. I will accept your generosity — if you will make extra time for me!"

Bookman abruptly put out his hand and smiled.

"Rabbi, it's a deal! My secretary knows my schedule. Pick out a time that's convenient for you and arrange it with her. Tell her to leave an hour and a half open."

He glanced at his watch and suddenly rose to leave. Uri grasped the Gemara and also rose.

"Wait, Mr. Bookman," he called.

The lawyer paused.

"Thank you, Mr. Bookman," Uri said quietly. "You know, this offer will change my life."

Bookman nodded. "Good! Let's hope it changes mine, too."

⚓ ⛵ ⚓

That evening, Uri returned to his small study and tried to grasp what happened. Suddenly, everything was changed…in a flash, just as Klonimos had promised, had blessed him. Bookman's offer would not make Uri rich, but there was a huge difference between earning a few dollars more than he spent, or having a few dollars too little.

For the first time since their marriage, Uri and Chaya had sufficient *parnasah*. They did not have to tremble at the end of each month that the yeshivah's executive director would call, demanding to drop by and pick up a late tuition check. He still had students, but now he could devote himself to his learning with an easier mind. Each morning, he strode into his study and attacked the *daf* with passion.

He had his suspicions... Was this part of Zeideh's game? Had he instructed Bookman to begin studying with him now, after three years, for a reason? Was Bookman's money really Zeideh's money?

With Zeideh, anything was possible.

He asked Bookman the same question a half dozen times, until the lawyer grew impatient: "Edwin, please tell me the truth — did the idea of learning Talmud come from you or from my grandfather?"

Finally, Bookman grew exasperated: "Rabbi Schiffman, please don't ask me that same question again! I told you, it was my idea to study with you! The honorariums come from me, not your grandfather's estate!"

So it was Hashem's doing, not a Zeideh game. Uri plunged into *seder Nashim*. It was so difficult! *Yevamos* was so hard! He bought all the illustrated *sefarim* he could find, holding them open on the desk next to his *shtender*. He struggled to understand as best he could. But there was no time to stop, little time to review. Each *daf* took longer and longer to master, down one side, then slowly rappel back down *amud beis*. Could Zeideh have really studied these difficult pages, even with Klonimos's help? It was hard to swallow. And yet...every few pages, Zeideh inscribed some comment, some little *chiddush*, all in his old-fashioned, fine script.

Zeideh's comments appeared more and more frequently, and the pages were sprinkled with occasional cash, like leaves dropped on the path. After Zeideh's generous gift in *Shekalim*, he pulled back. There was money, but in smaller amounts: ten and twenties. The hundred-dollar bonuses vanished. Even when he was alive, Zeideh always had his own reckoning, sometimes generous and then suddenly tightfisted. Why? Only Zeideh knew.

Finally, Uri completed *Yevamos* as best as he could, and began *Kesubos*. But here, new surprises greeted him. Zeideh apparently entered a new phase in his education. Up to now, all his comments were written in English. But Zeideh was not satisfied. In *Kesubos*, Zeideh began writing his comments in Hebrew. The first time Uri saw his tortured attempts, he stared in surprise, smiled, and perhaps even laughed. Whatever he did, he regretted it later, for soon he struggled not to weep. Zeideh had tried so hard. But as beautiful – even outstanding – as was Zeideh's English hand, so were his attempts at writing Hebrew awkward and tortured. The letters were crudely shaped, like he was struggling to imitate a sample of Hebrew writing Klonimos had provided him. And the language was impenetrable, even his few clumsy phrases.

Uri was ashamed of himself for having laughed at Zeideh's attempts. What courage Zeideh had! His grandfather had never learned to write in Galicia, and now, in his old age, he struggled like a child to shape these letters and to form phrases.

Out of loyalty, Uri tried to decipher his grandfather's Hebrew notes, to make sense of them, but finally he gave up.

But Zeideh did not give up. After the first few attempts in Hebrew, Zeideh temporarily reverted to more comments in English – probably meant for Uri's sake, like a little wave of a hand. But then, after two more chapters, the English notes stopped altogether, and Zeideh switched to Hebrew. But, his writing was absolutely unintelligible. The letters were small and neat, arranged in perfectly straight lines, but Zeideh seemed to have given up trying to form proper letters. His writing was absolutely indecipherable, like someone had taken an aleph-beis soup mix and chopped up the letters in a grinder. But – that was Zeideh!

Uri moved on steadily. *Kesubos, Nedarim, Nazir, Sotah,* and finally *Gittin* and *Kiddushin*. He wrestled through unfamiliar *sugya*s, and so had Zeideh. Each time Uri collected a new Gemara, the binding was magnificent, the paper was sparkling, but every few pages, Zeideh etched in his cryptic notes, like tiny blue waves lapping along a pristine white shore. But the notes were absolutely sealed – probably even to Zeideh himself.

Why were they there? Uri remembered all the years of Zeideh's self-imposed seclusion. So this writing had made Zeideh happy, like he was playing with the big boys, writing his own *hagahos*. Zeideh had always yearned to be a scholar. This was his *Shas*, and he could do what he wanted. Perhaps Zeideh was showing off to Uri!

So, this was Uri's lot – Zeideh's legacy – and he sailed on. Somewhere in the middle of Gemara *Kiddushin*, Uri crossed an invisible equator, entering the second half of *Shas*. But each *daf* was also a calendar of life itself. Each day the children grew bigger, hungrier, costlier, had new problems. And each day they gave tremendous *nachas*. Tova and Dina blossomed into womanhood and already daydreamed about *chassanim*. Dovid'l and Yisroel went to summer camp and won *mishnayos* contests. And Yirmiyahu grew into a determined *masmid*, remaining in *beis midrash* late into the night, and learning until dawn each *mishmar* night. *Baruch Hashem*!

Uri finally finished *seder Nashim* and entered the order of *Nezikin*. He sailed into the familiar waters of the three Grandmothers, the three Gates, recalling his carefree days in yeshivah, his beloved Rabbi Nevenensky, his many *chavrusas* and their endless arguments in *pshat*. When he learned *Bava Basra*, he owned fields and houses in Eretz Yisrael. Zeideh Elijah seemed to feel at home here also, for there were more of his notes and comments. Uri tried desperately to decipher his grandfather's words – something – but eventually had to give up. He was proud of Zeideh's attempts, proud, but frustrated.

It took more than a year, but he finally completed the three Grandmothers: *Kama, Metziah, Basra*. The morning of the *siyum*, Uri made a breakfast in shul after *shacharis*. Uri was surprised when Yirmiyahu, always extremely dedicated to his own learning, suddenly begged to join him. It was strange, but with Yirmiyahu you didn't ask questions.

That afternoon, Uri met Bookman and received the next volume, *Sanhedrin*. It was a thin, elegant Gemara, an absolute work of art. It looked like it had never been touched before. That evening, before going to bed, Uri peered inside the Gemara to see if Zeideh had written anything. It looked so spotless! But, no, sure enough, Zeideh had not only studied *Sanhedrin* with Klonimos, he had grown more ambitious. Zeideh's *hagahos* increased dramatically. Now, on almost every page, were beautiful, blue waves of commentary lapping across the sparkling white pages. All absolutely illegible! Uri sighed. *Zeideh, Zeideh...* He hid the Gemara on a high shelf and went to bed.

The next morning, Uri was up before dawn. It was a new day, a new Gemara! He dressed, recited *Birkas HaTorah*, and soon stood ready at his *shtender*. The first pink light of morning seeped through his window, and outside, little birds greeted the dawn. He opened the Gemara and gazed at the immaculate first *daf* of *Sanhedrin* that lay waiting for him.

This is my time, he thought. *I am alive, I am healthy, I have the privilege to learn Torah with an easy mind. Thanks, Zeideh!*

He lay the pen on the first words. Suddenly, he heard a low rapping at his door. At first Uri thought it was his imagination, or perhaps the air-conditioning, but when it persisted he became alarmed. Who could be knocking at this hour?

"Who is it?" he called, suddenly fearful to open the door.

"Abba, it's me!" a voice murmured.

It was Yirmiyahu. Alarmed, Uri ran to the door and opened it. His son was fully dressed, standing at the entrance.

"Yirmiyahu, is everything all right?" Uri asked, concerned. "I didn't know you were home."

"I came home last night, *Avi Mori*."

Yirmiyahu's formal tone unnerved Uri. "Are you not feeling well, Yirmiyahu?" he asked. "Why are you up already?"

"No, I feel fine, Abba. I came home to study with my father."

Uri studied his son closely. His son's tone was...stiff.

"Come in, Yirmiyahu," he said.

Yirmiyahu entered the room, and Uri closed the door behind him, so as not to disturb the rest of the family.

"What do you mean you want to learn with me?" he asked.

"You mentioned yesterday that you were beginning *Sanhedrin daf yomi* today. I want to start learning together with you."

Uri glanced at the clock. It was barely past five. He shook his head, perplexed.

"But, but you are in yeshivah, Yirmiyahu! You have your set *sedarim* there! How can you learn with me? It's too much!"

"But Abba, if I learn with you, I'll cover thirty *blatt* a month!" Yirmiyahu answered quickly. "I'll have *yediah*s in so many Gemaras. I'll be familiar with so many concepts, so much material. It'll help my regular learning."

Uri studied his son closely. This was...too strange. He didn't like this whole business. And what about sleep? This was not what a young yeshivah boy did — no yeshivah boy.

"But what about your night *seder*?" Uri asked. "Does that mean you'll come home every night and not dorm?"

"Is there a *chiyuv* to dorm?" Yirmiyahu asked. "I'll come home at night, and be back in the yeshivah for *shacharis*."

Uri shook his head firmly. "Listen, Yirmiyahu, did you ever hear of a thing called sleep? You need to sleep! You can't stay late for night *seder*, and then come here for a dawn *daf*."

"I can, *Avi Mori*."

"Yirmiyahu, please. I love you. Just call me Abba, okay? Look, I think it's too much. G-d forbid, you'll get sick."

"Learning Torah doesn't make a person sick, Abba."

"Did you ask your Rosh Yeshivah?"

"Yes."

"And what did he say?"

"He said...no."

"So, what are you doing here?"

"I asked him again."

"And?"

"And he said no again."

"So?"

"I asked him, I begged him again and again. Finally, he gave up. He said if I can take sleeping less and not lose out on my learning, he would let me try for three months."

Uri stared at his son in awe. He was always learning. He was so serious, so strong-willed. That stubbornness was how he acquired his expensive tefillin. Now he was forcing his way into Zeideh's *daf yomi* learning. *Yirmiyahu is as headstrong as Captain Zeideh was*, he thought.

Uri reflected silently. If Yirmiyahu's Rosh Yeshivah said he could try for three months, could he say no? Yirmiyahu did not take his beautiful blue eyes off him, and it was scary.

"Okay," Uri said. "We'll try. But if you suddenly fall asleep in the middle of *shiur*, don't blame me, you hear! There's a Gemara *Sanhedrin* in the living-room china closet. Go bring it in."

Yirmiyahu disappeared out the door and returned in an instant.

"I already had it in the hallway," he said. "I didn't want to waste time."

Uri's study was hardly large enough to fit himself and all his books, and with Yirmiyahu, there was hardly any room to move. Uri stood over his *shtender*, keeping his place with the pen, while Yirmiyahu, who had grown tall like a willow, crammed himself into the desk, leaning the Gemara over the side. Yirmiyahu's yarmulke floated alongside Uri's Gemara, so that his head was practically in Uri's *daf*. It was awkward and cramped, and Uri would not have tolerated such closeness with anyone else. But, Yirmiyahu was his pride, and fatherly love overcame all.

In truth, Uri hardly knew Yirmiyahu anymore. Since entering yeshivah, he had grown so quiet, so resolute, that this was a blessed chance to be together, alone. Uri did not like this new schedule. It was too much for Yirmiyahu, and he knew he could not keep it up. But as long as he was here, it was a chance for them to bond.

Sanhedrin had a lot of easy *aggadah*, and they moved briskly through the pages. If Uri read too fast, Yirmiyahu stopped him and asked him to repeat some lines. But mostly, his son leaned silently over his Gemara, listening, and occasionally peered into Uri's Gemara. They passed some of Zeideh's notes, Yirmiyahu glanced at them briefly, but otherwise took little notice. But when Uri turned over a *daf* to a new chapter, and a crisp fifty-dollar bill suddenly materialized in the margin, Yirmiyahu's sat up in astonishment – especially when Uri plucked up the bill and pocketed it.

He peered up from his seat, so that his handsome face seemed almost an extension of Uri's *daf*.

"Abba, what's that money?" he asked.

Uri smiled cryptically. "Oh, that's a tip from my Zeideh. Every once in a while he stuck in some cash, just to keep the learning interesting."

"And you keep the money?"

Uri was taken aback by the question. "Why not? Zeideh wanted me to have it, to be able to learn, to support the family."

"But is it still considered Torah *lishmah* if you take the money?" Yirmiyahu persisted.

Uri lay down his pen and turned to his son.

"Listen, Yirmiyahu. I would learn this Gemara if there were no dollar bills tucked away. Your Zeideh left us almost nothing in his will, and this was his way of helping us raise our family. Tell me, do you remember your Zeideh?"

"I remember he always wore a sailor's hat."

Yirmiyahu seemed impatient with the conversation, and turned back to his Gemara. "Abba, it's getting late. Can we go back to learning?"

Uri sighed and returned to the *daf*. Too bad Yirmiyahu had not known Zeideh, because they would have had a lot in common.

Daf followed *daf*, and chapter followed chapter. It was a grueling pace for Uri, and an impossible schedule for Yirmiyahu. Uri was very concerned about him. He still stayed late each night in the *beis midrash*, he stayed up all night on Thursday for *mishmar*, and yet, like a soldier he appeared each morning at five for the *daf yomi*. Yirmiyahu said the Rosh Yeshivah had given him a three-month trial period, and the three months were now up. But Uri still had not heard from anyone, nor had Yirmiyahu mentioned anything.

One Friday afternoon, as Uri was preparing the Shabbos *leining*, his wife suddenly opened the study door excitedly. She held the portable phone, and carefully covered the speaker with her hand. "It's

Yirmiyahu's Rosh Yeshivah," she whispered. "He says it's very important."

This was the call that Uri feared. He took the phone and closed the study door.

"*Shalom Aleichem*, Reb Dovid," he greeted the Rosh Yeshivah respectfully.

"*Ah gutten erev Shabbos*, Rav Schiffman," he answered. "I needed to talk to you about your son, Yirmiyahu. I thought maybe I should wait to next week, but it was important that I speak to you now, before Shabbos."

Uri steeled himself. "Yes...thank you —"

"Your son, Yirmiyahu — I wanted to tell you, so you should know what is happening. *Ehr vagst ah gadol b'Yisroel!* Do you hear? He has an *eizener kop*, a brilliant head! I felt you needed to know what a treasure Hashem gave you, and to look good after him!"

Uri was stunned. Pleased, but still stunned.

"But what about this business of his learning *daf yomi* every morning with me. He said you gave him permission. Is that distracting him, making him too tired?"

There was pause. "What *daf yomi*?"

Uri was surprised. "He said...he said that he asked your permission to learn with me early each morning. Is that not taking away from his *seder*?"

Again, there was a pause. "Oh, that? But that was such a long time ago! Did he ever start that?"

"We've been learning now for more than three months. We've covered ninety *blatt* of *Sanhedrin*!"

"Unbelievable! I'll tell you the truth, I forgot all about it! There is absolutely no change at all. His learning is getting stronger and stronger! I'm telling you, Reb Uri — Hashem has given you and your wife a treasure to guard! I have my eye on him for great things! *Ah gutten Shabbos* — and *shept nachas!*"

"*Ah gutten Shabbos!*" Uri answered weakly.

Stunned, Uri collapsed into his chair. His cheeks colored, he lay his head down over his *Tikkun* and wept for joy.

Deep Blue

⛵ ⛵ ⛵

It was like a calm summer cruise on Zeideh's old *Swift Current*. Uri and Yirmiyahu sailed briskly through *perek Chelek* in *Sanhedrin*, filled with legends and *mussar*. Occasionally, Uri stopped to study the Maharsha's explanations, printed in minuscule letters, column after column.

"There's so much to learn, " Uri sighed to his son. "But there's no time now for the whole *Maharsha*."

"Someday I'll come back and learn it," Yirmiyahu promised, with an earnestness that left no doubt.

Sanhedrin ended, and they began *Makkos*. Abruptly, the tone of their learning changed. Uri saw that Yirmiyahu was not happy. At first, he didn't say anything, but Uri saw his son's yarmulke shaking back and forth as he read the Gemara. Uri was unnerved, but Yirmiyahu said nothing, so Uri pressed on with his explanation. Yirmiyahu's yarmulke grew still, and Uri moved ahead. But in a few minutes, the yarmulke was again shaking back and forth, even more vigorously. Uri had moved down the page, but Yirmiyahu's finger was still stuck a few lines above, tapping stubbornly. It was too much. Uri put down his pen.

"Yirmiyahu, what's the matter?" he asked.

Yirmiyahu looked up to his father. His fathomless blue eyes were so magnificent, and his worried frown so sincere, that Uri wished he had a camera.

Is this really my son? Uri wondered. *What did I do to deserve him?*

"Abba, I don't think you're learning the right *pshat*."

"What's the matter with what my *pshat*?" asked Uri.

"We had this Gemara in *Bava Kama*, and what you are saying cannot be right. It contradicts a clear *Rashi*!"

"Fine!" said Uri. "So...you tell me *pshat*."

For the first time, Yirmiyahu read the Gemara and Uri listened closely. Uri had understood the Gemara totally differently from his son. But Yirmiyahu's *pshat* made much better sense. Uri studied the page again, and his face flushed. If how he learned now was wrong, then the way he had been learning for the last two days was also wrong! He turned back a page to the *mishnah*.

"Okay, let's start all over."

From that very morning in *Makkos*, the learning changed, like a ship turning delicately on a different course. If Uri thought that Yirmiyahu's presence was a short-lived whim, he soon discovered that he was in the battle of his life — just to keep up with his son!

Uri read the Gemara and said *pshat*, but when Yirmiyahu was not satisfied, his black velvet yarmulke twisted like a yardarm in a gale, signaling an objection. Uri wasn't always wrong, and sometimes they were both right — but Yirmiyahu would not let Uri continue until everything was clear and made sense. Uri struggled to hold his own against his son, and now he understood why Reb Dovid had gushed: "*Ehr vagst ah gadol!*"

Uri steeled himself for the next Gemara, *Shevuos*. It had taken just three weeks to complete *Makkos*, but it seemed longer. Before, Uri had been able to sail quickly through the pages, like a ship through calm waters, answerable only to himself. He was always right, even when he was wrong. The main thing was: sail on!

But now, Yirmiyahu would not let him escape so easily. With his permanently furrowed brow, his piercing blue eyes, his yarmulke that swung like a weather vane when he didn't like something... Yirmiyahu would not accept vague explanations. Uri struggled to respond as best he could, not to be embarrassed before his brilliant son.

Gemara *Shevuos* was uncharted waters. Uri had never learned it before, and he turned to the first *mishnah* with a grim sigh. He immediately felt a bump underneath. He turned over the page. A crisp one-hundred-dollar bill lay tucked in the margin. Yirmiyahu glanced up for an instant, no longer surprised at the money. Uri plucked up the bill and found a little yellow note folded underneath.

> *No easy sailing ahead, Eerie!*
> *Please don't forget your Zeideh!*
> Love, Zeideh

Deep Blue

Uri was perplexed by the note. Why would Zeideh suddenly be worried about being forgotten? But despite his bewilderment, Uri was also pleased – for the money, and that Zeideh had written something he could read! The note was in his beautiful handwriting, unlike his scribble scrabble Hebrew.

He attempted to show Zeideh's note to Yirmiyahu.

"Would you like to see a note from my Zeideh?" he offered.

But Yirmiyahu was already engrossed in the Gemara and shook his head without looking up.

Uri took a stab at humor.

"Maybe you'd like the hundred-dollar bill, then?"

Yirmiyahu looked up at his father impatiently. "Abba! We're wasting time!"

They plunged into the difficult waters of *Shevuos*, and yet they made surprising progress. Because it was unfamiliar Gemara, Uri worked harder to prepare. Yirmiyahu seemed pleased. His yarmulke shook less often, and he accepted Uri's *pshat*. But it was the calm before the storm. Soon they entered harder and harder Gemara. Uri explained as best he could, but Yirmiyahu's yarmulke started shaking, and he challenged Uri on almost every *daf*.

Uri tried his best, but *Shevuos* was tough! Yet, they could not stay mired in one place for long. Uri pushed on as best he could – half *pshat*, no *pshat*, maybe even wrong *pshat* – but they moved on to meet Zeideh's schedule. Yirmiyahu grudgingly followed.

But one morning, they reached a piece of Gemara that came crashing down on them like a huge tsunami wave:

It was the *sugya* of "*Yoshanti v'lo yoshanti, eshon o lo eshon...* – I take an oath that I have slept or have not slept, that I will sleep or not sleep..."

Uri gave his *pshat*, but Yirmiyahu immediately raised a fierce objection. Uri's explanation made no sense – and Uri soon realized it himself. They were stuck. There was no use going further unless they could work out a meaning. Uri frowned deeply and hunched over his *shtender*, poring over the *Rishonim* for an answer.

Yirmiyahu also huddled over his Gemara, trying to find a *derech*. The two sat hunched over diligently, seeking some answer. Yirmiyahu finally looked up from his Gemara, waiting for his father to complete his search. Almost accidentally, he glanced into the margin of Uri's Gemara that lay in front of his face. He peered harder, then leaned forward. He lay his finger on one of Zeideh's *hagahos*, studying it.

Uri saw his son's curiosity and smiled.

"Don't waste your time, Yirmiyahu. Zeideh wrote in a language that only Hashem can read! Let's go on!"

But Yirmiyahu was so intent on Zeideh's note that he didn't hear his father. Uri's curiosity was aroused.

"Yirmiyahu, what do you find so interesting?"

Yirmiyahu finally heard Uri and ran his finger quickly to the end of the note. He looked up, his face glowing.

"Abba," he announced, "Zeideh asked the same questions that we did!"

Uri's head shook almost imperceptibly. "Yirmiyahu, what are you talking about?" he asked.

Yirmiyahu tapped his finger on Zeideh's comment.

"It's right here, Abba! Our *kasha*! Almost word for word! Did Zeideh really write this?"

Uri, who was already edgy from not knowing proper *pshat*, was incredulous.

This was nonsense.

"What are you talking about, Yirmiyahu?" he demanded impatiently. "Who can read anything Zeideh wrote? Zeideh could barely read the Gemara itself! It's your imagination, Yirmiyahu! That's not writing, it's...scribble scrabble!"

"Abba," Yirmiyahu pleaded, "please, look closer."

He lifted the Gemara, holding the margin close to Uri's face. Uri took off his glasses and studied the *hagaha*. There was not one legible word! He looked worriedly at Yirmiyahu. His son was fantasizing all this, wishing it. Uri lay the Gemara back down on the *shtender*.

"Yirmiyahu," he said firmly, "you're studying too hard! Maybe you're not getting enough sleep! I promise you – there's nothing here but a lot of mish-mash scribbling."

Yirmiyahu looked up at him without answering, and Uri grew upset.

"Look, Yirmiyahu, this has to stop – you're trying too hard! It's not healthy! Maybe you're tired, or your desire to learn is transporting you. There is nothing here!"

But Yirmiyahu would not back down. He jumped up, standing almost as tall as his father. His eyes flashed with excitement, with more animation than Uri had ever seen in him.

"Abba," he cried, "I'm not going crazy! Let me show you! Give me your pen – just for a minute."

Reluctantly, Uri surrendered Zeideh's pen. Yirmiyahu leaned forward and pointed to the top line.

"You see, Abba! Every letter is here – I can read it clearly!"

Uri bent down to his Gemara. "Where? Where?" he pleaded. "There's nothing there!"

Yirmiyahu pressed the pen to the beginning of the top line.

"Zeideh has his own Hebrew writing style, Abba, don't you see? It's like shorthand! He wrote small, and he sort of wrapped one letter into another and one word ran into the next – but it's all there!"

"Where?" repeated Uri in frustration, concerned for his son's mental balance. "I don't see anything!"

Very carefully, Yirmiyahu pointed at the first pen stroke. "You see, Abba, a *tav* –"

Uri looked closely. There was a tiny curve and downward stroke. "That's a *tav*?" he asked.

"It's enough of a *tav* for Zeideh to go to the next letter. You see, right attached in the middle – a little *yud* –"

"That's a *yud*?"

"That was Zeideh's *yud*!" responded Yirmiyahu, pointing to a tiny blue thorn. "It's attached to the *tav*! And then there's a *mem*, and then there's a final *hei* – Zeideh wrote 'teimah.'"

Uri stared at the minuscule squiggles and lines. He swayed back and forth uncertainly.

"It could be," he admitted, "but who can read that stuff?"

Yirmiyahu turned to his father, his face flushed with joy. "Abba, I can read it! Just listen —"

Uri sat in stunned silence, his beard grasped in his fist, his face set tight, as Yirmiyahu carefully read through the *hagaha*. Even he had trouble deciphering every word, but if he was correct, Zeideh indeed had asked their *kasha*!

But even after Yirmiyahu finished, Uri shook his head in denial. *Yirmiyahu is seeing what he wants to see. He is reading what he wants to read.*

But Uri loved his son dearly and did not want to contradict him directly. He was very concerned, but he kept his silence. Perhaps Yirmiyahu was overtired, overstimulated — his imagination overheated. After all, he was just a seventeen-year-old boy!

"So that was Zeideh's question," he finally responded. "And what was Zeideh's answer?"

Yirmiyahu looked up at his father, the pen still pressed to the *hagaha*.

"Zeideh has no answer."

Uri laughed. "Good for Zeideh! So we are no worse off than poor Zeideh was! Come, let's move on, Yirmiyahu. Maybe we'll find a solution later."

Uri continued the *daf*, they completed the second side, and Yirmiyahu left for yeshivah. Uri remained alone, and turned back to Zeideh's *hagaha*. He removed his glasses and held the blue writing close to his face. He could see nothing, just meaningless strokes. Either way, it didn't make sense. If Yirmiyahu was making this all up, then it was very disturbing.

Was his brilliant son under too much pressure?

But if these lines somehow did make sense — then who wrote them? Not Zeideh, that was certain. He knew his grandfather better than anyone. Captain Elijah was a colorful businessman, a grand self-promoter, a loving Zeideh — but a *talmid chacham* he was not. He did not write these commentaries.

So...who wrote these lines? Or were they just a mirage created by Yirmiyahu's overwrought imagination?

A few days passed, the Gemara was easier, and Uri's unease faded. There were also no *hagahos*. Yirmiyahu seemed happy, fine and grounded. They reached the chapter of "*Shevuos Ha'Eidus.*" Uri read the Gemara and interpreted it. Yirmiyahu immediately challenged his *pshat*, and Uri argued back vigorously. A lengthy blue *hagaha* lay inscribed in the margin of Uri's Gemara. This time, Yirmiyahu did not hesitate. He leaned over Uri's Gemara and ran his finger quickly down the neat, thin lines.

Uri waited, fuming, as his son scanned the tiny markings.

"*Nu?*" he demanded impatiently. "What does it say?"

"Zeideh writes exactly like I said!" Yirmiyahu answered triumphantly. "He learns *pshat* just like I do!"

Uri was unconvinced. "No he doesn't!" Uri answered firmly. "He can't! Yirmiyahu, you're just imagining all this!"

Yirmiyahu's face clouded with hurt, and Uri felt sorry. But even so, Yirmiyahu remained strong.

"He does, Abba, I promise he does! See...see for yourself!"

Uri swept the Gemara from the *shtender*, whipped off his glasses, and held it close to his face. He scanned the writing, then turned to his son impatiently.

"There's nothing here, Yirmiyahu!" he cried. "All I see is little pen marks! It's your imagination!"

Yirmiyahu boldly tried to seize the Gemara out of his father's hands, but Uri held fast, stubbornly refusing to surrender the volume. He was afraid it would tear. In the end they stood shoulder to shoulder, and Yirmiyahu patiently deciphered the lines for his father, letter by letter, word by word. Even Yirmiyahu could not make up a perfect *hagaha*, word for word, out of thin air.

There was something there. Yirmiyahu could read it, and Uri could not!

Uri tugged endlessly at his beard, agitated. He held the Gemara close to his eyes, and studied the writing. Here and there the little strokes and points did begin to shape into words. He could discern a few letters, half letters, even — a word! Finally, he laid the Gemara back down on the *shtender*.

So, it wasn't Yirmiyahu's imagination. These were *hagahos*, and the *hagahos* had a point.

Uri turned to his son and put out his hand. He was proud of him.

"Yirmiyahu," he said, "I apologize — these are real *hagahos* —"

But who wrote these notes? Uri wondered. *Or, who had broken into Zeideh's Gemaras to write these hagahos?*

And so, things were suddenly different. Each morning, it was Uri, Yirmiyahu — and Zeideh's notes. They appeared regularly now, on every two or three *dapim*. Some were just a line or two, while others were more developed. Yirmiyahu was drawn to them like a bee to honey, not missing even one. For him, there was no question — these were Zeideh's writings! Uri did not want to disillusion him. Yirmiyahu scanned the notes easily, reading them out for Uri. The notes were to the point, good observations. Most were questions and began with the word "*Teimah* — It is to wonder..."

It is a teimah! thought Uri. *I wonder who wrote these notes!*

Many of Zeideh's questions were left unresolved, just as Uri and Yirmiyahu left much of what they learned still hanging — promising someday to return, to look deeper. Yirmiyahu was interested in the content, but Uri was obsessed with another question: who laid his hands on Zeideh's Gemaras to write these notes?

He felt there was an unknown stranger in their midst, and his mind dwelled on this riddle day and night. Was this part of Zeideh's game of hide and seek?

There was only one person he could ask — Reb Klonimos Kalman.

He had not spoken to the tzaddik in a long while, and Reb Klonimos greeted him warmly. Uri basked in the serenity and holiness of Klonimos's darkened study. Last time he had come, he needed help — and the tzaddik's blessing had come true. But now he needed an answer.

"So how is your learning coming on?" Reb Klonimos asked. "You must have finished many *masechtos*."

"*Baruch Hashem*, I'm making progress." Uri answered modestly.

"But where are you holding?" Klonimos pressed him.

"I've almost finished *Shevuos* – one more week."

Klonimos nodded and made a face, impressed.

"Soon you'll finish *Nezikin* and start *Kodshim*," he said. "You're only two years away from the *siyum* on all *Shas*. Your grandfather would be very proud!"

Uri looked away modestly. But inside he smiled, joyfully basking in the tzaddik's warmth and praise. Reb Klonimos always said kind things, always nice, always encouraging.

"My son started learning with me," said Uri. "*Baruch Hashem*, he has a good head – he keeps me on my toes."

"Who, Yirmiyahu?'

Uri nodded, surprised that Klonimos remembered his name. They sat silently for a moment, Klonimos gazing down patiently at his desk, waiting. Uri coughed nervously.

"Reb Klonimos, I am in a quandary. You know, I have been learning from the Gemaras that my Zeideh left me. He had a lawyer, a Mr. Edwin Bookman, and he has been giving me the Gemaras, one by one."

"I know Edwin Bookman," Klonimus said.

"You do?" asked Uri, surprised.

"Yes, your grandfather introduced me to him on some business. So...he gives you the Gemaras, one by one?"

Reb Klonimus smiled to himself and shook his head. He seemed amused by Zeideh's instructions.

"Yes, they're all perfect, like they were never touched. But I know that my Zeideh did use them! He left me...money – bills hidden in different *dapim*, like a game of hide-and-seek. I never know when I'll find money, or how much."

Klonimos smiled. "So, Reb Uri, what could be better? *Torah u'sechorah b'tzidah* – you get instant reward for learning Torah!"

"Yes, like Reb Klonimos once said, it is just like manna. That part I understand – Zeideh Elijah always like to play games with money. But there is something else. I found notes, *hagahos*, written on many pages."

First they were in English, and now, in Hebrew. At first I thought they were just Zeideh's attempt to appear learned. I couldn't even read them! But my son, Yirmiyahu — he can read them. They are real learning — to the point! I know that my Zeideh did not know that much. He could barely learn without *nekudos*. Reb Klonimos, you used to learn with Zeideh — where did the notes come from? Are they yours?"

Klonimos's face suddenly turned very earnest. He shook his head. "No, they were not mine."

"Then...who?"

"They are your grandfather's."

"Zeideh's?"

"Yes, your grandfather." He leaned forward earnestly. "Reb Uri, you did not know your grandfather at all! He was not a simple man. His whole life, he was like an actor playing a part. It is true — when he started with me he did not know how to learn. But then, week by week, month by month...he caught on. But how he caught on, Reb Uri, how he caught on! You think he knew the boat business? Try him on a *Tosafos*, or even a *Rashba*! I showed him *sefarim*, and he took to them like a bee to honey! As a child, he once learned how to write a little Hebrew, but he forgot. I taught him again. True, he had a strange, shorthand handwriting, a Captain Elijah handwriting — but he understood it, and that was enough! This is the truth, Reb Uri. These are his *hagahos*."

"And he really wrote them from what he learned from you?"

"At first! But in his last years, when he secluded himself at home, it was more from what he learned by himself."

"After the race?"

Klonimos nodded and averted his gaze.

"Yes, after the race."

Uri's eyes moistened. His grandfather was unbelievable — unbelievable!

A wave of intense anger coursed through Uri's body.

Why did Zeideh have to have run that foolish, foolish race? he thought. *Why did he have to demolish his whole life?*

"He must have been a wonderful *talmid*," said Uri.

Klonimos smiled sadly, and shook his head.

"*Talmid* you call him? By the time we finished learning, he was almost the rebbe!"

⚓ ⚓ ⚓

Uri sat in his study, waiting for Yirmiyahu. He had woken early, wanting to be alone before they began learning. His world had slid sideways, like a sloping floor in an amusement park. What he thought, was not really what was happening. He had begun studying *Shas* to fulfill Zeideh's wish that he complete the Talmud for his eighth *yahrtzeit*. He thought it was one of Captain Zeideh's sweet eccentricities, which he was fulfilling out of loyalty. He thought Zeideh a good-hearted, sentimental, unlearned Jew, who studied snatches of Gemara with Reb Klonimos.

Now, it turned out that Zeideh knew much more than Uri suspected. Zeideh was a *talmid chacham*!

And as for Yirmiyahu — what should he make of him?

He knew his son was brilliant, and he was proud of him. But like Zeideh, he was a puzzle. He came home each night from yeshivah past twelve, but was up at five each morning to learn Zeideh's *daf*. Even now Uri already heard his footsteps, hurrying to his study. When did he sleep? And yet, Yirmiyahu was not sullen or anti-social. He had three good *chavrusas*, his marks were outstanding, the Rosh Yeshivah was extremely pleased.

But his intensity, his single-mindedness to learn, was almost alarming.

Am I am envious of my own son? Uri wondered. *Already Yirmiyahu can learn better than I can — and he can understand Zeideh's hagahos that I can't even read!*

They finished *Shevuos* and began *Avodah Zarah*. It went well. Uri had studied *Avodah Zarah* with a student a few years before, and even remembered some *Tosafos*. Yirmiyahu also seemed at ease. He did not argue as much. Even when he was not satisfied, he did not object as fiercely. For now they had an arbiter who lay between them: Zeideh's *hagahos*. Often, when Yirmiyahu had a challenge, there was a Zeideh note to refer to. Sometimes Zeideh learned the Gemara differently from Uri, sometimes he posed the same questions that Yirmiyahu did. Uri had a rival for his son's attention — Zeideh. But it did not matter. Uri was happy, Yirmiyahu was happy, Zeideh in *Shamayim* was happy — so they sailed ahead. And as a bonus, Zeideh's bills would appear unexpectedly, sweetening the page even more.

Zeideh's *hagahos* played a greater and greater part in their learning. Uri leaned against his *shtender*, studying from Zeideh's Gemara. Yirmiyahu sat to his left, his head hovering just alongside Uri's volume. Although Yirmiyahu's own Gemara lay in front of him, whenever Zeideh's *hagaha* appeared, he instinctively turned his head and peered into Uri's Gemara. If the note was on the right side, Uri would pull his Gemara closer to the left, raising the page for Yirmiyahu's benefit. He waited patiently as Yirmiyahu deciphered Zeideh's *hagaha*. It slowed them down, but Uri was pleased because Yirmiyahu was happy.

But the peace did not last long. They reached halfway through *Avodah Zarah*, and Yirmiyahu grew more restless. He argued more and more with Uri about *pshat*, and spent more time scanning Zeideh's notes. Yirmiyahu seemed to be learning more from Zeideh's notes than from Uri himself. They reached *daf* thirty-seven.

"*Chazakah al chaver...* – It is an accepted principle that a friend does not leave a task incomplete..."

Uri and Yirmiyahu debated its meaning, and how far the rule applied. Yirmiyahu argued his point stubbornly, but Uri held his own ground. Floating between them like a little pool was one of Zeideh's blue *hagahos*. Uri slipped the Gemara to his son, and Yirmiyahu eagerly devoured Zeideh's precise shorthand — a handwriting that only he could decipher. Yirmiyahu spent even longer than usual scanning Zeideh's commentary. Uri grew impatient and peered into another commentary, looking for support for his position.

Suddenly, Yirmiyahu gave out a whoop of joy. Uri looked up, and saw a look of joy had colored his son's face.

"*Nu?*" he asked. "What did you find?"

"Zeideh has a great *kasha!*" Yirmiyahu exclaimed excitedly, like a diver who has recovered a precious pearl.

"What's the *kasha?*" asked Uri, feeling left behind.

Quickly, Yirmiyahu explained the contradiction Zeideh had found in the Gemara's words. It was very close to Yirmiyahu's own position, but better. Uri listened, studied the lines in question and finally nodded, pleased.

"You're right. It's a real *kasha* – something like you said."

"But I have a *teretz* to Zeideh's question," Yirmiyahu answered eagerly. "At least, I think I have."

"So, let's hear," Uri said.

He was pleased at Yirmiyahu's joyous enthusiasm. It was a pleasure to see a real smile on his face. Yirmiyahu rapidly restated the question, and then quoted a line from a passage they had learned a few days before that resolved the question. Uri turned to the earlier page, studied the passage carefully, and nodded.

He looked at his son and smiled. "Good! It sounds good! Thank goodness you're not a chip off the old block! Zeideh would be proud of you."

"Maybe I'm a chip off the old, old block," Yirmiyahu answered, in a rare show of cheekiness.

Baruch Hashem, that he is in such a high spirits! Uri thought. *He has not forgotten how to laugh.*

They shared a few moments of happy contemplation. Uri rejoiced in his son's brilliance, and then turned back to the *daf*. The clock was moving, and Yirmiyahu had to leave for yeshivah.

"*Vamanos!*" he shouted happily. "*Kadimah!* Let's go, Yirmiyahu."

But Yirmiyahu did not return to the Gemara. Instead, he turned to his father.

"Abba," he said, "I would like your permission –"

"Permission – for what?" asked Uri.

"I would like to write the *teretz* to Zeideh's *kasha* right under his *hagaha* – so that I don't forget."

Uri stared at his son. "What? Write in Zeideh's Gemara? Write in Zeideh's Gemara! Yirmiyahu, I've been learning Zeideh's Gemaras for almost five years. I haven't made a mark in them, not even a finger mark! He left the Gemaras for me absolutely spotless except for his notes. How can I let you start writing in them now?"

Uri reached for a piece of paper.

"Look, write your answer somewhere else, Yirmiyahu! I'll buy you a notebook. Okay?"

But it wasn't okay.

"Why can't I write in Zeideh's Gemara?" Yirmiyahu insisted. "He asked a *kasha*, and now I have a *teretz*! What's so terrible?"

Uri's eyebrows rose dangerously high, and his face darkened.

"Absolutely not!" he said angrily, shaking his head.

"But why not, Abba?" Yirmiyahu argued. "Is it *assur*? Is there a halachah against it? It's Torah I want to write Abba, an answer to Zeideh's *kasha* in his own Gemara."

Uri recognized Yirmiyahu's tone. His son spoke calmly, but with iron determination. It was the same determined tone that got him his expensive tefillin — and forced Uri to learn Zeideh's *daf* with him. And now it was the same unstoppable persistence that was leading him now. Uri knew that no argument could stop him — except one.

"Yirmiyahu, there's a simple reason you cannot write your *teretz* in Zeideh's Gemara —"

"What?"

"There's not one pen in the study, and there's no time now to go looking for one in the house!"

Yirmiyahu looked at him, wide-eyed.

"Abba, there's a pen in your hand!"

Uri looked down at Zeideh's gold-plated pen in his hand and laughed. He shook his head vigorously. "This pen? Are you kidding? This was Zeideh's pen ten years ago! Mr. Bookman gave it to me when I started learning Zeideh's *Shas*. It hasn't been used for years, and it's dry as a bone! Don't be ridiculous!"

"Can I see it?" Yirmiyahu asked.

Uri lost his patience. "What is there to see, Yirmiyahu? Come on — you're a *ben Torah* now, you're a smart young man! Don't suddenly act like a baby! The pen is dry! It's like a bone! Don't you believe your Abba?"

Yirmiyahu met his father's gaze, unfazed.

"Abba, of course I believe you! But can I see the pen anyway?"

Uri shook his head in frustration. He tsked his son, trying to embarrass him, shook his head, and even smiled with exaggerated disappointment. Yirmiyahu ignored his father's performance and put out his hand.

What a strange son I have, Uri thought. *Nothing stops him.*

He did not know whether to be proud or angry at Yirmiyahu's stubbornness. All he knew was that he loved this son very much. Reluctantly, he handed the pen to Yirmiyahu, like a runner exchanging a baton in mid-race.

"*Akshan*, see for yourself!" he muttered.

Yirmiyahu accepted the pen. Uri peevishly turned to his Gemara, studying ahead. After a minute he looked up, and his eyes grew wide with shock.

"Yirmiyahu, what are you doing?" he screamed.

Yirmiyahu had unscrewed the pen case, and had slipped the razor-sharp pen point into his mouth, touching the tip to his moistened tongue.

"Yirmiyahu, stop that!"

Yirmiyahu ignored him, continuing to moisten the point with his tongue. Uri stood by helplessly. He was afraid to move a finger, lest Yirmiyahu's tongue be ripped open by the razor-sharp point. Yirmiyahu glanced up to his father, and their eyes met. His eyes gleamed, and he grinned guiltily. Then he puckered his mouth and ran the pen over his lips, wetting the point with a little shower of white spittle.

Satisfied, he removed the pen from his mouth.

Uri looked at his son aghast, so relieved that Yirmiyahu had not been harmed that he spoke not a word of reproof.

Yirmiyahu turned calmly to his father.

"Abba, can I have a piece of paper?"

"Yirmiyahu, are you all right?" Uri asked frantically. Yirmiyahu did not answer. Uri quickly retrieved a sheet of paper. Yirmiyahu lay the paper on Uri's desk and ran the pen over it. Nothing happened.

"I told you!" Uri exclaimed victoriously.

But even as he spoke, a fine line of sea blue ink began flowing from the pen, like water from Moshe's rock. Uri watched in shock, his mouth agape. Yirmiyahu said nothing, but etched a few long, sharp lines over the sheet. He lifted the paper and admired his work. The lines were beautiful, sharp and fresh like Zeideh's own writing.

Yirmiyahu looked at his stunned father. "Abba, now can I write the *teretz*?"

Uri stood speechless, unable to answer. His world was suddenly turned upside down. The dry, useless pen he had been holding for five years was suddenly alive! He had been holding a dead instrument — but it had really been alive in his hand! He nodded, unable to speak.

Hastily, as though he was afraid that his father would change his mind, Yirmiyahu snatched Zeideh's Gemara off Uri's *shtender*, laid it over his own Gemara, and began writing his answer. Uri stood at his empty *shtender*, watching helplessly. He saw Yirmiyahu hunched familiarly over Zeideh's volume, treating it like his own. Where Uri had been afraid even to make the slightest mark, Yirmiyahu wrote recklessly, furiously, joyously.

Uri finally coughed. Still, Yirmiyahu did not look up.

"One more second, Abba, I'm almost finished."

He inscribed a few more lines, until his own comments grew to almost twice the length of Zeideh's original question. Satisfied, Yirmiyahu blew on his lines to dry them, and then placed the Gemara back on Uri's *shtender*.

Yirmiyahu sat over his own Gemara, primed to continue.

"Yirmiyahu, can I please have my pen back?" Uri asked.

Yirmiyahu looked at his father, and reluctantly surrendered the pen. Uri took the pen and pointed at the next line of Gemara.

But he knew – they both knew – that everything had changed.

Uri and Yirmiyahu met each morning, but a fine, subtle transformation had come over their learning. Uri still stood authoritatively at his *shtender*, opened Zeideh's Gemara, and read the *daf*. Yirmiyahu sat at his desk, leaning over the family Gemara. Uri used Zeideh's pen as a pointer, but now he felt like a...fool. Yirmiyahu looked up from his Gemara from time to time and eyed the pen hungrily, then made silent eye contact with his father.

He is disappointed that I am using the pen just as a simple pointer, Uri knew. *He is wondering how I could let all these years go by with the pen sealed, when it was capable of pouring out fountains and fountains of Torah!*

But the truth was that even if he had known the pen could write, what did he have to say? Uri could understand a page of Gemara, but he had no *chiddushim*, no deep insights.

They sailed through the remaining pages of *Avodah Zarah* like a ship in choppy waters, bouncing up and down. Yirmiyahu – confident, emboldened by Zeideh's notes – challenged Uri on almost every *daf*. Uri paid close attention as his brilliant son raised one objection after another. He battled through each *daf*, having to defend his *pshat*. But it was a three-way discussion: Uri, Yirmiyahu...and Zeideh. Yirmiyahu pored over Zeideh's notes, nodded, then stuck out his hand demandingly, not even looking up. Uri passed him the pen, surrendered Zeideh's Gemara, and waited with a mixture of pride and envy as Yirmiyahu wrote his own comments. There was no more arguing about writing in Zeideh's Gemara. Uri had lost, and Zeideh's pen flowed fresh Torah like water, each word glistening with a new, dewy shine.

They completed *Avodah Zarah* and began the final tractate of *Horayos*, only fourteen pages long. That was it – and then and they were done with *seder Nezikin*! It was a difficult subject: the whole Sanhedrin that erred in judgment, the greatest minds of Israel! How was it possible? And yet – it happened. Zeideh's notes dropped off sharply, as though he, too, struggled with these pages. Uri and Yirmiyahu were left at peace, to study alone with each other, and Uri felt joyous at the reprieve.

But Zeideh was still able to surprise. They reached the last *daf* of *Horayos*, and there, etched in blue on the margin, was a huge question mark. No note, no *hagaha* — just a mark.

Yirmiyahu saw the mark and, as the custodian of Zeideh's notes, turned to his father.

"Did Zeideh draw that?" he asked, astonished. Zeideh wrote in a fine, delicate hand, in thin, perfect lines. This question mark was bold and took the whole side of the border, like a shout!

Uri ran the end of his pen over the question mark, like he was following a road.

"Who else could it have been?" he asked.

He could not explain the huge mark, and there was no time to stop now and study it. Uri was thrilled to reach the last *daf* of *seder Nezikin* after more than two years of tough learning.

Uri lay his pen over the top line of the last *daf*, and immediately felt the familiar bounce underneath. Zeideh had left him a bonus! After completing a whole *seder* — he could only imagine how much it might be! But he did not want to show his excitement in front of Yirmiyahu.

Uri raced joyously down the final *daf*. There was no thrill like the thrill of a *siyum*, no joy like completing years of a struggle.

But the Gemara ended with an unanswered question:

"*Rabbi Zeira chorif u'maksheh. Rabbah bar Rav massun u'massik. Mei? Teiku* — Rabbi Zeira is sharp and asks brilliant questions, while Rabbah bar Rav is slower and deliberate, but reaches sound conclusions…Who stands first?"

"*Teiku*! Let it stand — there is no answer!"

Uri stood up, lifted his pen, and smiled broadly at his son.

"Yirmiyahu — I did it! I finished *seder Nezikin* — the first time in my life!"

Yirmiyahu glanced up earnestly at his father. "*Yasher koach*, Abba!"

Uri stared at his son, disappointed.

"That's it, Yirmiyahu? Just a little *yasher koach*? No *mazel tov*? No handshake? No smile? No nothing?"

He was hurt at his son's coolness.

Yirmiyahu realized his mistake, stood up, and shook his father's hand. He forced a smile.

"I'm sorry, Abba. *Yasher koach*! I am really proud of you!"

"So why the long face, Yirmiyahu?" Uri demanded. "It's a *yom tov* today! We finished *Nezikin*! Where's your enthusiasm?"

"I'm excited, Abba," Yirmiyahu answered. "But Abba, the Gemara finished with a *Teiku*! The whole Gemara is left standing!"

Uri smiled and shook his head. *Yirmiyahu is too serious.*

"Listen, brilliant son! If the Gemara doesn't know, how do you expect your poor father to know? The Gemara asked the question fifteen hundred years ago — so let it wait a few more days! Eliyahu will come soon and tell us everything! Cheer up, Yirmiyahu! Smile! *Mazel tov*! We finished *Nezikin* — that's what counts!"

Yirmiyahu smiled at his father's humor, but he still didn't look convinced. He left for yeshivah. Uri planned to meet him at *minchah* for a modest *siyum*, and then go downtown to Bookman's office to pick up the next volume. He was all alone. Uri lifted the Gemara from the *shtender*, kissed it warmly, and lay it on his desk. He was truly happy. He had finished *Nezikin*! And he was heading full steam ahead towards completing the whole *Shas* — all because of Zeideh!

He looked around to make sure that Yirmiyahu wasn't watching — although his son was already in yeshivah. Now came Zeideh's payoff — after completing the whole *seder Nezikin*. He turned over the final page of *Horayos*, and there lay one single hundred-dollar bill.

That's all?

Uri pocketed the money, surprised that it wasn't more. After all, he had completed a whole *seder* — in fact, four *sedarim*. He had expected more.

Underneath, Zeideh had pasted a note. Uri unfolded the yellow paper, and saw that it was longer than he had imagined. The paper had been folded over and over into a little square, but it opened into a small sheet.

> *Dear Eerie,*
>
> *Mazel tov for completing the section of Nezikin. This Gemara Horayos is strange, don't you think? It leaves you hanging – and I always like to know an answer. But – we shall see...*
>
> *Eerie! Up to now I sweetened things for you by sowing a few dollars here and there, like seed money, just to keep things interesting. But, Eerie, that's it! Don't expect to find any more. If you haven't kept track, I dropped you a total of thirty-two hundred dollars. Not huge – but better than a kick in the head, correct?*
>
> *But that's it. I'm sure by now you've found a way to get by without these little presents – anyway, I hope so. So that's it, Eerie. Now it's all learning, straight learning, just to make your Zeideh's soul shine!*
>
> *I wish you smooth sailing and a strong wind at your back!*
>
> *Mazel tov!*
Zeideh

Uri stared at the note, and shook his head in disbelief. He laughed to himself sadly. How did Zeideh know what he was thinking? It was true! The money had been so nice to find! But now it was over – and that was that.

"*Baruch Hashem*," he murmured to himself. "*Baruch Hashem* for everything!"

For now it was clear. No more money. Now he was learning...*lishmah!*

PART TWO

THE RACE

FIVE

"So, how's my favorite Rabbi?"

Edwin Bookman was in an expansive mood. Uri had studied with him now for more than a year, and the famed lawyer had taken a fatherly liking to him. Now Uri sat across from Bookman, the great polished mahogany table between them.

"Your favorite Rabbi has come to collect his next Gemara," Uri answered good-naturedly, reflecting Bookman's warmth. He had learned to respect Zeideh's old friend more and more. Bookman was a person of great kindness and integrity, and as they learned together each week, Bookman's soul bent more and more towards *Yiddishkeit*.

"I see that you are in high spirits today," Bookman said. "Did you win the lottery?"

Uri smiled. "No. As a matter of fact the jackpot ended. My Zeideh left a note that he was no longer going to sprinkle my Gemaras with dollar bills. It's so uncanny, I feel that he is still alive, even after all these years. He still leaves me notes, he leaves commentaries in the Gemara, he even knows what I think."

Bookman nodded. "There were no two Captain Elijahs, that's for sure," he answered. "He was larger than life."

"The money doesn't matter. But this volume that I came to collect is very special. My son and I completed the fourth Order of the Talmud, and now we are entering a new phase —"

"Oh?"

"We are starting to learn *Kodshim*. It has to do with the Temple laws. It's a different world, a world that no one alive has ever seen, but it's our dream of the future, of the Temple rebuilt."

"Sounds complicated."

Uri's mood suddenly changed. "No one said *Zevachim* was easy."

Bookman did not respond, but sat, reflectively. Uri watched him, wondering what was really going on in that great mind. Finally, Bookman broke out of his reverie, and snapped open the large black case that lay next to him. Carefully, he extracted a large Gemara and passed it ceremoniously to Uri.

Uri reached across the table and accepted the volume solemnly. Each passing of a Gemara had become a ritual between them, like the granting of permission to learn further. It was an honor bestowed from Zeideh to Bookman, from Bookman to Uri.

Uri laid down the Gemara solemnly before him. He knew that Bookman's time was precious, expensive.

"Reb Elisha," — as Uri now sometimes called Bookman — "do you mind if I just glance through it for a moment?"

"I would be disappointed if you didn't," the lawyer answered.

Uri ran his fingers lovingly over the cover and opened the Gemara. He opened to the first *daf*. It was spotless, as though he was the first human being ever to touch this page. But he knew Zeideh had been here before. He turned a few *dapim*, flipped quickly to the middle of the Gemara, to the end. Something was missing. Uri looked up at Bookman, who watched him silently, waiting.

"What's the matter?" asked Bookman.

"The Gemara — it's empty!" Uri said.

"Empty?"

"Empty of my grandfather's notes! The other volumes were filled with my grandfather's *hagahos*, his comments. Here the pages are empty — not a mark."

Bookman smiled slightly and nodded. "You're right."

"But why?"

Bookman opened his case again and extracted a thin, leather-bound volume.

"Try this," he said.

But instead of passing the volume across the table, Bookman rose and strode over to Uri's chair. Uri rose respectfully, but Bookman signaled him to stay seated. He lowered himself into the chair next to Uri, and handed him the volume. Uri looked at Bookman, confused.

"Rabbi, open it!" the lawyer urged. "It's yours —"

Still puzzled, Uri opened the volume. It was a notebook, filled with Hebrew handwriting. The handwriting was a work of great beauty, the letters perfectly formed, each stroke clear, precise, perfect. Uri slowly leafed through the pages, filled with commentaries on tractate *Zevachim* — questions, commentary, vast references. Unlike Zeideh's indecipherable margin notes, whoever wrote this had an exquisite hand, and was a tremendous scholar.

"Who wrote this?" Uri asked.

"Your grandfather," Bookman answered.

Uri stared at him in disbelief. "Zeideh?"

"Yes, Zeideh."

Uri stared at Bookman. "Let me understand, Reb Elisha... Did he write this in his own hand or did he dictate it to someone who wrote it for him?"

Bookman smiled, amused at Uri's shock. "Rabbi, this is Captain Elijah's handwriting! I give you my personal word..."

Uri gazed at the beautiful script, and read one of Zeideh's *hagahos*. It was a profound question on the Rambam's *Hilchos Isurei Mizbei'ach*.

Had Zeideh written this? Had Captain Elijah really been able to learn like this? How was it possible?

And yet, here it was — here it was in his own hand! Zeideh was...a *gaon*!

Uri suddenly remembered that he was sitting next to the famed lawyer, keeping him waiting.

"I can't believe it," Uri finally said, brushing his eyes. He looked up at Bookman, embarrassed, but saw that the old lawyer's eyes were also moist.

"I can't believe my Zeideh wrote this," Uri repeated. "I just can't believe it."

"He wrote it, Rabbi Uri," Bookman murmured, "make no mistake about it!"

Uri studied the notebook. As always, Zeideh did things his own way. Although there were pages and pages of copious notes, Zeideh had established a strange format. Zeideh's writing was small and precise, but very clear. He had chosen a notebook with narrow spaces between lines so that he could write as many *chiddushim* as possible. Yet, he had left the bottom quarter of each page blank, as though he planned to add on comments later. But he never did, so that the notebook had an odd appearance – the top three-quarters of each page was densely filled with the most closely written lines, while the bottom quarter was like an empty field, waiting to be used.

Uri pointed at the vacant bottom lines.

"Why did Zeideh leave these empty?" he asked.

"I don't know," Bookman answered. "Your grandfather gave me instructions that when I give you this new Gemara, I also hand you the notebook. But I never discussed its contents with the captain."

Uri closed the notebook and ran his hands over the soft, leather-bound cover, embossed with a decorative gold trim.

"It is so beautiful," he murmured. "Thank you for taking such good care of my Zeideh's things."

Bookman nodded. He did not seem to be in any rush to return to his clients.

"Let me show you something I discovered —" he said.

He took the notebook from Uri, and gently opened it on the boardroom table.

"I discovered this by accident," he said.

Bookman lifted one of the pages between two fingers. Very carefully, he drew a manicured fingernail swiftly over the edge of the page. The page emitted a thin, high, bird-like chirp. Bookman repeated the action, and the page sounded just like a chirping bird.

Bookman smiled with pleasure, closed the notebook, and returned it to Uri.

"What was that?" Uri asked, astonished.

"It's the paper. Your grandfather had this notebook custom bound for himself: the leather cover, the paper, even the binding. The paper is fine, old vellum, delicate like parchment. When you run your finger over it, it vibrates — like an instrument."

"It sounds like a birdsong," said Uri.

"Who knows?" Bookman shrugged. "With your grandfather anything was possible. Maybe he inscribed his soul into the pages, and now it's singing."

Bookman rose, Uri smiled, but for a single moment their eyes locked and Bookman stared with strange intensity at Uri, as though he had a secret he wanted to share, but was holding back. A violent shock suddenly coursed through Uri's body — a feeling that something was deeply concealed. But Bookman left without speaking, and Uri was left alone, to ponder.

Was Zeideh's *neshamah* really contained in these pages?

⚓ ⚓ ⚓

It had been a long, exciting, but unsettling day for Uri. He celebrated a joyful *siyum* of *seder Nezikin*. He met with Bookman and received the new volume of *Zevachim*. He had even managed to learn with three different students. He caught the last *ma'ariv* at eleven, and finally came home, exhausted. The house was silent. Chaya and the children had gone to bed, and Yirmiyahu was still in the *beis midrash*.

He had not glanced at the new Gemara or the leather bound notebook since the meeting in Bookman's office. He was too exhausted to look at them now. He entered his study and placed the two new acquisitions neatly on his desk. He even risked leaving out his gold pen overnight.

It was past midnight. He donned his pajamas and robe and prepared for bed. He lay his siddur on the dining-room table, and opened to *Hamapil*. He stared at the *berachah*, but then changed his mind and closed the siddur. He could not sleep yet.

Since meeting Bookman earlier, Uri had had no time to think. Now, all his thoughts flooded into his head. The new Gemara was without even a single *hagaha* — why? The unbelievably beautiful leather notebook, written in such a perfect hand, full of profound *chiddushim*. Bookman promised solemnly that it had been written by Zeideh...but how was it possible? How was it possible for Zeideh to write Torah like that? Captain Elijah? Who taught him? When did he learn? Why did he write such Torah?

Your grandfather was an actor...

You really didn't know your grandfather...

Uri had not really thought about Zeideh for years. He had just focused on the Gemaras, the learning, the hundred-dollar bills that appeared like manna, and Zeideh's indecipherable notes. Even now, he struggled to summon up Zeideh's broad, once happy face, like a rainbow fading in the heavens.

But this new notebook, this immense learning — it didn't make sense! Zeideh didn't make sense — he never did! He never made sense when Uri was young, and he was even more of an enigma in his last years. He locked himself away in his big house for almost ten years — why?

Uri was no longer a child. He was a grown man, a *ben Torah*, with children who were almost grown up, ready for marriage. He needed to know *pshat*...about Zeideh!

He switched off the house lights, walked silently through the kitchen and out to his back deck. The night was warm and clear, and a canopy of silver stars filled the sky like a chuppah. A half moon had just begun rising over the horizon. Two piercing eyes stared at him from the yard.

"Go home, Herb," he called out, "there's nothing to eat tonight!"

The eyes kept staring, and he clapped his hands.

"Go away, Herb!" he yelled louder. The gleaming eyes blinked once and then disappeared. The giant racoon that inhabited their back shed slunk away, insulted.

Uri stood at the deck railing, hands clasped behind his back like a sea captain. He began striding back and forth, just as his grandfather had paced the pilothouse of *Swift Current*, restless, thinking up new schemes, never at peace.

Now, Uri paced nervously, trying to understand. Who was his grandfather, and why did he do the strange things he did?

Zeideh Elijah had raised him and his brothers since their father died when they were children.

You were so generous, so loving – so why did you stick me with the name Eerie? It was torture – didn't you realize?

And the will, Zeideh, the terribly unfair will! It was terrible. It was terrible.

Zeideh wasn't stupid, wasn't naïve. He was a brilliant businessman. Zeideh knew Gortel was worthless. Where was your fairness, Zeideh? Alexander got the palatial estate, Solomon got the *Swift Current*, which was a license to print money...and he got – ha, ha, ha – Gortel.

Why, Zeideh, why?

And Zeideh had placed on his shoulders the responsibility of completing the whole Talmud for his eighth *yahrtzeit*. It was such a heavy burden, but he had no choice. He owed it to Zeideh – as a *hakaras hatov*. And Klonimos Kalman had practically commanded him to accept the mitzvah. But it was so demanding, every morning at five, *daf* after *daf*, like endless waves one after the other, a vast sea of learning without end!

And then, Zeideh's money game. Dollars suddenly appearing in the pages of Gemara like wildflowers along the road, teasing him, tempting him away from learning *lishmah*. Yes, that too was a challenge, learning *lishmah*, for pure reasons, holding back from shaking out the pages to see how much cash would fall out each time he received a new Gemara! And just when he became reliant on Zeideh's gifts, Zeideh suddenly yanked them away.

Why, Zeideh, why?

And now, this unbelievable notebook! Was this really Zeideh's own handwriting, as Bookman pledged, or was there some mystery he did not fathom? And the pen, what was the story of the pen? All these years he used it like it was a helpless object, just good for pointing, never suspecting that it flowed like an endless blue fountain, flowed with Torah waiting to be written...but not by him, by Yirmiyahu!

Why had Zeideh really given him the pen?

Uri paced furiously as he realized that he was trapped — trapped in a brilliant game that Zeideh had devised for him, a game that Zeideh controlled even after he passed on to the Next World.

Caught in his troubled deliberations, Uri paced back and forth across the dark deck, growing more and more agitated. He was...angry with Zeideh. He feared that hidden in all of Zeideh's great love and kindness and generosity there was a streak of cruelty...and cruelty was so alien to Uri's soul. All Uri wanted in life was to be kind, to do what's right and good and sweet. Never to hurt anyone — nor be hurt.

A sight of such beauty suddenly appeared that it dissolved his anger. The moon had risen to the top of the magnolia tree that bordered his house, and etched against the silvery moonlight was the shape of a beautiful cardinal that perched on a high branch. The little bird must have been inspired by the moonlight, or perhaps it mistook it for an early dawn, for it suddenly began whistling and tweeting a boisterous melody that rang out over the treetops. It was a song of love, of yearning, of hope. Uri listened as the cardinal sang his brave little heart out to Hashem. Had it been a sad song, it would have been a *kinah* for the destroyed Temple. But the cardinal's song was a paean of joy, greeting the dawn, and the Redemption of Israel.

Uri's soul suddenly flooded with peace and hope. He must be wrong. There was another answer, there must be. It could never have been cruelty. Zeideh was just like that little red cardinal, glowing in the moonlight, filled with joy and *bitachon*. Zeideh, also, longed deeply for the Redemption.

There was only goodness in Zeideh's heart.

So what was the answer?

Uri leaned against the railing and tugged reflectively on his beard.

So, then, the question: Who was Zeideh, and why did he do the things he did? And why did he change so completely after that terrible race?

That race, that race! It held the secret to Zeideh, down to its shocking end!

The cardinal grew silent and stillness reigned. Above, the moon with her train of stars sailed majestically through the night sky. Uri gazed out into the darkness, and into the past.

He conjured up those fateful days, days that changed everything — forever!

SIX

Zeideh Elijah Schiffman started at the very bottom — planting trees.

He came alone to Canada from Galicia. He didn't speak English, he didn't have an education. His first job was planting saplings in the north woods. When they wouldn't let him keep Shabbos, he ran away to Toronto, which had shuls and a community. But still, there was no work. He signed on to work on one of the lake ferries, dragging heavy cables and lashing them to the pier, mopping decks, cleaning engines — everything. But he loved the open water and working on Lake Ontario. There were no other Jews working at the lake, but there were other ethnics: Romanians, Ukrainians, Polish. He spoke all their languages, and soon he knew English also.

He befriended a ferry captain, and the old laker taught him how to manage a boat: from keeping the engines from exploding to gauging the tides and winds. He taught him how to seal the hatches from flooding and how to navigate around the islands without being dragged onto the sand bars. He also taught him how to handle a crew of hungover seamen, issuing orders quietly but firmly. In a few years, young Elijah earned a first-mate license and became a regular in the pilothouse, steering trawlers across the lake and ferrying tourists around the islands. All this time he dreamt of a boat of his own.

One week after he married Grandmother Esther, Zeideh bought his first boat. It was an old dinghy, capable of carrying two dozen anglers out onto the lake. It was small, but it was Zeideh's — he was the captain! From then on, and for the next sixty years, he stopped being little Elijah Schiffman, but became Captain Elijah — the Jewish Popeye of Lake Ontario. He dressed the part. He bought a set of captain's hats which he wore all the time — all the time. He wore them to work, he wore them to shul, he wore them weekdays, he wore them on Shabbos and *yom tov* — removing it only when he put on his tallis and tefillin. He wore one cap at work that turned gray from the fumes; at home, he wore a simple white sailor's cap; for Shabbos, he donned an embroidered sea blue cap, complete with gold braid; and for *yom tov*, a snowy white formal captain's dress hat, with insignia. At first people mocked, then people smiled — and, finally, people loved it.

Zeideh had craftily turned himself into a character, and Toronto started taking note. Toronto loved — yearned — for something colorful, and Zeideh was certainly colorful. But Zeideh was not satisfied. He developed a small, loyal following, but he was competing against boats that were bigger, faster, fancier than his dinghy, that could outspend him in advertising, that offered waitresses and air-conditioned lounges. All Zeideh had was his booming personality and his imagination. He taught himself to say "welcome" in a dozen languages, and "thank you" in Chinese and Japanese, but things were still rough. He needed to get more attention...and that's when Zeideh's legend took off.

Zeideh's Jewish birthday was in Cheshvan, but his English birthday was on October twenty-second. It was past the peak summer tourist season, and business had fallen. Zeideh sent a typed carbon-copy letter to all the local newspapers.

> *Captain Elijah, owner of the Ontario Express cruise vessel welcomes all Toronto to celebrate his birthday on October twenty-*

second. He will be giving out a free fiberglass fishing rod to everyone who comes to wish him a Happy Birthday from nine to twelve at Queen's Quay, Pier Five. And, two dozen lucky winners will be drawn by lottery for a free, four-hour fishing excursion on Lake Ontario.

It was a wild, seat-of-the-pants idea for what it was worth. Grandmother Esther typed the note on their small typewriter, tucked the letters in envelopes, mailed them to all the local newspapers — and waited to see if anyone took notice.

For a few weeks they heard nothing, as though they had thrown a letter into the lake and it disappeared. Meanwhile, Zeideh ordered three dozen fishing rods on consignment from MacJames Fishing Gear, just in case anyone showed up. Meanwhile, there was nothing.

Two days before his birthday, a reporter from the *Toronto Express* telephoned Zeideh. The paper was intrigued by the event. No one ever gave away something for free in Toronto. What was the catch?

"No catch," Zeideh answered huffily. "It's my birthday and I'm celebrating! Come on down and you'll see!"

"I might just do that," said the reporter, and hung up.

Zeideh was bemused that someone had even read his letter. He was even more surprised when two other papers contacted him, and a photographer knocked at his door. He wanted a picture of Captain Elijah.

"Is that really your name, Captain Elijah?" the photographer asked as he posed Zeideh for a picture along his boat. "Or did you make it up because it sounds like *Moby Dick* —"

"Who is Moby Dick?" asked Zeideh, puzzled.

"You know, Captain Ahab. Now you're Captain Elijah."

Zeideh scowled and flipped his cap impatiently. "Who is Moby Dick? Who is Captain Ahab? Are they from Toronto? I never heard of them."

The photographer laughed, took his picture, and went back to the newsroom. Even as he showed the photo to his editor, he smiled: "Mac, we got a real character here —"

When Mac the editor heard from his photographer that they had a real colorful story, he assigned a human-interest reporter to the event. This time, the reporter came the day before to talk to Zeideh, and did a long piece about little, spunky Captain Elijah who was celebrating his birthday with all Toronto. The story appeared the morning of the birthday on the front page of two newspapers.

That morning, Zeideh arrived at the boat early. He had a suspicion that there might be more people than he expected, so he ordered an extra dozen rods. As he walked up to the pier, he saw that something had happened. There was a crowd lined up on the dock. He grew worried — did something happen to his boat? He ran over and spotted Michael, his Newfie first mate.

"Michael, what's the matter?" he asked anxiously.

Michael shook his head. "Nothing's the matter, Captain! It's your people — they're all waiting for their fishing rods! Boy, you really started something."

Zeideh glanced at the crowd. There were probably a hundred people lined up and it wasn't even eight!

Zeideh scratched his head in bewilderment.

"Michael, I wasn't expecting this. All I ordered was a few dozen rods."

Michael spoke in his slow, calm, Newfoundland drawl.

"Well, Captain, you better get some more fishing rods quick or you'll have a riot on your hands."

He whistled for good measure, but even as they spoke a dozen more people exited the streetcar and rushed towards the boat.

For a moment, Zeideh was seized with panic by all these people. But when he saw photographers busily snapping pictures, he knew he had to do something. He ran to a pay phone and called MacJames.

"Listen, MacJames, Captain Elijah here! I have a crowd out here in front of my boat all waiting for fishing rods, and there are half a dozen photographers taking pictures. This is going to be on the front page of every newspaper in Toronto tomorrow! Listen, come down here with a few hundred fishing rods, and I'll see that your company's name is featured big in my birthday bash. It'll be worth thousands in free publicity!

But I need the fishing gear now! MacJames, you'll never get a chance like this again."

And so the legend began. Captain Elijah's birthday party was a sensational success. It was featured on the first page of half a dozen Toronto newspapers, and even carried across the country. For the next forty years, Captain Elijah's birthday became an annual city event. Torontonians and visitors alike lined up at the lakefront for the privilege of meeting the colorful Captain Elijah and shaking his hand. It became the fashionable thing to sail on the Captain's boat, and in a year Zeideh acquired a boat twice as big.

But it was not enough. The bug — the publicity bug, had bitten Zeideh. He loved the attention, he grew addicted to the notoriety. Zeideh lived for his write-ups and hung framed copies of his press on the boat's cabin walls, and all over his home. The city looked forward to his birthday bashes, which became more elaborate each year. Zeideh even gave out free turkeys, and crowds, salt of the earth people, lined up a block long to receive their birthday presents. But Zeideh grew restless — he wanted something more. He decided to do something that would grab the city's attention by the neck and hold it firm!

He kept the details secret, even from the family. Only Grandmother Esther and the boat builder in Halifax knew what was going on. Uri and his brothers were young men now, and they enjoyed going out on Zeideh's boat. He had brought them into his house after their father died, and he shared the fun with them — but even they were kept in the dark.

The first ones to get an inkling of what was coming were the newspapers. A month before the boat season began in May, Zeideh called all his friends, the reporters. By now, they all knew him, and knew he was good for a colorful story, especially on a dull news day.

Zeideh knew how to play the press like a piano. He called up his favorite reporters and warned them cryptically:

"Get ready for something that will knock the socks off the waterfront."

"When?" they asked.

"What is it, Captain?" they demanded.

"Can't tell you yet," answered Zeideh. "But it'll knock Lake Ontario on its side."

The reporter was enticed. "Oh, go on, Captain Elijah," she coaxed, "you can tell me."

The captain laughed significantly. "Not yet — but you'll be the first to know."

So Zeideh called half a dozen reporters, hooking them like a carp, whetting their curiosity.

A week later he called the same reporters again. "I hope you're getting your photographers ready," he confided. "I'm telling you, this will be front page!"

"Tell me what it is!" pleaded the *Telegram*'s star columnist. "I hear people talking about it on the waterfront. I heard you rented the whole quay. No other boats will be allowed to dock."

"Just wait," Zeideh promised. "You'll be the first to know."

When Zeideh called again two weeks before the start of May charter season, and let it be known that he had hired a marching band with bagpipes to present his new sensation, it was too much for the papers. Each one was afraid that the rival would get a scoop, so they sent investigative reporters snooping round the waterfront. They asked everyone: the coast guard, the waterfront police, and even the hot dog vendors who knew all the gossip. What was Captain Elijah up to? But no one knew. But little by little, the rumors hit the papers, first on the inside pages, and then, as the Captain's opening day grew closer, the headlines grew bigger.

Two days before Victoria Day, the *Star* ran a banner headline over its masthead:

TORONTO'S LAKEFRONT MYSTERY
WHAT'S THE CAPTAIN'S SECRET?

No one knew, except the shipyard in Halifax that had built the new boat and was even now secretly sailing it up the St. Lawrence River. The sides of the ship were wrapped in tarpaulin, like a ship being repaired or scraped. Just the top of its smokestack stuck out, but that had also been disguised. The boat left the St. Lawrence and traveled across Lake Ontario, keeping far from shore, out of sight of curious cottagers. Meanwhile, Toronto had been whipped into a merry frenzy. The city was held happily hostage by Zeideh's game of hide-and-seek, and the people loved it. Even the hard-nosed press corps fell in love with Zeideh's scheme. It was like a giant game, and they were the targets! True, Zeideh held all the strings, but it didn't hurt anyone – and it sold papers! It sold papers like a royal visit! But it wasn't the queen, it was Zeideh – Captain Elijah Schiffman from Galicia, who led the world-class city by its nose.

But Zeideh was not done with his showmanship. On Monday afternoon, Victoria Day, the new boat appeared on the horizon, and a cheer went up from the crowd of a thousand people who had gathered to see the new sensation. Slowly, like a dot growing larger, the boat closed towards the pier, and a small armada of motorboats and trawlers went out to greet her – even though they did not know what they were greeting. Whatever it was, was still shrouded in a huge black tarpaulin that covered her hull and cabin. Just one pilothouse window was exposed for the helmsman to see out. It was a big, three-story boat, and it finally slid into Pier Five. A gang of crewman tossed lines to the men waiting on shore.

The boat was lassoed to port, and the crowd waited eagerly. It was already late afternoon, and the reporters were getting impatient. They had been waiting since morning and still didn't have a story except that an oversized boat had landed – but that wasn't news.

"What's up, Captain Elijah?" they demanded. "Where's the big deal? You haven't snowed us, have you?"

Captain Elijah stared them down dismissively.

"Me, fool the fifth estate – never!"

He looked at his watch. "In two hours the sun sets – then you'll see! Just be patient!"

He signaled and the band struck up a march. To keep the crowd calm, Captain Elijah handed out free sandwiches and beer. Everyone was happy.

A reporter from the *Telegram* sidled discreetly up to the Captain.

"Now, Elijah, you promised you would tell me first. You can give me a little head start, okay?"

Captain Elijah raised his finger scoldingly. "Don't be so eager! I promised everyone the first exclusive – everyone at the same time." He checked his watch. "One hour to sunset – be patient!"

Finally the sun began sinking over Hamilton harbor to the west. The bright afternoon faded towards twilight. A few blocks away, the lights of the Gardiner expressway blinked on. It was the signal Zeideh had been waiting for.

He ascended a platform that had been erected in front of the boat, just he and Grandmother Esther. The reporters and photographers pressed forward, the band waited expectantly, the crowd hushed.

Zeideh addressed the crowd like a potentate.

"Ladies and gentlemen! Thank you for coming out to the launching of the new Wonder on Lake Ontario! What you will witness now has never ever been seen on this lake before, and nothing of such magnitude will ever be seen again! My wife will pull the cord, the curtains will drop, and we present to you…we present to you – "

Zeideh paused, and the crowd held its breath.

"We present to you the *Swift Current!*"

Grandmother yanked the cord. There was a loud electric hum, a reddish orange glowed out from under the tarpaulin, and then it fell away. The crowd fell back, stunned into silence. The ship's side was a dazzling wall of whirling orange, red, yellow, blue lights, shaped into exploding, multi-colored volcanoes and stars and brilliant rainbows, swirling and gyrating across the length of the boat in overflowing fountains of light. In the dusk, the huge wall of explosive neon color was mesmerizing. There was a moment of stunned silence, and then a spontaneous roar went up from the crowd.

"I don't believe it!" one of the reporters shouted. "It's fantastic!"

The photographers fell over themselves snapping pictures from every angle. The band began playing loudly, a choir burst out with sea shanties, the bagpipers wailed raucously – and the incredible lake cruiser, *Swift Current* – part charter boat, part Captain Elijah's circus, part Mississippi showboat and floating café — was launched. *Swift Current* made the front page of every paper in Canada, was shown on local American stations, and even made some European newspapers.

Zeideh was beside himself — he had entered the gate of publicity heaven!

So began the golden years of the Schiffman family. The *Swift Current* was a license to print money; it delivered endless cash. But it wasn't just money, it was pure fun! Zeideh's name was famous not only in Toronto, but all over Canada. His opinion on politics and new fashions was sought after. His birthday bashes were almost national observances, and for what? Zeideh standing at the helm of his beloved ship, captain's hat tilted jauntily on his round head, blasting the ship's horn in and out of the harbor, skirting the island sandbars, rubbing shoulders with political leaders and hockey stars. Or, exclusive nighttime cruises amidst shimmering stars and fresh lake breezes.

Mother was not well, father had passed away, but Zeideh and Grandmother Esther took their place. Alexander studied business, Solomon went into finance, but Uri was so inspired by his tenth grade rebbe that he was drawn into learning. Solomon urged Uri to learn a profession, but Uri cleaved to learning. They all married, Alexander to Ruby, Solomon to Zahava, and Uri to Chaya, who was one of ten children. Zeideh helped Uri with a down payment for his house, but that was it.

"You have to learn to stand on your own two feet and not count on me," Zeideh advised.

Occasionally, Zeideh slipped Uri a hundred dollar bill straight from the boat's cash register — especially after he had the beautiful twins, Tova and Dina, and then Yirmiyahu soon after. But Uri knew that Zeideh was there, and it made him feel more secure.

It was wonderful, halcyon time. Everyone was secure. Zeideh had his famous boat and had fallen into a contented routine. Even his publicity became a touch less flamboyant. As for Uri, he took on Gemara students and learned half a day in *kollel*. The family had respect, had *parnasah* — and then, to top it all off, Klonimos Kalman arrived in Toronto.

Sometimes one person can pull a whole city upwards: *tzaddik ba la'ir*.

Klonimos Kalman was a *shochet* and a *mohel*, but above all, he was Klonimos. He didn't lead a minyan, he gave no public *shiurim*, but he inspired Toronto just by being there. He didn't seek followers, but people were drawn to him like bees to honey. Why? Nothing — but when he prayed the *amidah* his face grew so contorted with fervor that people stood covertly and watched his every move. He never raised his voice, but even when he smiled there was a sadness that melted your heart. Somewhere, someplace, Zeideh met Klonimos and instantly fell in love with the tzaddik.

Perhaps it was Zeideh's natural restlessness. He began visiting Klonimos four, five times a week, maybe more — who knew? — with a Gemara tucked under his arm. Zeideh with a Gemara was like seeing a carpenter walking with a stethoscope, it was so strange looking. And yet, Zeideh stuck to it without telling anyone. And it showed on his face, ever so subtly. Zeideh changed, in his own hidden way. It was the best of times. Uri was in Torah, Zeideh had a restless joi de vivre, there were wonderful grandchildren.

And then, without warning, everything changed.

One morning, a full-page newspaper ad appeared in the *Toronto Star*:

ATTENTION TORONTO!
GET READY
FOR THE REVOLUTION
AT THE LAKESHORE!
COMING JUNE 17th
THE MOST FABULOUS,
STATE-OF-THE-ART
CRUISE SHIP THAT TORONTO
HAS EVER SEEN!
INTRODUCING:
DEEP BLUE

Alexander was the first to tell Zeideh about the ad. Apparently, Zeideh had been studying with Klonimus that morning and knew nothing about it.

Zeideh was shocked. "It's news to me," he said. "Who paid for the ad?"

"It doesn't say."

"Not to worry," Zeideh answered. "We've had competition before."

Zeideh went to his office on the *Swift Current* and studied the newspapers. The same ad appeared in all the morning papers.

"Whoever is behind this has deep pockets," he muttered.

It was still a month before the launch of the new boat, and Zeideh did not appear overly concerned. May was a beautiful month, and business was brisk on the *Swift Current*. The same ad for the new boat appeared each Sunday, counting down the days until the launch.

A week before the launch date, Zeideh began receiving calls from the press.

"What's this new boat, Captain?" they asked him. "Who's behind it? Do you know anything?"

Captain Elijah shook his head. "Can't say — and I don't really care! Whatever it is, it can't beat the *Swift Current*. By the way, what did you hear?"

"Well, the people at Port Authority heard it's some consortium out of Europe that's behind this. Plenty of money — really plenty."

"Consortium, eh?" Zeideh's interest was piqued. "So tell me, where exactly is this *Deep Blue* now? It should be out on the water somewhere. Has anyone seen it?"

"Whoever it is has taken a page from your book, Cap. He knows how to build up the excitement. Every paper has received a news kit. They say that when *Deep Blue* docks, it'll make every other boat on the lake obsolescent."

"Obsolescent? What's that mean?"

"It means old-fashioned, passé, out of style —"

Zeideh snickered. "Old-fashioned? *Swift Current*? Let them try! I'll take them on, head to head!"

Zeideh hung up and snorted in derision. Old-fashioned! But there was a shadow of worry on his face.

Whoever was in charge of publicity for the new boat knew his business. The company rented not one, but two piers, for the launch. Huge blue banners hung all along the waterfront, and billboards sprung up all over the city.

TORONTO: THE WORLD-CLASS CITY
THAT DESERVES
A WORLD-CLASS SHIP!
NOW SHE'S GETTING ONE!
A BOAT
CANADA WILL BE TALKING ABOUT!
DEEP BLUE!!!
COMING JUNE 17TH

Zeideh passed the signs and banners and snorted. What were they making such a big fuss about? What was this, a new Hollywood movie? But the family saw Zeideh grow more agitated by the day.

June seventeenth was a glorious spring Sunday. The weather could not be more pleasant, with a soft breeze blowing over the lake. It was a perfect day for *Deep Blue*. Zeideh knew there would be a lot of commotion about the new ship. The TTC scheduled extra busses to the lakefront, and the Premier of Ontario and federal ministers promised to attend. There would be no raucous pipers like the launching of the *Swift Current*, instead, a choir of inner-city children would sing, and each child was given a new, sparkling uniform. There was a swell of pride in the city, a sense that *Deep Blue* was not just a commercial venture, but the wave of the future, almost a movement.

Zeideh promised the family that he would not let this day be different from any other. Michael, his Newfoundland helper, was still booking tickets for *Swift Current* at a good clip. The gaudy rainbow of lights still blinked and flashed bright as always. Zeideh went to learn in the morning with Klonimos Kalman. *Deep Blue* was scheduled to arrive at

2:00 p.m. sharp, and the young Swiss director of opening day ceremonies promised the press they could set their watches to *Deep Blue*'s arrival.

Zeideh headed downtown at one. He promised himself that he would drive straight to the *Swift Current* office, but his curiosity overcame him. He parked his car under the expressway, and walked the eight blocks to the *Deep Blue* pier at the foot of Queen's Quay. He walked with his cap pulled low, blending in anonymously with the crowds, who were even now rushing down to the pier to catch a glimpse. He didn't want to be noticed. When he arrived at the *Deep Blue* pier, it was jammed. The young choir was singing hip-hop sea hymns, and the dock was jumping. It was a bash. This crowd was younger and more stylish than the people who had come out to see *Swift Current*'s launch. The *Deep Blue* management had erected huge television screens, and in the distance the silhouette of the approaching ship could be seen. This was a new hi-tech world that Zeideh had no knowledge of, but the crowd was enthralled.

There she came!

Zeideh hid himself in the crowd. The dock was so crowded he could not even see the lake, but he watched the boat approach on the big screen. Suddenly there was a close-up view of the new ship, and a cheer went up from the crowd. Zeideh leaned forward and stared at the screen.

What was that?

Rising from the hull of the boat were two large, vertical sails, one at the bow, and the other leaning off the stern. What was this *Deep Blue*, a sailboat? It couldn't be, because the boat also had a sharply angled funnel, so it obviously had an engine. Zeideh was puzzled. *Deep Blue* drew closer, and Zeideh pushed himself forward. He wanted to see this boat straight on, not from some television screen. He found a gap in the crowd, and for the first time saw *Deep Blue* as it pulled majestically alongside the dock. A hush fell over the crowd, like it was holding its collective breath. There was no cheering, no applause, just awed silence.

Deep Blue was…magnificent. It was not just a ship; it was a fantastic work of art! Not only had it obviously been designed by a brilliant ship maker, but it had been painted like no other ship in the water. Unlike the *Swift Current*'s circus of flashing, racing, garish lights, *Deep Blue* was an exquisite study in the beauty of blue — long, flowing splashes of cobalt and azure and sapphire, sky blue and sea blue, indigo and teal. The sides of the ship seemed to flow into the lake itself. The huge, rectangular billowing sails added to the overall effect, like pure, floating white clouds.

Deep Blue was absolutely beautiful.

After a few moments of awed silence, the crowd reacted in the strangest way. The people began applauding, like at a concert. They stood tall, lifted their hands over their heads, clapped and applauded and hurrahed and whistled like they had just seen an opera or heard a symphony. *Deep Blue* was a magnificent work of art, a triumph!

Zeideh watched the crowd go wild. The inner-city children began singing, balloons were sent aloft, and Zeideh decided it was time to escape before anyone noticed him. He had had enough. He was almost free when a microphone was suddenly thrust in his face.

It was one of the reporters he knew.

"Captain Elijah, are you here to secretly check out the competition? What do you think of *Deep Blue*?"

Zeideh scowled and tried to escape without answering, but other reporters saw what was happening and raced to cover the breaking story. Zeideh was trapped. They surged around him in a pack, attacking him with cameras and microphones.

A reporter shouted: "Captain Elijah, what do you say to *Deep Blue* on its opening day?"

Zeideh tried to run off, but there was no escape. They had him cornered, and he had to say something. He was embarrassed to be caught spying on the new boat.

Zeideh knew what he should say: "I came here to congratulate *Deep Blue* and wish her well on her maiden voyage! May she have good winds in her sails and a safe harbor!"

Instead, Zeideh let loose: "There is more real heart and soul of Toronto in one rivet of *Swift Current* than *Deep Blue* will ever have! We'll beat her hands down — just go watch!"

Then he burst through the circle and ran off.

The press loved it. The next morning, the papers were filled with the photos of the magnificent *Deep Blue*, and underneath, in bold headlines:

CAPTAIN ELIJAH DECLARES WAR ON *DEEP BLUE*

The radio talk shows were full with nothing else but *Deep Blue*, *Swift Current,* and Captain Elijah's crusty comments. Were they ungracious? Was it sour grapes? Had the Captain's time passed? Or was he a man who spoke from the heart?"

One thing was clear: nothing would be the same again.

Zeideh was struck deeply by the new ship and all the accolades it received. For a few days, he seemed in shock. He did not go down to the lake, he hid away with Klonimus Kalman and his Gemara. The family watched him and worried.

And then Zeideh came out fighting. He took out a full page ad in the *Toronto Sun*:

Swift Current is True Grit Toronto!
Cruise in a real Great Lake boat
Not someone's floating watercolor!
Swift Current!
Still the Queen of Lake Ontario

On the corner of the every ad and billboard that Zeideh bought was a picture of Captain Elijah's round, friendly face, his trademark captain's cap, a full color photograph of the *Swift Current* in the background. Wherever you turned, Zeideh's face beamed down.

But who owned *Deep Blue*? No one knew anything, except that the boat had been built in Europe and the investors had deep pockets. Captain Elijah's insults were met with dignified silence. There was no need to respond — *Deep Blue*'s glory spoke for itself. It was a breathtaking work of art, like a floating Picasso or Van Gogh. Despite all of Zeideh's bluster, it made a stunning show on the lake. And when it set out on the water, its two huge sails caught the lake breezes and billowed out like fleecy summer clouds, so that it stood out for miles. What *Swift Current* did with its gaudy circus lights, *Deep Blue* accomplished by trapping sunlight in its sails. But these were not just simple sails. They were state-of-the-art, hi-tech equipment connected to advanced computers. They were able to twist and arch in sections, exploiting the slightest breeze, using less fuel, causing minimal pollution. It was the environmentally friendly craft of the future, tomorrow's technology, and Friends of Lake Ontario loved it.

Then there was the matter of image. *Swift Current*'s captain was Zeideh, assisted by Michael Harran, the tall, grizzled Newfoundland first mate. They made a colorful, old-fashioned team. *Deep Blue*'s captain was Izaak Vanderlerner, a Rhine River veteran of many years. Zeideh pursued the press, pleaded for interviews. Vanderlerner was tall and taciturn, with movie-star looks, and he spoke like each vowel he uttered cost him money. The less he said, the more the press adored him. He was the real thing. Poor little Captain Elijah was trying to play captain. Vanderlerner had the smell of the sea.

Subtly, the bloom faded off Zeideh's rose. Long articles appeared in nautical magazines about the excellence of *Deep Blue*'s sleek lines, its fuel-efficient, majestic sails, the breathtaking beauty of its impressionistically painted hull, the reserved professionalism of its shy, good-looking captain — and always a contrasting jab at the *Swift Current*. *Swift Current* was a floating circus, an anachronism. Its captain was a poor immigrant boy trying to play captain. Izaak Vanderlerner was the real thing.

Zeideh fought back like a wounded bear. The more he was pushed into second place, the more he responded with entertaining publicity stunts, surprise prizes, sunset cruises to mystery destinations. He slashed prices at an hour's notice, and the crowds rushed down to take advantage. Every time an article appeared lauding *Deep Blue*, Zeideh called a press conference to say that he was real grit Toronto – not some magazine-writer idea of a captain.

The rivalry grew fiercer. Meanwhile, business flourished on both boats. The docks were crowded with tourists, and all the buzz about the extraordinary *Deep Blue*, and Zeideh's salty response, kept the pot boiling. The press loved the rivalry – it sold papers. The city chuckled and ate it up. Zeideh was the character actor, and Vanderlerner was the leading man. Business was booming better than ever. *Swift Current* was booked with passengers for months ahead. The family was proud and happy.

And then, Zeideh made his dreadful mistake. There was no end to the interviews and photo ops that Zeideh pursued. He said what came to mind, and always with a jab at the competition, the *Deep Blue*. Even Alexander and Solomon were getting worried.

"Boost yourself, Zeideh," they cautioned, "don't attack the competition."

But Zeideh was Zeideh, and couldn't be stopped. As for *Deep Blue*, the management ignored Captain Elijah's remarks. But after much goading, Captain Vanderlerner finally agreed to be interviewed. He was especially gracious, and gave the reporters a personal captain's tour of the elegantly outfitted upper and lower decks, the state-of-the-art restaurants, the computerized guidance systems and mainsails.

Finally, Vanderlerner was asked about the *Swift Current*. The tall, Viking-like captain looked at the reporters and broke into deep laughter. "*Swift Current*? *Swift Current*? That's not a boat – it's a floating circus. We could sail circles around her with our engines running at half power."

"And what about Captain Elijah? What is your professional estimate."

Vanderlerner laughed scornfully. "Captain Elijah? You call him a captain? He's no captain!"

The next morning the *Telegraph* ran a banner headline.

VANDERLERNER CALLS *SWIFT CURRENT* A FLOATING CIRCUS
DEEP BLUE CAN SAIL CIRCLES AROUND *SWIFT CURRENT* CLAIMS VANDERLERNER
VANDERLERNER'S VERDICT: "CAPTAIN" ELIJAH IS NO CAPTAIN

Zeideh was so busy with Klonimos Kalman that afternoon that the reporters had no time to get his reaction, and they ran the story as is. The first Zeideh knew of it was the next morning, before *shacharis*. He only scanned the headlines and his blood pressure shot up dangerously high. Right after prayers he raced downtown to his boat and spread all the morning papers on his desk. Each one was the same. A striking picture of Captain Vanderlerner and *Deep Blue*, and the same quote.

SWIFT CURRENT IS A FLOATING CIRCUS
"CAPTAIN" ELIJAH IS NO CAPTAIN

Zeideh was outraged. He was in shock. He was furious. He had been sailing Lake Ontario for thirty years, and the *Swift Current* had been sailing for more than ten! Who was this interloper to say he was no captain?

He was furious at his friends at the press. He saw their bylines on the articles. Richard! Marilyn! Mario! Mario — his friend Mario! He sent him a forty-ounce bottle of Chivas Regal every New Year, and this is what he wrote? He reached Mario on his cell phone.

"Mario," he cried, "my friend Mario, ...this is what you write about your old friend?" He was near tears.

"Captain, I didn't say those things," Mario explained. "I interviewed Vanderlerner like I interview you. He said those things and I have to write it."

"But you're my pal! What about my Chivas Regal?"

There was a moment's cold silence. "Captain Elijah, I am a professional first and a pal – second." Mario hung up, insulted.

Zeideh stared at the phone. This wasn't getting him anywhere. Reporters were reporters. They had to do their job. Zeideh's feelings had been deeply hurt. His reputation. His Shabbos and *yom tov* sailor's hat. Now people would laugh. His dignity was at stake, his place in Lake Ontario history.

The old joke rang in his ears: "My child: by me and Poppa you're a captain, but by a captain are you a captain?"

Zeideh leaned on his elbows, face glum. Who was this handsome stranger to come to Toronto and insult him? Not a captain! There was a rap at the door, and Newfoundland Mike entered. Zeideh looked up sourly.

"Mike," he asked glumly, "am I a captain or not a captain?"

Mike thought for a moment. "Yep, sir! You are a captain, Cap, and a darn good one at that."

"This Vanderlerner fellow says *Deep Blue* can sail circles around us – is he right?"

"Let him try, Captain. He doesn't know the *Swift Current*. You let me tone up the engines, install a new DPD booster, we could beat *Deep Blue* hands down, any day."

Zeideh's face brightened. "Are you sure, Mike? They have those new computerized sails, a digitized engine, satellite tracking systems."

"And I have saltwater in my Newfie veins, Cap! I just need to jig up and oil the engines. It'll cost some, but we'll beat 'em."

Zeideh considered just for a moment. He was furious at Vanderlerner's insult. He couldn't let it pass. Zeideh slammed his fist against the desk.

"That's it, Mike! We're going to take on *Deep Blue*, head to head. Winner takes all!"

The captain of *Deep Blue* had miscalculated badly. Vanderlerner had played right into Zeideh's publicity-loving hands. Captain Elijah was relentless. He summoned the press almost every day and challenged *Deep Blue* to a head-on-head race across Lake Ontario.

Zeideh comments were not timid.

"Vanderlerner says I'm no captain. And I say I know more about sailing Lake Ontario in my sleep than he will ever know in his lifetime."

The management of *Deep Blue* studiously ignored Zeideh's taunts. They issued a terse statement.

"We will not respond to Captain Elijah's remarks. *Deep Blue*'s excellence speaks for itself."

But Zeideh would not give up. "What are they afraid of?" he chided. "*Swift Current* is ready to challenge *Deep Blue* any time, any distance."

Zeideh placed *Deep Blue* under siege. The owners of the boat tried not to respond, but Captain Elijah's daily challenge caught the city's feisty spirit. People liked a good fight, and the personal interest built.

But *Deep Blue* remained aloof. "We have said all we have to say," the administration responded coolly.

Zeideh rented a huge electric sign overlooking the Gardiner Expressway that counted the days since Captain Elijah first challenged *Deep Blue* to race. It was seen by tens of thousands each day and read boldly:

DAY __!
DEEP BLUE:
WHAT ARE YOU AFRAID OF?

Zeideh was having a great time. It had been a long time since *Swift Current* and Captain Elijah had received such publicity, but the family was worried. "These are powerful people, Zeideh," Alexander and Solomon warned. "You are goading them too much. Be careful — you may get hurt!" They even summoned Uri out of the *beis midrash* to intervene. Uri was Zeideh's favorite, and they wanted him to convince Zeideh to tone down his campaign.

Uri did not want to get involved. He made one quick phone call to Zeideh asking him to slow down — but that was all.

"You know you can't stop Zeideh," he told his brothers.

Later, Uri regretted that he did not try harder. Perhaps it would have prevented what happened.

The season was almost over. *Deep Blue* remained firm. Whatever Zeideh said, *Deep Blue* would not agree to race. And then, with one slip of the tongue, everything changed. Zeideh was asked by a reporter why he thought *Deep Blue* did not take up his challenge. Zeideh adjusted his captain's cap impatiently and blurted out:

"You really want to know what I think? I think that Vanderlerner is coward, that's all. Coward is spelled c-o-w-a-r-d!"

It was just a quick remark, made almost offhandedly. But it was a slow news day, so the next morning the *Telegram* ran it as a front-page banner headline:

CAPTAIN ELIJAH CALLS *DEEP BLUE*'S CAPTAIN A "COWARD"

Later that morning, Zeideh got a call from *Deep Blue*'s director of public affairs.

"Captain Vanderlerner read your remarks this morning and takes personal offense."

Zeideh, who was surprised by the call, answered sharply. "So let him race me if he's insulted!"

"He will!" answered the director. "We accept your challenge. We tried not make this personal, but you left us no choice. We'll set up a meeting with your people and work out the details. We didn't want this, but Vanderlerner will teach you a lesson, believe me!"

Zeideh snorted in disdain.

"I have no 'your people!' " he answered. "I am my 'your people' — me and one Newfie helmsman. Tell Vanderlerner we'll see who teaches who a lesson. There's only one condition that I insist on —"

"What's that?"

"This race was my idea. It's going to bring us both a ton of free publicity. I want it held on October twenty-second —"

The *Deep Blue* spokesman hesitated. "That's late in the season, isn't it? We don't know what the weather is going to be like."

"October twenty-second is my birthday! I always do something special on my birthday — for the last thirty years! It's only October, after all. I know the lake and I'm not afraid. What's the matter, is Vanderlerner chicken?"

"Captain Vanderlerner is not chicken of anything!" the director responded angrily. "I'll get back to you —"

"Well, you know where you can find me!"

Zeideh hung up and pulled his cap triumphantly down over his forehead. He smiled to himself. He would show the world: *Swift Current* beats *Deep Blue*, any day!

Zeideh played the next five weeks like a master pianist, and Toronto was his piano. There was not a day that his name or picture did not appear in the paper — boasting, challenging, inviting dignitaries, stirring the pot.

As for Vanderlerner, his face was not to be seen.

"Why is Captain Vanderlerner hiding?" Zeideh taunted. "What is he afraid of?"

But Vanderlerner's concealment was a perfect foil for Zeideh's noisy pronouncements. An aura of mystery and refinement surrounded the Rhine River captain, and he evoked curiosity and wonder.

The intense rivalry between the circus-like *Swift Current* and the aristocratic *Deep Blue* caught the city's fancy. Blue banners hung from cars that favored *Deep Blue* (mostly BMWs and Audis), and bright orange ribbons for *Swift Current* (Fords and Chevrolets).

Captain Elijah plastered ads around the city touting *Swift Current*:

SWIFT CURRENT IS REAL TORONTO!
BEAT THAT, VANDERLERNER!

Deep Blue countered with a sign of its own, understated and elegant:

DEEP BLUE'S BEAUTY SPEAKS FOR ITSELF

In late September, a meeting was held to discuss the details. The owners of *Deep Blue* sent their technical staff and public relations people. They arrived at the hotel meeting room looking like a national delegation — half a dozen men and women attired in snappy deep blue uniforms embroidered with the ship's twin-sail logo. Zeideh showed up in a battered jacket and his workday captain's cap. His only assistant was Newfoundland Michael, who hovered over him like a bent CN Tower.

The two sides met for an hour. Interest was high, and reporters camped outside, waiting to hear the race route. Finally the two sides emerged. Captain Elijah stepped forward, triumphant.

"The race will be held on October twenty-second, at 3:30 p.m. from Queen's Quay. The finish line will be —" Zeideh paused for effect, "Niagara on the Lake, Ontario, the last docking berth on the Canadian side of the border."

A whistle went up from one of the reporters.

"Hey, great timing. You'll get there just in time for the Shaw Festival curtain call!"

The reporters laughed, but Captain Elijah shook his head. "Captain Vanderlerner can go to the Festival all he wants. But *Swift Current* is going to win this race, trust me!"

The leader of the *Deep Blue* delegation suddenly jumped forward, turned angrily, and pointed a finger at Zeideh:

"Captain Elijah, your boat is going to lose, make no mistake!"

There was a shocked silence, and Captain Elijah strode off in a huff. So it was set...and both sides prepared for a real battle.

SEVEN

It was the night before the race and the city was in a happy froth. Zeideh had succeeded beyond his wildest imagination. *Swift Current* and *Deep Blue* were probably the two most famous boats in North America. Only one family member fought to ignore the tumult. Uri held to his schedule of *kollel* and teaching and prayed that he would be overlooked. So far, he had succeeded.

The phone rang in Uri's home.

"Eerie?"

"Hello, Zeideh."

"How are you doing, grandson?"

This was the call that Uri dreaded — but expected.

"*Baruch Hashem*, Zeideh. Are you all ready for tomorrow?"

"Ready as I'll ever be. Eerie —"

Uri steeled himself inwardly.

"Yes, Zeideh."

"I want you to come along tomorrow, on the boat."

There was a pause. Uri tried to find the right balance, to say no without hurting Zeideh's feelings.

"Zeideh, I can't."

"Why not? Alex is coming. Solomon is coming. Ruby, Zahava. You are my special grandson. It means a lot to me. This is the race of my lifetime."

There was no use beating around the bush.

"Zeideh, I have to learn! You know me! How can I leave the *beis midrash* two weeks after the start of the new *zeman* to go on a boat cruise?"

Zeideh's voice rose heatedly. "Boat cruise? Boat cruise? You call this a boat cruise? The papers call this the race of the century! There's been nothing like it on Lake Ontario — ever. There will be reporters from Vancouver and Halifax and New York! Eerie...I need you there, next to me, helping me."

"Zeideh, I need to learn! I need to learn! What help will I be? I don't even know to push a button on the boat."

"Because you are my truly righteous grandson," Zeideh argued. "Just your being there will guarantee that I beat *Deep Blue*! And didn't I help you buy the house?"

"But Zeideh, how can I leave my learning? The ship will be full of people, you know that... All sorts of people! What shall I do, wander around the deck shaking hands? Waste six hours, there and back?"

There was a pause. The two Schiffmans were locked in love and stubbornness. Uri knew that Zeideh was thinking on his feet.

"Okay," Zeideh finally said. "I hear what you are saying. Let's compromise. I really need you on board, but you don't want to waste time. So I will make you a deal. I'll take you up with me into the pilothouse. The only people who will be there are Newfoundland Mike and me. I have a desk built into the corner, and you'll have nothing to do with me or anyone. You'll sit there with your Gemara and you'll learn."

"Where, in the pilothouse?" asked Uri incredulously. "While you're trying to win a race? How can I learn there, Zeideh?"

"What does the race have to do with you, Eerie? I'll race, you'll sit and learn. Please!" Zeideh was pleading.

Uri had to laugh. "Zeideh, where do you come up with these ideas? Whoever heard of a boat race with someone sitting in the pilothouse learning Gemara?"

Zeideh's tone brightened. "So, do you agree to come? Say you agree to come — please, Uri."

Uri could not believe himself. He was giving in. But how could he say no to a beloved Zeideh who had raised him, and for whom this crazy race meant so much? If Zeideh lost, he would never forgive him.

"Okay, Zeideh, I'll come. What time?"

"The boats will set out exactly at four. Be there by three thirty, sharp! I'll tell the boys to be on the lookout for you. And bring Chaya and the children. You can study, but they'll have a good time. It's supposed to be beautiful tomorrow!"

"Yes, Zeideh," Uri answered resignedly. Uri felt like a twelve year old all over again — a twelve year old who adored his crazy, brilliant Zeideh.

There was a pause on the phone. *What now?* wondered Uri.

"By the way, you asked me how I came up with the idea of your coming along. It wasn't my idea — it was Klonimos Kalman's! He said you would be a *segulah* for my success."

October 22, 3:40 p.m.

It was mayhem downtown. Uri and Chaya took a taxi, but they almost didn't make it. The streets were packed with throngs of people rushing to see the start of the race. Uri and Chaya jumped out of the taxi two blocks before the lakefront and ran the rest of the way, Yirmiyahu and a stroller hanging from each arm. Thankfully, they had left the twin girls home with a babysitter. The streets were bedlam. Pier Six was mobbed. A huge red banner, hung across the entrance:

THE GREAT BOAT RACE

The dock separating the two boats was a wall of humanity. Uri and Chaya fought their way towards *Swift Current*. In the bright afternoon sun, its orange and crimson and yellow lights flashed and sparkled wildly, and a huge orange *Swift Current* banner hung proudly from its stern.

"Let us through, let us through!" Uri yelled as they elbowed their way through the crowd. They were late. Chaya held on desperately to Uri's backpack, afraid that she would lose him. They fought their way closer to the *Swift Current*'s gangplank. Zeideh stood anxiously outside the pilothouse, scanning the crowd, searching for them. They waved and screamed, and finally Zeideh spotted them. He nodded, signaled to his crewmen, and they swam into the crowd to help them through the last few yards. *Swift Current* was crammed with passengers, reporters, old friends. Zeideh was not willing to compromise on anything, even though it made the boat heavier for the race. The crew fought to pluck Uri and Chaya out of the crowd and aboard the boat.

Zeideh looked down from the deck above and smiled. He cupped his hands over his mouth.

"You made it! You made it!" he screamed.

Uri did not try to yell back. He gestured with his thumb at the backpack that contained his Gemara and pointed up to the pilothouse. Zeideh had promised – he could sit upstairs and learn! Meanwhile, Alexander and Solomon and their wives ran to greet them. He placed Chaya and Yirmiyahu in their welcoming arms. Satisfied that Chaya was happy and looked after, Uri ran up the wide staircase to the upper deck, found the narrow, steep stairs to the pilothouse and quickly clambered up.

Zeideh was waiting for him at the top of the stairs, on the narrow ledge between the pilothouse and railing. Captain Elijah was in his glory, waving to well-wishers, gesturing thumbs up, beaming, posing for hundreds of photos. He wrapped his arm around his grandson's shoulders and grinned.

"Thanks for coming," he yelled, still waving. "I hope you davened for me!"

"You have a gorgeous day, Zeideh," Uri answered. "It's like summer!"

Indeed, it was a beautiful Indian summer day on the lake. Huge, white cumulus clouds swept lazily across the hazy sky, and there was just the slightest breeze. Across the pier, their rival, *Deep Blue*, rocked gently up and down in the water. Unlike Zeideh, Captain Vanderlerner was nowhere to be seen. Uri had never seen *Deep Blue* before. He caught his breath in amazement. It was an incredible work of art, its delicate, tinted bands of blues upon blues, like the sea and sky blended into one breathtaking whole. Her two huge, oversized, snow-white sails gleamed exotically in the afternoon sun, like some ship of the East.

Uri forgot himself and blurted out, "She's beautiful."

He turned apologetically to Zeideh, embarrassed at his praise for Zeideh's rival. He was shocked — there were tears in Zeideh's eyes.

"I know," he murmured even as he smiled and waved. "She is more beautiful than the *Swift Current*. But I will still beat her because I said I would!"

Tension built as the time for the race approached. Newfoundland Mike was still below, working on the engines. Zeideh called down and summoned him to the pilothouse. With just minutes to go, the lanky seaman appeared on the top deck, limping badly. He shook his head, grimaced, and grabbed at his knee.

"Boy, it's hurting bad. There's gonna be rain."

"Not today, Michael," Zeideh promised. "It's beautiful, just perfect! Let's go inside."

With just minutes to go until race time, Captain Elijah saluted the crowd below and gave one grand sweep of his arm towards *Deep Blue*. The three men entered the pilothouse, where a young seaman held the helm and scanned the control console, packed with dozens of dials and indicators that controlled engines, radar, ship-to-shore communication.

Uri peered out the large pilothouse windows. Lake Ontario stretched blue and peaceful past the islands. He looked back towards the boat, but Chaya and Yirmiyahu were far below, out of sight, on the covered lower deck. He would not see them again until they crossed the finish line. He hoped they were having a good time.

One minute to go

The mayor stepped forward and stood on a platform at the end of the pier, starting gun in hand. Uri, swept up in the excitement, wanted to watch the start.

This was what he was afraid of.

"Zeideh," he announced, "I have to learn."

There were just three minutes to go.

Zeideh sat in his captain's chair, hands at the helm. He did not turn around.

"The corner, Eerie," he shouted. "The corner desk is yours."

Michael stood, tense, in front of the control panel, his hands ready to thrust the engines into full power. Below, the crew had freed the ropes from their moorings. *Swift Current* was like a prancing racehorse, ready to charge from the gate.

The excitement was unbelievable. Down below, the crowds were cheering and whistling.

Uri murmured to himself, "This is my test. I must learn!"

Uri laid his backpack on the desk, extracted a small Gemara *Bava Basra*, and opened to a light section: Rabbah bar bar Chana's sea stories.

Race Time

A huge roar rose from the crowd. A silver ball started dropping from a pole atop one of the nearby buildings.

The crowd began counting: thirty, twenty-nine, twenty-eight...

The mayor lifted the starting gun: Ten, nine, eight, seven...

Uri placed his hands over his ears and peered one final time around the cabin. Zeideh's hands trembled excitedly at the wheel, while Mike watched over the control panel, all the time grimacing from his painful knee.

"Three... Two... One..."

Unknown to the passengers and crew, a monumental battle was about to erupt over Lake Ontario. Two awesome giants, each of whom towered tens of thousands of feet tall and stretched fifty miles wide, were preparing for war. At four o' clock, a giant, hazy, low-pressure blanket of warm air reigned over the lake. It was laden with tons of tiny moisture droplets, suspended high in its massive core. The giant, low-pressure weather system was warm, indolent, heavy, content to lie sluggishly over the lake forever if no one disturbed it, like an overfed buffalo snoozing in the midday sun.

Unseen even by weather radar, another giant descended swiftly towards the lake from the northwest. This weather system had been spawned by the frigid open waters of Lake Superior, and it roared down on the back of a powerful jet stream. This high-pressure giant was swift and bone-chilling, determined to deliver the first icy breath of winter to the lower lakes.

Still, at four o'clock, the oncoming system was a hundred miles away, and the lake stretched forth placidly and warm, still blissfully unaware of the fierce battle about to erupt over her.

October 22, 4:00 p.m.

The gun went off!

The crowd roared, and the two boats lurched out of their berths. *Deep Blue* immediately jumped into the lead. Although it was heavier than *Swift Current* and lay low in the water, it had surprising power.

"Look at those sails deploy!" whistled Michael, as *Deep Blue* pulled in front of them.

Although there was little wind, electronic sensors attached to *Deep Blue*'s sails sensed every lakeside breeze and exploited it, delicately adjusting the angle of its panels to harness the wind power. Coupled with its streamlined engines, it gave *Deep Blue* an early advantage.

Zeideh watched grimly as *Deep Blue* widened the distance between them. He tried to control his voice so as not to disturb Uri.

"We have to overtake her and stop her from passing," he said.

"But how, Cap?" wondered Michael. "She's in front of us!"

Zeideh's face stiffened with determination, and a thin smile crossed his lips. "Watch this —"

Before the two boats could enter the open lake, they had to curve past the Toronto Islands. The shallows along the outer island were treacherous, and ships gave it wide berth. But *Swift Current*'s draft was six feet shallower than *Deep Blue*'s. *Deep Blue* moved further to the right to avoid the shallows, but Zeideh aimed *Swift Current* directly at the tip of the island, cutting sharply inside of *Deep Blue*'s track.

"Full engine!" Zeideh ordered, forgetting Uri's presence. "Full engine! Give it everything!"

Swift Current surged ahead, and she quickly caught up with her rival. Zeideh tacked her sharply leeward, widening the distance between them.

Captain Elijah smiled grimly. "Keep her to full engine, we're pulling ahead."

Deep Blue tacked hard left to regain her lead, but her wide sails slowed her turn, and she fell further back.

"Wherever she moves, we have to stay right in front, to block her," Zeideh said. "We have to check her, turn for turn — it's our best chance."

"You want me to open the thruster?" Mike asked.

Captain Elijah shook his head. "Not yet. Save the extra power for when we need it. If we can check her moves, she won't be able to pass us easily. She'll be too busy tacking back and forth, trying to avoid us... Check the wind speed."

Michael studied the gauges. "Dead in the water — it's fallen to nothing. There's a real low-pressure cell over us right now, like soup."

Zeideh glanced back and saw *Deep Blue* desperately trying to catch up. *Swift Current* had pulled nearly three hundred yards in front. Zeideh smiled — let Vanderlerner try! Even with all his state-of-the-art gear, the sails were a huge drag in zero wind. *Swift Current* was the lighter, narrower ship — like a swift stallion.

Who did Vanderlerner think he was playing with? Captain Elijah had cruised this lake for thirty years! He knew every angle, every bit of coastline.

The pristine, blue waters of Lake Ontario beckoned to him like an old friend, and Zeideh pointed *Swift Current* straight as an arrow towards the goal: Niagara on the Lake.

Zeideh had promised to keep the cabin still and quiet, but even his muttered commands were more like a roar. Now that the boats were launched, it was impossible to concentrate. Uri cupped his hands over his ears and forced himself to learn.

"*Amar Rabbah: ishtayu li nechusei yama...*"

"Said Rabbah bar bar Chanah: The seafarers told me...the wave that sinks a ship has a fringe of white flame at its crest, but when it is beaten with clubs engraved with the words 'I am what I am... Amen, Amen, Selah!' it sinks back down..."

Instinctively, Uri peered out the window. *Baruch Hashem*, there were no flaming monster waves out there! Instead, the sky stretched blue and hazy, and giant, white cumulus clouds piled atop each other like a mountain of pillows.

Never mind the clouds! Uri commanded himself. Never mind Zeideh's race! Get back to learning!

The question was, What were these mysterious *nechusei yama*, monster waves that traveled the sea? And what was this awesome *tzuzitza d'nehura*, the white flame that flashed atop the wave that threatened to destroy the ship? And what was the *allavusa*, this mighty staff engraved with G-d's name that could beat down the monstrous wall of water?

He turned to the commentary of the holy Maharsha at the back of his small travel Gemara. Uri's Gemara was small enough, but the Maharsha's commentary was even smaller, the letters were tiny!

But who could understand Gemara without the Maharsha?

> *The waves...are the waves of our terrible exile. Each surging wave is a new enemy who rises up against us, generation after generation. And the fierce white flame is the enemy's Guardian Angel, leading the way. But every enemy is beaten down by the holy allavusa, the rod of Moshe, with the Almighty's name inscribed upon its side! The waves rise to the heavens, but they all fall back, beaten down by the Almighty — and Israel survives!*

Uri studied the minuscule letters of the Maharsha. He forgot all about the silly race, Zeideh, even Chaya and Yirmiyahu in the lower deck. These tiny words of the Maharsha, this was his sea, his waves, his race. He did not even notice his surroundings of lake and cabin – or the heavy, leaden clouds that had begun rolling in above...

October 22, 4:40 p.m.

"Yirmiyahu, you see the beautiful clouds Hashem made?"

Chaya held her three-year-old son on her lap and pointed high above. A huge, snowy white cloud passed overhead, and Yirmiyahu looked up, fascinated. It was such a beautiful fall day, it couldn't be more perfect. Chaya was glad that Uri had agreed to come, and that she and Yirmiyahu could share this special day.

The boat was a great big party. Carousel music played from the speakers. Everyone mingled and enjoyed the free refreshments. Chaya knew that Zeideh was keen on winning, but who cared? *Deep Blue*, their rival, was not far behind, and Zeideh was swinging the boat this way and that, so that she couldn't overtake them. What did it matter? *Swift Current* was beautiful, *Deep Blue* was beautiful, Lake Ontario was beautiful, Hashem's world was beautiful: it was a day to cherish. The music played, *Deep Blue* passengers leaned over the side of their boat, smiled, and waved to *Swift Current* passengers, and vice versa.

"Look up, Yirmiyahu, you see the clouds? What do you see?"

Yirmiyahu had the most piercing blue eyes, made even bluer by the sea and sky. He pointed up. "I see a cow!"

"Yes, it looks like a cow. It has legs and a head – and now, it blows away. Look, here comes another one. What do you see now?"

"A doggy, there's a doggy!"

"Right, a doggy. Does it go bow-wow?"

Like a box of animal cookies, the clouds rolled by, now a little denser than earlier in the afternoon.

"I brought you a water, *glatt* kosher." Solomon brought a bottle of ice-cold spring water from the galley. Everything was free on the trip, courtesy of the Captain Elijah. The afternoon was growing muggy, and

Chaya gratefully shared the water with Yirmiyahu.

"Beautiful, isn't it," said Ruby, who sat on her other side. "Zeideh picked a perfect day for the race."

Chaya watched as the clouds clustered closer overhead. "Look, Yirmiyahu, you see the mountains up in the sky, big mountains!"

The clouds had accumulated in great white columns over their heads, beginning to spread like an anvil. Yirmiyahu hid his face in Chaya's dress.

"What's the matter, Yirmiyahu?"

He peered up from his hiding place. "Scary mountain!" he whimpered. "Big, scary mountain!"

Chaya was about to answer when a powerful gust of wind suddenly swept across the deck, scattering cups and almost blowing her *sheitel* off. A startled whoop went up from the passengers.

"Whoa! What was that?" they asked each other. Soon after, a great gray wave suddenly lifted its foaming head alongside the lower deck, sprayed some passengers, and disappeared as suddenly. The *Swift Current* plunged sharply in its trough, and a surprised howl went up on deck. The clouds were growing thicker, the temperature dropped sharply, and the wind lifted strongly.

"Hey, what happened to summer?" joked Alexander.

Right above *Swift Current* and *Deep Blue*, the invisible battle had commenced. The huge cold front had reached the north edge of the lake and demanded possession of its vast waters. Lying in its way was the thick, moisture-laden blanket of heated gulf air. Like two giant warriors battling for the rule of a kingdom, they fought for supremacy over the deep blue waters of Lake Ontario.

The lazy warm front refused to budge, so the fierce, cold, north wind attacked angrily, driving off the warm air with its powerful gusts, chasing the lighter heated air into the frigid upper atmosphere above. As high and low pressures fought for equilibrium, the waves swelled higher and higher. *Swift Current* and *Deep Blue* bobbed helplessly in the giant swells, and the wind swept over them in ever stronger gusts.

"She's gaining on us, Captain. The wind's come up — it's helping her!"

Captain Elijah turned and saw *Deep Blue* closing quickly. The wind had suddenly given her the advantage. Her two huge sails had come alive, stealing the wind, adding tremendous thrust to her already powerful engines. Meanwhile, the waves were growing taller, and both ships rose and fell wildly, fighting to make headway.

He'll have to trim those sails or they'll rip right off their masts! thought Zeideh.

But Vanderlerner was determined to overtake *Swift Current*, no matter what. They were already halfway across the lake. Captain Elijah looked back. *Deep Blue* was making her move. Vanderlerner was maneuvering far to starboard, overtaking *Swift Current*. *Swift Current* would have to shoot ahead to block him.

"Mike, give me full engine, thrusters, full power!" Captain Elijah shouted, forgetting Uri. "I need everything now!"

"Captain, be careful," the Newfoundlander warned. "Those waves are getting high. It'll be hard on the pumps. We have to ease off some!"

"Give me power, Michael!" Zeideh shouted. "We have to stay in front!"

Michael shook his head. "I don't like it, Cap."

Deep Blue was the steadier boat. It lay wide and solid in the water, and crested the billowing waves easily. *Swift Current* was narrower, top heavy, and swayed drunkenly back and forth as it climbed every oncoming wave and then plunged headlong into the watery chasms in its wake. *Swift Current* responded sharply to the extra power, and Zeideh leaned his ship sharply starboard to head off Vanderlerner.

This is some way to learn Gemara, thought Uri.

Zeideh had invited him for a nice lake outing, but it was getting rougher and rougher. The skies had grown dark, rain began splattering on the windows, and the boat rose and fell sickeningly, like a carnival ride. Uri had trouble keeping his finger stuck to the Gemara. *Don't waste time*, he told himself angrily. *As long as you don't bring up, you can learn.*

He bent over his Gemara:

"Said Rabbah: The seafarers told me: There is a distance of three hundred *parsangs* from one wave to the other, and the height of the wave is also three hundred *parsangs*. Once, we were on a voyage, and the wave lifted us so high that we saw the resting place of the smallest star and there was a brilliant flash... And if it had lifted us up still further, we would have been consumed by its heat..."

A coast guard emergency signal suddenly wailed in the cabin. Michael quickly turned to the warning system:

"Immediate warning to all boats on the western end of Lake Ontario! A severe thunderstorm warning is in effect. An unexpected high-pressure cold front has swept in from the north, and we are expecting severe weather, with the possibility of spin-off tornadoes. Gusts could exceed seventy knots, and waves could threaten some vessels. Proceed to shelter as quickly as possible! We repeat, severe weather is about to descend on Lake Ontario. Seek immediate shelter!"

Uri looked up from his Gemara and peered out the window. The bright day had suddenly turned dark like night, and the black clouds were tinged with a frightening greenish border.

Chaya and Yirmiyahu – he had to go down to them!

"And one wave called to the other: My friend, have you left anything in the world that you did not wash away? I will go and destroy it."

The *Swift Current* passengers had suddenly grown very still.

In a matter of minutes, a fun-filled afternoon had turned into a nightmare. The skies had turned leaden, and the once-graceful white cumulus clouds welded into a huge, black anvil that threatened to drop down on them. The winds blew stronger and stronger, ripping off part of the lower deck's canopy. Just behind them, *Deep Blue* was also struggling through the rising waves, and her passengers had all run into the enclosed decks seeking shelter. *Swift Current* was the smaller, less stable vessel.

Chaya and Yirmiyahu had been sitting on a bench near the open stern of the lower deck. But the waves began crashing over the railings, the passengers were getting soaked, and they retreated towards the back of the deck. But even there, they could not escape the splattering of the waves.

"Mommy, it's too much water," Yirmiyahu complained, not comprehending the unexpected shower. "Stop the water, Mommy."

"Why don't we go up to Zeideh in the pilothouse," Solomon suggested. "At least there we'll be dry."

"Are you kidding?" Alexander answered. "You have to climb a ladder to get up there! Eerie will stay dry."

Chaya ignored the stab at her husband. Up to now, it had been such a beautiful trip. It was the first time that all the brothers and sisters-in-law had been together, having fun, in a long time. But she did wish she had Uri at her side now. He couldn't help them much, but Yirmiyahu would be reassured. What was he doing up there now, with the winds howling?

Uri closed the Gemara and lurched out of his seat. "Zeideh, I'm going down to the deck! I have to find Chaya and Yirmiyahu."

Michael whistled and shook his head in disbelief.

"Are you nuts, Eerie?" shouted Zeideh. "You'll fall overboard, G-d forbid!"

Uri struggled uphill towards the cabin door. Suddenly there was a blinding flash of lightning, followed almost immediately by a monstrous thunderclap. The whole sky was ripped open, and the rain began falling in torrents. Staggered by the blinding flash, Uri retreated. The storm was unleashed in all its fury, and Uri sought refuge next to Zeideh and Michael.

It was the awesome battle of the mighty forces of nature! The powerful cold front, spawned hundreds of miles north over Lake Superior, now chased the southern warm air higher and higher into the upper reaches of the atmosphere, where the temperature reached minus forty. The huge cumulonimbus, laden with millions of droplets of moisture, flash froze, and each frozen droplet attached to another. The clustered raindrops became giant hailstones, which fell from thirty thousand feet, bombarding the ships that sailed helplessly below. The winds roared unimpeded over the open waters, and the *Swift Current* struggled blindly through the roiling waves, pitching this way and that, trying to stay afloat — and maintain its lead over its unseen rival, now hidden behind a blinding curtain of torrential downpour.

Chaya, Yirmiyahu — the whole boat — was terrified. The waves shattered over the deck, flooded down into the salons and engine room below. The hail fell thunderously, like a Biblical plague, assaulting the thin canopy that sheltered the back half of the lower deck. The sky took on a sickly, greenish hue, with flashes of light as the clouds were momentarily split by tongues of white lightning and deep rumbling thunder.

Yirmiyahu dug his head into Chaya's shoulder, afraid to look out. Everyone was soaked by the waves and the wind-swept rain and hail. There was no escape.

"Zeideh or no Zeideh," screamed Solomon, "I'm going to sue the *Swift Current* if we ever get out of this alive!"

But that was the question: would they get out of here alive? Somewhere out there, *Deep Blue* was in the same danger they were. The race had turned into a nightmare.

Where is Uri? Chaya wondered. *What was happening up in the pilothouse?*

"Radio's out... Compass is out... Radar's out! We're sailing blind," Michael announced. "The storm has knocked out the communications tower."

"Can anyone see *Deep Blue*?" Zeideh asked. "Where is she?"

But no one could see anything in the blinding storm.

"Maybe she pulled ahead of us," Zeideh worried. "Michael, are the thrusters on full?"

Michael did not respond.

"Michael, I asked you about the thrusters — turn them up."

"Cap'n," Michael argued, "we don't know where we are, or what's in front of us! How can we run the ship at full engine?"

"Who doesn't know where he's going? I can tell exactly where we're going! We're heading straight south, just where we're supposed to be! Michael, I'm ordering you to open up the thrusters full!"

"Sorry, Captain Elijah. No can do."

"What do you mean, 'no can do'? I'm the captain!"

Michael turned angrily to Zeideh.

"Listen, Cap'n, you can report me later to the coast guard. We're not going down like the *Edmund Fitzgerald*. Remember her, Captain Elijah? Nine hundred feet of iron ship, and she just headed straight down into the deep without even one SOS! There wasn't even a peep of distress signal! We're taking on the water now, Cap'n, I can feel it! You give it more speed, you meet one of the Three Sisters, and we're done for."

"What's the Three Sisters?" Uri asked Michael.

"There's a story that before the *Edmund Fitzgerald* went down, three giant waves — the Three Sisters — attacked her from the stern. That's why she broke up and went down so fast that she couldn't even issue a call for help."

"Aw, that's just rumor!" shouted Captain Elijah dismissively. But Zeideh had to yield to his first mate, who was at the controls.

"All right, Michael," Zeideh snorted angrily, "no thruster power. But give me everything you have from the diesels."

Michael shook his head glumly, but obeyed.

There was the slightest easing off of the hailing. It still rained heavily, but the deafening beat of hailstones against the pilothouse roof had quieted.

Uri had waited long enough.

"Zeideh, I'm going down to Chaya."

Zeideh, already humbled by Michael, looked at Uri angrily. "Eerie, are you crazy? It's terrible out there! Wait a few minutes until the storm quiets down — it won't last. It's too dangerous now!"

"Zeideh, I'm going," answered Uri firmly.

"Eerie, no!" Zeideh shouted. "It's crazy!"

Uri turned to escape and Zeideh grabbed him by the sleeve, trying to hold him back. Uri yanked his arm fiercely, breaking free of his grandfather's grasp, and ran to the door. He paused at the doorway, heard the terrible storm howling outside, and turned apologetically to his grandfather.

"I'm sorry, Zeideh, but I have to go."

Bracing himself against the wild swaying of the boat, Uri pulled the door open. He was immediately met by a windswept torrent of rain that slapped across his face. The boat pitched forward, then flung backwards, almost knocking Uri over. He clung desperately to the outside door handle and shut the latch tight. He was all alone with the howling storm.

Uri stood on the narrow ledge, clinging to the railing. Below, the gray, dark waves foamed and beckoned, like tongues of an underwater creature licking at the sides of the boat. Uri grabbed the railing of the narrow staircase that led down to the upper deck. The railing was coated with a thin, icy sheen left by the hailstones, and he struggled to grasp it. One misstep and he would be thrown overboard into the lake. The conditions were much worse than he ever thought. Zeideh had been right — he had made a terrible mistake…but there was no turning back now! The pilothouse door was locked above him, and the twenty feet of frost-slicked stairs dropped almost vertically below him. There was no way to go but down — one way or the other!

Hashem, he prayed, *Hashem please help me — for the sake of Yirmiyahu!*

Uri slowly descended the first three steps. Every step was treacherous, uneven, ice-coated, and slick. He slid his foot from step to step. The boat heaved violently like a carnival ride, and his fingers held desperately at the frozen railings. Suddenly, there was an eerie whoosh, and the air was sucked out of his body. The boat seemed to hang suspended in mid-air, and an enormous black wave suddenly rose alongside, rising taller than the boat. The wave hung there momentarily like it was rejoicing in its huge mass, and then it crashed down thunderously against the side of the *Swift Current*, swamping Uri in its powerful grasp, almost dragging him from the staircase and hurtling him into the foaming lake below. The wave was like a sentient being, with a will and brain, malevolently trying to pull him from his thin perch into the depths below.

"Hashem, Hashem, help me!" he screamed. "*Shema Yisrael…* Hashem please help me!"

The wave held him in its crushing embrace, toyed with him sinisterly, pulled at his shoes, at his pants, so that one leg was dragged off the step. Uri held on desperately to the railing, resisting the force intent on plunging him into the foaming waters below. And then, just as suddenly as it rose, the wave was gone. The boat fell steeply into its wake and then righted itself. His whole body gasping for air, Uri struggled to regain his foothold and hold on tighter. He was afraid to move up or down.

Was that the First Sister? wondered Uri.

There was a momentary eerie silence, and suddenly a second wave snuck up silently from behind, even darker and more monstrous than the first. It lifted its immense head, paused to rejoice in the brief moment of awesome power that its Creator had granted it, and then crashed down with a thunderous roar against the side of the ship, engulfing Uri in its raging waters.

For a few seconds, Uri was completely submerged, unable to breath. He panicked, not sure whether to abandon his hold and swim free. But then the wave broke, and his head was suddenly above water. Uri gasped for breath. The wave was a like huge wall, tons and tons of raging water, whose foaming tentacles reached out savagely at his legs and arms and body, trying to drag him away from his feeble hold. He couldn't fight a hundred tons of water!

"What's happening, Hashem," Uri sobbed. "Hashem, what's happening? How did I get here? What did I do wrong? Help me!"

Uri fought a losing battle to hold on. First one foot was drawn off the step, then his left hand slid off the soaking, ice-slicked railing. With his one right hand, with just a few fingers that threatened to slide off in a second, he held on with all his might. Just a few fingers separated him from the seething cauldron below. His hands were bleeding, he was blinded by rain and tears, and his half-suspended body flapped crazily from the staircase. The wave held him in its crushing embrace seemingly forever, and then, suddenly, its moment of glory was over! Stripped of its awesome power, the wave fell meekly into the lake below.

I have to get down from here, Uri knew. *One more wave, and I am gone!*

The Second Sister was over...what was next?

There was a sudden lull. An ominous silence descended over the lake. The rain had almost stopped — but still the wind blew unrelentingly. Uri took advantage of the lull. He carefully lowered himself down a few more steps. There were only a dozen stairs to the safety of the deck below. There was an expectant hush, then the sound of a great, deep whoosh, like the lake itself had taken a breath. Uri looked up. He could not believe what he was seeing. A third wave rose, still, silent, majestic, awesome. It was a towering, huge Titanic of water. It rolled closer and closer, rose higher and higher, racing towards the puny hull of the *Swift Current*, to where Uri held on with only his ten torn fingers. The incredible wave curled fearfully overhead, twice as tall as the ship itself! It was a watery monster spawned by the mighty north wind, ready to overwhelm everything, Uri, the boat, Chaya, Yirmiyahu — maybe the world itself! Uri stared at the wave in disbelief. A white flame glowed at the crest of the wave — the *tzutzia d'nehura*! This was the monster that was going to down the *Swift Current*. The Third Wave! It had come!

I am gone, Uri thought, *we are finished!* He gazed down at the waters below that waited patiently for him, and he knew that he, too, would soon join them in their depths.

Hopelessly, Uri cried out his final prayer: "Hashem, in the merit of the holy Maharsha, save us!"

Uri watched the wave expectantly, steeling himself for its thunderous arrival. But instead...the wave fell back down the way it had risen, almost meekly. Uri gazed up. The *tzutziza d'nehura*, the white flame...it wasn't on the top of the wave! It was a cluster of bright stars on the horizon! The skies were clearing! Even as he stood there, suspended between heaven and sea, holding on for his life, a calm suddenly descended on the waters. The wind abated. The storm was over! It was a crisp, beautiful, autumn evening on Lake Ontario. The *Swift Current* had survived! Uri half climbed, half fell down the steps to the deck below, and raced to find his wife and baby.

"Chaya, Chaya, where are you?"

Uri raced down to the lower deck, searching through the darkness for his wife. "Chaya! Chaya!"

There was a lot of confusion. Night had fallen, the lights were out. Everyone was soaked, and a light but steady cold wind blew, chilling everyone to the bone. But...they were safe!

"Chaya!" Uri yelled over and over, "Where are you?"

Suddenly, it was as if Shabbos had just ended. The lights that had been doused suddenly flashed on dazzlingly. The speakers began blaring their cheerful carousel music again. Everyone looked around, and a huge cheer went up from the passengers: cheers, tears, and laughter as they saw what a storm-swept, terrible condition they were all in. Everyone was soaked. Women's hair hung limp. All the cute sailing outfits were destroyed. Everyone laughed and cheered and smiled — because they were not going to drown!

And then Uri saw them — all of them — Chaya clutching Yirmiyahu, Alexander and Solomon, a very wet and unhappy Ruby and Zahava. They were safe. They were safe! *Baruch Hashem*!

Uri rushed to his wife. She cried when she saw him. He took Yirmiyahu from her arms. He kissed his child, and held him close. Yirmiyahu was shivering and tear-stained, but okay.

He held his son's face close to his: "Yirmiyahu, are you okay? Did you get wet?"

His son looked back at him with those blue eyes, so serious. "There was so much water, Abba," he whimpered. "Mommy and me got washed!"

Uri reassured him. "No more water, Yirmiyahu. It's okay now. Water went away."

"Eerie! Eerie! I bet you were nice and dry up there in the pilothouse while we were getting soaked!"

Uri turned to Alexander impatiently, controlling his words. "Oh, right, Alex! It was just so warm and *cozy* up there. Look how nice and dry my clothing is!"

"Uri, you're so soaked to the skin — and look at your fingers! — what happened?" asked Chaya.

"There was leak in the roof," he answered quickly. "Listen, Chaya, the race isn't over yet. Has anyone seen *Deep Blue*?"

In the excitement of the storm, the race had been forgotten. They looked out onto the lake. Uri was worried. There was no boat in sight.

"Where's *Deep Blue*?"

Uri turned to his wife, and handed Yirmiyahu back into her arms. "Chaya, I'm going up to Zeideh. Will you be okay? Something is funny here. I want to be up there with him."

Chaya looked at him, disappointed that he was leaving them again. She put on a brave face. "We're okay now, Uri," she answered. "Do what you have to do."

Uri ran back up to the upper deck and approached the narrow pilothouse staircase with dread. The stairs were still very slippery. Just a few minutes before, he had almost been dragged off these steps and thrown into the lake. He looked up the narrow staircase. This was the place where a *neis* had transpired for him. He would surely have to recite *hagomel* tomorrow! Impulsively, he kissed the metal railing that had saved him. He quickly but carefully walked up the staircase, pulled open the pilothouse door and entered.

Zeideh sat like a rock at the helm, not turning, not saying a word.

"Zeideh, I'm back," Uri announced.

Still no answer. "Zeideh, what's the matter?" He approached his grandfather and looked into his stony face. His face was stained — he had been crying.

"Zeideh, what's the matter?" Uri asked.

"He thought you fell overboard!" Michael finally spoke out. "He thought you drowned!"

"What, me drown? It was a piece of cake getting down!"

Hashem, forgive me, Uri thought. *But one way or another, I would have gotten down!*

Zeideh finally broke his silence.

"Did you see Chaya and the boys?" he asked.

"Everyone is okay," Uri said. "Everyone is soaked, but they're happy we survived."

Zeideh snorted. "Soaked? Too bad! What did they expect? You go on a boat, you get wet."

"Zeideh," asked Uri, "where's *Deep Blue*? Did you see her?"

Captain Elijah smiled tightly. "I saw her. Didn't you?"

"No. Where?"

Zeideh gestured backwards. "Look back about a mile, towards the west, towards Catherines. He lost his nerve, our Captain Vanderlerner! Look, he rolled up his sails, lowered speed and called it quits. Don't you get it? He gave up! In the worst of the storm I pushed ahead! I wasn't afraid, Eerie! Captain Elijah wasn't afraid! To me every one of those waves was like a page flapping in the wind! I just dived ahead, page after flapping page! I wasn't afraid, Eerie! I didn't slow down! Look, Eerie, what's she doing now?"

Uri turned and gazed hard. In the darkness of the lake, *Deep Blue* was hard to locate. Finally he saw her bluish glow. "She's turning to land," he said.

Zeideh laughed triumphantly. "Ha! She won't even make it to the finish! Vanderlerner must have lost his radar and couldn't figure out where he is! Some great captain! Big, tall, silent, handsome Captain Vanderlerner versus little Elijah Schiffman from Stretin! And we won Eerie, we won! Look, ahead — you see, where the lights are flashing. Niagara on the Lake! We beat her! Even without Michael's thrusters, we beat her straight!"

Zeideh lifted a microphone and spoke excitedly to the passengers and reporters below. "Folks, if you're worried about *Deep Blue* — don't be! You can spot her right out there, a mile to the stern, trying to find a harbor! Folks, straight ahead — see the flashing lights out there? Niagara on the Lake! We're going to land in twenty minutes! I promised you — Captain Elijah is still the boss of Lake Ontario!"

The cheer of the passengers below was so loud it penetrated the sealed windows of the pilothouse. The passengers gathered along the prow of the boat to witness the oncoming coast. Already, cameramen were testing their flashes for the big moment when *Swift Current* made her triumphal landing. The cabin was dark except for the greenish glow of the control panel, but there was a little lamp hooked to the corner desk. Uri turned on the lamp, and tried to read a few last symbolic lines of Gemara before the exciting landing.

"Eerie," Zeideh shouted. "Come here. We're landing!"

Uri closed the Gemara and approached the windows to witness the triumphant docking of *Swift Current*. A whole caravan of official cars and vans awaited their arrival, and their crimson lights flashed beckoningly. Uri took one final glance back. *Deep Blue* was nowhere to be seen. She must have turned into the other port for safety. He felt bad for Zeideh's rival. It was such a beautiful ship — too bad that both boats could not win!

Like the arrival of a monarch, *Swift Current* swept into Niagara on the Lake, horn blasting. The pier was darker and much shorter than Toronto's, and Michael had to abruptly reverse engines so as not to crash into the end of the dock. Finally, he cut the engines. There was a moment's blessed silence, and then a burst of applause went up from the passengers. They had landed! The crew threw out the mooring ropes, and helping hands on the land quickly secured them to the pier posts.

Captain Elijah stood up stiffly from his chair, walked to the pilothouse door and stood on the narrow deck outside. Smiling broadly, he waved triumphantly to the passengers below, throwing kisses, his face flashing on and off from dozens camera flashers below.

He turned to Uri. "Come on," he said, "you're part of this too!"

He climbed briskly down the still, slick staircase like a youngster, crossed the upper deck and then descended the wide staircase to the lower deck. A gangplank had been thrown onto the dock, and officials were already there waiting to meet him. On shore, half a dozen police cars flashed bright red and white beams. Zeideh smiled and waved, smiled and waved, posed for more pictures, and when he saw Chaya and Yirmiyahu, he grabbed his great-grandson and kissed him for the cameras.

"Me and him, folks," he yelled, pointing at Yirmiyahu. "We won! We beat *Deep Blue*!"

Followed by Uri, Alexander, and Solomon, Zeideh stepped jauntily onto the gangplank. The reception committee had already ascended the gangplank, and the reporters and photographers stood ready for the official welcome.

The reception committee consisted of uniformed police.

"Hello, Niagara!" Captain Elijah greeted the half dozen officers waiting for him.

Their response was much less friendly.

"Sir, could we see your passport, please, and those of your passengers?"

Zeideh stopped short, frowned, and looked sternly at the officer. "Passport? What passport? We are all full-blooded Canadian citizens!"

"Right you are, Captain! And we are full-blooded U.S. border customs officers. Can we see your passports, please. And those of everyone on board."

"Passports? Who needs passports for Niagara on the Lake?"

The custom officials glanced at each other for an instant, and a touch of a smile formed on their lips.

"Niagara on the Lake? Canada? Captain, don't you know where you are?"

"Where am I?"

"You are in Upstate New York, the United States of America! You missed the Canadian border by three miles! You're in the U.S.A. now!"

Zeideh was in shock. "What? This isn't Niagara on the Lake!"

The custom officials began laughing. "Niagara on the Lake? You don't get it, Captain? You're outside of Buffalo! Niagara on the Lake is three miles that way! You're part of that race, aren't you? Well your rival docked at Niagara on the Lake twenty minutes ago!"

Zeideh looked back across the lake, stunned.

A buzz went up from the passengers, and then the buzz turned into a roar...of laughter! The whole boat was screaming with laughter! Even the custom officers were laughing. Captain Elijah had missed his port! He wasn't even in the right country! Zeideh stood there, his face white with shock, cameras snapping, custom guards besides themselves with laughter, Michael trying to escape, Alexander and Solomon skulking away, Uri, totally bewildered, holding on to his grandfather's arm so that he shouldn't fall, Yirmiyahu wailing and cold.

It was a disaster!

NICE PORT, WRONG COUNTRY!
SWIFT CURRENT, OOPS!
WRONG COUNTRY — SO SORRY!
PASSPORTS, PLEASE!
YOU'RE IN AMERICA NOW!

There was not a newspaper in Canada that did not have a headline mocking Zeideh's terrible gaffe. Captain Elijah had raced his circus boat straight...to the wrong destination. Every newspaper had the same two photographs: a stricken, white-faced Captain Elijah confronted by U.S. customs agents, and a beaming, proud Captain Vanderlerner, waving from the bridge of *Deep Blue*. Her sails had been shredded by the wind, and, like the *Swift Current*, her radar and compass had been knocked out. But, unlike *Swift Current*, *Deep Blue* had lowered its speed, been cautious in her directions, and had taken bearings frequently.

One headline that appeared not in Canada, but in a Miami sports section, summed it all up:

THE DIFFERENCE BETWEEN —
A CAPTAIN AND A "CAPTAIN"!

The tone of most of the articles were a combination of mockery at Captain Elijah's unbelievable mistake, respect for his seamanship during the terrible storm, and sympathy.

But, paraphrasing another famous quote, the paper summed it up: "Admit it, Captain Elijah – you're no Captain Vanderlerner!"

Nor was the publicity limited to Canada, or even the U.S. Papers all over the world reported the humorous climax to the race:

"SO SORRY — BUT WRONG COUNTRY!"

And then, worst of all, what became the catch phrase for the next three months on every talk show and comedy skit:

"Sorry Elijah — but you ain't no Captain Vanderlerner."

Poor Zeideh became the object of Canada's ridicule.

Something happened to Zeideh after that. Perhaps it was the shock of his terrible error. Or the ridicule. He became a different man. He changed. Before, Captain Elijah had been the toast of Toronto, an eternally cheery smile on his face, a wave, a hello, a telephone call, a man with a thousand friends, known by all, by politicians, reporters, the plain people on Queen Street. He was here, there, everywhere, always in the papers, always on the boat, always greeting everyone at synagogue.

He changed. The family was even afraid that he had suffered some undetected stroke. His whole world changed. Gone was his sailor's cap. Gone was his jaunty walk, his easy manner. He became a recluse. He placed his business in the hands of Edwin Bookman and appointed Michael the Newfoundlander as captain. He stayed hidden away in his house for days at a time, just emerging to attend minyan each morning. He still took care of himself, but he stopped shaving and let his beard fill in, white and silver, so that suddenly he was an old man.

When he spoke to the family, it was just briefly, before Shabbos and holidays. He asked about his great-grandchildren, he asked Eerie about his learning, but otherwise, Zeideh disappeared from the city's radar.

The only person he kept in close contact was with Klonimos Kalman, whom he saw a few times weekly, and his old friend, Edwin Bookman. And so he lived out his last years, until one day, he was suddenly gone.

Uri stood at the railing of his deck and looked out. His eyes had adjusted to the darkness, and the bright moonlight lit up the yard. Herb the raccoon peeped out shyly from behind the shed, waiting for him to disappear so he could begin his night inspection of the garbage pails. Somewhere up in the magnolia, the cardinal had begun singing again, anticipating the dawn. It was past two. Uri was played out, exhausted, still bewildered. It was enough. Uri went inside. Uri climbed into bed, recited *hamapil*, and finally closed his eyes. It had been a long, tumultuous day, but he needed desperately to understand the mystery of his Zeideh.

He sighed, and finally fell into blessed, hard-earned sleep.

"Uri —"

He heard a voice call his name. Uri turned away, still asleep.

"Uri!"

He forced his eyes open. He saw the digits on the clock: two minutes past four.

"Uri, are you awake?" It was Chaya. She was whispering, a panicky sound in her voice.

"What is it, Chaya?" he asked, eyes finally open.

"Uri, there's someone in the house!"

He lifted his head and listened. He was so tired. "No, there isn't, Chaya. You're dreaming." He dropped his head again.

"No, Uri, I'm not dreaming," Chaya hissed. "I heard footsteps, and the sound of voices. Someone is in the house!" She kept her voice very low.

Uri groaned. He was so tired. "Maybe it's Yirmiyahu, come in late?"

"Yirmiyahu came home after one o'clock and went right to bed," she whispered. "It's only four o'clock. He wouldn't be up now. Listen —"

Uri heard the voices for the first time. He bolted upright. Someone was in the house.

"The children..." Chaya warned. "The children are in their rooms, the girls — you have to go out there, Uri — "

He did not have to be convinced. Uri was instantly fully awake. The house was pitch dark, the two sets of twins were in their rooms, Yirmiyahu was in his basement bedroom. They were all in danger. Uri stood up quickly without making a sound, and donned his robe. Their bedroom door was closed.

I can't confront them with my bare hands, he thought.

He had nothing in the bedroom, no hammer, no weapon. Fear made him think quickly. The wide shade over their window had a long, thin shaft at its bottom. Swung sharply it could do a lot of damage, like a whip. Quickly, he forced it out of its sheath and opened the door. There was a long, narrow hall that crossed the house. Uri could hear the intruders' voices clearly. *What business do they have in my house*, he thought angrily! Uri walked very slowly, not sure when he would confront them face to face. He stopped and listened. He heard whispering, but it was uncanny, almost like an animal had gotten inside. Maybe he had forgotten to close the back door in his exhaustion. Was that stupid raccoon in the house?

He looked towards his study door, and a chill went up his spine. The door was open slightly, and a light shone from it. He had been in the hall less than two hours before, and the house had been dark. Raccoons didn't turn on lights. Someone was in there! He could hear talking. Instinctively, he wanted to scream and race to the phone to call Hatzolah. But it was too dangerous. He approached his study door slowly. An odd sound came from the room. Shaking, he grasped the rod with all his might, ready to strike out, and peered in the doorway.

Yirmiyahu was bent over his desk. Zeideh's Gemara *Zevachim* and his beautiful notebook lay opened in front of him. Zeideh's gold pen was in Yirmiyahu's hand. Yirmiyahu bent over Zeideh's notebook, learning from it carefully. As he studied, he...sang. Yirmiyahu was reading Zeideh's notes in a beautiful, soft *niggun*. Suddenly, Yirmiyahu paused and began writing his own notes in the empty lines at the bottom of the page. As he wrote, the vellum paper responded to each stroke with a tiny chirp, just as Bookman had shown. The chirps blended into a hushed birdsong.

Satisfied with his writing, Yirmiyahu laid the pen back down and continued studying Zeideh's *hagahos*, singing the words as he read. Uri had never heard Yirmiyahu sing since his bar mitzvah. He had never heard his son so contented before! Again, Yirmiyahu paused, lifted the pen, and began writing underneath Zeideh's notes. Again, the book sounded a joyous chirp with each pen-stroke.

Zeideh and Yirmiyahu were singing to each other!

Uri laid the rod gently down against the wall and watched his son.

What should he do? Should he retreat back to the bedroom? Chaya was watching him anxiously from the far end of the hall. He gave her a silent thumbs-up, and placed his finger over his lips. And then Uri did what his heart told him. He slid silently into the study, and sat down at the *shtender* alongside Yirmiyahu.

Yirmiyahu did not seem startled by Uri's entrance. Perhaps he knew all along that he had been watching him. He continued studying the notebook, but his singing stopped.

"Yirmiyahu, it's four o'clock in the morning," murmured Uri. "You have to sleep, my son."

Yirmiyahu turned to his father. His beautiful, serious face glowed with joy. "I slept enough, Abba. I was excited to start *Zevachim*, so I woke up early. I found Zeideh's notebook. Abba, did you know this paper sings — like a bird!"

Uri smiled, unfazed. "Yirmiyahu, with our Zeideh, anything was possible."

Yirmiyahu's face suddenly grew intense.

"Abba, Zeideh was a *gaon*! These *chiddushim* are tremendous!"

Uri looked at his son. He was joyous at Yirmiyahu's happiness.

"Yirmiyahu," he answered. "I thought about it a lot tonight. I realize that I never knew who Zeideh really was — and I still don't know... What are you writing in his notebook?"

Yirmiyahu looked down, guiltily. "Just some *hagahos*... I'm sorry, Abba, I didn't ask your permission."

Uri gazed at his strange, intense child. He wanted to embrace him, kiss him for joy, like the day of the great storm.

"Yirmiyahu, Zeideh did not leave those empty lines for me. He left them for you!"

PART THREE
SHIDDUCHIM

EIGHT

It was such a wonderful time. Uri surrendered to his son. How could he fight him, or try to change him? Yirmiyahu was an exceptional boy. He was like Zeideh: he did what he did his way. And he was so happy. For the first time, Uri saw his son content and fulfilled. He even surrendered his precious gold pen to Yirmiyahu.

At first Yirmiyahu refused to accept it. "Abba, this pen is for you. I can borrow it."

But Uri insisted, and when Yirmiyahu still argued, Uri commanded him as his father — *b'mitzvas kibbud av* — to accept the pen. He put Yirmiyahu in control of Zeideh's notebook, and control it he did. Uri and Yirmiyahu began their *daf* every morning at five, but Yirmiyahu was usually there even earlier — who knew from when — already learning, looking into Zeideh's notes, chirping away with the pen, a look of pure joy on his face.

This was crazy. A boy going to *yeshivah gedolah*, doing very well in his *shiurim* and *sedarim*, the Rosh Yeshivah bursting with compliments, good *chavrusa*s, staying up all night for Thursday *mishmar*, a few normal friends — although Yirmiyahu rarely socialized — and he was up every morning long before dawn, delving into the complexities of *Kodshim*. And Yirmiyahu was joyous.

So what could Uri say, or Chaya?

"Yirmiyahu, you don't get enough asleep —"

"Yirmiyahu, maybe you should go play basketball on Friday afternoons just to relax —"

"Yirmiyahu, don't burn out —"

Yirmiyahu was Yirmiyahu, a treasure that Hashem had placed in their hands for safekeeping.

And then, there was a subtle change in their learning... How could it be described? Like the race between *Swift Current* and *Deep Blue*? It was true! Yirmiyahu was *Deep Blue* and Zeideh's pages were his beautiful, white sails. And as they learned, although Uri read the page and *Rashi*, it was *Deep Blue* who forged ahead. It was Yirmiyahu who asked the deepest *kashas*, who read out Zeideh's profound insights, his unbelievable *chiddushim*, his knowledge of all *Shas*. When did it all happen? When did Zeideh become such a *gaon*?

Uri realized that he did not know anything! He did not know Zeideh. He did not know Yirmiyahu. He did not know the Gemara very strongly. And he even had trouble knowing himself.

Eight months, eight beautiful, halcyon months. *Zevachim* was one hundred and twenty folios, and *Menachos* was one hundred and ten. Eight months of pure Torah learning, of closeness between father and his oldest son, two *chayalim* of Torah, breaking through the lines, fighting for highest ground.

And then, suddenly, the glory stopped, like a plane that runs out of fuel, mid-air.

The day before Uri and Yirmiyahu were to begin *Chullin*, Uri made an appointment to see Reb Elisha, Edwin Bookman. He never knew what surprises lay in store for him when he went to collect a new Gemara from Bookman. There had been a leather-bound notebook for *Zevachim* and an even thicker one for *Menachos*. What had Zeideh left him for *Chullin*? Uri waited an unusually long time for Bookman to appear in the boardroom.

Over the years, Uri and the aging lawyer had grown very close. Uri taught Bookman Gemara, but Bookman took a great personal interest in Uri and his family. He even reprimanded Uri in a fatherly fashion if he thought he was negligent in some financial manner — almost like Zeideh himself. Uri peered into a small pocket Mishnayos and waited. It was a long time before Bookman finally appeared through the double oak doors.

One look at Bookman's face and Uri sensed that something was not right. *What? Is he angry at me about something?* But Bookman smiled at him paternally, so he knew that it was not that. And yet, what?

Bookman sat down across the table from Uri.

"So, how is my rabbi doing?" he asked. "Are you still learning with your son?"

"*Baruch Hashem*," Uri answered mildly. He did not want to boast of his great pride.

Bookman and Uri gazed at each other for a moment. Bookman studied Uri's noble, honest face, while Uri's gaze fell towards the Gemara. His eyes searched for a notebook. Bookman followed Uri's look. He laid the Gemara on the table.

"This is it, Rabbi Schiffman. Just the Talmud. There are no more notebooks."

He smiled, but there was sadness in his face.

Uri reached over and took the Gemara *Chullin*. He looked to Bookman for permission to inspect it.

"Go on, look inside!"

Uri opened the Gemara to the first *daf*. It was snow white. He turned a few pages, then flipped though the back. Not a mark, not a word.

"What happened to Zeideh's notes?" he asked.

"Your grandfather passed away after learning the last volume I gave you. Those were his final writings. The rest — the last three volumes — are his inheritance to you. But you will find nothing of Captain Elijah in them, no folded money, no commentaries — just the Talmud itself."

Stunned, Uri looked at Bookman almost beseechingly, not wanting to believe what he said. A tear rolled down his eye. Bookman's eyes also reddened.

"I feel like Zeideh has died right now," Uri murmured, shaking his head. He ran his hands over the first untouched *daf* – a *daf* without Zeideh.

"It feels so empty," he said.

Bookman gave Uri a reproving look. "Rabbi," he said, "is the Talmud empty without your grandfather?"

⛵ ⛵ ⛵

Uri entered his study early the next morning, but Yirmiyahu was already waiting for him. He rose for his father and watched him as he laid the new volume on his *shtender*. Uri had deliberately hidden the Gemara in a different room so that Yirmiyahu would not find it. He wanted to show Yirmiyahu the unmarked Gemara himself, to prepare him.

"Yirmiyahu," he warned, "you are going to be disappointed."

He opened the beautiful volume to the first *daf*. There was not a mark or a note anywhere. Yirmiyahu looked into the Gemara but did not seem surprised. Zeideh had not written in *Zevachim* or *Menachos* either.

"Where are Zeideh's *hagahos*?" he asked. "Where is his notebook?"

"There is no notebook, Yirmiyahu. Nothing! Zeideh passed away before he could start *Chullin*. It's just you and me."

He studied Yirmiyahu closely to see his reaction. Yirmiyahu shrugged and turned to the first *mishnah*: "Hakol shochetin..."

Uri paused, astonished. "Wait, Yirmiyahu – is that all you have to say? Don't you miss Zeideh and his beautiful *hagahos*?"

Yirmiyahu looked up at his father, his finger already pressed to the first *Rashi*. "Abba, Zeideh's not gone and his Torah is not gone."

He pointed up to the bookshelf that now contained almost the complete set of Zeideh's *Shas*, filled with his notes, and next to it, the two leather-bound notebooks of Zeideh's commentaries on *Zevachim* and *Menachos*.

"Abba, we hardly did *Zevachim* and *Menachos*! We rushed through them, and I only studied some of Zeideh's *chiddushim*. We skipped almost all the *Tosafos*! I am going to go back to those *masechtos*."

Uri sighed and shook his head.

"Yirmiyahu, please! When will you have time to study *Zevachim* and *Menachos*? We're just starting *Chullin* — and *Chullin*'s really hard — the *siyum* is less than a year away, you have to finish your last year in yeshivah and prepare for *farheir*s to get into a good *beis midrash*. Yirmiyahu, there's a limit — even for you! Here —" he handed Yirmiyahu the gold pen that his son had returned after finishing *Menachos*. "This was Zeideh's and now it's yours, for keeps! His *neshamah* will be with you, even when there are no *hagahos*."

At first Yirmiyahu refused, but Uri was implacable. "In honor of starting the countdown to the *siyum*, take it!"

Reluctantly, Yirmiyahu took back the pen, using it as a pointer, just as Uri had. But he wrote no notes in *Chullin*. Zeideh did not write, so Yirmiyahu did not write. It was a different learning. Zeideh was no longer there in their midst, learning with them. There were no more indecipherable *hagahos*, no more little yellow notes, and no more cash surprises. It was learning for learning's sake, *daf* after *daf*, father and son. Uri saw now why Yirmiyahu's Rosh Yeshivah was so excited about him. Yirmiyahu had a tremendous head. There was not a line where he did not have a tough question, a *sugya* that he could not match up with another Gemara. Uri had been afraid that his son's spirit might be dampened without Zeideh's *hagahos*. But Yirmiyahu learned with a fire, with a joyous *bren*!

Where was his ardor, his joy coming from? And then Uri discovered the answer. His son was leading a secret life that he did not know.

Uri was a person who needed sleep. Without sleep, he was a robot. He could not learn, could not daven properly, could not think properly. Each morning he rose at four thirty to start learning with Yirmiyahu at five. And so, Uri disciplined himself to go to sleep right after *ma'ariv*. He read from a light *sefer* in bed, recited *Hamapil*, and was soon fast asleep.

One night, he had to break his routine. A member of their minyan was in the hospital, and the *chevrah* took turns sitting at his bedside.

Uri was supposed to stay until midnight, but his replacement did not arrive until one. Uri had no choice. He sat next to the bed, watched his friend toss and turn fitfully, reciting *Tehillim*, giving his friend a drink and tissues. Finally, his replacement showed up.

When Uri arrived home, it was already past two in the morning. He checked his watch and sighed. He would be a zombie tomorrow. The house was dark, except for a light on in his study. Probably one of the twins had done his homework at his desk and had forgotten to switch it off. He entered his study. There was Yirmiyahu, sitting at the desk. In front of him lay Zeideh's Gemara *Zevachim*, and next to that was Zeideh's notebook! Yirmiyahu was busy writing in the notebook and the paper sang happily.

Uri was aghast. "Yirmiyahu! It's two o'clock in the morning! What are you doing?" He struggled to contain his voice. "Yirmiyahu, enough is enough!"

His son answered him calmly. "Abba, if other boys my age can play video games all night, why can't I be up learning what I really want to learn?"

Uri was nonplussed. His son was so self-assured, as though it was the most normal thing in the world to be up two o'clock in the morning, learning! But what could he do? Yirmiyahu was already taller than he was, he was a man! Uri approached the desk and peered into the Gemara. Yirmiyahu's finger lay pressed on the middle of a giant *Tosafos* on *daf nun-aleph*. The gold pen was held at the ready, Zeideh's notebook was laid out at a slant, ready to be attacked. His son looked delighted.

What could he say? He nodded his head. "You really love *Kodshim*, don't you?"

Seeing that his father had calmed down, Yirmiyahu just smiled.

Uri shook his head. He was helpless. Yirmiyahu was out of his control. He did what he wanted to do, and that was it.

"Yirmiyahu," he pleaded, "please, we have to learn in a few hours. Please, go to sleep already!"

Yirmiyahu nodded, finally agreeing with his father. He had to admit that he was exhausted. He laid down the pen, closed the Gemara and notebook, and went to bed.

Uri smiled wearily to himself. "Who would imagine?" he murmured to himself. "I'm a Stretiner, and I produced a son who's a Brisker!"

⛵ ⛵ ⛵

But not everything was the *daf*. Uri and Chaya entered a beautiful time in their lives. They were multi-millionaires, for they had children who were fine and beautiful. Besides Yirmiyahu, there was Tova and Dina who had just turned nineteen, and the twins Dovid'l and Yisroel.

But when Dovid'l and Yisroel turned bar mitzvah, the frolicsome, irrepressible twins molted into young yeshivah boys. They were not as intense as Yirmiyahu – they were full of life and joy – but they were ripening into beautiful, serious learners.

One day, the Rosh Yeshivah said to Uri: "When you have an older brother like Yirmiyahu, then you grow up into a Dovid'l and Yisroelnik."

The twins dressed beautifully: always crisp white shirts and black hats that were neat and brushed clean. And they took to learning: learning with *chavrusas* in class, learning with each other at home, always into learning. They were in the *bikkurim* years, the first precious years of manhood, and they ripened into handsome young men, full of good qualities.

Tova and Dina were graduating Bais Yaakov and deciding on their future seminary. Already some girls in their class were becoming *kallahs*.

"We're not in a rush," Chaya told Uri. "When the time comes, we'll start looking."

Uri was content, the girls were content, everyone was content...but in *Shamayim*, they were not content. For, *shidduchim* happen when Hashem decides!

Unbeknownst to Uri and Chaya, trailing behind and all about them was the glow of good deeds and golden reputation. Yirmiyahu's genius was the talk of the famous Walden Pond Yeshivah, and Uri himself was looked up to as a tzaddik and true *ben Torah*.

Uri and Chaya were multi-millionaires, for although they had a modest house and measured income, they had children who were jewels, a name that was golden, and their merits piled up high in *Shamayim*.

And in Heaven it was decreed: this was the *eis dodim*, the time for Tova and Dina to find their *shidduch*. Both of them!

⚓ ⛵ ⚓

Uri came home one evening after *ma'ariv*, and Chaya was standing outside the door, waiting for him.

He grew concerned. "Chaya, what's the matter?"

"Uri," she whispered excitedly. "There's a *shadchan* on the line. He wants to talk to you about Tova! I told him you would be home now, and he called to the minute."

"Tova? Is she ready to go out yet?"

Chaya's eyes grew wide with wonder, and she smiled with amusement. "Do I know? Go, Uri, talk to him!"

Uri ran into his study, sat down at his desk, and lifted the phone.

"Hello?"

"Rabbi Schiffman?"

"Yes. *Shalom Aleichem*. Who is this?"

"Rabbi Messenger, from Walden Pond Yeshivah."

Uri caught his breath. Reb Moishe Messenger was a world famous Rosh Yeshivah. "*Shalom Aleichem, Mori v'Rebbi*. It is a *kavod* for me to speak to you —"

"Never mind *kavod*, I called about a *shidduch* for your daughter. I hear that you have two daughters, twins."

"Yes," he answered nervously. "Tova and Dina."

"I assume Tova is the older."

"By seventeen minutes."

"Good. Seventeen is good, *tov*. I have a *shidduch* for her."

"I don't know if she's ready to go out yet!"

"Listen, Reb Uri, first hear what I have to say. Go back to your daughter, speak to her, speak to the *bnei bayis*, and then you can decide! Will you hear me out, at least?"

"Of course, Rosh Yeshivah! What a great honor it is to talk to you...to have you call me!"

"Leave me alone with the honor, would you! Now listen, this is a boy, an excellent boy. He comes from a wonderful family, a *Torahdik* family. His father is a rebbi in a small yeshivah nearby, and the boy – he is one of thirteen –"

"One of thirteen?"

"A beautiful family. Now, he learned in Eretz Yisrael, and has been by us for a few months. He just came out of the toaster."

Uri was confused. "Toaster, Rosh Yeshivah? Doesn't the Rosh Yeshivah mean 'freezer'?"

"Such a boy was not in a freezer!" Rabbi Messenger exclaimed. "Such a boy was in a toaster! He learns with such a *bren*, such fire...he was in a toaster, not a freezer! He has beautiful *middos*, he wants to learn, and his father heard of you and your wonderful family. I am telling you – he is the best *bachur* in Walden Pond!"

Uri hesitated, unsure of what to say. "May I ask his name?"

"His name? His name? Hold on...his name is Zerach Yerushalmi. A wonderful boy!"

"From that Yerushalmi family?"

"Aha! You see, you heard of them?"

"Very *chashuv*, very *chashuv*!"

"Three uncles are Rosh Yeshivahs, his grandfather is a *dayan*. A Torah family for generations! Listen to me, Reb Uri, everything is *bashert*. Speak to your *rebbetzin*, speak to your daughter, and then get back to me. Is that a deal?"

"I am so honored –" Uri checked himself mid-sentence, but it was too late.

"Leave me alone with honors, please!" The Rosh Yeshivah objected once more. "Honor belongs to Hashem, not to flesh and blood!"

"Forgive me," Uri said. "But what can I say? I am overwhelmed that you even heard of us – much less took the time to call."

"Enough said! Do what you have to, and get back to me."
"*Yasher koach.*"
"*Bruchim tihiyu* –"
And the phone went dead.

Uri replaced the phone on its cradle, laid his head on the desk, and buried his head in his arms. He closed his eyes tight. He couldn't believe it! Had he really just spoken to the great *posek*, Reb Moishe Messenger about a *shidduch* for Tova, or was he just dreaming it? He lifted his head, opened his eyes, and looked at the slip of paper where he had written down the Rosh Yeshivah's phone number and the boy's name – Zerach Yerushalmi.

No, it was no dream. It was a gift from *Shamayim*!

That very night, the family held a meeting: Uri, Chaya, Tova...and Dina.

When Dina sat down next to her sister, Chaya was very direct. "Dinaleh, we love you very much, but this meeting concerns a *shidduch* for Tova. It is a very sensitive issue, perhaps we should discuss it alone."

Dina was astonished. She and Tova were twins. They looked alike, dressed alike, thought alike, talked alike – they were never separated. Dina looked at her sister, not knowing what to do.

"Imma, please let her stay," said Tova. "Dina is part of this also."

So they all huddled together and decided Tova's fate. Uri told her the details. The Yerushalmi family was very *meyuchas* – and extremely poor. The boy was one of thirteen! And he came recommended by Reb Moishe Messenger, *shlita*. What did she think? Was she ready?

Tova looked at Dina, Dina looked at Tova. They didn't even have to talk – they could read each other's mind. Tova and Dina turned to their parents, squinched up their faces, and lifted their thumbs: "Yes!"

The conference did not take more than fifteen minutes.

Everyone knew: this was not up to them, but everything – everything – was happening from *Shamayim*. That very night, Uri called back Rabbi Messenger. The *shidduch* was on, and a date was set.

But arranging the first date was not so easy. This was Uri and

Chaya's first child to go out on a *shidduch*, and they were unsure of how to make plans. The boy needed a place to stay and a car to drive. Also, Zerach was a serious *masmid*, and he wanted to wait for *bein hazemanim*. So, the first date was put off for two weeks, when *bein hazemanim* began. Yirmiyahu would be off also, and it might be nice for him to meet the prospective *chassan*. There was a charge in the Schiffman household, an adventurous thrill: *shidduch* time had begun! Dina seemed as excited as Tova, and there was a lot of laughter.

Uri watched his daughters' joy with delight and nervousness.

The date was set.

But life is full of tricks. The Schiffmans had done everything right. They had arranged a place for Zerach to stay, and borrowed a car from a friend so that he would not have to spend unnecessary money renting. The date was set for Monday evening. Tova bought a beautiful outfit — two outfits, in case there was a second date. The house sparkled, Yirmiyahu and the twins were tucked away safely in the back rooms. Everything was perfect. Except...Tova had disappeared!

Tova had gone cross-town to have her hair done, and the battery on their five-year-old car went dead. Even now, one of Chaya's friends was on the way to retrieve her with Dina, but she would be a half hour late.

At seven o'clock — to the second — the doorbell rang. Uri opened the door and there stood Zerach Yerushalmi. He gazed at Zerach, and Zerach gazed at him.

Perfect, thought Uri, *perfect! Baruch Hashem!*

Perfect, thought Zerach, *perfect! Baruch Hashem!*

It was Zerach's first date. It was Tova's first date. It was Uri and Chaya's first date, but somehow, nobody seemed nervous. Uri and Chaya welcomed Zerach into their dining room, and they sat around the family table.

"Zerach," Uri apologized, "I don't know how to tell you this, but I have to tell you the truth. My car battery went dead, and Tova is stuck across town. She'll be here in about twenty minutes or so."

Zerach didn't bat an eye. He looked at Uri, and smiled. "Not to worry, Rabbi Schiffman. My father's car has been stuck at the mechanic for two days."

He's so charming, thought Chaya. *What fine middos. Baruch Hashem!*

She laid a beautiful bowl of fruit and a plate of chocolate chip cookies in front of him. "Tova baked the cookies," she said.

Uri cleared his throat. "So, what *masechta* are you learning at the moment?" he asked companionably. Chaya watched proudly as Uri and Zerach exchanged *he'aros*. There was a pause in their conversation, and Uri cleared his throat again. Zerach looked at the cookies, and then at Uri. "Rabbi Schiffman, you say that Tova will be about twenty minutes?"

"Yes, I'm sorry."

He waved his hand tranquilly. "No problem. But —"

"Yes —"

"Maybe there's a room where I can just sit down and learn?"

Baruch Hashem, thought Uri and Chaya.

Uri rose excitedly. "Of course, Zerach. Come into my study. We'll leave you alone until Tova comes."

"You don't think I'm being rude, do you?" Zerach asked nervously.

Uri smiled. He wanted to hug this young man. "*Chas v'shalom!* Twenty minutes of learning is twenty minutes. Here, let me show you."

Zerach rose, and Uri led him down the hall to the study. The door was closed. Uri opened the door, urged him inside, and shut the door behind him for privacy.

"Don't worry," he called, "when Tova shows up, we'll call you!"

He returned to the dining room, where Chaya excitedly waited for him. "He's such a wonderful boy," she whispered. "Look at what fine *middos* he has! Look how he didn't want us to feel bad about Tova not being here."

"And how he doesn't waste a minute!"

They sat there, watching the clock. Tova had called. Her friend was delayed, but they were heading home now — she would be there in fifteen minutes. Uri took a *Chumash* from the cabinet, munched on a cookie, and prayed that the two children would like each other. Chaya opened her *Tehillim* and recited psalm after psalm.

And then, a loud shout suddenly came from the direction of the study. Uri and Chaya stared at each other in shock. They both jumped up. More yelling.

"Uri," she gasped, "it sounds like a fight!'

Uri laid down the *Chumash* and rushed down the hall. There was a terrible argument going on inside. It was Zerach's voice — Zerach and Yirmiyahu, arguing over a piece of Gemara! Uri banged his fist against his head. He didn't know that Yirmiyahu was in the study! The two must have met, and they were going at it like wildcats.

"That's not *pshat*!" screamed Yirmiyahu at the prospective *chassan*.

"That is *pshat*!" Zerach screamed back excitedly. "There is a *befeireshe* Chazon Ish that says just like I said."

"Show me!" Yirmiyahu demanded. "We have the *Chazon Ish* — show me!"

Uri stood outside the study, listening. Should he go in? Mediate? He ran back to Chaya.

"Chaya, Yirmiyahu was in there! I didn't know he was in the study. They're having a terrible argument!"

Chaya flapped her *Tehillim* up and down, not sure whether to put it down or open it up and recite another psalm.

"Maybe you should go in there just to soften things."

Just then, the doorbell rang, and Tova and Dina rushed in. Dina covered her face with her hands and ran to her bedroom.

"Where's Zerach?" asked Tova. She looked beautiful.

Chaya pointed towards the study and burst out laughing. "They're having a fight —"

"Who's having a fight?" asked Tova.

"Zerach and Yirmiyahu. Listen —"

But the yelling has ceased. Uri took a deep breath and approached the study. He opened the door. Yirmiyahu and Zerach were huddled over his desk, shoulder to shoulder, peering into a *Chazon Ish*. Zerach had taken off his hat and jacket, and the two young men looked like they were brothers.

"Zerach, Tova is home. She's just going to take a drink and catch her breath."

Zerach looked up. "Fine. I anyway want to finish this piece with Yirmiyahu. We'll be at it a couple of minutes longer."

Uri went back into the dining room. Chaya looked at him. "Uri — you're crying?"

It took almost five minutes for Zerach to extricate himself from Yirmiyahu. He met Tova, and they went out on their date... And went out...and went out. It was past one before their daughter finally came home.

"How did it go?" asked Chaya, breathlessly.

Tova shrugged coolly. "It was okay... We'll see."

But she spent the next two hours telling Dina everything that happened.

The next afternoon, Tova and Zerach went out again. She returned six hours later. Uri and Chaya were waiting anxiously at the dining-room table. "Tova, what do you think?" they asked.

She looked at her parents sheepishly. "First I want to hear what Zerach has to say."

"But tell us, was it good, was it bad? Is he interesting?"

"Yes, he's interesting. But...ask the *shadchan* what Zerach thinks."

Uri called Rabbi Messenger. "Rosh Yeshivah — have you heard from the boy?"

There was a pause. "Ah... Yes... He is willing to put off his flight back to Walden Pond, if your daughter would like to see him again."

A little bell went off in Uri's head. "Yes, I believe she is very interested."

"Excellent."

So, on Wednesday, Zerach and Tova went out for the third time. He picked her up at five and by twelve that night they were still not home. Chaya waited up at the dining-room table and recited *Shir HaShirim*, while Uri gave up and went to bed. He had to be up for learning at five.

"Uri —"

Uri woke up and glanced at the clock. It was one thirty. He sat up, still half asleep.

"What...what, Chaya? Is everything all right? Is Tova home?"

"She came home an hour ago. I had a long talk with her. Uri, I think our daughter is going to become a *kallah!*"

Uri washed his hands and turned on his table lamp. "Become a *kallah*? So fast? After only three dates?"

"She wants to go to Walden Pond next week to meet his parents."

Uri sat up in a state of shock. "So fast? The first boy she ever went out with? The first girl he ever went out with?"

Uri was shocked, Chaya was thrilled, Tova was overwhelmed, and Dina could not stop smiling.

But when Heaven decrees it, then a *shidduch* happens in a blink!

Tova went to Walden Pond and stayed at friends of the Yerushalmis. They were as taken with her as she was taken with them — and with all of Zerach's eight sisters, who thronged to meet her. She returned to Toronto under tight secrecy, and Uri waited for matters to unfold.

"Hello, Rabbi Schiffman?"

"Shalom *Mori v'Rebbi!*" Uri answered.

"*Un vee gait dus?*"

"*Baruch Hashem yom yom!*"

The Rosh Yeshivah cleared his throat. "I hear that your daughter and Zerach are very serious about each other."

"They have the same *hashkafos*," Uri answered. "They are both dedicated to a life of Torah."

"*Baruch Hashem —*"

"Yes...*baruch Hashem —*"

"Now, here is the situation. Zerach and the family are very interested in proceeding with an engagement. But there are certain practical matters to iron out."

"I understand," answered Uri.

"Zerach, you understand, wants to learn for a number of years."

"Of course,"

"But not here. He insists on learning in Eretz Yisrael. He says the very *kedushah* in the air helps him to *shteig —*"

"I understand."

"Now his family, *baruch Hashem*... Thirteen children, *bli ayin hara*."

"*Bli ayin hara* —"

"They can't help with a penny, you understand. Not a penny! They are just scraping by — and what with the wedding, the photographer and orchestra... — sure, there's *hachnasas kallah* to help them, but afterwards...the burden, unfortunately, will have to fall on the *kallah*'s side —"

That means me, Uri said to himself.

"Now...you must remember — he's a very serious boy. He doesn't waste a minute. You see that."

"Yes, *baruch Hashem*."

"He would like a commitment from you to support him in learning for...seven years."

"How many years?" gasped Uri.

"Seven years, like Yaakov Avinu. Seven years of pure learning in Eretz Yisrael!"

Uri caught his breath. "Seven years! Rosh Yeshivah, that's a long time! And how much support are we speaking about?"

"Things are not cheap in Yerushalayim, and we know that you have limited resources. The minimum would be thirteen hundred dollars a month — U.S. money."

Uri made a quick calculation. That was a huge amount in Canadian!

Uri hesitated and the Rosh Yeshivah understood.

"Listen, Rabbi Schiffman. I know that it sounds like a lot. But this boy is a gem, a real gem! Do you know that I have a list as long as my arm of girls whose fathers would be happy to support him! But, your family has a golden reputation and comes highly recommended. And, of course, he is quite taken with your Tova. But still, this is what the family is looking for. Now, what do you say?"

Uri cleared his throat. Thirteen hundred dollars U.S. times twelve months times seven years was a huge commitment! But there were not many Zerach Yerushalmis out there. And Tova and he obviously liked each other very much.

"Rosh Yeshivah, we are very interested in Zerach. We feel like he's part of our own family — already. And Tova felt so much at home with his family. But still, it's a big decision. It's a lot of money for us, and I should discuss it with my wife. Can I get back to you tomorrow?"

There was a prolonged silence on the other side. Then the Rosh Yeshivah coughed.

"Nu, nu..." he finally said. "Reb Uri, discuss it with your *bnei bayis*. But listen, don't wait too long to decide."

"Rosh Yeshivah, *bli neder* you'll hear from me tomorrow."

"Good!" he answered abruptly, and the phone went dead.

That night, soon after the children had gone to bed, Uri and Chaya held an urgent meeting.

"Thirteen hundred dollars U.S. means more than sixteen hundred dollars Canadian," Uri said. "And it's a commitment for seven years — seven years! How can we make such a promise?"

"But Uri, he's a wonderful boy," Chaya answered. "It's not like he wants the money to go out and buy a tennis racket. Zerach's whole life is learning — and so is Tova's. They need that money just to live. And, *im yirtzeh Hashem*, they'll have a family... Seven years. It's not so long."

"But where do I get such money?" Uri wondered. "We're doing fine now because my learning with Bookman and a few other *talmidim* covers us just okay. But now what?"

Chaya smiled at her husband. "We have to have *bitachon*. This *shidduch* is from *Shamayim* — you could see that even before he met Tova, from that first second when Zerach met Yirmiyahu. Look, let's make a list of exactly what we are short."

Uri laid down a sheet of paper. He listed their expenses and their income. There were Uri's lessons, Chaya's morning job of running the cheder breakfasts, child benefit checks from the government. Their expenses included tuition, mortgage, food, clothing, tzedakah.

"How much are we short?" asked Chaya.

"If we assume the responsibility of supporting Zerach and Tova, we need twelve hundred dollars more a month," he said.

"That's three hundred dollars a week —"

"Exactly. At least —"

"That's not so much!" argued Chaya. "They always need substitute teachers in the high school. And I could find private students! Can you find any more students?"

"I would have to work very hard to find them."

"Uri, Hashem will send. Don't worry!"

Uri gazed at his wife admiringly. "You have so much faith, Chaya."

"We have no choice, Uri. We can only live with *bitachon*. Otherwise, how does anyone survive?"

Uri took a deep breath. He smiled, relieved. His wife had said what was hidden in his heart but couldn't articulate.

"*Mazel tov*, Chaya," he murmured. "Should I call Rabbi Messenger now?"

They looked at the clock. It was past eleven.

"Call," she urged. "Don't let this drag on. Tova is so anxious."

With hope in his heart, Uri dialed Rabbi Messenger with the important news. But the Rosh Yeshivah did not answer. He was probably on the phone making other *shidduchim*. Uri left a brief message.

"Rosh Yeshivah, we have decided to accept the Yerushalmi family's proposal for seven years support at the amount you mentioned. It should be with *berachah* and *mazel*! Please get back to me as soon as possible!"

He went back to his wife, who had prepared a cup of tea for him. "Should we wake up Tova and tell her?" he asked.

"Wait," Chaya answered. "Let's hear back from the *shadchan* first, make sure that everything is confirmed."

They stayed up to one o'clock, hoping to hear back from Rabbi Messenger. But he did not call. Maybe he had a *chasunah*. Uri learned with Yirmiyahu in the morning, went to shul, and rushed back to the house.

"Did you hear from the Rosh Yeshivah yet?" he asked Chaya.

She shook her head. "Perhaps he didn't get the message?" she suggested. "Maybe you should call again?"

Uri hesitated. "I'm sure he got my message. He's a very busy man, remember. Let's wait."

And so, Uri taught his lessons, Chaya did her breakfast program and hit the phone to try to find more work. Still they heard nothing.

"Mommy, what's happening with Zerach?" Tova asked.

Chaya looked at her beautiful, gem-like daughter, and wanted to hold her in her arms like when she was a little girl. "Oh, everything is fine, Tova. Be patient, we're just waiting to her back from the Rosh Yeshivah."

She saw the disappointment and worry in her daughter's face, how much she yearned to be married to Zerach. Chaya promised herself: come what may, they would find the money.

How do you rob a bank? she wondered.

Uri came home for dinner after *minchah*. He did not have to ask. He looked at Chaya, and she shook her head.

Uri shrugged. He gave up worrying — whatever would be would be. But this not getting back did not look good. Who knew what went on in people's heads?

Yirmiyahu was in the *beis midrash*, Dovid'l and Yisroel were in class, and it was just Uri and Chaya and the two girls. They were just finishing their soup when the phone sounded with a long-distance ring. Tova, Dina, Chaya...they all popped up like a white-water raft that's hit a bump. Uri smiled. He lifted his hand and placed his finger over his mouth.

"Absolute quiet!" he whispered.

He ran into his study.

"Reb Uri?"

"*Shalom Aleichem, Mori v'Rebbi!*" he answered respectfully. The Rosh Yeshivah certainly sounded cheerful.

"I'm sorry I couldn't get back to you before. You have no idea how *farnumen* I am! *Shidduchim, she'eilos,* tzedakahs...there's no end!"

"Hashem should give you *koach!*" Uri answered. "Rosh Yeshivah, is everything all right?"

There was a pause on the other end. "All right? About what?"

Uri's voice grew shaky. "About the *shidduch* of Zerach Yerushalmi and my daughter Tova. Did you get my message that we agree to the proposal?"

There was a momentary pause. "That? That?" roared Reb Moshe.

"What are you talking about? That's old news! Of course the family agreed. The family is crazy about Tova, they're crazy about your whole family. That's old news, Reb Uri. *Mazel tov!* I didn't call you about that! Didn't I tell you this morning that it's all agreed?"

"No, Rosh Yeshivah!"

"Ach!" he shouted. "So why didn't you call me back? The *shidduch* is a done deal! It should be with *mazel* and *berachah*! The family will come to Toronto in a week to meet you."

Uri turned to the door, where Chaya, Tova, and Dina were huddled. He smiled broadly, and gave a deep, broad, thumbs-up, even as he held the phone. There was a burst of whispered glee.

Uri waved for them to get out of his study.

"Hello, are you there?" asked Rabbi Messenger.

"Yes."

"But I didn't call you up about that."

"No?"

"No! Tell me, Zerach tells me that his *kallah* has a twin sister —"

"Dina."

There was pause. "Let me write this down. Just Dina?"

"Dina, Dina —"

"Dina, Dina. Now, here's the story. Zerach has a first cousin, Avraham, who is also just out of the toaster. The best boy in Walden Pond —"

"I thought Zerach was the best boy in Walden Pond?"

"So, they're both the best boys in Walden Pond — what does it bother you? Anyway, his cousin is also his *chavrusa*. He very much wants to meet your daughter Dina. Can it be arranged?"

"You mean the son of the famous Rosh Yeshivah in Yerushalayim?"

"That's it!"

Uri caught his breath. He couldn't believe his *mazel*. "Rosh Yeshivah, can I impose on your precious time and ask you to wait a moment? My wife and daughter are right here — let me ask them. Do I have your *reshus*?"

"So, what are you waiting for?"

Uri put down the phone and raced into the kitchen.

"Chaya, Tova, *mazel tov*! The *shidduch* is all agreed! Chaya, Rabbi Messenger now has a *shidduch* for Dina, Zerach's first cousin, Avraham Yerushalmi. Dina, what do you say?"

Dina blushed red and she smiled. Her eyes grew wide with excitement. Yes, yes, she nodded excitedly.

"Zerach's cousin?" squealed Tova under her breath. "Oh, wow!"

"Chaya, quick, what do you say?"

"I can't believe this is all happening so fast!"

"Can I say yes?"

Chaya lifted her hands heavenwards and nodded. "Hashem, how can we thank you for your *chesed*?"

Uri did not bother to return to the study. He lifted the handset in the kitchen.

"Rosh Yeshivah, how can I thank you for what you are doing for our family? My daughter would be very pleased to go out with Avraham. I just can't believe how fast everything is happening!"

"Reb Uri, forgive me, but what does this have to with what you expect or don't expect? When Hashem makes the bell goes off in *Shamayim* that it's time for a *shidduch*, then that's it! It's not up to us! But tell me, do your daughters recite *Shir HaShirim*?"

"Yes, every Friday night for the last year, right after the candles are lit."

There was a moment's pause. And then the Rosh Yeshivah said almost in a whisper. "Aha! Now I understand everything."

Dina's first date was set for the next week. The new *zeman* had begun, but no one wanted to put things off. It was such an odd feeling, like a Heavenly hand had taken hold of the family. Things were moving so fast! But, who could know? Zerach was *bashert* for Tova, that was obvious. But now it was Dina's turn, and as seven o'clock drew closer, the family waited nervously.

"No more late arrivals," Chaya said.

Dina had her hair done that afternoon, rested, and said some *Tehillim*. Tova was as nervous for her twin sister as if she herself was meeting the boy for the first time. She stayed together with Dina in their room and tried to calm her.

Seven o'clock came, and to the minute, the bell rang. Uri took a deep breath, whispered a *tefillah*, and opened the door. He looked at the boy in shock. It was…Zerach!

"Ze…Zerach?" he asked, stunned.

The boy smiled and shook his head. "Not Zerach — that was last week. I'm Avraham Yerushalmi."

Still bewildered, Uri stood at the open door and didn't even invite him in.

"But you look…just like Zerach!"

The boy laughed. "I know, people think we're twins. What can I do? May…may I come in?"

Uri broke out of his daze and threw his hands to his head in embarrassment. "*Gevalt*, what's the matter with me? *Shalom aleichem*, Avraham. Please, welcome to our home. Forgive me!"

The smile did not leave Avraham's face. "Don't worry, Rabbi Schiffman. It happens to Zerach and me all the time — not to worry."

Uri led Avraham into the dining room and saw the shocked look on his wife's face. "Chaya, don't be nervous. I promise you, this is not Zerach — this is Avraham! But go, call Dina — and you'd better warn her."

And so Dina went out on her first date with Avraham. It was his first date, her first date. The next day they met again, and by the third day (Avraham had extended his visit) it was clear. Dina was also going to become a *kallah*! A week later she went to New York to meet her *chassan*'s uncle and aunt.

⛵ ⛵ ⛵

"Hello, Rabbi Schiffman?"

"Shalom aleichem, *Mori v'Rebbi*."

"Rabbi Schiffman — Reb Uri — I don't know what you've done right in your life, or your *rebbetzin* — but you hit the jackpot! The Yerushalmi family is crazy about Dina, and everything is set for a *vort* —"

The Rosh Yeshivah paused and cleared his throat. Uri knew what was coming. "You see that you are blessed! Avraham is just like Zerach — they're cousins, but they are more like twins. They are even *chavrusas*. The family wishes to make the same arrangements that you made with Zerach — seven years' support."

Uri took a deep breath. "What amount?"

"Everything the same. Thirteen hundred dollars U.S. a month. Reb Uri, I'm telling you, these days, it's a minimum for a couple living in Eretz Yisrael! If we can just settle this matter, then *baruch Hashem*, we'll have an unbelievable *simchah*. Imagine! You are being *meshadech* twice into the Yerushalmi family. What a *zechus*!"

There was a silence, a deep, profound silence. No one spoke, not Uri, not Rabbi Messenger. The silence lasted for almost half a minute.

"*Nu, nu*, Reb Uri," urged the Rosh Yeshivah. "What should I tell the other side?"

"Tell them...tell them...that we accept their proposal! May it be with *berachah* and *mazel*."

The Rosh Yeshivah was ecstatic. "*Mazel tov! Mazel tov!* What an unbelievable *simchah*! Two such wonderful *shidduchim* in one month! Unbelievable! You can see it's straight from *Shamayim*!"

Uri was afraid the Rosh Yeshivah would hang up. "Wait, Rosh Yeshivah, just one thing!"

"Yes?"

"Before you go, please...give me a *berachah*! I have no idea how I'm going to pay for all this!"

"You have no idea?" exclaimed the Rosh Yeshivah. "Who needs you to have an idea? Did you have an idea a month ago that both your daughters would become *kallahs*? Did you arrange it? Did you plan it? Jump, Reb Uri, jump! Jump like a child jumps with joy! You open up your siddur tomorrow morning and say to Hashem: You sent me two beautiful *shidduchim*, now send me the *parnasah* to pay for them! It'll come — you'll see!"

"Amen!"

"It'll come, Reb Uri! Such *shefa* and *berachah* that you will not believe it!"

"Amen! Amen!"

And the phone went dead.

Uri returned to his wife and daughters and told them the news. Dina was a *kallah*! Tova and Dina burst out with whoops of pure *simchah*. They called their friends, Uri and Chaya called family, the two family phone lines were busy non-stop.

Amidst the bedlam, Uri whispered to Chaya, "I know I didn't ask you, Chaya — but how could I say no? But I got a *berachah* from the Rosh Yeshivah."

Chaya did not answer. She gazed at her husband and whispered: "Uri, you're the *berachah*."

The Schiffman house was filled with blessing and joy and love and faith.

NINE

The next morning, Chaya received half a dozen phone calls from anxious mothers.

"Who was the *shadchan*?"

"How did you do it — two girls in one month! *Peh, peh, peh!*"

"Chaya, Hashem must really love you!"

Uri seized the next day with tremendous *bitachon*. His friends showered him with a thousand *mazel tovs*, and he shared the Rosh Yeshivah's cell number with a few fathers who were looking for *shidduchim*. Even though he had stayed up celebrating, he and Yirmiyahu learned that morning with a strength and determination that came from joy.

But even as he rejoiced, a little voice whispered into his ear:

"So, Reb Uri, where are you going to get an extra three thousand dollars a month — for seven years?"

"*Bitachon*," he whispered back quickly. "Have *bitachon*."

And that night, like a sign from Heaven, Uri received an incredible phone call about Yirmiyahu. It was Rabbi Mordechai Levi, Yirmiyahu's high school Rosh Yeshivah.

"Reb Uri, you have a moment?"

"For you, Reb Mordechai? I have all the moments in the world."

Reb Mordechai chuckled. "*Yasher koach*, but I'll make this short and...very sweet."

Uri listened intently.

"I don't have to tell you, your Yirmiyahu is *oisergevainlich*, an outstanding student —"

"*Baruch Hashem* —"

"Here's the story: Our board has approved plans to start a post-high-school *beis midrash*, right here in the yeshivah. We are sending out scouts to all the best yeshivahs, and we hope to gather at least thirty of the best *bachurim* —"

Uri whistled in amazement. "Thirty *bachurim* — that's a wonderful start!"

"Not only thirty, but the best thirty. Excellent boys, *metzuyanim!*"

"I hope the Rosh Yeshivah is *matzliach*."

"Amen! But listen — here's the best part. Your son has an excellent reputation even out of town. His presence will draw boys to our yeshivah. So the board has authorized me to make you the following offer. We want Yirmiyahu to come to our *beis midrash* absolutely tuition free! The board will cover everything. He can sleep in our dorm so he has that out-of-town feeling. Food will be free, he will have a generous allowance for *sefarim*, and the board will grant him a thousand dollar scholarship for personal needs, clothing, a chance to visit *gedolim* — whatever!"

Uri whistled with amazement. "That — that is so generous! Please tell the board thank you! I'll tell you, Reb Mordechai, we just made two fine *shidduchim*, but it's going to cost me a fortune. This offer will help me greatly."

Reb Mordechai smiled over the phone. "Yes, we heard about the *shidduchim*. You've done unbelievably, Reb Uri! So now — what shall I tell the board?"

Uri hesitated. "Listen, Rabbi Levi, if it were up to me, I would accept your offer in an instant. From my part, it's wonderful, a tremendous help. But Yirmiyahu has been *farheir*ed by three yeshivahs and they all want him. You know he has his own strong will. I have to speak with him."

Reb Mordechai coughed meaningfully. "I know, Reb Uri, do I ever know! But please, do your best! It would help our new *beis midrash* immensely!"

Uri hung up the phone, and his spirits soared. What an honor for his son! And if Yirmiyahu agreed, it would save seven, eight thousand dollars a year, just when he needed it!

The next morning, Uri and Yirmiyahu sat down to learn at five.

It was mid-June, and already, bright daylight poured through the study window. They had long finished *Chullin* and almost all of *Kodshim*. They fought through the small, difficult tractate of *Kinim*, and now were rushing through *Tamid* and *Middos*. Uri watched his usually restrained son shake nervously with enthusiasm as they studied the *avodah* of the Holy Temple. Uri was also in high spirits — they were less than three months to finishing the whole Talmud — the Great *Siyum*!

Their *seder* was usually from five to six. Uri watched the clock, and at ten minutes before six, he abruptly closed his Gemara. Yirmiyahu looked up in surprise.

"Yirmiyahu," Uri said, "close your Gemara for a moment. We have to talk."

Yirmiyahu tried to protest, saw that Uri was firm, and finally shut his Gemara.

"What is it, Abba?"

"You know, your yeshivah ends in another three weeks or so. I'm very proud of how well you did in Rabbi Levi's yeshivah —"

Yirmiyahu did not answer, he just watched his father carefully. "You were *farheir*ed in three yeshivahs, and they all want you very much — you should be proud of yourself."

Uri watched his son's eyes narrow warily. *He's no dummy*, thought Uri.

"Now, here's the thing. I don't know whether you've made up your mind which *beis midrash* you want to go to —"

"I have, Abba."

"Wait, Yirmiyahu, just listen! I received a call last night from Rabbi Levi. They are starting a new *beis midrash* right here in Toronto, just ten minutes away. They'll have the best boys from all over America —"

"Abba, please —"

"Listen!" Uri continued, talking ever faster. "They're willing to pay all your expenses! No tuition, free dormitory — you won't have to come home even for Shabbos! It'll be just like out of town! They'll even give you money for *sefarim*, pay for visits to meet *gedolim* —"

"Abba —"

Uri was almost pleading. "It'll make it so much easier for us, Yirmiyahu! You know, we're going to have to support Tova and Dina in Eretz Yisrael! I don't know how we'll do it! This will take a financial burden off us, save us so much money —"

Uri was talking faster and faster, trying to block whatever argument his son would make. But finally, he ran out of words — and breath.

"Abba," Yirmiyahu answered, "I have already made up my mind where I want to learn."

Uri looked at his son with great intensity. "You have? Where, Walden Pond?"

"No, Abba."

"Then where?"

"Abba, I'm going to learn in Eretz Yisrael!"

"What? Where in Eretz Yisrael?"

"Abba, I want to learn in a yeshivah where they study *Zevachim* and *Menachos*."

"You mean, in Reb Chaim's yeshivah?"

"Yes, Abba! I made up my mind."

Uri was flabbergasted. "But...that's...that's *Kodshim*! *Korbanos*! What about *Kesubos*, what about *Gittin*, what about *Shabbos* and *Sukkah* and all of *Nezikin*?"

"Abba, some day, *im yirtzeh Hashem*, I'll learn it all. But I want to learn in Eretz Yisrael, in a *Kodshim* yeshivah."

"But you're too young, Yirmiyahu! First learn in America for a year or two, then go to Eretz Yisrael!"

But Yirmiyahu was firm. "Abba, I'm sorry. I made up my mind. I am going to learn in Eretz Yisrael. Tova and Dina will be there, Zerach and Avraham — I won't be alone."

Yirmiyahu's decision was a shock to Uri. What eighteen-year-old boy goes off to Eretz Yisrael to learn *Zevachim*? He looked up and caught sight of Zeideh's notebooks. *Zeideh did this!* he thought.

Uri lost his composure. "And, and who is supposed to pay for this, Yirmiyahu?" he asked, almost in tears. "I don't know how I'm going to pay for Tova and Dina, and now you place another burden of ten thousand dollars for air-fare and tuition? Yirmiyahu, how am I going to afford this?" Uri was almost crying.

Yirmiyahu saw that his father was upset and tried to calm him. He spoke deliberately, in a voice that was mature beyond his years.

"Abba, listen! I know you have tremendous obligations now. If you can't afford it, I'll find the money myself, another way."

"How?"

"The boys in my yeshivah — some of them are very wealthy. I know their fathers and they like me. I will go and ask them for help, for a scholarship..."

Uri reeled with horror. "What? A son of mine go begging for money? Absolutely not!"

"I'm not begging for money, Abba, I'm begging to learn Torah! They, they can lend me the money, I'll pay it back."

Uri snorted derisively. "Pay back? How will you ever pay back such an amount? Listen, my brilliant son! Consider the generous offer your own yeshivah has made — you've earned it!"

Uri paused, and pointed a sharp finger at his son. "But one thing I am telling you, whatever you do. Do not ask anyone for money! Your mother and I have struggled all our lives never to ask from others! I forbid it, you understand clearly? Listen, if you insist on learning in Eretz Yisrael, Mommy and I will find the money somehow! But do not go to strangers. Do you understand? I forbid you that as your father!"

Yirmiyahu nodded solemnly and left the room. Uri sat in his chair and gazed at Zeideh's notebooks.

This was all part of Zeideh's game. Zeideh realized that Yirmiyahu would eventually discover his writings and be captured by *Zevachim*, by everything to do with the Beis HaMikdash. It was Zeideh who was sending Yirmiyahu to Eretz Yisrael! Uri rose, approached the bookcase, and laid his hand on the beautiful, leather-bound spine of Zeideh's notebook.

He knew: Zeideh was still here, directing everything!

⚓ ⚓ ⚓

Things were happening faster and faster, almost spinning out of control. Everything was wonderful. It was almost too wonderful. Matters were set in motion, and they had no control. Uri felt like he was back clinging to the treacherous steps of the *Swift Current* in the midst of a monstrous storm. A huge wave had risen, huge as the Titanic, to sweep him overboard — and there was no way to halt it!

The wave was money — big money — that he needed for two weddings, to support two beautiful families in learning, and send his son to a wonderful yeshivah in Yerushalayim. Everyone smiled, everyone wished him *mazel tov*, he had tons of *bitachon* — but meanwhile, how was he supposed to pay for everything?

Once, he had been Captain Elijah Schiffman's grandson, and wanted for little. But now, all he held was a portfolio of pitiable Gortel shares and the roof over their heads. What was next?

Uri and Chaya sat down and set a plan of action. They advertised for students in the local community bulletins. Uri found two new pupils and Chaya was offered a job to teach a high school *Navi* class. It helped, but they were still short of more than two thousand dollars a month. And the days were passing swiftly. They planned two separate *vorts* for the twins, as their *rav* had advised them. The two weddings — just two weeks apart — were a scant three months off. There would be *sheva berachos*, the two couples would be off to Eretz Yisrael, and then the calls would come in: "Abba, it's the first of the month — could you please send money?"

Then...what would he do? Beg? Go around to rich men and ask for a handout? Not Uri Schiffman. Not Elijah Schiffman's grandson!

So I ask you, Uri, where's the money going to come from?
Bitachon!
Okay, I have bitachon also – but Tova and Dina are counting on you – what will you do?
Bitachon!
Yes, but show me the money!

Uri spent many sleepless nights. Tova's *vort* was just two days away. The house was in a frenzy, everyone was joyful, the *mazel tovs* were endless. And then, in a flash of inspiration, Uri thought of a plan that was so bold and so simple that it might work!

You see, bitachon works!

But it affected their whole household, and he could not attempt it without consulting Chaya. The night before the *vort*, after the girls had finished decorating the walls and hanging banners, after some friends had brought the first cream-dipped fruit salads and cakes, Uri laid out his plan before Chaya.

"Are you sure you want to do that?" she asked.

"Why not?" he asked. "It's good for everyone – and we need the money!"

⚓ ⛵ ⚓

It was the night of the *vort*.

The Schiffman's modest home sparkled like a mansion. Uri and Chaya were blessed with wonderful friends, a dozen sincere yeshivah families who lived modest, earnest, joyous Torah lives like them. One brought a cake, another brought a horseradish mayonnaise dip, others brought salads, cherry cakes, and more dips and more cakes and more salads and more dips. At first there was a scattering of people, but then guests streamed in one after the other, in droves. They came, and no one wanted to leave. The men crowded into the dining room, while the women packed the kitchen, the hallways, the back deck, and even the side yard – wherever there was room. Uri stood alongside the *chassan*, beaming, while Reb Yitzchak Yerushalmi — of the Yerushalmi dynasty — stood proudly on his son's other side. Each father heard wonderful compliments about his new *mechutanim*. Zerach looked like a prince: tall, handsome, gracious, modest.

"*Baruch Hashem*," whispered Uri to himself over and over. "*Baruch Hashem*! Hashem will help!"

Meanwhile, he kept his eye out for the one guest he was looking for. *Show up, Alexander,* he prayed. *Please, show up!*

Just past ten, Uri's oldest brother, Alexander, slipped unobtrusively into the room. Uri looked around. Everyone was having a great time. Zerach's *chaveirim* had arrived, and he was busy with them. Rabbi Yerushalmi was discussing a halachic issue with Yirmiyahu's Rosh Yeshivah.

Forgive me folks, Uri whispered to himself, *but business is business*!

He shook hands through the crowd, accepted *l'chaim*s, exchanged *berachos* and *mazel tov*s, and finally caught up with his brother.

"*Shalom aleichem*, Alexander," he said. "I am so glad that you were able to make it."

He hadn't seen his brother in a few months, and he seemed to have lost a few pounds. His brother grasped his hand with unaccustomed warmth — warmth he had never shown before.

"Shalom, Uri. *Mazel tov!*" He swept his arm towards the crowd. "This is beautiful, beautiful! I wish you lots of luck!"

"Is Ruby here?"

"Yes, I left her at the side door. Your daughter took charge of her. I hope she finds Chaya."

Uri led his oldest brother to Zerach.

"Zerach, this is my brother Alexander —"

Zerach broke free of his *chevrah* and extended his hand. "I'm so glad to meet you. *Mazel tov!*"

Alexander looked around the noisy, packed room. "Uri, I haven't been in this house for years. Everything looks so beautiful —"

Ten years, thought Uri.

"*Baruch Hashem*," he answered. "It's not big, but we manage. Er...Alexander, I wanted to talk to you privately for a moment —"

Alexander laughed nervously. "It's going to be hard to find privacy in this place," he said.

"Follow me —"

He took his brother's hand and led him through the crowd. One hand held his brother and with the other, Uri shook hands and exchanged toasts. He felt his inside jacket pocket to make sure the paper was still there.

Finally, they broke free of the living room, walked up a few stairs and past some of Tova's friends who had gathered in the hallway. He pushed open a door and led Alexander into the one quiet room in the house — his bedroom. He closed the door behind them.

"Whew!" said Uri. "It's hot out there. Alexander, sit down, please."

Alexander sat down self-consciously on Uri's bed. Uri sat down across from him. The brothers had never been close, especially since the reading of Zeideh's will. Alexander and Solomon had entered a different social sphere, like a plane flying at higher, rarefied altitudes. But this...this sitting together on one bed, like brothers, brought back a flood of memories.

Alexander smiled. "Remember, Uri, when we were kids, and we shared a big bed together?"

Uri forgot about the crowd outside and was caught up in memories. "Yes, Zeideh did not want us to have our own rooms, so that we would grow up close, like brothers."

"Poor Uri! Zeideh didn't know how much we teased you... *Eerie eerie shir dabeiri.*"

"I remember."

"I'm sorry, Uri, if we tortured you! To Solomon and me it was just a stupid joke. But...it must have been torture for you."

Uri looked at his brother. Alexander had never spoken so warmly to him in his life. "It doesn't matter. That was then — we were kids."

"But look at this out there, Uri! Look at that crowd! Look at those people! I don't know them, but I can see they are wonderful! You have beautiful children, and now you are getting a beautiful son-in-law —"

"Two of them."

Alexander shook his head in envy. "Two of them. G-d bless you, Uri!"

"*Baruch Hashem*," Uri murmured.

He reached into his jacket pocket and extracted a sheet of paper. "Alexander, I asked you in to talk some business."

Alexander's face abruptly stiffened. "Business? Oh, what is that?"

"You see all that out there? Do you know why it is so beautiful? Because it's all based on living a Torah life! I don't mean just study. I mean living a life dedicated to Torah, to learning, to raising children to learning. It means every moment spent in Torah achieves blessing in this world and an unbelievable portion in the Next World!"

"You make me jealous," Alexander said.

"*Chas v'shalom*," Uri answered quickly. "I don't mean to make you jealous, G-d forbid. I want to make you a partner in all this!"

"I'm not the learning type, Uri, you know that."

"No, but listen." He unfolded the sheet and held it against his chest. "There is such a tradition among Jews, a contract —"

"Contract?"

"Yes. It's called *Shimon achi Azariah,* Shimon the brother of Azariah."

Alexander looked perplexed. "Never heard of it."

"It's a *mishnah* in *Zevachim*. Shimon wanted to study Torah, but he couldn't afford to. He had a brother, Azariah, who was a businessman. They made a deal between them: Shimon would learn and Azariah would support him. Shimon agreed that Azariah would get part of his reward for learning Torah, in return for Azariah's support.

"I'll tell you the truth, Alexander. We haven't been that close, but you are my oldest brother, and I love you and respect you! I've taken upon myself tremendous obligations with these marriages, and I can't afford them! G-d has blessed you financially, and this is a chance for us to share my *berachah* and your *berachah* — and you will have an important share in all this *simchah*. It'll be blessing for both of us. Here, just look at the letter of understanding I made up —"

Uri tried to hand the paper to Alexander, but Alexander waved it away.

"Don't bother," he said. "Uri, don't waste your time."

Uri stared at his brother in disbelief. He hadn't known whether or not Alexander would accept his offer, but he didn't expect an immediate brush-off!

"Alexander," he said hotly, "I'm surprised at you! I didn't expect you to just say no just like that —"

Alexander took a deep, deep sigh. And then he burst out with such a cry of pain that Uri grew frightened.

"*Oy*, Uri! You don't know what happened, do you?"

Alexander dropped his head into his hands, and covered his eyes.

Uri dropped the paper down on the bed and moved next to his brother. "No, Alexander. Tell me, what happened?"

Just then there was a sharp knock at the door. Uri stood up, raced to the door, and opened it. Dovid'l was standing there.

"Abba, everyone is looking for you! They want to take pictures. Where have you been?"

Uri was impatient. "Tell whoever it is that I'm sorry."

"But Mommy say you have to come out to the guests."

"Tell Mommy, I can't come out for a few minutes — something urgent has come up. I'll be out in a few minutes. Listen, go take my place! You be the honorary *shver*."

He slammed the door closed, and locked it securely. He sat down next to his grieving brother.

"Alexander, what happened?"

Alexander lifted his head. "Poor, Uri! You thought you had a rich brother! It's all gone, Uri — the house, the money we had invested in it —"

"What happened?" asked Uri, shocked.

"I don't know! We inherited the house. We started spending: furniture, vacations. Those condominiums I invested in — they just went south! They lost all their value — like your Gortel stocks! We made other bad investments, too! We fell behind, we took out a second mortgage, we fell behind in that mortgage. We took a third mortgage at high interest rates, the debts piled up, and I was near bankruptcy!"

"You, Alexander? The house was a palace!"

"I know. We called it Alexander's Palace – and Queen Ruby! But it's gone now! We had to sell it, just to pay off all our debts –"

"Zeideh's house, sold? I can't believe it! We grew up in that house. Who bought it?"

Alexander took a deep breath. "I sold it to Solomon."

"Our Solomon? Our brother?"

"Yes, he's doing well with *Swift Current* and his gold investments. I sold it to him straight, without an agent so we got a few more dollars – just to pay off our debts!"

"I didn't know!" said Uri in amazement. "So where are you living now?"

"We're renting a house on Laurelcrest."

Uri whistled with amazement. "You are renting?"

Alexander's face grew wide-eyed with horror.

"Shh!" he pleaded. "Don't say it so loud!"

"You're renting?" repeated Uri in a whisper. "After owning Zeideh's palace?"

Alexander dropped his head in shame and nodded. Uri did not know what to say.

Goodbye Shimon achi Azariah! Goodbye Yissachar and Zevulun! He placed his hands lovingly on his oldest brother's shoulders and consoled him.

"Alexander, have *bitachon*! I hope that everything you lost comes back to you."

Alexander placed his hand on his brother's and cried like a baby.

"Renting," he sobbed. "Imagine, Alexander and Ruby Schiffman renting!"

Uri left Alexander in his bedroom, still crying. So much for *Shimon achi azariah*, unless...

Where was Solomon?

Uri had called him a half dozen times, left messages at home and on his cell phone – no Solomon!

Now he understood. Solomon had acquired Alexander's massive estate, all the land, and who knew what other investments. Solomon was a world-wise entrepreneur. He was brilliant: Solomon the Wise who never stopped doing deals. Now he had Zeideh's beautiful home in his pocket. What next? Who knew where he was, what corner of the world?

Tova's *vort* was a smashing success, attended by all the *rabbanim* and all the *roshei yeshivah* in the city, plus many *chashuve* guests from out of town. Dina deserved no less. It had to be equally beautiful – and yet have her very own stamp. Besides, the *mechutan* was Reb Dov Yerushalmi, the famous Rosh Yeshivah from Yerushalayim.

Where was Solomon? And then, a miracle occurred. After trying unsuccessfully a dozen times, Uri decided to just give it another try one day before the *vort*. He called, and there was Solomon on his cell phone.

"Solomon, where are you?" Uri yelled.

And Solomon answered with the most unexpected warmth: "Kid brother, you wouldn't believe the places I've seen!"

"Is this Solomon?" Uri asked, surprised at his warmth. It was the first time Solomon had ever called him "kid brother." After being reassured that it was indeed Solomon, he invited his brother and Zahava to attend the *vort*. Again, much to Uri's surprised delight, he did not hesitate a minute.

So, Alexander had told the truth! The family did respect what Chaya and he had achieved.

He recited over and over to himself: *Shimon achi Azariah... Shimon achi Azariah... Shimon achi Azariah...* Let's go for it!

The night of the *vort* arrived, and the Schiffman house again sparkled magnificently. More *mazel tov* balloons, carrot dips, six types of banana cream cake, radish dips, squash pies, creamed avocados, a huge bouquet of flowers from the *mechutanim*, and the same crowd of *rabbanim* and *roshei yeshivah*, and, of course, the good friends Uri and Chaya had acquired over the years like fine wine. Avraham stood handsome and princely between Uri and his distinguished father, and Uri murmured "*Baruch Hashem*" over and over to himself.

But where was Solomon? Uri felt the sheet of paper that lay folded in his jacket pocket and hoped for the chance to convince his brother.

Just before ten o'clock, Solomon strode into the living room. Even in the thronged room, full of distinguished people busy conversing with each other, his appearance drew stares. Uri had not seen his brother in more than a year, and he hardly recognized him. Solomon had turned...brown! Although it was midsummer and everyone had a nice deep color, Solomon looked like he had fallen asleep on a tanning bed!

Uri excused himself, and rushed through the crowd to his brother.

"Solomon, *shalom aleichem*!" he greeted him warmly. He took his brother by the hand, and led him through the crowd of well wishers to meet the *chassan*.

"Avraham, I would like you to meet my older brother, Solomon."

Avraham, who was talking to a Rosh Yeshivah, turned and gaped at Solomon's deep tan.

"*Shalom aleichem*," Avraham greeted him. "Where did you get that tan?"

"New Guinea," answered Solomon in an embarrassed voice. "I spent almost a month there."

"New Guinea? Wow!" exclaimed Avraham, very impressed. "*Mazel tov*."

Uri introduced Solomon to the *mechutan*, and then whispered into Avraham's ear.

"I have to have a meeting with my brother. It'll only take a few minutes, but it's very important. Please tell your father to excuse me — just a few minutes!"

Avraham nodded with great poise, even as he greeted another well-wisher. Uri took Solomon by the hand and led him out of the crowded room. But he was better prepared now. The bedroom had been an awkward place to talk to Alexander. This time, Uri had posted a sign on his study door: Please do not enter.

This meeting was with Solomon — Solomon, who held so much power, who could make or break everything. He opened the door of his study apprehensively. Good, the room was empty. He led Solomon inside, locked the door, and sat him down in his desk chair.

"Solomon," he said, "I need to talk to you."

But Solomon was gazing around the study, looking at all the *sefarim*.

"Uri, I am really proud of you! Look at all these books! Have you studied them all?"

"I'm working on them," said Uri, "very slowly."

"You know Uri, when Zahava and I came to the side door, she was really nervous. She doesn't really know anyone here! But then your daughter — Tova — she came out and brought her right in! How did you get children to be like that?"

"The Almighty has been kind to me."

Solomon looked at Uri, and there was a great sadness on his face. Uri wondered why. *He is so rich, yet he is so unhappy*, thought Uri.

"You look fit yourself," said Uri. "Not like me." He pointed at his expanding waistline.

The two brothers gazed at each other silently.

"*Eerie eerie shir dabeiri* — why have we been so far apart?" Solomon asked.

He has become so warm, Uri thought. *He's finally acting like a brother — just like Alexander!*

Uri carefully extracted the sheet of paper from his pocket and unfolded it. He took a deep breath. This was it.

"Solomon, I need a favor from you — I want to make a special business deal with you."

Solomon leaned forward and frowned. "What business deal?"

Uri held the sheet in front of him. Quickly, he explained the obligations he had assumed towards the new couples, and his lack of money. Uri swept his arm towards the packed bookshelves, towards Zeideh's almost completed *Shas*.

"This mitzvah of Torah study that I have, and that the children will have in Israel — you can be a partner in all of it with this *Shimon achi Azariah* contract." He dangled the sheet in front of Solomon's face.

Solomon stared at the sheet, looked up at Uri's hopeful face, turned suddenly to the desk, and banged it so hard with his fist that Uri thought it would break.

"Phooey!" Solomon started shouting. "Phooey! Phooey! Phooey!"

He banged the desk again like a madman, and threw his head down so violently that Uri was afraid that he would harm himself. Solomon sat there, his arms stretched across the desk, his head hidden, mumbling "Phooey! Phooey! Phooey!" over and over, like a madman.

Just at that moment, someone rapped on the door.

"Abba! The photographer is waiting!" It was Dovid'l.

"Dovid'l, get away from here!" Uri ordered.

"Leave me alone about the photographer — I have an emergency here."

"Abba, is everything okay?"

"Just go, Dovid'l..."

Uri fell into the chair next to Solomon and wrapped his arm around his brother's shoulder.

"Solomon, what's the matter?"

Solomon looked up. "You don't know! No one knows — not even Alexander!"

"Knows — what?"

Solomon caught his breath, sniffled, and sat up. "It's all gone, Uri! *Swift Current*, Zeideh's mansion, all the investments, the land, the deckhouse restaurant. I lost it all —"

"What? How? When?"

Solomon gasped for air.

"It happened just a week ago, but it'll hit the papers any day, you'll see! You remember — I told you to put everything in gold? Gold is gold. There was this big property in New Guinea owned by a gold company — Greex. They claimed it was the richest gold vein in the world! Gold was literally bubbling up out of the ground! I sent my man to assay the gold there. He came back, and he said it was the richest mine he had ever seen. He said that the ground literally shone with the stuff. I went there myself for a month, under the blazing sun. You could see the gold glittering right in front of you! I took a loan against all my assets: the boat, the house, everything! I would be the richest man in the world, Uri, the richest man in the world!

"And you know what?"

"What?"

"Do you know what that glittering gold was?"

Solomon reached into his vest pocket and took out a gold toothpick just like the toothpick he had once given Uri.

"Those crooks! I gave the owner of the company — Greex — I gave him two boxes of my gold toothpicks as a gift. That gave him an idea. You know what he did? He took my toothpicks and melted them down into gold nuggets. His people salted the ground with my own gold! They used my own toothpicks! Then they made up all sorts of false projections, fake surveys. They had dozens of people on their payroll, even government inspectors. They fooled everyone — my own experts, my own assayers. The mine was worthless, the lowest grade ore in the world! But it wasn't just me! I convinced a hundred investors to come in on the deal, to put in all their money! Oh...phooey!"

Again, Solomon lost control of himself, threw himself down on the desk, and began sobbing.

"Solomon, Solomon," Uri calmed him. "Solomon, it's just money! You lost money! You are still alive, you are still healthy!"

Solomon lifted his head.

"Uri, I didn't lose my money. I lost all my money. I lost investors' money. They wanted to lynch me, have me charged! I had to do something: sell my assets, pay back my creditors, get back my name. Zahava wouldn't even look at me anymore. She said I was a fool. 'Solomon, where's all your wisdom?' she snickered. 'You're so smart, so where's all the money?' "

"I'm sorry," Uri said. "Solomon, I'm really sorry."

Uri looked at the clock. There were people outside and he was being rude. He had to go back to the *vort*.

"Tell me, so what happened to the house and *Swift Current*?"

"I had it to sell them all – in one package – to pay back my creditors, to get my investors off my back. Everything was under the *Swift Current* company name, Zeideh's company."

"And who did you sell it to?"

Solomon did not answer at first. He sat there, glumly staring into the air, his chin tucked morosely into his hands.

"Solomon, who did you sell *Swift Current* to?" Uri asked again.

Solomon lifted his head and took a deep breath. He turned to Uri.

"I sold it to the only people I could. I sold it to...*Deep Blue*."

Uri stared at his brother in shock. "What? You sold *Swift Current* to Zeideh's biggest rival? You sold it to the people who humiliated Zeideh? Solomon, how could you do such a thing?"

Solomon rose up angrily. "Oh, the wise Rabbi Uri Schiffman! Who else could I sell it to? How many companies want to buy a thirty-year-old cruise ship that looks like a floating circus? Did I have a choice? I did what I had to do!"

Uri was furious. "But it means that *Deep Blue* owns everything that was precious to Zeideh – the boat, the house, everything he worked for for so many years! Zeideh must be spinning in his grave!"

"What could I do?" Solomon said glumly. "And they bought me, too. I had to agree to stay on and run *Swift Current*, as a hired employee!"

Uri stared at his brother with pity and shook his head. He glanced at the clock – it was so late! He had to go back to his guests, to Avraham and Rabbi Yerushalmi, but he was numb from shock.

He still needed to know just one thing.

"Tell me, Solomon, who owns *Deep Blue*? Who is behind it?"

Solomon shook his head. "No one knows – not even the lawyers who handled the sale! It's like a spider's web, a mystery company hidden behind another mystery company that's impossible to trace. Maybe it's Europeans. Maybe Japanese. Who knows, but boy, are they ever clever – and rich!"

Uri looked at his brother. Solomon looked so totally defeated. What a bizarre evening. Outside was joy and laughter, *simchah* and *mazel tovs*, and here was absolute gloom and failure. Uri saw his *Shimon achi Azariah* contract lying on the *shtender* and laughed bitterly to himself.

Nice try, Uri.

He lay his arm on his brother's shoulder and comforted him. "Solomon, I hope the Almighty replaces your lost fortune — yours and Alexander's. I'm sorry, I have to return to my *simchah*. Stay here until you're ready to come out."

Solomon nodded like a child, and Uri returned to his guests.

Bitachon, bitachon, Uri whispered to himself. *Don't lose heart — you see that it's all in G-d's hands!*

PART FOUR

THE SIYUM

TEN

Uri was on a wild ride.

It was such a blessed time. A brilliant son who wanted to learn Torah in Yerushalayim, two wonderful *shidduchim* that were the envy of the whole city. Uri was like a soaring aircraft cruising at the highest altitudes...but he was out of fuel in midflight! The *vorts* were over, the invitations were being printed, the *chassanim* were negotiating for apartments in Sanhedriah... But where was the money supposed to come from?

Meanwhile, Uri's joyous ferment grew daily. He and Yirmiyahu had already learned half of the final *masechta*, and the *siyum* was just a month away, and drawing closer every day. Everything was transpiring so fast!

Meanwhile, the Almighty had given him a new, terrible challenge, right in the midst of his joy: Alexander and Solomon. In their childhood, they had tortured him: "*Eeerie eerie shir dabeiri...*" They mocked him because he was different; he was the dreamy, lonely one. And then, Zeideh's will was read. They received fortunes, and he was left with barely anything — and they would not help him.

Now it had all changed. Alexander and Solomon had been reduced to bankruptcy and debt; they had lost all their possessions. Uri had the beautiful children, and the Torah learning. And it was so pleasant, so sweet, so easy...to gloat, to relish their downfall, their humiliation.

But the Torah says it is forbidden!

It was a terrible challenge, tougher than keeping Shabbos, tougher than kosher, tougher than learning. To beat back jealousy, to crush gloating and pride, to feel your brother's pain, his loss, to feel it like your own.

Only love could overcome these natural feelings, only love, absolute love for those who hurt him. He recited special *Tehillim* every day just in the name of Alexander and Ruby, Solomon and Zahava, that G-d restore their fortune.

Meanwhile, the invitations were sent out, the girls were getting ready for their weddings, Yirmiyahu was accepted in Reb Chaim's yeshivah, and a little voice hissed into Uri's ear: *Show us the money!*

Every night, after the children had gone to bed, Uri and Chaya sat and discussed money. Chaya was trying hard to get a third job, while Uri pursued new students — without luck. He shared his dilemma with Edwin Bookman. As he expected, the lawyer immediately offered to lend him money.

"That's not the answer, Reb Elisha," Uri answered. "I can borrow a bit, but I need wealthy students like yourself to teach."

Bookman was sympathetic and he tried, but there were not many lawyers on Bay Street looking to study Gemara.

"Uri, we may just have to ask the community for help," Chaya suggested gently. "It is no shame — other people do it."

"I just can't do it," Uri answered. "I am Captain Elijah's grandson! I would rather eat bread crusts than come on to people's charity."

So it went, as day quickly followed day.

Everything was happening so fast! The *siyum* was in three weeks, Tova's wedding two weeks later, and Dina's wedding just two weeks after that.

So, where's the money?

Have bitachon!
I have bitachon – show me the money!

Uri had trouble sleeping at night. He lay in his bed, the amber street light filtering in through the blinds. He lay, open-eyed, part davening, part worrying, part pondering. He looked up at the bedroom ceiling and the beautiful molding around the walls. Their light fixture was thirty years old, elegant and charming. He leaned against his elbow and admired the old-fashioned window casing. The house was about fifty years old, and everything had been finished with finest oaken wood. The house oozed charm.

A giddy, fanciful mood struck him. He got up, put on his robe, and went for a tour of his own house. Not the house of benching and homework and Shabbos meals and *zemiros*, but a tour of 95 Grant Avenue, the charming bungalow just off Bathurst, on a quiet, tree-lined cul-de-sac. He padded silently through the hallway, into the living room.

"And here, folks," he said in a low tone, "is the wood-paneled dining room. Please notice the polished wood floor, and there, the ribbed, stained-glass window over the fireplace."

He wandered into the kitchen. "And here is the ultra-modern kitchen and breakfast room, remodeled just five years ago, with two sinks. Downstairs is a full Passover kitchen."

He opened the front door and stepped onto the porch. "As you see, the steps were completely repainted a few years ago, with a stone walkway, and newly painted railings. Just peer down the street and you will see that this charming bungalow is on a cul-de-sac leading down to Earl Bales ravine. An utterly charming house on a desirable street, near schools, synagogues, and shopping."

"Uri, what are you doing?" Chaya asked. She was standing in the doorway, watching him as though he had lost his mind.

"Chaya, what are you doing up?" he asked, surprised. "I thought you were sleeping."

"I dreamt that a real estate agent came to sell our house, and I woke up. Then I heard talking in the living room, and I couldn't tell whether I was asleep or awake, so I came out. Uri, what are you doing?"

He smiled at her reassuringly. "I couldn't sleep, so I decided to get up and play 'tour the house.' " Uri laughed, sheepishly. Chaya laughed back nervously. They looked at each other: husband and wife who had spent almost every day of the last twenty-two years together and raised five children — and they knew what was in each other's mind.

But no one dared speak.

I cannot ask her to do this, Uri thought to himself.

And Chaya knew, *this house is Uri's whole world, his study, his Shabbos table — without this, what does he have?*

Days passed and matters grew critical. Money flowed out like blood. Everything cost: the down payment for the caterer, new suits and hats for the boys, *sheva berachos* outfits for the girls, registration and plane tickets for Yirmiyahu in Yerushalayim... There were no secrets between Uri and Chaya. They both knew where every penny was coming from and going to — and they were fast running out of pennies.

One evening, after supper, Chaya appeared very nervous. Uri was also jumpy. They spoke very little that night. Finally, just after washing the dishes, before Uri went to *ma'ariv*, he turned to Chaya and announced: "Chaya, I have to talk to you after *ma'ariv* —" which was hardly audible, because at that very same instant, Chaya had turned to her husband and said the very same thing:

"Uri, I have to talk to you after *ma'ariv* —"

They looked at each other and, in an instant, their tension cracked like ice. They both laughed, for they both knew.

Uri came home from *ma'ariv* late, past ten thirty. His friends must have looked at him curiously, because long after the *chazan* had finished *Aleinu* and Kaddish, he still stood in his southeast corner, *shuckling* and davening the *Shemoneh Esrei*. He was praying his heart out, for he knew that he and Chaya must make a decision that would affect the rest of their lives. He asked for wisdom, he asked for forgiveness, he asked that the decision they made would be correct in G-d's eyes.

I do not ask for what I want, Hashem. I pray for what is Your will.

When he finished davening, he was all alone in the shul. He locked up and drove home, full of — *bitachon*.

The house was still when he arrived home. Chaya had prepared a piping cup of mint tea and had baked fresh chocolate chip cookies. *This is serious*, Uri thought.

They sat down together like two crafty politicians, neither wanting to begin.

"What did you want to speak to me about?" Uri asked.

"What did you want to speak about?" she countered.

He looked at her. "I have an idea, but I don't know if it's fair to even mention it to you."

"What?"

"The house, our house —"

"To sell it?"

His eyes widened with alarm. "Yes."

"That was also my idea."

"It was?"

"Of course, you know — the night you played real estate man."

"But how can I take you away from this house that you love?"

"And I was thinking that this house is your castle —"

Uri gazed at his wife. "Chaya, you are my castle, you are my home, you are my joy. I can live in a basement apartment the rest of my life. But I didn't want to do that to you —"

"And you are my home and my joy," she responded. "You are my pride — your Torah and your sincerity. I will not be living in a basement apartment, Uri. I will be living in a palace, with the *nachas* of my daughters and sons-in-law, my grandchildren living in Yerushalayim, studying Torah day and night. I will be the richest woman in the world."

"Our house has gone up in value. We have good equity," Uri said.

"So, that is the answer," Chaya said. "Who needs the house? Who needs the polished floors? If we have each other, we will have everything."

They looked at each other with profound love.

Uri lifted up his cup of tea ceremoniously and smiled.

"*L'chaim!*" he said.

Chaya lifted her cup in return.

"*L'chaim*! May we see only *nachas* from all our descendants."

Uri put down the cup, nibbled thoughtfully on one of the cookies, and said. "So it is agreed, Rebbetzin Schiffman — we will put the house up on the market —"

"Agreed, Rabbi Schiffman."

Uri lifted a hand. "One thing. This is a big, big decision. I want to get the approval of Reb Klonimos Kalman."

So, they had come to a momentous decision — the house for the children!

⛵ ⛵ ⛵

Uri called the next morning for an appointment to see Reb Klonimus Kalman. For the first time since the engagements his mind was at rest. He was filled with happiness, full of *bitachon*!

But it was not easy to meet with Reb Klonimos. He was busy with *brisim*, visiting the sick, and seeing the many people who sought his blessing and advice. Uri had to wait almost a week before he could speak privately with the tzaddik. Meanwhile, time grew short. The *siyum* was only a few weeks away, responses for both weddings were coming back, the real-estate market was hot — but for how long?

Uri had not visited Klonimos for more than a year. It was enough that they davened together, that he could gaze secretly at Reb Klonimos's face and be strengthened. The *Shechinah* rested on the tzaddik's forehead.

It past eleven o'clock on a warm August night when Uri knocked at Reb Klonimos's house. Reb Klonimos himself opened the door and led him to his dim, book-lined study. As always, he gave Uri a warm, enigmatic smile, although he did not say much.

"Sit down, Reb Uri, sit down," he said. "Can I bring you an iced tea?"

Uri demurred. "I am sorry to keep you up so late," he apologized. "But my wife and I have a big decision to make and we wanted your opinion."

Reb Klonimos laughed. "Late? The night is just starting. *Mazel tov* again on your wonderful *simchahs*. You made unbelievable *shiduchim*."

"Amen."

"Tell me, how is it going with *parnasah*? These weddings must be a heavy strain."

Uri sighed, and then smiled. "Reb Klonimos, you don't know the half of it. But, *baruch Hashem* for everything!"

Reb Klonimos's face creased with concentration. He ran a hand over his eyes. "You had a situation, I remember... Your grandfather left a will, and your brothers received most of the fortune. Am I right?"

Uri hesitated. "Er...yes —"

Reb Klonimos's great eyes opened and he stared knowingly at Uri. "Nu, are they helping you?"

Uri looked down. *I must not gloat*, he whispered to himself.

"Unfortunately, they cannot —"

The tzaddik leaned forward. "Oh, why not?"

"Because your words came true, Reb Klonimos. Money is a *galgal hachozer*, a ball that bounces from person to person. They each received fortunes, and each, in turn, lost his —"

"*Azoy!*" Reb Klonimos answered, astonished. "So fast? They each received great amounts, I believe?"

"One got the house. The other was given Zeideh's boat. They both lost them in bad investments! And, to make matters worse, all of Zeideh's fortune was acquired by Zeideh's rival, *Deep Blue*."

Klonimos looked shocked. "*Deep Blue*? The boat that beat your Zeideh's boat?"

"None other." Uri shook his head in dismay.

Reb Klonimos seemed truly disturbed. He sat upright and shook his head in disbelief.

"*Deep Blue*," he murmured over and over. "*Deep Blue* owns everything —"

"Just like you predicted, Reb Klonimos! The ball bounced away from our family and went to others."

Reb Klonimos recovered from his shock. He gazed at Uri. "And what about you, Reb Uri? I heard the new couples are going to live in

Eretz Yisrael — you will probably have to help them. Where will you get the money?"

"It will cost a fortune to support them!" Uri answered. "We had to commit to supporting our *chassanim* in learning for seven years."

"Seven years?" Reb Klonimos whistled with amazement.

"Plus my own son Yirmiyahu is going to learn at Reb Chaim's *Kodshim* yeshivah in Yerushalayim. He insists! And then there are the twins, Dovid'l and Yisroel. It all adds up to tens of thousands of dollars a year — for seven years!"

"So, what will you do, Reb Uri?" Klonimos asked.

Uri slid his finger nervously across the edge of Reb Klonimos's desk. "My wife and I have decided…we will sell our house. It's the only way."

"And if you sell your house, where will you live?"

"We can rent. It's not a shame."

"But renting costs money too. Isn't rent expensive?"

"We don't need much. The children will all be out of the house. Even the youngest boys can live in dorms. It's just Chaya and I. And we decided — we can live anywhere! We can rent a basement apartment, they're very cheap. We can even make do with one bedroom if we have to…"

Reb Klonimos drummed his fingers on his desk, then looked at Uri. "You, Reb Uri, you? You are one of the most *chashuve talmidei chachamim* in our community! How will it look — living in a basement apartment at your age? And after living in a nice home for so many years! What will people say?"

Uri became upset and confused by the tzaddik's response. He leaned forward excitedly. "What can I do, Reb Klonimos? My children are dedicated to learning Torah in Eretz Yisrael! This is the only way we can do it —"

"But why not go to Amram Glicklich? Why not ask some of the wealthy *ba'alei batim* for help? Everyone does!"

"It's not necessary, Reb Klonimos!" Uri answered heatedly. "We have something of value that we can sell and do it ourselves! I don't want to go to people for charity. Whatever Hashem has given me, He has given me! Reb Klonimos is it an *aveirah* to live in a basement apartment? Is it a *de'Oraisa*? A *d'rabbanan*?"

Reb Klonimos smiled, then his face grew very serious.

"And you will not ask anyone for help?"

"No! We have the house — we can sell it! We'll survive!"

"And you would sell the roof over your heads so that your children can study Torah in Eretz Yisrael?"

"What else is there in life?"

The tzaddik stared silently into space, stroked his beard, and then shut his eyes. Uri looked down, near tears. The silence in the room was palpable, a dome of utter stillness. Reb Klonimos dropped his head on the desk and buried it in his arms, like he had suddenly fallen asleep. Uri watched him with dismay, but dared not speak. Uri's eyes grew heavy in the heat, and he felt dizzy. The room was very warm — it burned with *kedushah*.

Suddenly, Reb Klonimos lifted his head. Uri was overcome with alarm. Reb Klonimos's face was awash in perspiration, and he seemed to have transcended into a different world. The tzaddik lifted his huge eyes and stared wordlessly at Uri.

"Reb Klonimos, what is the matter?" Uri asked.

Reb Klonimos swayed from side to side, and then he smiled.

"Stand up, Reb Uri, stand up!" he ordered.

Bewildered, Uri stood up.

Reb Klonimos rose from his chair, walked around his desk and took Uri's two hands in his. There was a euphoric smile on his face, and the tzaddik closed his eyes. He began dancing around the room with Uri. Uri, bewildered, was forced to follow.

Reb Klonimos began singing:

> "*Nichsefah v'gam kalsah nafshi l'chatzros Hashem, libi u'vseari yiranenu el Keil chai...* – My soul yearns, indeed it pines, for the courtyards of Hashem, my heart and my flesh pray fervently to the living G-d!"

"Sing, Reb Uri," Klonimos cried. "Sing, Reb Uri, for this is your song!"

Awkwardly, Uri sang the holy words of *Tehillim*.

"*Nichsefah v'gam kalsah nafshi l'chatzros Hashem —*"

They danced for what seemed like an hour, although it was only a few minutes. Then Reb Klonimos abruptly stopped. His face was flushed and full of perspiration. He retrieved a handkerchief from his pocket, wiped his forehead, and addressed Uri.

"Reb Uri, Reb Uri, do you know what you have done?"

"No."

"You — you and your wife — you pulled the *nichsefah* out of the *klippos*, out of the impure shells that it had fallen to! The love of Hashem that the world has corrupted into lust for wealth, for money, more money, more money, more things — by your sacrifice, by your love of Torah, you released a million sparks of holiness from the shells they were trapped in, and they are soaring Heavenwards in a storm!"

Uri stared at Reb Klonimos and shook his head.

"No, Reb Klonimos!" Uri cried, "I haven't done anything! We do just like everyone else! Who wouldn't sacrifice for Torah? For us it was just a little harder —"

"No, Reb Uri!" the tzaddik answered. "You are willing to give away the roof over your heads, to live the rest of your life in a tiny apartment not even on a ground level — just for Torah! *Oy*, Reb Uri, what you have done, what you have done! You don't know what you have accomplished!"

Reb Klonimos raised his hands, lifted his head heavenwards, and shouted: "*Nichsefah v'gam kalsah nafshi l'chatzros Hashem!*"

Uri saw there was no use arguing. He had done nothing special. *What we are doing, others would also*, he knew.

They stood there silently in the dark, warm study. Uri knew it was time to go.

"Reb Klonimos, do we have your *berachah* that we should sell our house?"

Reb Klonimos lifted his hand. "You always have my *berachah*, for everything. But, what is the rush, Reb Uri? *Teshuas Hashem k'heref ayin*, Hashem can change things in a moment! You're making a *siyum haShas* for your grandfather, is that not right?"

"Yes, in two weeks. How did you know?"

"My friend Mr. Bookman told me."

"Could you be there, Reb Klonimos?" Uri asked excitedly. "It's going to be held in Mr. Bookman's office, just as Zeideh requested."

"I'll be there if you invite me," Reb Klonimos answered.

"Oh, Reb Klonimos! What a *kavod* it will be — for my Zeideh's sake, and for me!"

"*Bli neder.* Meanwhile, go slowly with your house. Don't rush too fast. May the mitzvah of your *siyum haShas* bring you a *berachah* that you can't even imagine!"

"Amen!" Uri answered fervently. "Amen v'amen!"

Reb Klonimos escorted Uri to the door of his study, and Uri soon found himself on the darkened, tree-lined street.

Uri paused, tugged his beard, and pinched his cheek to make sure he wasn't dreaming. Did this really happen tonight? Did Reb Klonimos really dance a *mitzvah tantz* with him?

It did happen, and Uri could not stop dancing in his head for days to come!

ELEVEN

Three more *dapim* until the *siyum*, not even! The final page of the final Gemara was not even one whole side, and Uri and Yirmiyahu were already on the seventieth page.

Each morning for the last three and a half years, Uri and Yirmiyahu had risen together, learned together, debated and battled over *pshat*. Reb Uri stayed Reb Uri, the same Reb Uri as he started, with a little more Torah — and pounds — under his belt. But Yirmiyahu had grown up before his eyes. A fiercely stubborn young boy, who knew no hours of day or night in his determination to learn the *daf*, had become a *talmid chacham* with a brilliant head, and an iron will.

Is this really my son? Uri wondered.

Uri had a good head. But Uri was not the Vilna Gaon, nor the Shaagas Aryeh, nor a Reb Chaim — he was a simple foot soldier slogging it out among Hashem's legion of Torah learners.

But Yirmiyahu! Someday he would become a commanding general!

So the learning drew to its climax, and Uri shook inside. He had never completed the whole *Shas* before, learned every word in *Talmud*

Bavli, every *Rashi*. He lost his appetite, he slept fitfully. Uri Schiffman was going to complete *Shas*!

Yirmiyahu, on the other hand, took it all in his stride. It wasn't a *siyum* for him. It was *daf* seventy, the *daf* before seventy-one. If he was excited for his father's achievement, he kept it under wraps. Each morning, Uri opened his Gemara with a flourish. "Four more pages to go, Yirmiyahu! Three more pages to go!"

Yirmiyahu would nod politely, turn to the *daf* and mumble: "Abba, let's learn!"

Uri realized that Yirmiyahu's heart lay not here, but in *Zevachim*, in the laws of the Temple, and in poring over Zeideh's notes. Yirmiyahu still held the beautiful gold pen on permanent loan, and Uri would find him writing notes in the empty lines of Zeideh's notebook, the lines that Zeideh had reserved for him.

In Uri's heart, the *siyum* took over everything. Tova's wedding was in two weeks, Dina's just over a month. It seemed ages away. The invitation replies were piling up, Chaya and the girls were negotiating with the *mechutanim* and the caterer, but for Uri, the *siyum* was a great, holy mountain that he needed to ascend, to conquer.

Nothing could shake him and nothing frightened him – not even all his money worries and the heavy commitments he had made to Tova and Dina.

"*Aron nosei es nosav* – The Holy Ark carried those who bear it." His love of learning, his joy at completing *Shas*, inured him from any fear, any doubt.

Chaya and Uri agreed that the children must not know what sacrifice they were about to make for their sakes. 95 Grant Avenue was the only home the children had known. Chaya had brought them home from the hospital when they were born, had nursed them, had raised them there. If they knew that the house was to be sold, it would darken their whole *simchah*.

Uri and Chaya were very discreet. One of Uri's fellow *mispallelim* was Aron Sweet, a real estate broker. One morning, when Uri knew that children would be away, Uri walked Aron through every room of the house: the bedrooms, the basement, the back deck, all around the outside. Uri was proud of their large, country-like backyard. Aron followed, pad in hand, nodded, grunted, made notes. Finally, they had covered every corner.

"What do you think we can get for it?" asked Uri.

Aron looked over his notes, coughed, and crunched in some numbers on his calculator.

"The market is hot now," Aron said. "But they say it won't last. In two months there'll be a glut of houses on the market, and the bubble may burst. If you move fast, you can probably get four hundred thousand, or close —"

"How much?" asked Uri, astonished.

"Four hundred thousand — but that's now — this week, next week or two, maybe a month. In two months, it may go down by fifty thousand, maybe more — if the market crashes."

"What should I do? What do you suggest?" asked Uri.

"I told you what to do, Reb Uri," Aron answered briskly. "Put it up for sale! In fact, I'm pretty sure I have a buyer for you already — at a good price!"

Bitachon, Uri whispered to himself, *have bitachon and you see it pays off!*

When Chaya came home that night, Uri wanted to share the good news immediately. If they got even near four hundred thousand, they could pay off their mortgage, put away a large sum, and have enough money to support the new couples and cover Yirmiyahu's expenses and the twins' tuition. There would be no fat, no luxuries, they would have to live very modestly...but there were plenty of decent basement apartments in the homes of the wealthy.

But who could get in a word alone with Chaya?

The girls grabbed her before supper and held her prisoner for hours. There were phone calls to make, responses to record, and then they ran out to check which color *gemach* flowers to rent. They held debates whether to style their *sheitels* up or down or sideways, the best place to buy watches for their *chassanim*. Uri watched this frantic planning with joy and peace, even more than Chaya — because he already knew where the money was coming from! He tried to signal to her; he winked, he nodded, he wiggled his fingers, but to no avail. All Chaya could do was raise her eyebrows and point with her eyes in the direction of the children.

"Later," she whispered to him in passing, "they'll get tired eventually."

Meanwhile, Uri hid himself in his study, and *chazer*ed over the last pages of the Gemara. He *shuckl*ed harder and harder, like an oarsman in the last hundred meters of a canoe race; shaking, learning, singing, happy.

Baruch Hashem for everything!

Finally, there was quiet in the house. Uri closed the Gemara and went out to tell Chaya the good news. The children had all retired. It was a warm, late August night. The air-conditioning was no match for the humid air. Chaya was in the kitchen, putting away the last of the dishes.

"Chaya," Uri said quietly. "I've been trying to talk to you the whole evening. I have good news."

Chaya turned to him and smiled. She looked exhausted, and her face was perspiring.

"Let's go into the dining room," she whispered. "It's the only room that's cool."

Uri switched off the lights in the kitchen and hallway. The house was completely dark, but it was cool. Uri and Chaya sat at the dining-room table, gazing out towards the amber streetlight coming through the living room window. The air was cool and lighter here, and they sat reflectively.

"Chaya," Uri said, "I spoke to Aron Sweet, the real estate man. Do you know how much we can get for the house if we sell it right away?"

"Three-hundred thousand?"

"Four hundred thousand, Chaya. Four hundred!"

"*Baruch Hashem —*"

"It'll take care of everything, Chaya. We won't have to worry about where to find support money every month! We can live on what we earn, and the money will support the children."

"*Baruch Hashem*," she answered. "But you know, the children will be upset. This is their home also."

"They mustn't know anything," Uri agreed, "not until after all the weddings. They'll go to Yerushalayim and start their own homes."

"What did Reb Klonimos tell you when you said that you wanted to sell the house?"

"He gave me his *berachah*. But —"

"But what?"

"He said I should wait a bit."

"So shouldn't you wait?"

"But Aron said the real estate bubble might burst any day now. In a month, maybe before! If we wait too long, the price may drop like a stone! We have to act quickly."

"But Reb Klonimos said not to rush."

"Who's rushing? Look, he said that the *siyum* will bring us a blessing. Selling this house *is* a blessing — our children will be able to study Torah all their lives. The *siyum* is in two days. We'll wait that long. Reb Klonimos will also be at the *siyum*. I'll tell him what Aron said, and then, then we'll do what we have to do." Uri's voice rose with emotion.

"Shh —" Chaya whispered sharply. "Keep your voice down. We don't want the children to hear anything."

They sat together quietly in the dark room. The house was dark, but their hearts were alight with hope. Finally, Chaya broke the silence.

"This has been a wonderful home for us, Uri."

"*Baruch Hashem.*"

"We've made many *simchahs*. *Brissim*, bar-mitzvahs, *sheva berachos* for our friends —"

"You remember the parlor meeting for *hachnasas kallah*?"

"The *orchim* we took in when other people had *simchahs* —"

"The Russian families at the seder —"

They sat quietly, remembering.

"Chaya, how many *berachos* have we made in this house?"

"How many *berachos*? What do you mean?"

"I mean *berachos*. How many *al netilas yadayims*, how many *asher yatzars*, how many *hamotzis*, *birkas hamazons*, davening when we couldn't go to shul..."

Chaya added to the list. "How many *hadlakas neiros* of Shabbos, how many *l'hadlik ner shel yom* – "

"How many Havdalahs, how many *shehechiyanus*, how many *hamapils*, how many *Birchos HaTorah* –"

"How many times have we kissed the mezuzahs –" Chaya said.

"How many times have we blessed the children," Uri added. "How many mitzvahs have we done, how much Torah we have learned in these four walls! Chaya, no wonder the house is warm! It's packed with all our Torah. The house is burning with mitzvahs, Chaya!"

"And when we sell it, what happens to all that *kedushah* that is here?" asked Chaya.

"Every mitzvah leaves a mark," answered Uri, "a *roshem*, like wax dripping on the table. It will always be here."

Chaya started crying. "Uri, you're making me so sad."

Uri leaned closer and spoke passionately.

"But we're going higher, Chaya. We are offering all these mitzvahs to Hashem like First Fruits in the Temple, so that our children, and our children's children can learn Torah, can learn Torah in Yerushalayim!"

"Shh," Chaya said through her tears. "I'm going to miss this house so much, Uri."

There was a silence.

"So...we shouldn't sell it?" he asked, finally.

"We have to," Chaya answered through her tears. "We have to, and we will have to be happy wherever we live!"

"Amen," he answered.

Uri suddenly felt very miserable. This house meant so much to Chaya, and to himself. But, there was no choice, no choice. They had to do what they had to do.

Uri lowered his voice. "But, remember, Chaya. Not a word of this to the children, not a hint! They can find out about it only after the weddings."

Chaya wiped her tears, and she nodded her head in agreement. Everything must proceed just as they planned.

But Uri and Chaya made one mistake.

They did not know that in the stifling heat of his bedroom, Dovid'l decided to sleep that night on the living-room couch.

He overheard every word they said!

On the morning before the *siyum*, Uri and Yirmiyahu began the penultimate *daf*: page seventy-two.

Their learning began as usual. Uri read and Yirmiyahu listened silently until he had a comment, a question, or he disagreed with Uri's *pshat*. They traveled down the long narrow Gemara column, past the *mishnah*, past the *machlokes* between Beis Hillel and Beis Shammai, and then they turned the page to the second side.

Uri stopped reading.

There she was! Across the other side of the page was *daf* seventy-three and...the finish! The *Hadran*. The *siyum*. The goal line!

Uri smiled: There she was! Columbus must have felt this way when he spied the coast of America for the first time, or the astronauts as *Orbiter* swept down towards the moon's surface.

There she was!

"Abba, let's go!" Yirmiyahu remonstrated. "It's getting late."

"Look —" Uri answered. "Look, Yirmiyahu — there's the goal line, it's so close!"

But Yirmiyahu was not impressed. "Abba, we can celebrate tomorrow. We're even having a *seudah*. But now, let's learn, please."

Uri looked at his son, crestfallen. "Yirmiyahu, does nothing shake you up?"

"Abba, I'm all shaken up! Look at me, I'm shaking! But, please, let's go on learning!"

Uri looked at his son, sighed, and smiled. He was proud of

Yirmiyahu's determination, but wished that he felt more empathy for his father. They pushed forward down the page, paused to learn one short *Tosafos*, and stopped five lines from the bottom of the page.

Uri took a deep breath and closed his Gemara. Tomorrow!

Yirmiyahu did not close his Gemara. Instead, he turned to his father. "Abba, I want you to know...I am very proud of what you are doing. Your *siyum* means a great deal to me —"

Uri stared at his son with astonishment, surprised by this show of emotion.

"*Baruch Hashem*," he answered.

"Abba, I want to do something special to celebrate the *siyum* — just you and me. Tonight is also Zeideh's *yahrtzeit*."

Uri looked at his son, amazed at Yirmiyahu's enthusiasm. But then, why should he be? Yirmiyahu was always his own person.

"What is it, Yirmiyahu?" Uri asked.

"Let's hold a *mishmar* tonight, Abba, in honor of the *siyum* — and in honor of Zeideh!"

"A *mishmar*?"

"A real *mishmar*, Abba, like when you were in yeshivah — an all-nighter. Like Shavuos night. We'll start at ten thirty, right after *ma'ariv*, and learn until *neitz*. We can daven *shacharis* at the *neitz* minyan —"

Uri was flabbergasted, yet filled with joy! This was the first crack in the dam, the first sign that Yirmiyahu really felt for his *siyum*!

He hesitated just for a moment.

"Listen, Yirmiyahu! You know how hard it is for me to stay up even Shavuos night. I don't know if I can do it. But...it's a deal! If the *siyum* really means so much to you, and Zeideh's *yahrtzeit* —"

"It does, Abba."

"Then I will give it the old yeshivah try. What will we learn, though?"

"Well, we have to finish the *masechta* — we'll do that at the end. Let's review the last three *dapim*. There are lots of *Tosafos* that we skipped, and maybe you can find something to say at the *Hadran*."

Uri smiled and shook his head.

"Listen, Yirmiyahu, I'm no Yirmiyahu Schiffman! I'm just your plain, old Abba, Uri Schiffman! I'm happy if I get the words straight! Don't count on any great *dvar Torah*!"

Yirmiyahu smiled one of his rare, open smiles, a smile of absolute, radiant beauty.

"Abba, you can try!"

Everything faded into insignificance.

Two weddings, two *aufraufs*, a house for sale (secretly), five round tickets for Eretz Yisrael to purchase, four students to teach privately. It all faded.

For Uri it was like *erev Yom Kippur*, *erev* his grandfather's *yahrtzeit*, *erev* the Great *Siyum*. That was all that was on his mind. Woven in with his practical preparations were the chapters of *Tehillim* that he recited waiting for the red lights to change, and a very long *Shemoneh Esrei* at *minchah*.

It was like the *minchah* before *Kol Nidrei*. Uri had to do one final, sincere *teshuvah* for the past, prepare himself for the holy day when he would cross the goal line — the *siyum*!

He spoke to Edwin Bookman's secretary. A meal was ordered from "Milk and Honey," trays of salads and fish, bagels, coffee. As per Zeideh's request, the *siyum* was to be held in Bookman's elegant boardroom, the same room where Zeideh's uneven will had first been read, and the same room where he had received, in turn, each volume of Zeideh's *Shas*. Zeideh's *Shas* was now complete — and it was magnificent!

Then there was the question of having a minyan for the *siyum Kaddish*. They were close: Uri, Yirmiyahu, Bookman, Reb Klonimos, Dovid'l and Yisroel, and Alexander and Solomon who had been invited — almost summoned — to join, by Bookman. Two more men were needed. Again, the boys pitched in. They guaranteed Uri that they would bring two more men to make the minyan, probably from Rabbi Levi's yeshivah.

So it was all set. The minyan, the place, the *seudah*, the time — 11:00 a.m. sharp — all that was necessary for the *siyum*. Amidst all the preparations, amidst the phone calls about the weddings, between the students, Uri tried to rest. At five o'clock he lay down for a nap. But he slept fitfully, wrestling with his sheet. He closed his eyes, thought about sailboats and lapping waves — but it didn't help. He was too excited. At five thirty he jumped out of bed, washed his hands, went back to his study and learned. Chaya was proud. She treated Uri like a king, made him his favorite dishes, but served him small amounts. Uri didn't want to get sleepy by overeating.

At eight thirty, he went back to shul, listened to a halachah *shiur*, and served as *ba'al tefillah* for *ma'ariv* in honor of his grandfather's *yahrtzeit*. He kept the *siyum* to himself, fearing that to boast of it would damage its *kedushah*.

Only those who had to know, knew. Only his own family.

Uri entered his study at ten thirty, and Yirmiyahu was already sitting at the desk, his Gemara open. Uri saw that his son had brought out Zeideh's gold pen in honor of the occasion, and was using it as a pointer. Uri had not seen it used this way for many months, and it was a signal what this night meant to his son.

Uri dropped wearily into his seat, pulled his *shtender* close, and opened his Gemara. He looked at the clock.

"Yirmiyahu, I haven't done an all-night *mishmar* since I was in yeshivah. But, I'll try. Where do we start?"

Although they still had two-thirds of the final *daf* to finish for the *siyum*, they went back three *dapim* to do *chazarah* — including all the *Tosafos*. Uri looked at the clock: quarter to eleven. Dawn was not until five thirty, a long six and half hours to go.

Uri turned to his son. "Yirmiyahu, I'll start, just to stay awake. You can take over later."

It was sweet learning, good learning. What Uri had thought was *pshat*, he discovered was often wrong. Now, with *chazarah*, he got it right. He and Yirmiyahu struggled with one *Tosafos* after another, breaking their teeth over the *Maharsha* and *Maharam*. They shouted at each other, pulled out books from the shelves to prove a point, and even quoted Zeideh's *chiddushim*! It was good learning.

Uri checked the clock. It was one fifteen. Only four hours until daybreak. They had already covered two whole *dapim* in review. They turned to the *mishnah* on *daf* seventy-one.

Uri eyed it wearily.

"Come, Abba," Yirmiyahu urged, "let's go for it! There's only a few hours until *neitz*, and we still have to finish the *siyum*."

But Uri called for a time out.

"Yirmiyahu, listen," Uri answered. "I'm getting very tired. I don't know if I'll hold out all night. Let's finish for the *siyum*, and then in whatever time is left, we'll do *chazarah*."

Yirmiyahu agreed. Uri turned to the bottom of page seventy-two and began learning. Slowly, carefully, Uri read down the page and then crossed over to the final *daf*...

His voice grew shaky as he read down the final *daf*, line after line, stopping here, struggling there, *pshat, pshat, pshat*... heading...heading for the final goal...

"*Talmud lomar... Talmud lomar...*"

Down, down the page...

Like a child, Uri counted how many lines were left to the finish: eighteen lines...

"*Talmud lomar... Talmud lomar...*"

twelve lines...

"*L'Rabbi Akiva kera'i...l'Rabbi Elazar ben Azariah hilchesa...*"

seven lines...

"*Tana dvei Eliyahu...*"

three lines...

"*Kol hashoneh halachos b'chol yom...*"

two lines...

"*Al tikrei halichos...*"

two words...

"*Ela halachos...*"
SIYUM! SIYUM! SIYUM! SIYUM!
Bells rang, sirens sounded, the huge scoreboard flashed yellow letters on and off, the crowd went wild.
URI SCHIFFMAN CROSSES GOAL LINE!
SIYUM! SIYUM! SIYUM! SIYUM!
But there were no crowds, no cheers, no roars, no horns. Just Uri and Yirmiyahu sitting next to each other, as they had done for years, and now they had finished.

There were no more words in the Gemara.

Uri had completed all of *Shas*.

Yirmiyahu turned to his father. "*Mazel tov*, Abba," he murmured. No more.

"*Mazel tov*," Uri responded solemnly. And he murmured over and over, "*Baruch Hashem...baruch Hashem...baruch Hashem* a thousand times!"

Uri gazed at the clock. It was exactly two thirty in the morning. There were still three hours to daybreak. Uri was exhausted, physically, emotionally, spiritually.

He turned to his son.

"Yirmiyahu, I'm very tired. I don't know if I can stay up all night."

"Try, Abba — we're so close."

"I'm going to go outside for a few minutes, to catch my breath. I'll come back and we'll continue."

Filled with absolute joy, but exhausted to the bone, Uri closed his Gemara, walked through the kitchen, and opened the door to the back deck. A cool night breeze blew through the trees, and he immediately felt revived. A half-moon had just risen, and Uri gazed upon its white, glistening face as it climbed through the branches. It was a magnificent August night.

Uri raised his hands towards the star-spangled night sky.

"Hashem, You have made such a beautiful world, and You have let me live to complete your holy Talmud!

"How can I praise You? How can I thank You for the holiness of every word that I have learned?

"How can I thank You for a son who was my *chavrusa*, for wonderful children who inspired me and are going in the proper way, for a wife who is an indescribable *eishes chayil*?

"*Lecha Hashem – hagedulah...v'hagevurah...v'hatiferes...v'haneitzach...v'hahod!*

"For Yours, Hashem, is the greatness...the strength... the splendor...the triumph...the glory!"

Uri lowered his voice to an intimate whisper.

"For You and I know the truth, Hashem: You are everything, and I am...zero!"

There was a sudden ruffle of wings in the magnolia tree along the deck. Uri looked up. His old companion, the cardinal, had landed on its topmost branch. It perched there grandly, its crimson feathers glowing fiery red in the luminescence of the huge, rising moon.

The little bird raised its head and began singing its tiny heart out. Its whistling and chirping and warbling were so sweet, so full of melody, so longing, so enchanting, that they almost sounded like words.

I wish I was King Solomon, thought Uri, *and knew the language of the birds!*

The glorious little creature was singing its heart out to the Creator, welcoming the pale dawn light that would soon break in the east. The little cardinal had no clock and no watch. It did not know any weariness or fatigue, but sang its morning song over and over, its *tefillah* to the Almighty.

Maybe he is wishing me mazel tov, thought Uri. *Maybe he wants to be at the siyum.*

Enough! Uri looked at his watch. It was past three o'clock! It was not fair to Yirmiyahu, waiting for him inside.

"*Boker tov!*" Uri greeted the little bird. "You do your *avodah*, and I shall go back to the Gemara and do mine!"

Uri turned and went back inside.

Nothing fazed Yirmiyahu.

It was past three o'clock, but he still sat, bent over his Gemara, writing notes as though it were ten in the morning. He lifted himself respectfully when Uri entered.

"How do you feel, Abba?" he asked.

"Tired. But I'm all right."

Yirmiyahu turned to the *mishnah* on *daf* seventy-one.

"Come, Abba, do you want to read?"

Uri shook his head wearily. "I'm too tired, Yirmiyahu. You read, I'll listen."

Yirmiyahu lifted his Gemara and began reciting the *mishnah*. Uri listened, silently. Then Yirmiyahu moved to the Gemara below. Uri suddenly put down his Gemara and shook his head.

"It's no use," he mumbled. "Yirmiyahu, I can't concentrate. My head is clouded, I'm too tired."

Yirmiyahu looked up at the clock. "Abba, there are less than two hours left. Hold on!"

Uri looked up wearily and smiled at his exceptional son.

"Listen, I'll make you a deal. This Gemara right now is too difficult. Let's find a piece of *aggadeta* – that's also Torah. Maybe we can study the holy *Maharsha* on it."

Yirmiyahu saw that his father's eyelids were drooping. "Okay, Abba. Can we go back to *daf lamed*?"

"Why not?" Uri answered, turning back to page thirty.

Yirmiyahu rolled the pen down towards the bottom of the page. Uri was struggling desperately to stay awake, and Yirmiyahu deliberately raised his voice.

The lyrical Gemara described the formation of an embryo in its mother's womb, its growth from two little dots into a human being. An angel taught the whole Torah to the new baby even as it lay curled inside its mother. Uri listened to his son read and nodded drowsily to himself. Yirmiyahu's voice was like a melody, like the sweetest birdsong. Uri's head dropped down onto the page...

"Abba, you're falling asleep!" Yirmiyahu warned.

Uri jerked his head up. He smiled.

"Yirmiyahu, I'm not falling asleep. I'm listening to every word you're saying! I'm just closing my eyes for a second to concentrate, but I hear every word."

He shut his eyes and lay his head on the open *daf*.

Undeterred, Yirmiyahu read on:

"*V'eino yotzei misham ad shemashbi'in oso...* — And the child does not leave his mother's womb until he is made to swear...

"*U'mah hi hashvu'ah shemashbi'in oso* — And what is the oath that he is made to swear?

"*Tehi tzaddik v'al tehi rasha* — Thou shall be righteous and not wicked.

"*V'afilu kol ha'olam omrim lecha tzaddik atah, he'yei b'einecha k'rasha...* — And even if the whole world says that you are a tzaddik, in your own eyes you shall consider yourself wicked!

"*V'hevei yodei'a sheHaKadosh Baruch Hu tahor, u'mesharsav tehorim, u'neshamah shenasan becha tehorah hi...* — And know! The Holy One is pure, and His heavenly servants are pure — and the *neshamah* He placed in you is pure!"

Uri's arm fell to his side, and his yarmulke near slipped off his head. His son's voice was putting him to sleep. Uri fought a losing battle to stay awake.

Yirmiyahu leaned over to his father.

"Abba," he whispered gently. "Abba, you're falling asleep."

Uri lifted his eyes open and peered into Yirmiyahu's sky blue eyes, eyes innocent and pure as the heavens themselves.

He rolled his head over on the page.

"Forgive me, Yirmiyahu! I can't do it — I'm so sorry." His eyes closed.

"Abba," Yirmiyahu urged anxiously, "say *hamapil* before you fall asleep."

Eyes closed, Uri mumbled the blessing. He lifted his eyes open one last time and gazed into his son's face. Uri frowned — he had disappointed Yirmiyahu.

Yirmiyahu drew close to his father, their faces almost touching. He took Zeideh's pen and slipped it halfway into his father's open hand, and held the other half in his own. Uri looked up. The pen felt so warm.

"Abba," Yirmiyahu whispered, "I am so proud of you."

Uri smiled, his eyes closed over the open *daf*, and he dropped into a deep, deep sleep.

TWELVE

Uri's Dream

A bell rings, and a tiny, pure *neshamah* is summoned before the Heavenly Throne.

"*Neshamah*, it is time for you to descend to earth and be garbed with human form."

The *neshamah* cries:

"O Master of the Universe! I beg You, please don't send me away! Here I am so pure! Here – I stand before You! Look where You're sending me! Like Joseph's brothers, You are casting me into a dark pit."

And the Almighty answers:

"*Segulasi*! No, you must go – for this is your purpose in creation! You must descend into the Lower World, a world of myriad, myriad temptations, of veils and concealments and partitions – and there still cleave to Me through My Torah and mitzvahs...until you return!"

The *neshamah* pleads further:

"*Dodi*! But I will become sullied! I will be ashamed to return to Your Holy Presence!"

The Holy One responds:

"*Aymasi*! That is your purpose. You must struggle each day to stay pure! And even if you come back imperfect, you shall still stand higher than the angels – if you truly try!

"The angels will say to you: 'O, holy *neshamah* that descended into the lowest worlds and stayed faithful to Hashem, how we envy you! For we have no choice between good and evil, but you performed one mitzvah after another, studied one word of Torah after another, and gathered up the fallen sparks of holiness!' "

The *neshamah* answers:

"*Dodi*! O how shall I be away so long from You? I shall be gone for a hundred and twenty years before I can return to Your Heavenly Presence!"

But the Holy One consoles her:

"*Segulasi*! Each night you will fly up to the Heavenly Court and recount all the Torah and mitzvahs that you performed that day! Each night you will visit Heaven for an instant of an instant! And then – you shall return!"

The tiny, pure *neshamah* trembles before the Holy One. The Heavens rumble, and the soon-to-be-born *neshamah* is given its final Oath:

> "*Tehi tzaddik v'al tehi rasha* – Thou shall be righteous and not wicked.
>
> "*V'afilu kol ha'olam omrim lecha tzaddik atah, he'yei b'einecha k'rasha...* – And even if the whole world says that you are a tzaddik, in your own eyes you shall consider yourself wicked!
>
> "*V'hevei yodei'a sheHaKadosh Baruch Hu tahor, u'mesharsav tehorim, u'neshamah shenasan becha tehorah hi...* – And know! The Holy One is pure, and His heavenly servants are pure – and the *neshamah* He placed in you is pure!"

And in a blink the *neshamah* descends to earth and a new baby is ready to be born...

Uri laid his head on his Gemara and dreamt holy dreams, even as his *neshamah* soared Heavenwards.

"*Shalom aleichem*, Reb Uri! *Shalom aleichem!*"

Uri gazed as two dignified gentlemen rushed forward to welcome him. They were dressed in fine Babylonian robes and turbans, and their faces were wreathed in smiles. They approached, hands outstretched.

"*Shalom aleichem,*" Uri answered uncertainly. "My masters, who are you?"

The older gentleman bowed courteously.

"I am Chanina bar Papa! And this is my younger brother, Rami."

Uri's eyes opened wide with delight.

"Are you *the* Chanina and Rami bar Papa? Of the *siyums*?"

The brothers smiled warmly. "Yes! We heard from the Heavenly Court that you completed *Shas* this morning and we have come to greet you! *Mazel tov! Mazel tov! Mazel tov!*" they shouted.

Uri looked down, embarrassed. "*Baruch Hashem,*" he murmured.

"We have been ordered by the Heavenly Court to present you with your medals for learning," said Rami.

"Medals?" asked Uri, surprised. "I didn't know you get medals for learning."

"Why not?" asked Chanina. "If swimmers get medals for swimming, and runners for running, and jumpers for jumping — should you not get medals for learning?"

Uri was nonplussed. Medals? A *berachah*, yes... A fiery *chuppah* in *Shamayim*...but medals?"

The brothers saw his hesitation.

"Why are you waiting, Reb Uri?" said Chanina. "You finished all of *Shas* — come, come!"

Like a *chassan* being led to the *chuppah*, they led him down a long, red carpet and into a great chamber. A crowd of Heavenly faces stood ready to welcome him.

"Reb Uri," the brothers said, "rise up here on this platform and accept your first medal!"

Uri stopped short. It was all too much.

"I don't need medals, oh holy sons of Reb Papa!" he argued.

Chanina bar Papa raised his hands imploringly, like Uri was a child.

"Reb Uri, if they have decreed in *Shamayim* that you are to receive medals, who are you to argue?"

So Uri stepped onto the small platform, watched by the crowd. He closed his eyes, lowered his head, and waited.

Rami bar Papa cried out:

"Reb Uri of Toronto! For completing *masechta Berachos*, you are awarded a gold medal!"

Uri waited, sighed, but nothing was placed around his neck. Instead, his face suddenly felt warm. He opened his eyes.

"Where's the medal?" he asked.

"You are wearing it." Rami answered.

Uri looked down. "Where?"

"What are you looking for?" asked Chanina. "A chunk of gold around your neck? Touch your face — it's shining! The holy words of *Berachos* are glowing on your face!"

Uri felt his face. It was warm. He looked at his fingers, and they sparkled from the shine of his face!

"*Mazel tov!*" everyone shouted.

"Come," said Chanina. "It is getting late. We will pass you on to our next set of brothers, Nachman and Achai. They will escort you for your next awards."

Uri stepped down quickly, his face aglow. He hadn't expected this!

"*Shalom aleichem! Shalom aleichem!*"

Uri was greeted warmly by the next two brothers, who met him under the *Mo'ed* archway. They led him to the foot of a tall platform.

Uri looked up. "Why is this platform so high?" he asked.

"Every step is for a Gemara you learned," answered Achai. "Twelve Gemaras, twelve steps!"

Uri sighed and climbed to the top of the platform. He looked down at all the holy faces smiling at him. Embarrassed, he closed his eyes tightly.

"Reb Uri of Toronto, *amod*! Prepare to receive your medals for *seder Mo'ed*!"

Uri lowered his head. Even with his eyes closed, he could tell that a white light glowed from his face – all of *Shabbos* and *Eiruvin*, *Pesachim* and *Shekalim*, *Rosh HaShanah*, *Yoma*, *Sukkah*, *Beitzah*, *Ta'anis*, *Megillah*, *Mo'ed Katan*, *Chagigah* – all the holy words washed over his face, drenching it with *kedushah*.

Finally, he opened his eyes and felt his face.

"My masters!" he cried. "I don't deserve all this!"

But the brothers did not even listen. They hastily escorted him out of the chamber and to the next set of brothers, who waited impatiently at the *Nashim* entrance.

Abba Mori and Rafram bar Papa greeted him warmly, but they also seemed in a great hurry. They quickly led him to the next platform.

Uri paused at the bottom of the platform. "Please, my masters!" he implored them. "Enough honors – I don't need any more medals!"

"Reb Uri! This is what the Heavenly Court has decreed for you!" said Abba Mori firmly.

Uri still hesitated. The brothers took hold of Uri's arms like he was a prisoner being led to the gallows, and walked him briskly up the platform.

"Reb Uri of Toronto..."

Uri shut his eyes. A different holiness washed across his face: *Yevamos* and *Kesubos*, *Nedarim* and *Nazir*, *Sotah*, *Gittin*, *Kiddushin* – the *sefer hayichus* of the Jewish people, a nation of modesty and chastity, *kish'silei zeisim u'k'gefen poriyah* ... – beautiful olive shoots and fruitful vines...

Uri shut his eyes and basked in this new *ohr*.

But there was no time to pause. They were urging him forward. Uri opened his eyes.

"Reb Uri," pleaded Rafram. "Hurry! More medals await you and time grows short! We will escort you to the next chamber."

Uri was so exhilarated by this last *ohr*, he no longer hesitated. These were not honors that he was receiving, but holy gifts.

The next two brothers, Rachish and Surchav, met him at the *Nezikin* entrance.

"*Shalom aleichem*, Reb Uri!" they greeted him. "Come, we will lead you to the next platform. You will find a nice surprise!"

A surprise? wondered Uri. *After all these medals, what more surprises could there be?*

Uri stopped and gazed around, trying to discover the surprise.

"No, no!" said Rachish. "This is no time to pause! They are all waiting for you in the Heavenly Court! You must not keep them waiting!"

What Heavenly Court? wondered Uri. *Who was waiting?*

They hurried Uri through the *Nezikin* chamber, through even greater crowds of *neshamah*s who came to rejoice with him. Uri did not look right or left, nor did he recognize whom he was passing. If he had, he would have known that these *neshamah*s were his grandfathers and grandmothers, his great-grandfathers and great-grandmothers of a hundred generations past, all rejoicing in his Torah and good deeds.

He reached the platform and eagerly mounted its stairs. Suddenly, Uri heard footsteps climbing alongside. He looked — and there was Yirmiyahu!

"*Shalom*, Abba," said Yirmiyahu. "*Mazel tov!*"

"Yirmiyahu!" cried out Uri in shock. "What are you doing here?"

"Abba, remember? I started learning with you in *Sanhedrin*! So they let me escort you the rest of way!"

Uri was stunned. What a wonderful surprise! They stood side by side at the top of the platform.

"Reb Uri of Toronto, stand and receive your medals for *seder Nezikin!*"

"Close your eyes, Yirmiyahu," Uri warned. Uri shut his eyes, and the brilliance of *Nezikin* poured over his forehead: *Bava Kama, Bava Metziah, Bava Basra, Sanhedrin* and *Makkos, Shevuos, Avodah Zarah, Horayos, Eidiyos* — such difficult, difficult Gemaras, so many *kashahs* and so many *teirutzim*, so many *sefarim* and so many *pilpulim*, so much genius! All that holy brilliance now washed over his brow, and Uri felt his mind open with new clarity.

Baruch Hashem, murmured Uri to himself. *They gave me new seichel for my old age.*

Uri and Yirmiyahu descended the platform. The brothers were worried.

"Reb Uri, we are approaching your Great *Siyum*! The Heavenly Court has gathered. You must move on quickly to the next chamber!"

Uri lost his shyness. Each medal was a profound gift! With Yirmiyahu proudly at his side, Uri led the way briskly, and the two ancient sons of Rav Papa ran hard to keep up with them!

The two youngest sons of Rav Papa, Ada and Daru, met him at the *Kodshim* entrance.

"*Shalom aleichem*, Reb Uri," they greeted him.

But it was a different, solemn greeting from these sons of Rav Papa. The other brothers had welcomed him with warm handshakes and beaming smiles. But these sons of Papa were subdued, even somber.

Have I done something wrong? Uri wondered.

They led him quickly towards the raised platform. But the whole mood of this chamber was quieter. Unlike the other glowing chambers, here the lights were dim, and the faces in the crowd were downcast.

Uri, troubled by this melancholy chamber, turned to Rav Ada.

"My master," he whispered, "why is this hall so much darker and sadder than the rest? Everyone looks so...downcast."

Ada gazed at Uri in amazement.

"Reb Uri, Reb Uri, do you need to even ask? This is the *Kodshim* chamber: *Zevachim, Menachos, Bechoros, Tamid*. Tell me — where are the *zevachim* and where are the *menachos*? Where is the *ketores* and where are the *hazayos*? Do you see the *kohanim* perform the *avodah*, or the Leviim rise up in *shir*? The Mikdash is in ruins, the *mizbei'ach* is destroyed, and we may not step even one foot on the Har HaBayis! How shall we rejoice here?"

The brothers grew anxious.

"Reb Uri, they are waiting for you! Quickly, please, go up to receive your medals!"

But Uri would not budge.

"My masters, if this chamber is in mourning, I do not want medals!"

"Reb Uri!" Daru bar Papa retorted. "Don't tarry! You have been called forward to receive your medals! The Temple is no more — but you have learned *Kodshim*! Step up swiftly to the platform!"

Left with no choice, Uri and Yirmiyahu approached the high platform. Uri looked at his son, sighed, and began climbing up.

"Yirmiyahu," he whispered, "stay near me!"

Uri reached halfway up the tall staircase when he sensed that someone was walking on his other side. He turned and stood frozen with shock.

"Zeideh Elijah!" he cried.

He stared at his beloved grandfather, not believing his eyes. "Zeideh, is it really you?"

Zeideh smiled at him. It wasn't the somber Zeideh of his old age, after the *Swift Current*'s infamous landing. It was the Zeideh of his childhood, full of life.

"*Shalom aleichem*, Eerie!" Zeideh greeted him.

"Zeideh, what are you doing here?" Uri asked, astonished.

"The Heavenly Court has given me permission to escort you to the top of the *Kodshim* platform!"

Uri was flabbergasted. What did all this mean? But the brothers called up from below: "Reb Uri, hurry!"

Uri strode briskly up the last steps and stood atop the platform. Zeideh Elijah stood to his right, Yirmiyahu to his left. Below, countless *neshamah*s gazed up to him, melancholy *neshamah*s longing for Tzion and the Mikdash.

Uri shut his eyes and lowered his head. A holy flame leaped forward and danced over his head like a fiery angel. It was a flame of the *mizbei'ach*, a throne that he had fanned awake by his *Kodshim* learning!

The whole chamber lit up joyously from the blazing flame, like lights after Tisha b'Av! Uri opened his eyes — the room radiated with his *Kodshim* learning! Uri gazed at the thousands of *neshamah*s, and in place of despair, now was *bitachon* and *emunah*!

The Beis HaMikdash was on its way!

Rav Papa's sons called from below.

"Reb Uri, please, it is almost sunrise!"

Uri turned to his grandfather. "Zeideh! Come with me to the *siyum*!" But Zeideh shook his head sadly.

"No, my Eerie! This is as far as I may go! I was permitted to stand next to you for *seder Kodshim*, for my notebooks helped you and Yirmiyahu! But now you must go forward, and I must go back —"

Uri grasped Zeideh's arm to hold him back. Zeideh looked at Uri, and shook his head reprovingly. Embarrassed, Uri released his grip. But he pleaded with his grandfather:

"Zeideh, before you go! Tell me the secret. How did you do it? How did you become a great *talmid chacham* in your last years?"

Zeideh stared at him, moved his lips, but Uri could not hear. It was not time for him to know — yet. Zeideh saluted one last time, and vanished.

Uri turned to Yirmiyahu.

"Yirmiyahu, you were my *chavrusa*, please don't disappear on me! Not now, when I am so close to my *siyum*."

They climbed down the platform and, hurried along by the two brothers, headed towards the final gateway.

The brothers escorted them to the entrance, and then stopped.

"Reb Uri," proclaimed Ada bar Papa. "We, the ten sons of Rav Papa who gave our lives for Torah...we, whose names summon up the ten *ma'amaros* of Creation and the ten *sefiros* of Holiness — we say to you: *yasher koach* and *mazel tov*!

"You carry the blessings of every word of Gemara you learned! Every crease of your brow on a difficult *Tosafos*, every tug of your beard to understand a *Rashi*, every joyous sigh at mastering an intricate *sugya* — it is all recorded!"

He paused, and Daru bar Papa continued:

"But now, Reb Uri, you must proceed alone to the great Heavenly Court that awaits you! Do not fear! Whatever test you face there, do your best — and Hashem will be with you!"

Wait a second, thought Uri, *fear what?*

He asked the sons of Rav Papa:

"My masters, what test will I face before the Heavenly Court?"

But the two brothers had already drifted far away.

"We can go this far…and no further," they shouted. "Now you are on your own!"

"But what do I have to fear?" he asked.

But it was too late. They were gone.

Filled with uneasiness, Uri turned to Yirmiyahu.

"Yirmiyahu, I must appear before the Heavenly Court! What will I say? What will they ask me? Maybe they will *farheir* me?"

"Abba," answered Yirmiyahu, "you learned the whole *Shas* — what do you have to fear? I will stay at your side to help —"

"But I am afraid, Yirmiyahu."

His son smiled his brilliant smile, a smile of youth and courage.

"Here Abba," he said, "grab onto this! This will give you strength!"

He reached into his pocket and extracted Zeideh's gold pen, the pen that had been Uri's companion throughout *Shas*, the pen that, after many years of being dry as a bone, now flowed beautiful wellsprings of Torah. Uri took the golden wand in his hand and, so armed, proceeded through the great archway.

Yirmiyahu and Uri walked a long, ascending path, passing under archway after archway, climbing higher and higher. So must the High Priest have ascended: upward from the deep Kidron valley to the Temple Mount, upward to the *chayil,* up the high steps to the Women's Court, up the fifteen steps into the Israelite courtyard, up the great ceremonial steps into the *Ulam*, into the *Heichal*, into the Holy of Holies!

Uri looked up — they had arrived! Before them sat the great Heavenly Court, waiting for him.

Uri looked up in fright. His legs trembled. What a huge, holy Court it was! All the *Tana'im*, all the *Amora'im*, all the *talmidei chachamim* whose names he had recalled in his learning — they all rose in his honor!

"Look Abba," whispered Yirmiyahu. "Look how they stand up for you! I am so proud!"

The faces of the scholars shone like the moon, and Uri sighed with relief. What was there to fear in this place?

The Head of the Heavenly Court addressed Uri:

"Reb Uri, grandson of Elijah, *yasher koach*! This morning you completed *Shas* in *Shamayim*, and in a few hours you will recite the *Hadran* on earth! *Yasher koach, yasher koach*! You already received medals for each Gemara, but now the Heavenly Court will award you the holy Crown, the *Keser Torah*.

Uri trembled with fright before this great assembly, unable to open his mouth. But he had to speak before it was too late.

In a voice trembling with fear, he said:

"My holy masters! You wish to bestow on me a crown that I do not deserve! I just learned quickly through *Shas*! How much did I miss, and how little do I remember? My masters, I raced to meet Zeideh's deadline! How can I don a *Keser Torah*? A *melech* wears a crown...but I am no king! I am the simplest, plainest learner of anyone who ever sat over a page of Gemara! Please, do not give me what is too large for my small head!"

"Silence!" cried the Head of the Court. "Reb Uri, Heaven forfend to speak so! Did you not study the whole *Shas* as best as you could? Every king has a different size kingdom: some great, some small, some just a few little hills — but they are still kings, and they wear crowns! And you, Reb Uri, shall also receive your *keser*!"

Without further delay, a Heavenly voice called out:

"*Amod*, Uri the grandson of Elijah, and be crowned with the *Keser Torah*!"

The great *Tana'im* and *Amora'im* whom Uri had mentioned day in and day out, Rabbi Yehudah and Rabbi Shimon, Rabbi Akiva and Rabbi Eliezer, Abaye and Rava, Rav Ashi and Ravina — thousands of Talmud luminaries — they all stood in Uri's honor.

It was too much for Uri. He didn't want a crown, he didn't want *kavod*, he didn't want the great *Tana'im* and *Amora'im* to rise in his honor! But they gave him no choice. He closed his eyes in embarrassment and shame, prepared to endure his honor.

"*Shalom aleichem*, Reb Uri, *mazel tov*!"

It was a familiar voice! Uri opened his eyes and there, standing next to him, was Reb Klonimos Kalman. In his hands he held the great crown.

"Reb Klonimos!" Uri cried. "Are you here also?"

Klonimos smiled like the sun.

"Reb Uri! I have been given the honor of placing the *Keser Torah* on your head – I, together with Yirmiyahu."

Uri could not help himself, he began to cry with joy. It was too much! On one side, Yirmiyahu. On the other, Reb Klonimos Kalman. Uri reached out and felt the *Keser Torah*. It was purest gold, the same pure gold from which the holy Menorah had been beaten – for the light of the Menorah and the light of the Torah was one! On the crown were thirty-six sparkling jewels, one for each of the thirty-six *masechta*s he had studied. Thirty-six holy lights like those of a Chanukah menorah – for they were all one, the *ohr haganuz* of *neis* Chanukah and the *ohr haganuz* of Torah!

Uri stood tall, and Reb Klonimos and Yirmiyahu placed the crown firmly over his forehead. Uri opened his eyes and peered upward – he was crowned!

Overcome with joy, Klonimos whispered in his ear:

"*Mazel tov*, Reb Uri. You are now a *melech*!"

"Abba, I am so proud of you," murmured Yirmiyahu.

Indeed, with the jeweled crown upon his head, the golden pen a scepter in his hand, Uri looked like a *melech*...he was a *melech*!

Uri stood proudly, his face wet with perspiration, his beloved son on one side, his rebbi on the other side.

What do I have to fear? he reassured himself.

But, it was too soon.

The Head of the Heavenly Court banged for silence.

"Reb Uri, soon you will recite the great Kaddish in honor of your *siyum*. But, before you recite the Kaddish, the Heavenly Court is anxious to hear your *pshetl* –"

"My...my what?" stammered Uri.

"Your *pshetl*, Reb Uri, your *pshetl*! Look, we are all waiting. Rabbi Yochanan ben Zakkai is waiting, and Rabbi Yehudah HaNasi! Rashi is listening and Rambam! They all want to hear your *chiddush*!"

Uri turned white.

"O Holy Master!" he cried. "I told you, I am just an ordinary student! I struggled just to understand what I was reading!"

He turned desperately to his side.

"Here is Reb Klonimos, and — and my brilliant son Yirmiyahu. They have *chiddushim* to recite, ask them!"

"No!" thundered the Head of the Heavenly Court. "We want to hear *your* Torah, Reb Uri!"

Uri was in tears. "O Holy Master, I have nothing!"

"No, Reb Uri!" he answered. "You must have something! Every Jew has a portion in Torah that only he brings into the world! You have your portion, great or small! Reb Uri, tell us your Torah!"

Uri's knees started knocking in fright, and he turned desperately to Yirmiyahu for help. But Yirmiyahu turned away. Uri turned to Klonimos and pleaded, but the tzaddik also stood silent.

The Heavenly Court was waiting for Uri's Torah.

There was a great, terrible silence. All eyes were on poor Uri.

Uri prayed to Hashem:

"Oh, *Ribbono shel Olam*, I tried my best. Please, let me not be ashamed before the Heavenly Court, before all the great Sages of our people!"

In the absolute silence of the Heavenly Court, with all eyes upon poor Uri, he suddenly heard a tiny, whistling sound. He listened closely as it grew louder. It was the sound of...chirping. Uri turned his head carefully so as not to drop his sacred crown, and there, racing cheerfully to the Heavenly Court, was...the little cardinal from his magnolia tree! The bird waved its wings joyously, and whistled and chirped its little heart out, just like in Uri's backyard.

The little bird rustled its wings high above the Heavenly Court, seeking a place to roost. There was no magnolia tree, so it alighted atop the high archway just above Uri. And there, in front of Uri and the

Heavenly Court, it began whistling its joyous song.

"Chirp, chirp, chirp, chirp!" it warbled. "Chirp, chirp, chirp, chirp!"

Uri was embarrassed — the little bird had followed him right into the Heavenly Court! But what could he do? The bird's song resonated such deep longing for Hashem, it was so laden with *yiras Shamayim*, that even the Heavenly Court was pleased. The bird's excited chirping and whistling sounded like holy words, but words that Uri could not understand...

"Listen, Reb Uri," whispered Klonimos, "the bird is singing your *pshetl*!"

"It is?"

Uri looked up and tried desperately to understand. He listened with his ears to what seemed like words, but he still did not understand.

He listened with his head, with his brain, with all his wisdom and knowledge, but still, he could not understand.

He listened with his heart, with all his human feelings and emotions and love of Torah, and the words started to become more distinct, they seemed to form into sentences and *pesukim*, but still, still he could not comprehend.

And then...he completely forgot himself, he forgot his *anochi*, and listened with his *neshamah*, the *neshamah* that had now soared to its *shoresh* in *Shamayim* — and the little bird's song turned into letters and words, and the words became Torah.

He looked up gratefully and murmured:

"Thank you, little bird. Now I understand!"

The little bird became silent, and Uri bowed to the Heavenly Court:

"My holy Masters and Teachers!"

"Hashem has given me just a tiny, tiny *pshetl* that is mine — but as it is, so I will recite it! The Torah is not mine alone: I heard it in the little bird's song to Hashem: four little chirps, four little sounds."

Uri began singing in a Gemara *niggun*, like the Four Questions at the seder.

"What are the those four little sounds?

"The final Gemara in *Shas* ends with these holy words:

" *'Tana dvei Eliyahu*: Whoever learns halachos every day, is assured a place in the World to Come... For it is written:

" *'Halichos olam lo* — The ways of the world are his:

" 'Do not read *halichos* but *halachos*, for he who studies Torah law every day is guaranteed a place in the World to Come.'

"So ends the Talmud, with those few words.

"But the very first word in the Talmud is '*Mei'eimasai*!' "

Uri swung his thumb like a yeshivah *bachur*.

"Now, we know that the Torah has no beginning and no end. So the end of the Talmud is attached to the beginning, like a great wheel. If so, the question is, What is the connection between *halachos olam lo*, the end of the Talmud, and *Mei'eimasai*, the beginning of the Talmud?

"The answer is —"

Suddenly the cardinal lifted its voice:

"Chirp, chirp, chirp, chirp!"

Uri lifted his hand for silence.

"The little cardinal has sung the answer! For he is whistling four holy notes:

"*Mei – ei – ma – sai!*

"*Mei – ei – ma – sai!*

"The first word of our holy Talmud is —

"*Mei-ei-ma-sai!*

"Why? The word *mei'eimasai* has two meanings. *Mei'eimasai* means 'when?'... But *mei'eimasai* also means *eimah* — awe of Hashem, awe of His holy Torah.

"My holy Masters, when the holy Torah was received at Sinai it was with *kolos u'vrakim*, thunder and lightning!

"It was with *eimah*, with *yirah*, with *reses*, with *zei'ah* — with dread, with awe, with trembling, with fear!

"Now, the Talmud ends with the words *halachos...lo*! The word *lo*, *lamed* and *vav*, equals thirty-six in *gematria*, like the thirty-six volumes of the Talmud.

"And the very first word of *Shas* is: *Mei'eimasai!*

"What is the connection? The very first word, *Mei'eimasai*, is proclaiming:

" 'So, Reb Yid, you wish to learn *lo*, the thirty-six books of my Torah?

" 'How will you study this Torah? Will you study it just with your head — or with your whole *neshamah*?

" 'Will it be *me'eimasai* — *b'eimah*, with awe? *b'yirah*? *b'reses*? *b'zei'ah*, with trembling?

" 'What kind of Torah, Reb Yid, hot or cold?

" 'Will you study *lishmah* — or for honor?'

Mei'eimasai!

" 'How will you begin a page of Gemara? By gazing at the clock and announcing — it's time to start... Or will you first stand trembling and awestruck, *b'yirah, b'reses, b'zei'ah* — and cry, "*Ribbono shel Olam*, I am not worthy to stand before Your holy Gemara! How shall I thank You for the honor?"

" 'When you finish a page of Gemara, will you be the same old person — or will your Torah set you on a higher path?

" 'And when you leave the *beis midrash*, will everyone see the Shechinah hovering over you?'

Mei'eimasai!

" ' Will the Torah make you kinder? Will it teach you to say *shalom aleichem* to a stranger you pass on Shabbos?

" ' Show me the *kedushas haTorah*! Show me how you cannot bear to gaze on something that is not *tznius*, not be able to abide improper speech, improper thoughts — because Torah cannot dwell with *kedushah* one minute, and *tumah* the next!

" '*Mei'eimasai*, Reb Yid! You begin a great journey, may it be with *d'chilu u'rechimu*, two mighty wings of awe and love! May every page of learning ignite like the fire of the *mizbei'ach*, amen!' "

Uri abruptly stopped. He was embarrassed, for he knew that he himself had not fulfilled the mighty words he spoke. But — that was it. That was his whole *pshetl*. He looked down shamefacedly, embarrassed that he could not deliver a real *pilpul*, full of brilliant *kashah*s and profound answers.

But this was his tiny *cheilek* of Torah.

There was a long, profound silence, and Uri finally forced himself to look up. The Head of the Heavenly Court smiled at him.

"Reb Uri! *Yasher koach*. Your *pshetl* was excellent."

Uri shook his head shamefacedly. It could not be!

"Master," he cried, "it was too simple! A child could have said it! You see, I am no *gaon*!"

"Reb Uri," answered the Head of the Court firmly, "there are *geonim* and there are *geonim*. There is a *gaon* in Gemara. There is a *gaon* in Rambam. And there is a *gaon* in *yiras Shamayim*! You are a *gaon* in *yiras Shamayim*, for your *neshamah* spoke, and your words touched every heart! In that merit, may you have children's children who will someday sit in the *Lishkas Hagazis*!"

"Amen," murmured Uri.

There was a great hush, and a Heavenly voice roared forth:

"*Rabbosai*, prepare yourselves! It is time for Reb Uri of Toronto to recite the Great Kaddish!"

Uri opened his Gemara, cleared his throat, and was ready to begin. Klonimos Kalman hurriedly whispered: "Wait, Reb Uri! Everyone must first stand in honor of the Kaddish!"

There was a hush, and a Heavenly voice rang out:

"Our Holy Masters! Reb Uri of Toronto has completed *Shas*, and now he will recite the Great Kaddish! *Amod! Amod! Amod!* Prepare to rise in honor of the Kaddish!

"Holy *Acharonim: Amod! Amod! Amod!*"

There was a great sweep of chairs as all the great scholars of the past five hundred years rose up: the Vilna Gaon and the Chasam Sofer, the Shaagas Aryeh and the Pnei Yehoshua, the Maharshal and the Bach, thousands of *geonim* who labored day and night over Torah — they all stood in readiness.

The voice rang out again:

"Holy *Rishonim: Amod! Amod! Amod!*"

In the echelon above, thousands of *Rishonim* rose: Rif and Rambam, Rashi and Rabbeinu Tam, Rashba, Ritva, and Meiri, and thousands of holy *Rishonim* of the Middle Ages who persevered amidst indescribable waves of hatred and slaughter — they all rose in preparation for Reb Uri's Kaddish.

Again the clarion call:

"Oh, holy *Amora'im: Amod! Amod! Amod!*"

Above, the great file of *Amora'im* arose: Rabbi Yochanan and Reish Lakish, Rav and Shmuel, Rabba and Rav Yosef, Abaye and Rava, and thousands of holy sages who caused the Torah to flourish in Eretz Yisrael and Babylonia under the harshest conditions — they all stood in readiness for Uri!

And again the great shout:

"O holy *Tana'im: Amod! Amod! Amod!*"

The next to highest row stood up: Shmayah and Avtalyon, Hillel and Shammai, Rabban Yochanan ben Zakkai and Rabban Gamliel, Rabbi Akiva and Rabbi Shimon and Rabbi Meir, and thousands of *tana'im* whose holiness was like that of the angels themselves — they stood up for the Great Kaddish.

There was a great, anticipatory hush. Everyone waited expectantly for the last, loftiest Heavenly row to be summoned.

Who can that be? wondered Uri. Higher than the *Amora'im*, higher than the *Tana'im* — gathered in a great assembly right under the legs of the *Kisei HaKavod*. Who?

Everyone waited. All eyes were closed. Every soul in the Heavenly Court swayed with concentration and readiness.

Finally, in a voice so filled with awe it sounded like a whisper, a whisper like a roar, was called out:

"*Kedoshim* of Israel: *Amod! Amod! Amod!*

Rise up, for this Kaddish is in your honor!"

With absolute, holy stillness, the *kedoshim* rose. Oh, how they rose! They rose by the thousands, they rose by the tens of thousands, by the hundreds of thousands, they rose by the millions. *Neshamahs* of innocent men, women, and little children, the *neshamahs* of Auschwitz, the *neshamahs* of Kishinev, the *neshamahs* of Damascus, the *neshamahs* of Lvov and of Uman, the *neshamahs* of Mainz and Worms and Frankfurt, the *neshamahs* of Beitar and Yerushalayim, ancient *neshamahs* and fresh *neshamahs*, those who died by sword and by fire, by gas chambers and by bus bombings – all the *kedoshim* rose! Uri could not gaze upon them for their faces shone *k'zohar harakia mazhirim*, they shone as bright as the sun at noontime! The *kedoshim* stood and waited, the whole Heavenly Court waited for Uri's Great Kaddish.

Klonimos Kalman whispered into Uri's ear. "It is time, Reb Uri!"

Uri raised his Gemara. High above, the little cardinal suddenly flapped its wings and began soaring back and forth in excitement.

"*Yisgadal v'yiskadash shmeih rabba!*"

"Amen!"

In the momentary pause, Uri heard a deep rumble coming from the distance.

"*B'alma d'hu asid l'ischadeta, ul'chya mei'saya, ul'asaka l'chayei alma –*"

Uri paused. The rumbling drew closer. He heard great waters rolling towards him.

Frightened, he raced on:

"*...ul'mivnei karta diYerushaleim, ul'shachleil heichaleih b'gavah, ul'me'ekar pulchana nuchra'ah mei'ara, ul'asavah pulchana d'Shmayah l'asrei –*"

Uri paused and listened. The rumbling grew to a mighty thunder, the waters rushed ever closer...

"*...v'yaztmach purkaneih vikareiv meshichei!*"

"Amen!"

The roaring of the waters became deafening, a huge wall of deep blue waters that swept up to engulf him –

Kol Hashem bakoach! Kol Hashem behadar!

The voice of Hashem is in power!

The voice of Hashem is in majesty!

There was no more time. The mighty waters surrounded him, the great, thundering roar of Hashem's waters! High above, the little bird leaped upwards in fear, its two little, holy wings beating furiously, ascending higher and higher —

"*b'chayeichon uv'yomeichon uv'chayei d'chol beis Yisroel —*"

Uri squeezed his eyes tight with all his might, and screamed out with all his soul:

"*ba'agala u'vizman kariv v'imru —* "

"Abba, wake up!"

Uri sat up with a start. Yirmiyahu was shaking him.

"Abba," he whispered, "it's past seven. You're going to miss minyan!"

Uri blinked, and sat up. His neck was stiff from lying on the Gemara. He looked at his son, dazed.

"What time is?"

"Almost quarter after seven. The sun is long up!"

Uri blinked again and shook himself awake. He sat up straight. "I really fell asleep," he said.

Uri noticed that his son was staring at him strangely.

"What's the matter, Yirmiyahu?"

"Abba, in your sleep —"

"Yes?"

"In your sleep, you were saying Kaddish!"

"I was?"

"Yes. I heard you, the *siyum* Kaddish: *b'alma d'hu asid l'ischadeta.*"

Uri smiled with embarrassment. "I did? I don't remember a thing."

But his son continued to look at him curiously. *Yirmiyahu is too serious*, thought Uri.

Uri bolted up straight. "Come on, Yirmiyahu," he said. "Today's a big day! Let's go!"

Little did Uri know how big it would be!

THIRTEEN

There was a lot to do for the *siyum* and little time to do it.

The *siyum* was called for eleven o'clock sharp in Bookman's law office. Uri had to daven, collect enough Gemaras for everyone, pick up his wife and children, drive downtown, and try to find affordable parking. The twins, Dovid'l and Yisroel, were to meet him downtown, in front of Bookman's building. They promised they would bring two more men for the minyan.

Although it was not his custom, Uri drove to the *mikveh* and immersed himself. This day for him was like *erev Yom Kippur*, a day of holy celebration. Under the water, he prayed that his *siyum* would be accepted in *Shamayim* – and that he would find a good buyer for his house.

He davened at a late minyan and borrowed five Gemaras from the shul. He had two more of his own, and people could share. He drove home; everyone was waiting for him. It was getting late, nearly ten. Bookman did not like anyone to be late for his appointments.

Chaya and the girls climbed into the back seats of the van. Yirmiyahu helped Uri carry the seven Gemaras over and put them in the back. The Gemaras were heavy, but together they set them in place quickly and closed the back door.

"Get in the front seat," Uri told Yirmiyahu.

But Yirmiyahu stayed planted on the street. "Abba, I want to tell you something," he said.

Uri had noticed that Yirmiyahu had been acting strangely this morning. Something was on his mind. Had the Kaddish that he had recited in his sleep disturbed him that much?

Uri glanced at his watch. They still had a few minutes grace. He approached his son.

"What, Yirmiyahu?" he asked.

Yirmiyahu stepped back from the car towards the house, and Uri followed him. Obviously, his son didn't want anyone in the car to hear. Uri became concerned. He lowered his voice and asked in a gentler tone, "What's up, Yirmiyahu?"

Yirmiyahu avoided Uri's gaze. He hesitated for a few moments and then plunged in.

"Abba," Yirmiyahu said. "I've thought about it. I think I should accept the Rosh Yeshivah's offer and learn here in Toronto."

"What?" asked Uri, astonished. "When did this happen?"

Yirmiyahu still avoided looking his father straight in the face.

"I thought about it. It's good for everyone. It'll help the Rosh Yeshivah start his *beis midrash*. I owe him that *hakaras hatov* —"

"And —"

"And...it'll help the family..."

Help the family?

Uri gazed at his son. "Yirmiyahu, why don't you look me in the face?"

Yirmiyahu would not turn his head. Uri cupped his hand under his son's chin and raised Yirmiyahu's face to him. His son had tears in his eyes.

Suddenly, Uri understood everything.

"Yirmiyahu, what do you mean 'help the family'?" Uri asked.

Yirmiyahu caught his breath and wiped a tear away. "Abba, I was selfish! It's too much for you and Imma! You have to support Tova and Dina, and it'll cost you a fortune. I don't want you to sell the house —"

"Who told you we wanted to sell the house?" asked Uri in shock.

Yirmiyahu shook his head. "Abba, don't ask me who! But I know. Don't sell the house, Abba! It your and Imma's home! I can learn Torah in Toronto also."

Uri stared at his son, and his heart swelled with pride and love till he thought it would burst. He put his arm around Yirmiyahu and drew him even further away from the car. Then he spun him around to face him.

"Listen, Yirmiyahu! You are not going to learn here in Toronto! You are going to learn in Reb Chaim's *Kodshim* yeshivah in Yerushalayim. Do you understand?"

Yirmiyahu shook his head, but Uri looked him squarely in the eyes. "Listen: I am the father and you are the son! You listen to me! Whether we sell our house or not is not your business — it's for Imma and me! You will become a *gadol* someday, and we will have that *zechus*! Forget about it! If we have to sell the house for you to learn in Yerushalayim, we'll sell the house! And if I have to sell my car, or my Shabbos tallis, or my shirt — you are going to become everything you can become!"

"Abba —"

"Yirmiyahu," Uri hissed heatedly, "not another word! Wipe your face clean and get into the car. We'll go over my *vort* on the way down!"

They drove down almost in silence. Although Chaya had not heard the conversation, she knew something was afoot. She glanced once at Yirmiyahu when he entered, and then made eye contact with Uri through the rearview mirror. Uri nodded reassuringly.

But soon, nature took its course. Tova and Dina were unstoppable. This was the first time they had all driven downtown in a long time, and they pointed out all the new buildings going up. The girls were animated and excited. Uri wanted to go over his brief *vort* for the *siyum*, but Yirmiyahu was engrossed in a *sefer*, and Uri did not want to interrupt him.

It was getting late, twenty to eleven. Traffic at Bloor Street was blocked by construction, but there was nothing he could do. They soon passed the obstruction and sped on. But where could he find reasonable parking? Uri drove to the front of Bookman's office building. There were just a few parking spaces, and by this time they would be taken. He planned to drop off the women and find parking wherever he could.

But, there was an empty space right in front of Bookman's building. Unbelievable! And then he saw why — Dovid'l and Yisroel had been guarding the space for him. They had parked a bike in a free space, discouraging anyone else from parking there. When they saw the family car, they removed the bike. Uri didn't know how they had gotten downtown so fast, but they had! He hoped they had brought two other men for the minyan. Dovid'l signaled his father, and Uri parked. Yisroel came running with a two-hour parking receipt. What a *kavod*!

The family climbed out of the car. They greeted each other happily on the eve of this holy ceremony.

"Chaya, you go up with the girls, and we'll bring up the Gemaras."

But Tova and Dina had disappeared down the street towards another car. Uri watched them with interest. Did they have friends there? In a moment, two men emerged from the car and came running to greet them. Uri stared in disbelief. It was Zerach and Avraham! The girls walked proudly back down the street with their *chassanim*, and approached Uri.

Uri recovered from his shock and smiled. "Zerach! Avraham! What are you doing here?"

"We came for your *siyum*," Zerach said. "We wouldn't miss it!"

Uri looked at his daughters, at his wife, at his children. "Did you know they were coming?" he asked.

Everyone seemed to have known except Yirmiyahu and he. Uri was overwhelmed. He hugged his future sons-in-law, and beamed with sheer pleasure.

"What can I say!" he said over and over. "What can I say!"

Uri glanced at the round street clock overhead. "It's eight minutes to eleven. It's getting late. We have to bring up the Gemaras!"

Carrying platters of cakes and cookies, Chaya and the girls had already disappeared into the building. Zerach and Avraham each grabbed a few of the heavy Gemaras and began walking inside. Uri stood free like a king.

Avraham entered the building, Yirmiyahu at his side. Zerach deliberately fell behind. When everyone else had disappeared, Zerach suddenly paused.

"Rabbi Schiffman," he said, "can...can I talk to you for a moment?" his face was very solemn.

Concerned by his demeanor, Uri stopped short. Uri pulled Zerach to the side of the entrance.

"What is it, Zerach?" he asked, a surge of fatherly love rushing through him.

Zerach cleared his throat and lowered his voice. "Rabbi Schiffman, I have to tell you something. But it had to be just between us. I don't want anyone to know – especially not Avraham."

Uri looked at him, now very concerned. "I give my word," he said.

"Rabbi Schiffman, when we worked out the details of our *shidduch*, it was agreed that you would support Tova and me for seven years in Eretz Yisrael –"

"Yes."

"That was worked out by my parents. But...but it's not fair to you! It's too much – you can't afford it! Tova and I spoke about it all last night. We are releasing you from your agreement! If you can help us for a year, maybe a little longer – that is plenty! We know that you promised Avraham and Dina what you promised us. Use your money to help them!"

Uri looked at his future son-in-law. He wanted to hug him, but he restrained himself.

"Zerach," he answered, "my wife and I have found the money to support both you and Avraham. Please, don't worry!"

"You mean you're going to sell your house?"

Uri looked at Zerach in shock. "Who told you that?" he asked.

Zerach didn't answer.

"We can't let you do that. You and your wife are the best father- and mother-in-law that I could ever want. Tova is my *bashert*! Please, Rabbi Schiffman — one year, a year and half — is plenty."

Uri looked up at the clock.

"Zerach, I have no time to talk. But listen, the answer is no! Hashem sent me a gift of such a wonderful *ben Torah* like you, and I have the *zechus* of helping you learn in Eretz Yisrael! You won't take that away!"

Zerach wanted to argue, but Uri cut him short.

"Come," he said, "they're waiting for us upstairs! Bookman's time is valuable. Let's go, Zerach!"

That was the end of the conversation.

Like a man who had just been bestowed with a bouquet of roses, Uri rode the mirrored elevator up to the thirty-second floor. Zerach stood silently beside him. Uri saw himself in the mirror — *boy, do I look scruffy! But boy, did Hashem give me a son-in-law who I could be proud of before the world!*

They exited the elevator on the thirty-second story. Bookman and Bookman offices took up the whole floor. There was a long hallway to the glassed entrance of the law office. Uri and Zerach had almost reached the doorway when Avraham intercepted them in the hallway. He still held the Gemaras.

He turned to Zerach.

"Zerach, they're waiting for us inside. Please take my Gemaras, I just have to do something in the hallway for a moment."

He piled his three Gemaras on Zerach, held the heavy glass door open for him and Zerach disappeared. Uri was about to follow, but Avraham put his hand out.

"Rabbi Schiffman, before you go to the *siyum*, could I talk to you for just a second?" he asked.

Uri checked his watch. There was still a few minutes. But it didn't matter — if Avraham wanted to talk to him, he had to listen. He walked Avraham back down the hallway towards the elevator, and they rounded a corner for privacy.

Uri was having a busy day. Everyone wanted to talk to him. Avraham looked nervous. Everyone looked nervous – except Uri.

Uri smiled reassuringly. "What is it, Avraham?"

It was strange talking to Avraham – it was just like talking to Zerach, they looked so much alike.

"I...I want to tell you something," Avraham began, "but it must stay just between us. I don't want Zerach to know anything about it."

"Yes, Avraham – it will stay between us."

"Rabbi Schiffman, when my family agreed to the *shidduch*, they set conditions that you would support Dina and me for seven years in Eretz Yisrael – is that right?"

"Yes."

Avraham cleared his throat.

"Dina and I talked it over for a long time last night. It is too much to ask of you and Mrs. Schiffman! You have too many obligations already! You and your wife are the best father- and mother-in-law that I could ever ask for, and Dina and I feel like we knew each other from the day we were born! If I were offered any other *kallah* in the world I could never accept – Dina is my *neshamah*!

"You promised Zerach and Tova seven years first, and we came along after! They come first. Please, use your money to help them. For Dina and me, whatever you can do – a year, two years – it'll be enough."

Uri gazed warmly at his beautiful, *ehrlich* future son-in-law. What was going on here?

"Avraham, why are you and Dina so worried? My wife and I have worked it all out! There'll be enough money for both Zerach and you to learn in Yerushalayim as long as you want. Don't worry!"

"But you're going to sell your house to support us!" Avraham said, "It's too much to ask!"

Uri threw up his arms in exasperation. "Is it in the *Globe* and the *Mail*?" he cried. "How does everyone know that we are going to sell our house?"

How do they know? wondered Uri. *How do they all know?*

Uri lowered his voice and spoke firmly. "Avraham, you are a wonderful young man! My wife and I dreamed of the day that we could marry off our daughters to real *bnei Torah* who would sit and learn and become great *talmidei chachamim*. And here you and Zerach are! Listen – clear! Not only will I sell my house, I will sell my shirt. I will sell my car. I will sell my lawnmower. I will sell myself into seven years *avdus* for the *zechus* of supporting you and Zerach in Torah!"

"But –"

Uri placed his hands firmly on Avraham's shoulders. "Reb Avraham, do you want me to miss my own *siyum*? Come, let's go! *Schnell!*"

He grabbed Avraham by the arm and dragged him back down the hallway to Bookman's offices. Dovid'l and Yisroel were there standing outside the entrance, looking for him.

"You see," he said. "We're late."

Uri strode quickly to the entrance. "Are they all there yet?" he asked.

"Mr. Bookman says he'll be a few minutes late," they answered. "Reb Klonimos is here – and Uncle Alexander and Uncle Solomon."

Uri opened the heavy glass doors for Avraham, but Dovid'l and Yisroel suddenly stepped forward.

"Abba," Dovid'l said. "Could we speak to you –"

Avraham paused in the open doorway. Dovid'l looked at him. "Just alone, for a minute."

Avraham understood, and stepped inside the office. Uri, curious what these two wanted now, walked down with them to the far end of the hall, out of sight of the entrance.

"What is it boys?" he asked.

"Abba," said Yisroel. "We have something for you."

Yisroel took out an envelope from his jacket and handed it to his father. Uri looked at the envelope and then at his boys.

"What is this?" he asked.

"Abba," said Dovid'l. "We decided to take the money from our bar mitzvah account and give it to you and Imma to help pay for Tova and Dina –"

"Help pay for them?"

"Yes. They are going to learn in Eretz Yisrael for seven years, and it's going to be very hard for you. We want to help out."

Uri looked at his sons. "How much is in here?"

The boys looked at each other.

"Four hundred dollars —" said Yisroel.

"Four hundred dollars?" said Uri. "That's the whole account!"

"We want you to have it," said Dovid'l. "We don't want you and Imma to have to sell the house!"

Uri looked at his sons. They were still his unstoppable, irrepressible twins. This was all the money they had!

"Will you take it, Abba?" Dovid'l asked.

Uri looked from one to the other.

"Yes — I will take it. *Yasher koach!*"

And then, with great formality, he shook hands with them both.

"Come," he whispered, "come boys, let's to go to the *siyum* — "

They entered Bookman's elegant office suite. The receptionist immediately rose to greet them.

"Rabbi Schiffman?" she asked. "They're all in the boardroom waiting for you. Mr. Bookman is delayed a few minutes, but you can go right in. I believe you know where it is."

Even so, she led Uri and the twins through the long carpeted hallway, past a gallery of precious works of art, into the inner recesses of Bookman and Bookman.

Uri suddenly paused. "Boys, go ahead to the boardroom. Tell them I'll be a few minutes."

He turned to the young woman.

"If you don't mind, this is a very special time. I want to be alone for a few minutes before I enter the boardroom. Is there a private room I can use?"

She hesitated for an instant, gave him a curious look, and then recovered.

"Certainly, Rabbi! You can use any of the conference rooms along the corridor. I don't believe there are any meetings going on now."

He thanked her, and she returned to the front desk. Uri was blessedly alone. He opened the first door to the right and peered in. To his surprise, two nurses sat there, guarding an oxygen tank equipped with a breathing mask.

He immediately thought of Edwin Bookman and grew concerned.

"Is everything all right?" he asked worriedly.

But the nurses smiled cheerfully.

"Oh, everything is fine," they answered. "We're here just in case someone needs help."

Uri closed the door and shook his head in wonder. He knew that Bookman and Bookman was high powered, but to have nurses on call seemed a bit much.

But Uri had his own agenda. He walked quickly to the next door and opened it. The room was empty. Good! Uri quickly closed the door behind him and locked it. A tall, deep-set window looked down on University Avenue.

Uri stood by the window, gazed into the brilliant morning sky, and closed his eyes.

"*Ribbono shel Olam*, we are alone just for a few minutes. What can I say and what words can I find? How can I thank You for Your kindness to me? Look what happened today! All of them, all of them: Yirmiyahu, Zerach, Avraham, even Dovid'l and Yisroel — they showed how much goodness flows in their veins! Yirmiyahu was willing to sacrifice his Yerushalayim yeshivah! He so much wants to learn there! Zerach and Avraham fought so that we should have enough money for the other one!"

Uri reached into his jacket, took out Dovid'l and Yisroel's envelope, and waved it in front of him.

"Look, *Ribbono shel Olam, habeit ur'ei!* Look at the money that Dovid'l and Yisroel gave me — it was all they had! Just so that Chaya and I would not have to sell our home!"

Uri lifted his voice in prayer: "It is all in Your hands, Hashem! I give up! You are the Boss! If You want us to sell our house to support our children, we are ready! If you have a different way, we are also ready! I surrender — You are in charge!"

He lifted Dovid'l and Yisroel's envelope over his head, like he was waving *kapparos* money.

"For here, *Ribbono shel Olam*, here inside this envelope is the manna, the manna you give us every day, *b'yodin u'vlo yodin*, whether we see it or not! And here," he ran his fingers over the crumpled envelope, "is the *tzintzenes* in which everything is hidden and disguised. But it is all from You, Hashem, every penny, every drop of *parnasah* — it is manna that has fallen from the holy *shechakim!*"

Uri paused, took a deep breath, and *shuckl*ed with all his might.

"Hashem, as the prophet Elisha commanded the poor widow to take a little bit of oil, and it turned into a fountain that filled jug after jug — for Your way is to bestow *yeish mei'yeish*, something from something — so may Dovid'l and Yisroel's money be the *yeish mei'yeish* from which *parnasah* flows to us like a fountain!

"But if it be Your will that Chaya and I struggle in poverty for the rest of our lives to help our children in Torah, then we accept Your will with *simchah!*"

There was a knock on the door. "Abba, everyone is waiting!" It was Dovid'l.

"Tell them sixty seconds!" he called.

Uri took a deep breath, opened his eyes, and wiped his face dry. He slipped the boys' crumpled envelope into his jacket pocket and, thus fortified, prepared to begin the *siyum*.

Uri opened the mighty boardroom door and shyly stepped in. Immediately, everyone rose. Uri was overwhelmed by this show of respect. His whole world — the world who mattered — was there. Edwin Bookman stood at the head of the long boardroom table, with Reb Klonimos Kalman at his side. On one side was Yirmiyahu, standing alongside Dovid'l and Yisroel. Across from them stood Alexander and Solomon, and next to them his future sons-in-law, Zerach and Avraham. The women — Chaya, Tova and Dina, his sisters-in-law, Ruby and Zahava, stood at a tastefully appointed table that had been prepared for them.

Uri smiled, embarrassed at the honor paid him, and shook his head.

"No, no," he mumbled, "don't stand up. Please —"

"Rabbi Schiffman," began Edwin Bookman, "welcome to your own *siyum*. Zeideh Elijah would be proud of this day. We set up washing stations, so let's get right to it if you don't mind!"

The boardroom table was covered with trays of food: rolls, bagels, cakes, all types of lox and fish salads. Everyone washed for the meal. A place had been reserved for Uri between Yirmiyahu and Reb Klonimos. Uri washed and took his place of honor.

Uri ate half a roll, put a spoonful of tuna fish on his plate to be polite, but he had no appetite. This was not a party. It was a *siyum*, a *siyum* that was being held in one of the most powerful law offices in Canada. This was the room where million dollar deals were sealed, where people spoke in hushed, refined, respectful tones. He was excited and nervous. Even as everyone ate, there was a deferential silence, a respect for the place and the moment.

Uri glanced furtively at his brothers, Alexander and Solomon. He had greeted them briefly when he entered, but now he studied them more closely. Poor Alexander and Solomon — they looked so down! This room must conjure up sad memories for them. They had once walked out of this room instant millionaires, whooping and high-fiving. Now it was all gone. All three brothers were the same now, in the same league, except that Uri had the whole Talmud Bavli under his belt — and they, sadly, had nothing but the *Financial Post*.

He watched Chaya interact awkwardly with her sisters-in-law. They hardly spoke. Ruby chewed silently, while Zahava looked straight ahead, distant and uncomfortable. Even Tova and Dina were subdued and spoke hardly above whispers. Only Reb Klonimos brought some life to the meal, making conversation with Bookman, congratulating Uri, talking briefly to his sons-in-law in learning. Uri realized that the relationship between Edwin Bookman and Reb Klonimos was much closer than he had thought. They made an odd couple — the worldly Bookman and the utterly unworldly Reb Klonimos — but Zeideh had somehow bonded them together.

In less than fifteen minutes, the meal was over. It was time to begin the *siyum*. The waiters silently removed the dishes, poured fresh coffee, and disappeared. Yirmiyahu and the boys brought over the Gemaras that had been piled on a side table and laid them open before the participants. Bookman and Klonimos shared one Gemara, Uri used the volume of Zeideh's *Shas*, while Zerach and Avraham switched seats to share with Alexander and Solomon and help them follow. The final page had been set off with bookmarks, and everyone soon found the *daf*. All eyes were on Uri.

Uri became very emotional. His hands trembled, and his voice caught. All he really had to do was recite a few words, complete three familiar lines, and recite the final *Hadran*. But the awesomeness of the moment suddenly overwhelmed him like a great flood, so that he could hardly speak. Zeideh's presence was watching over him — he felt it. He tried a few times to begin, but his voice caught. He couldn't speak. Reb Klonimos bent over and murmured.

"Take your time, Reb Uri. Everyone understands."

Uri looked around at the group. He had no reason to be afraid or embarrassed. They were all his family. He glanced at his brothers, who watched him with envy. They had never been close, but they were still his brothers. Bookman was like a father, Reb Klonimos was his precious rebbi, the children were his children...and Chaya was his life.

Get a hold of yourself, Uri, he whispered to himself angrily. *You're worried about money — that's why you are really nervous! Bitachon, Uri, bitachon! Hashem will help!*

For, in truth, money was his greatest worry. He was shaking from worry. He had everything: the *siyum*, the children, his wife, he just needed a little oil, a *sach shemen*, to land his plane safely. But he had a secret weapon that no one knew. He pressed his hand against his jacket and felt the little bump made by the envelope the boys had given him.

Yeish mei'yeish! Yeish mei'yeish! Yeish mei'yeish! Hashem — You can do anything!

Uri took a deep breath, sat up straight, and spoke determinedly.

"Rabbi Klonimos, Mr. Bookman, my brothers Alexander and Solomon and their wives, my beloved children, and above all, my partner in this *siyum*, Chaya.

"I thank Hashem that I have reached this point after seven years of difficult study, many of them with Yirmiyahu. It has been very hard. Gemara is hard, and I just scratched the surface. But when you scratch a golden surface, even what sticks under your nails is gold —"

He heard Solomon groan. "Er, sorry, Solomon," he apologized.

"But I persevered, because Zeideh's *neshamah* was always near, because all this learning was in his honor. As you all know, when his will was read eight years ago, I was left very little money. But Zeideh left me something even greater, for I have inherited his *Shas*, and I have finished it, as best as I could...

"Please follow, three lines from the bottom:

" '*Tana dvei Eliyahu*:

" 'Whoever learns halachos every day is assured a place in the World to Come. For it is written "*Halichos olam lo* – The ways of the world are His." Do not read *halichos* but *halachos*, for he who studies Torah law every day is guaranteed a place in the World to Come.' So ends the Talmud — with those words."

Uri lay down his Gemara and looked up.

"What does the Talmud mean by those few final words? Why does *Shas* end this way? For nothing in this world is permanent. Wealth comes, and wealth goes!"

Alexander and Solomon nodded sadly in agreement.

"And even if it does not go, then it is inherited by another — so what gain is there for the person who has toiled for it all his life? What does he have from it? It's all left to others! But *halachos – olam lo*! When a person studies Torah, it belongs to him — himself — *lo*! It adheres to his *neshamah* like glue, it never abandons him! For his Torah becomes a *chuppah* of fire in the Next World! It becomes the food and drink of his *neshamah*."

Uri paused and reflected. "Somehow, in his old age, Zeideh Elijah became a *talmid chacham*. I don't know how, I don't know why."

Uri looked to Bookman and Reb Klonimos as though hoping for an answer, but they just looked down, listening.

"I am sorry that Zeideh became so very serious in his last years — but he left this world full of Torah!

"On this, his eighth *yahrtzeit*, I am grateful to Hashem that I was able to fulfill his wish that I complete *Shas*. I thank Mr. Bookman for taking the time to present me personally with each volume, I thank Yirmiyahu for being my *chavrusa*, and, above all, I thank my wife, Chaya, for without her encouragement it would not have been possible."

Uri lifted his Gemara.

"Now, with Mr. Bookman's permission, I will recite the final *Hadran*!"

Uri rose, and everyone rose with him. Uri shook his head.

"No, no. Not yet! You can stay seated until the Kaddish."

There was a sigh of relief, and almost everyone sat down. Just Yirmiyahu, Dovid'l, Yisroel, Zerach, and Avraham remained standing in their father's honor.

Uri began the *Hadran*:

"We shall return to you, Talmud Bavli, and you shall return to us... We will not forget you, Talmud Bavli, and you will not forget us..."

Uri paused, took a deep breath, and rattled off the names of Papa's sons —

"Chanina bar Papa, Rami bar Papa, Nachman bar Papa Achai bar Papa, Abba Mori bar Papa, Rafram bar Papa, Rachish bar Papa, Surchav bar Papa, Ada bar Papa, Daru bar Papa..."

He stopped, caught his breath, and smiled. *Why do we mention them?* he wondered.

But there was no time to linger — everyone was waiting. "May we all, our offspring, and the offspring of your people, the House of Israel, know Your name and study Your Torah!

"We thank You O Hashem! For we rise early and they rise early — we rise early for words of Torah, and they rise early for idle matters!...

"*Va'ani evtach bach* — but I will trust in You!"

Uri paused and lowered his Gemara. Reb Klonimos was already on his feet, and the others quickly followed. Uri strode from the table, approached the boardroom window, and turned to face Jerusalem. He pressed his head against the heavy, maroon drapery, and began the final — final — *siyum* Kaddish, on this, the eighth *yahrtzeit* of his beloved Zeideh, Eliyahu ben Elazar...

"*Yisgadal v'yiskadash shmeih rabba* — May His great name be exalted and sanctified!

"*B'alma d'hu asid l'ischadeta* — In the world that will be renewed...and He will revive the dead and raise them up to eternal life... And rebuild the city of Jerusalem and complete His Temple within it —

"*B'chayeichon uv'yomeichon uv'chayei d'chol beis Yisrael — ba'agalah u'vizman kariv v'imru Amen!*"

The minyan in Bookman's office responded quietly:

"*Y'hei shmeih rabba mevorach l'olam ul'olmei olmaya* —"

This was it!

This was what the Heavenly Court was waiting for!

Not Uri's Kaddish in *Shamayim*, for Heaven is full of perfect praises, day and night! *Cherubim, Seraphim, Ophanim, Chayos Hakodesh!*

Asher ometz tehilasecha!

For Hashem's praise is given by Heavenly angels! By beings that glow like lightning! By lofty bands! By flaming legions! By those whose names are unknowable! By myriads of chariots!

V'ratzisa shevach!

But Hashem desires praise from below, from the hidden Jewish spark, the Yoseph HaTzaddik who descends into *olam hazeh*, a world of veils and curtains and masks, of infinite temptations and distractions...

For the *neshamah* was sworn:

"*Tehi tzaddik v'al tehi rasha!*"

"Thou shalt be righteous, and not wicked!"

— This was it!

This is what the Heavenly Court so longed for! A *neshamah* that remained faithful to its oath! To Torah! To mitzvahs! To *chesed*! To *shemiras ha'einayim*! To *bitachon* and *emunah*! To *kedushah v'taharah*!

For the *neshamah* was commanded:

"*SheHaKadosh Baruch Hu tahor, u'mesharsav tehorim, u'neshamah shenasan becha tehorah hi* – The Holy One is pure, and his servants are pure – and you, beautiful *neshamah*, you are pure!"

A great cry resounded in the Heavenly Court:

"*Amod! Amod! Amod!*"

All the glorious ranks of *Rishonim* and *Acharonim*, of *Tana'im* and *Amora'im*, of tzaddikim and *geonim*, the infinite legions of holy martyrs of Israel, *kedoshim* whose faces flamed *k'zohar harakia* – they all rose for Reb Uri's Kaddish!

The roar of the mighty waters grew louder –

Kol Hashem al hamayim...Keil Hakavod hir'im Hashem al mayim rabbim!

The voice of Hashem is upon the waters! The G-d of Glory thunders, Hashem is upon mighty waters!

The holiness of Uri's Kaddish flooded the darkest channels of the earth, it washed up in foaming waves of holiness to the very feet of the Heavenly throne...

Heaven waited, breathless.

The Kaddish of Reb Uri of Toronto!

There was a great silence.

There was a terrible shaking.

And then – from every voice in *Shamayim* rose a mighty chorus...

"*Y'hei shmeih rabba mevarach l'olam ul'olmei olmayah!*"

Uri stepped back slowly, bowed left and right, and completed:

"*Oseh shalom bimromav, hu ya'aseh shalom aleinu v'al kol Yisrael v'imru amen.*"

He turned around, almost shyly. That was it. He crossed the goal line. He did it all. He learned the whole *Shas*. He had said the final Kaddish for Zeideh. He sought out Chaya, and their eyes met knowingly. Her eyes glowed with pride, and she smiled to him. This was her *siyum* too!

The moment of calm lasted just a few seconds. In a flash, everyone left his place and surrounded Uri to wish him *mazel tov*. Reb Klonimos hugged him tightly and kissed his cheek. Bookman was more reserved but equally impressed. He shook Uri's hand firmly, and whispered:

"I am very proud of you Rabbi Schiffman — the Captain would have been overjoyed."

Yirmiyahu shook his father's hand formally, and gave him an embarrassed half hug. Dovid'l and Yisroel danced around their father proudly, while both Zerach and Avraham squeezed their future father-in-law so fiercely that he could hardly breathe. Only Alexander and Solomon held back. They didn't seem to know what to do. They approached Uri but stood at a distance, letting the others draw close. Uri broke free, approached his brothers, and hugged them both warmly:

"It means so much that you are here!" he whispered to them.

Suddenly, Edwin Bookman, who had seated himself once more in his chair, rapped his glass sharply on the table.

"Ladies and gentlemen, I congratulate Rabbi Schiffman on his great achievement. But it is getting late, and we still have legal business to conduct. I ask you all to please be seated, and we'll finish the ceremony!"

There was a short debate as to who would lead the *bentching*. Uri wanted to give the honor to Reb Klonimos. Reb Klonimos at first refused to accept, but Uri was adamant.

"Reb Klonimos, if it was not for your encouragement, none of this would have happened!" he insisted. There was a brief standoff. Reb Klonimos pushed the wine to Uri, Uri pushed it back. Everyone waited. Bookman glanced up at the clock. Uri absolutely refused.

Reb Klonimos sighed, saw that it was getting late and Bookman was growing impatient, and gave in. He led the *Birkas HaMazon* with great fervor, closing his eyes throughout. Even Alexander and Solomon fell into the earnest mood.

The Grace ended, the Gemaras were removed, and again the room took on the appearance for which it was designed — the prestigious executive boardroom of Bookman and Bookman. The time was exactly twelve noon — the whole *siyum* had taken less than an hour.

Up to now, Edwin Bookman had been reserved but informal. But now, Bookman turned completely businesslike. He called for order.

"Ladies and gentlemen, as you know, we came here to observe Captain Elijah Schiffman's *yahrtzeit* and the completion of the Talmud. But as I mentioned to you, and especially to Alexander and Solomon in our correspondence, there were still a few matters regarding Captain Elijah's will that had to be disposed of, and we will proceed to that now."

He signaled to one of his assistants, and a young lawyer entered from the side door, carrying a thin folder. He laid it in front of Bookman. Bookman opened the folder, adjusted his reading glasses and studied the fine sheet in front of him. Then he cleared his throat and looked up to the group. Before he began speaking, he called the younger lawyer and whispered something in his ear. The lawyer nodded. Satisfied, Bookman turned to the gathering.

"As you all know, we all met here more than seven years ago to hear the reading of Captain Elijah Schiffman's will. At that time, I informed you that the will had been almost totally executed, with but one item still to be disposed of. As Captain Elijah's attorney and trustee, and according to his wishes, I will execute that one final matter now."

He looked down and wiped his glasses. In the pause, Uri leaned over to Yirmiyahu: "I bet Zeideh left a set of *Shulchan Aruch* that he wants me to learn."

"I wish," whispered Yirmiyahu.

Bookman put back his glasses, gazed sternly around the room, and began reading:

"I, Elijah Schiffman, have already disposed of the vast bulk of my possessions, assigning each to my grandchildren. I awarded the great house to Alexander —"

Bookman gazed at Alexander. Alexander's head was bowed, and he stared glumly at the table. The house was gone.

"I bestowed my beloved *Swift Current* to Solomon —"

Solomon looked down morosely. He sighed.

"And I left my beloved youngest grandson, Eerie, who dedicated himself to Torah study, a hundred thousand shares of Gortel.

"Unfortunately, the Gortel shares collapsed before my eyes — but that was the Almighty's judgment, and we have no say in what happens whatsoever. The Almighty rules all things, takes and gives as He determines — we are helpless. To help comfort Eerie from his terrible loss, I shared with him my precious set of Talmud, with all my penned commentaries. I also gave him my notebooks on *Zevachim* and *Menachos*, which were very precious to me, for I struggled over them even into the small hours of the morning.

"If the Almighty is kind to my poor soul, and things have proceeded as I wished, you should be gathered now in Edwin Bookman's office at about twelve noon of my eighth *yahrtzeit*."

Everyone looked up at the clock. How did he do it?! After eight years, Zeideh hit it almost perfect — it was just ten minutes past noon!

Bookman scanned the paper. He frowned as though he did not want to read the next lines. But he controlled himself, looked up briefly, and read the next lines in a hurried, businesslike manner:

"Edwin Bookman was like a brother to me, just as Rav Klonimos was my Rabbi. Those two speak for me. Their words are my word, and I do not envy anyone who will challenge this will — or their instructions!"

Bookman read through the words of praise quickly. He seemed relieved to have read them. He took a sip of water and lifted the sheet. All eyes were glued on him. Uri glanced over to Chaya. He whispered silently: "Thank you, best wife!" She smiled back discretely.

"And so, to complete the assigning of my property, I bestow upon my grandson, Eerie Schiffman, the one item that has not been disposed of.

"I bestow upon Eerie Schiffman, my boat — *Deep Blue*."

A profound silence descended upon the room. Uri frowned, and sat, absolutely fixed. He did not hear what Bookman said, his heart rejected it.

Bookman waited, watching Uri with concern. No one spoke. The silence was broken — by Solomon. He raised his head.

"What?" he cried. "What?"

But in his shock, Solomon's voice rose, high-pitched and dry, so that it sounded more like a quack.

"What? What?" he repeated.

Bookman smiled to himself ever so slightly.

"I shall read this line of the will again: I bestow upon my grandson, Eerie Schiffman, the one item that has not been disposed of. I bestow upon Eerie Schiffman, my boat — *Deep Blue*!"

Alexander stood up angrily. "But that's...crazy!" he shouted.

Bookman stared him down. "Alexander, I would appreciate it if you calmed down. What is crazy?"

"*Deep Blue* was Zeideh's fiercest competitor!" shouted Alexander.

Bookman nodded. "Yes, you are absolutely correct! *Deep Blue* was Zeideh's fiercest competitor and rival!"

"So, so what does it mean, 'my boat — *Deep Blue*?' "

The angrier Alexander grew, the calmer Bookman spoke.

"Alexander, if you sit down, I will explain everything."

Alexander finally sat down. Bookman removed his glasses.

"You see, Captain Elijah owned *Swift Current*. He also owned *Deep Blue*!"

"You mean he bought them out?"

"No, he built *Deep Blue* himself!"

"What?" asked Solomon. "What?"

Bookman waited for Solomon to quiet down.

"It was all Zeideh's brilliant scheme — the greatest publicity scheme he ever dreamed up! He decided to compete against himself — create a real fight! Like Toronto versus Montreal, Edmonton versus Calgary! He built *Deep Blue* to challenge *Swift Current*! Elijah Schiffman built *Deep Blue*! He designed it, he even chose the blue colors! He found Captain Vanderlerner and hired him because he was the exact opposite of himself! What a contrast — little Elijah Schiffman versus, tall, handsome, strong and silent Captain Vanderlerner! Captain Elijah planned the challenge race to Niagara! Don't you remember how the whole country was caught up in it — like the World Series? It was worth millions in free publicity and revenues!"

Alexander stared at Bookman, flabbergasted. He still could not believe it.

"But he lost, Edwin, he lost to *Deep Blue*! Everyone laughed at him."

"Ha!" Bookman's voice rose. "Whom did he lose to? He lost to himself — so he really won, right? You're right, everyone laughed at him." Bookman's voice dropped to a confidential whisper. "But he was laughing harder at them! They were all fooled! The clever media! The talk show hosts! The whole world — the whole world was fooled! Only the Captain, Rabbi Klonimos, and I knew! And that, ladies and gentleman, is the whole story!"

But poor Solomon was still in shock.

"What?" he repeated over and over. "What? What? What?"

Alexander turned and shouted angrily at his poor brother.

"Solomon, would you please stop quacking like a duck!"

Solomon broke out of his stupor. He suddenly jumped up.

"That means...that means that Uri now owns *Deep Blue* and *Swift Current* —"

Ruby, who had been stonily silent the whole morning, suddenly stood rose up, angrily.

"And now he owns the great house, also."

Zahava rose next. She pointed an accusing finger at Uri like Madame Lafarge at the guillotine, and shouted:

"Uri — Uri — he owns everything!"

All eyes turned on Uri. His head had fallen to the table and he buried his face in his arms. The young lawyer walked up quickly to him and whispered with concern. "We have nurses on standby. Do you need oxygen?"

Uri, still bent over, shook his head. Finally he raised his head, finishing the last line of *Mizmor l'Sodah*.

"*Ki tov Hashem l'olam chasdo*... For Hashem is good, His kindness is forever, from generation to generation is His faithfulness..."

He sat up and looked towards Chaya. She was crying in Tova's arms.

Edwin Bookman turned to Uri. "Rabbi Schiffman, is there anything you want to say?"

Uri looked down, a deep frown on his face. If one did not know, one would have thought by Uri's countenance that he had just lost a fortune, not acquired one! He looked over to his brothers, and spoke softly.

"Alexander, Solomon — I can't talk. I don't know what happened here. I don't know. But if it is really true, if it is true that I have suddenly acquired wealth, I will not let you down! You will share in it also, I promise! If I am okay, then you will be okay... We will all be okay! We will all be okay! We will all be okay!"

Reb Klonimos reached over and laid his hand on Uri's, to calm him. "Easy, Reb Uri, easy," he murmured, "everything is okay."

Uri looked down, shook his head and tried to understand: *Why has Hashem done this to me?*

Bookman rapped for attention. He closed the file and he spoke extemporaneously.

"Yes, ladies and gentlemen, it is all true! I know it is hard to comprehend, but Captain Elijah was a genius! A promotional genius! He led the country by the nose!"

Bookman reopened the file, took out a second sheet, and coughed significantly.

"The appraisal of Rabbi Schiffman's inheritance has not yet been completed. There is a question of depreciation on one side, and eight years' accumulated revenues by *Deep Blue* on the other. However, a very broad, conservative estimate of these assets: *Deep Blue* and *Swift Current*, the docks and surrounding port lands, the great house, plus various accumulated revenues from other sources belonging to the *Deep Blue* Corporation — the best low end, conservative estimate is that Captain Elijah's bequest is worth between two hundred and three hundred million dollars. It will take a few more months to reach a more exact figure."

He turned to Uri and broke into a broad smile. "*Mazel tov*, Rabbi Schiffman!" he said. "You are a very, very rich man!"

Uri looked at Chaya. Her face was tearstained, but she was smiling happily. It was unbelievable, unbelievable! He reached into his jacket to find a tissue to wipe his face, and his hand brushed the boys' envelope of money tucked away in his pocket.

"Hashem," he whispered, "Hashem, this is Your doing! Your doing, nothing else!"

Bookman looked up at the clock. It was late. He closed the file firmly and prepared to end the meeting. Reb Klonimos leaned over to him, whispered something, and Bookman nodded in agreement. The lawyer tapped on his glass. Everyone looked up.

Mr. Bookman nodded at Reb Klonimos, who began speaking.

"I will hold you just for five more minutes.

"Mr. Bookman told you the story of Captain Elijah and *Deep Blue*, and all he said was a hundred percent correct. *Deep Blue* was a wonderful means to generate excitement, and it reaped millions!"

He turned to Bookman.

"But, that is not the whole story, Edwin, or even the main story! There is another story hidden here."

Bookman frowned in surprise. He bowed his head, listening intently.

Klonimos continued: "The idea for *Deep Blue* came one evening from a piece of Gemara that Captain Elijah and I studied at the end of the tiny tractate — *Horayos*.

"The Gemara asked: '*Rabbi Zeira charif u'maksheh. Rabbah bar Rav masun u'masik. Mai? Teiku!*

" 'Rabbi Zeira is sharp and asks profound questions, while Rabbah bar Rav is slower and more deliberate, but produces clear answers. Who stands first?' And the Gemara responds: '*Teiku!* — Let it stand!'

" 'What is "*Teiku*"?' Captain Elijah asked.

"I gave him the traditional answer: When the Talmud does not have an answer, it declares: *Teiku: Tishbi yetareitz kushiyos u'ba'ayos* — Elijah the Tishbite will answer doubts and questions!'

"But the Captain was not satisfied. 'I am also named Elijah,' he insisted, 'so I can also answer!'

"And you know, he was right. A person's name is a prophecy, for it reveals the spark of his soul. So I said: 'Go ahead, find us the answer!'

"To me, that was it — but not to the Captain. It bothered him more than I knew. He thought about it, and came up with an idea. He already owned *Swift Current*, a boat that was sharp and quick like Rabbi Zeira. Now he would build himself another boat that was deep, heavy, and more deliberate — like Rabbah bar Rav. He even had it painted with all shades of blue, blues upon deeper blues, to symbolize learning upon deeper learning, *iyun* and *amkus*! And then he gave *Deep Blue* two great snow-white sails, like two sides of a *daf*, *amud alef* and *amud beis*..."

Uri raised his hand like a child in class. "Reb Klonimos, my holy teacher — you must be making this up, aren't you?"

Reb Klonimos smiled.

"Reb Uri, *chas v'shalom*! *Deep Blue* is your boat now — don't you want to know about your own boat?"

Reb Klonimos turned to Bookman. "So, Edwin, you were correct! Captain Elijah did have business on his mind. He intended the great race from the start — to generate excitement! But in his heart it was a different race, a race with himself. What was better, to learn fast, *schneller*, page after page without stopping, without reviewing, as he had been doing, or to be slower, deliberate, delve deeper...

"And so...came the great race... What a race! What a wild, frightening race! The Captain told me that he pushed *Swift Current* full engine straight ahead despite the terrible lashing! Wave after giant wave shattered against the boat. The lake churned like a boiling kettle, and he saw his whole life and all his learning rise like a great wall before him! But still he leaped ahead! Because that had been his whole life of learning — *daf* after *daf*, always next page, next page, next page! He sailed *Swift Current* over every monster wave, just to steam ahead, just to finish first!

"And he thought he won!

"His *Swift Current* reached port first, way ahead! But then he realized — he had missed his whole mark! He wasn't even near! He had missed the port, the town — even the whole country! He had rushed ahead just to err all along — while *Deep Blue*, slower, deliberate, tattered and battered, reached its proper port!

"He came back to me two days later, the papers howling with derision, but he was very pleased — pleased and determined — because he had found his answer."

"What about all the press laughing at him?" interrupted Uri.

Reb Klonimos made a scornful face and waved both hands in disdain. "Who cared, Reb Uri, who cared? Did Zeideh care? Who mocked him? The world? The papers? Reb Uri, they were all fooled! He laughed ten times louder at them!

"The Captain said to me: 'Reb Klonimos, it's no good. My learning up to now has been no good! Either I learn right, or I'll always race to the wrong port! I want to really understand a *daf* Gemara! I have to learn slower — I have to learn right!'

"And he was good to his word — unbelievable! After that, he put his business affairs into Mr. Bookman's hands, and he sat down and began learning like a true *masmid*, day and night. He woke up at three or four in the morning, and sat over his Gemara till late at night."

"But he seemed so serious, Reb Klonimos," asked Uri. "He changed. He rarely smiled or joked."

"Yes," Reb Klonimos answered. "He was serious, determined — but sad? *Chas v'shalom!* Your Zeideh was the happiest man in the world. He loved learning with all his heart! And you know, he stayed clear minded even to the day he passed away.

"And...today, on his eighth *yahrtzeit*, we are all gathered for your *siyum* in his memory — what more could a person ask for, Reb Uri?"

Reb Klonimos grew silent, looked to Bookman and nodded. The lawyer peered back over his glasses reflectively, and then turned to the gathering. He surveyed everyone silently for a moment, reserving especially long looks for Alexander and Solomon, as though daring them to contest Captain Elijah's will.

Finally, he smiled thinly.

"Ladies and gentlemen, thank you for attending today. It was a very profound morning! Our meeting is now adjourned."

He tapped the bottom of his glass against the table and rose. Everyone stood up. Uri got up quickly. He wanted to be near Chaya. He was still in deep shock and bewilderment. But before he could move a step, Bookman stood alongside him, cornering him.

"Rabbi Schiffman," he murmured, "I know you want to join your wife, but I would like to speak to you privately, for just two minutes."

He led Uri out of the boardroom through a private side door, and Uri found himself in a small hallway. Unlike the elegant, cool, curtained boardroom, strong sunlight poured in through a huge, old-fashioned casement window, and the room was extremely warm.

Edwin Bookman turned to Uri.

"Rabbi Schiffman — Reb Uri — I am so very proud of you! All these years of struggle...I don't know how you did it!"

"G-d helps."

"It was very hard for Rabbi Klonimos and me not to tell you, believe me! We knew all along that the fortune was there for you, that some day you would be wealthy beyond your imagination! I saw how much you struggled! But that was Captain Elijah's instruction — that we not even hint, not even raise an eyebrow that might give away what was in store! If you are angry, I beg your forgiveness."

"G-d forbid!" answered Uri.

For the first time, Uri saw that Bookman was holding a large white envelope.

"Here," said Bookman, handing him the envelope. "This is the final act of Captain Elijah's little drama! It is a letter that your grandfather wrote to you, to be handed to you at this moment. I am sure you will want to read it when you are alone."

Uri accepted the envelope from Bookman without looking at it, but held onto it tightly.

They gazed at each other, the elderly, experienced lawyer, and Uri, the newly minted multi-millionaire.

Bookman cleared his throat self-consciously.

"Rabbi Schiffman, before we part, I would like to ask one final favor."

Uri watched him, waiting.

Bookman hesitated, then murmured.

"Give me your blessing, Rabbi Schiffman."

Uri stared at him in astonishment. "What?"

"Yes," Bookman insisted. "Rabbi Schiffman — Reb Uri — your grandfather Captain Elijah was a truly holy person, and so are you! Please, give me your blessing!"

Uri stood there, dumbfounded.

But they could not stay there much longer in the little hallway. The sun poured in like a furnace; the brilliant noontime sunlight glistened off their wet foreheads like a fountain of gold.

Uri took a deep breath and placed his hand on Bookman's bowed head. Uri closed his eyes, felt the glow of his Zeideh's *neshamah* hovering alongside, and murmured:

"Edwin — Reb Elisha... As my Zeideh Elijah heard the still, soft voice of Hashem amidst the storm, and it awoke his heart to find a great place in Torah, so, too, may all the wisdom and experience you have acquired be transfigured into serving the Almighty with all your heart and soul! May your kindness to me be repaid many times over — to you and all your descendants."

Uri paused, gathered all his being, and recited:

"*Yesimcha Elokim k'Efraim Uchi'Menasheh!*"

Then there was a silence. Bookman raised his head and gazed intensely at Uri. The heat in the tiny room scorched like fire.

"Thank you, Rabbi," he murmured, barely audible.

And then Bookman disappeared quickly through a side door.

FOURTEEN

The family gathered downstairs on the street in front of Uri's car. It was a warm afternoon, and the twins had taken off their jackets, but Yirmiyahu and the *chassanim* remained formally dressed in hats and jackets, and Tova and Dina stood proudly alongside them.

"How long are you staying in Toronto?" Uri asked his *chassanim*.

"We're just going to go out to lunch, and then we're heading back to Walden Pond," Zerach answered.

"Reb Moshe is giving a *shiur klali* tomorrow morning, and we can't miss it."

Uri smiled at his two *chassanim*.

"It means so much to me that you came for the *siyum*. May you merit to make many *siyumim* yourselves!"

Zerach and Avraham smiled, and they shook hands with Uri — a bit quickly, he thought.

"Abba, we have to go now," Tova said.

"Go in good health," Uri said to his sons-in-law to be. "But...maybe you can do me a favor. I want to spend some time alone with Imma.

Can you give my boys a lift up to yeshivah?"

Zerach and Avraham's rented car was only medium sized.

"No problem," said Avraham. "We'll manage."

Uri embraced his two wonderful *chassanim*, and then shook hands formally with his own sons.

"Please G-d," he said, "may you all start and complete many, many Gemaras!"

Again, the boys murmured amen, and shook hands quickly with their father.

Something's the matter, thought Uri, *they are all so – cool.*

Uri and Chaya watched their children as they squeezed into the car. Since the reading of the will this was the first moment that Uri and Chaya were alone.

"Come," he said, "let's go home."

They climbed into the car, and Uri drove into the crowded traffic on University Avenue. Uri had only slept a few hours the night before, and he suddenly felt utterly tired. They drove in silence.

Finally, Uri spoke. "How do you feel, Chaya?"

"I – I don't know," she answered.

Uri didn't pursue it. They drove past the roadworks and headed north to familiar territory.

"Chaya," Uri wondered. "Was it my imagination, or were Zerach and Avraham acting a little...distant?"

"Not distant, Uri," she answered. "They were shy of you."

"Shy? Of me? Why?"

Their eyes met his through the rearview mirror.

"You don't understand, Uri, do you? You are a multi-multi-millionaire now! People are suddenly afraid of you!"

Me, thought Uri, *afraid of me? Ridiculous!*

They drove up towards Bathurst in silence. It was hard for Uri to speak. He was still in deep shock.

You are multi-multi-millionaire! You are very, very rich!

He broke his silence.

"Chaya, I'm very scared! I feel like a great wave has broken over our lives! You heard what he said: boats, docks, the mansion, lakefront lands, accumulated revenues — what are we supposed to do with all of it? All I wanted from Hashem was enough money to pay Tova and Dina's support for seven years and the boys' yeshivah tuition! What are we going to do with all this money? I don't even know what we need it for."

"Uri," Chaya answered, "you're very nervous and tired. Could you just pull up the car somewhere."

They were driving through a quiet street. Uri nosed the car under a shady maple tree and switched off the engine.

"Uri," she said, "you remember eight years ago when they first read Zeideh's will and we thought we were left with almost nothing? We said it was Hashem's will, and that we would accept it, and live with it. Zeideh's will seemed so unfair at that time! Alexander got the house, Solomon got the boat, and you received almost worthless stock! Yet, we thanked Hashem for what He gave us, and we moved on — because we had *emunah* that everything is from Him, and there was a purpose! So now, we have a new situation. We are suddenly unbelievably rich! It's like a dream! But it's real! Hashem has a purpose in that also!

"Oh, Uri! What *tzedakah* we will be able to do! How many yeshivahs and suffering people we will be able to help! How much *ma'aser* we can earn and distribute, and how much more *hachnasas orchim* we will be able to afford...

"Uri, listen! We inherited the money, the money didn't inherit us! We are its master! It does not order us around — we order the money about!"

"It's not even our money," Uri said.

"It's Hashem's money, Uri! It was His, it is His, it will always be His! He put us in charge, as overseers, and we must never let the money dictate to us! We will live like we always lived —"

"I don't want a bigger house —"

"You will learn like you always learned —"

"I want to keep my *shiurim*, and my students at forty dollars an hour —"

"And we will be quiet about our wealth, and private, and modest!"

"Okay!" Uri answered cheerfully. "Okay, Rebbetzin! If that's the case...maybe we can live with our millions!"

Chaya smiled. "Uri, you're overtired. Overtired and overstimulated. Let's go home!"

Uri restarted the car and drove back onto the street. He took a deep, exhausted breath. He was utterly drained.

Baruch Hashem, he whispered over and over to himself, *Baruch Hashem* that I have a wife like Chaya!

Uri collapsed into the chair of the study. He was so completely exhausted. He sat back and pulled the *shtender* against his chest. The late August day was warm and muggy, and even the air-conditioning working full blast couldn't remove the heaviness. Uri laid his hat on the desk, pulled out two envelopes from his jacket, and let the jacket slip behind him on the chair. One envelope was from the boys, with their donation of four hundred dollars. He stared at the tattered envelope, with its green bills peering out from the cracks.

He could never forget — these bills were the *yeish mei'yeish* before Zeideh's final will! He kissed the envelope lovingly and laid it on the desk. Then, it was Zeideh's turn — the white envelope.

He laid it on the *shtender*. Before he opened it he played a final game with his grandfather— could he preempt Zeideh? What was in the letter? What could he write to him from more than eight years ago? Probably *mussar*: *mussar* not to neglect the fortune he had been given, to look after it wisely, and then — goodbye.

He needed something to open the envelope neatly, without demolishing it completely. He searched his desk, and then noticed for the first time that Yirmiyahu had returned the gold pen to him. They had finished *Shas* together, and that was it — it was his again. Uri lifted the pen and pressed it close to his lips. He held it all in his hands now — Zeideh's letter, Zeideh's pen, Zeideh's fortune. But the pen was too blunt an instrument to press under the flap. He reached into his pocket and retrieved a key. Carefully, he slipped the edge of the key under the flap and slit it open across the top. The paper was dry and cut like straw.

And the answer is…

Uri closed his eyes, and dropped his head into his hands. Did one say a *l'sheim yichud* before reading such a letter? He felt as though he should. He blinked himself awake and extracted the long, pristine, white inner envelope. He laid the outer envelope on the desk and placed the sealed second envelope on his *shtender*. It looked as perfect as if it had been sealed today. He turned it over. On the back was pasted a thin, long, yellow note.

> *Dear Eerie:*
>
> *I am sure that you are very anxious to read this letter. But I ask you for a final favor – please wait!*
>
> *I am taking a long guess that you will be reading this between two and three o'clock in the afternoon –*

Uri looked up. It was two twenty-five p.m. *How did Zeideh do that?* he wondered.

> *but this is not when I want you to read my letter. If you love me, Eerie, please wait to read it at daybreak, just as the day is growing light before your eyes. Dawn is my favorite time, when everything is still and holy, and Heavenly joy abounds. That was when I learned the sweetest and clearest, and felt so close to G-d!*
>
> *Please, Eerie, just a few more hours!*
> *Love, your Zeideh!*

Uri shook his head. Zeideh was Zeideh to the last! Even eight years after he was gone, he still ran things his way. And yet, it was also comforting, it was as though he was still alive, still close…

There was no question – he would honor Zeideh's wish. He sat there, his eyes drooping from tiredness and the oppressive heat, yet unable to find rest. He tapped the gold pen reflectively against Zeideh's note. A profound question began seeping into his head, amorphous and undefined at first, and then it took shape and coalesced like a cloud into a great question mark.

He tapped the pen on the words:

Dear Eerie... Dear Eerie...

Over and over the pen tapped, demanding an answer, like Moshe banging against the stones for water.

So, Zeideh! If you believed so much in the power of names, why didn't you call me by my proper name, Uri?

Did you not remember — my name is Uri, not Eerie? Why were you so careless, even to this last letter?

But Uri could tap all day, and no answer flowed. Zeideh was Zeideh, and that was that!

Despite his exhaustion, Uri did not sleep that whole afternoon. As the day wore on, his shock wore off. He slowly came to grips with his new reality: he was no longer a poor man, struggling to support his children. He was now very, very rich. Slowly but surely, he grew into the news, into his fortune. As Uri became accustomed to his new situation, so the whole day became one great recital of praise and thanksgiving to the Almighty. He could not stop murmuring "*Baruch Hashem, baruch Hashem!*" The wheel of wealth had stopped at his door, and as long as Hashem wanted, he would do his best to guard it and use it for good.

Despite his tiredness, he learned strongly the whole afternoon. He was determined to start *Shas* all over again, but slower, deeper, to take whatever time it took to do *chazarah*, to seek out the commentaries, to extract the meaning of each line of Gemara and *Rashi* until he really — really — understood clearly. He went to shul that evening, davened *minchah* for Zeideh's *yahrtzeit*, and learned *mishnayos* between *minchah* and *ma'ariv*. He was the same Uri. No one saw a difference, and no one even guessed at his incredible good fortune.

He returned home right after *ma'ariv*. His exhaustion finally caught up with him. He murmured a quick goodnight to Chaya and the girls, who were busy with the final wedding plans, and went straight to bed.

He set his clock for four thirty, tried to read a little, but in a minute descended into a deep sleep.

⛵ ⛵ ⛵

In the undulating wave of deep sleep and dreams, Uri walked along a long country road. Where it came from and where it led he had no idea. It wound all about, up and down in waving hills, but why he was on it, he had no idea. But he marched ahead, hoping he would find its purpose.

But it was a road without end, past trees and farms and quiet ponds *Where am I? Why am I here?* He had no idea. And it was such a silent place: no people, no birds singing, no crickets chirping, or frogs croaking.

It is so still here, he thought, *and I am so lonely! If I could hear just one sound!*

Suddenly, he stopped to listen, for a sound was coming his way. It was very distant, but he could tell that the sound was very loud, quickly drawing closer his way. But there was no time to stop. He marched along, even as the sound grew ever more raucous. He stopped and listened — he recognized the sound! It was the honking of geese as they migrated across the skies. Their loud honking escalated into a huge cry, like a wave descending upon him, and he hastened his step to outrun them.

Are they flying north or flying south, he wondered.

But there was no time to wait, for he had to march quickly wherever the road led! Soon the flock was straight overhead, their raucous honks and screeches deafening! He lifted his eyes, and above him flew a huge V-shaped formation, like a giant arrowhead pointing across the blue morning sky. The geese passed right overhead, and as they screeched and honked, Uri heard them call his name:

Eerie! Eerie!

Eerie! Eerie!

The great arrowhead was pointing neither north nor south, but eastward to the sea, and still the great flock called down to him:

Eerie, Eerie, Shir Dabeiri!

Uri gazed at the beautiful vision and smiled with delight. He ran off the endless road that led nowhere and hurried to follow them. But they were too swift, too high — for already they were well over the sea.

But even from a far distance, he still heard their call:

Eerie! Eerie! Eerie! Follow us!

Uri sat up with a start.

It sounded like a bomb was going off outside!

He listened. It wasn't a bomb, but a tremendous clap of thunder. The heat had finally broken, and torrents of rain fell outside. He checked his clock — the alarm was set to go off in just five minutes. The Almighty Himself had woken him this morning! He quickly cancelled the alarm and climbed out of bed.

Uri washed his hands and recited the blessings. It was still early. First dawn would not come for another twenty minutes, and he wanted to fulfill his Zeideh's wishes exactly. He entered his study and turned on the lamp. Outside, the rain fell noisily, but it was a pleasant sound — the oppressive heat was finally breaking. But even so, his study felt close.

He stood at the *shtender* and opened his battered *Tehillim*. He looked at the clock: still fifteen minutes to *amud hashachar*. Uri sighed deeply. He suddenly felt very lonely. For three years he had studied with Yirmiyahu every morning. Now it was over. Yirmiyahu had stayed in yeshivah last night, and he was busy with his preparations for flying to Eretz Yisrael right after the weddings. There was no more problem of money...but how he would miss him! How he would miss gazing into his earnest, deep blue eyes, and seeing such *kedushah* and love there.

He was a multi-millionaire now, but all his money could not replace learning with his son every morning!

Uri opened his *Tehillim*. Zeideh's envelope lay on the desk, waiting for him. It had waited eight years, now it would have to wait eight minutes more. He *shuckle*d gently and read his daily section. The dawn grew nigh, and Uri finished his reading. He kissed the *Tehillim*, laid it back on his desk, and took up the envelope. He laid it on his *shtender*. His hands trembled. Suddenly, the room felt oppressively warm. Outside, the rain still fell loudly, but there was a protective eavesdrop outside his window. He twisted open the narrow window and a rush of fresh air filled the room. Uri breathed in deeply. Through his window he could see beyond the next house towards the east. The clock announced dawn. But the rain fell like a heavy curtain, and it was still dark as night.

But it was dawn.

Uri took a small penknife and slit open the top of the envelope, careful not to damage the precious contents inside. He reached in for the letter when he heard a tiny noise at the window.

He looked up, and smiled.

"*Tzafra tava*, little *tzipor*," he called, "where did you come from?"

A little cardinal, soaking wet from the deluge outside, sought refuge in his windowsill.

Uri was delighted at his visitor.

"Make yourself at home," he said quietly, not to scare off the bird. The little cardinal settled comfortably, and Uri returned to the letter.

Refreshed by the clear morning air pouring in through the window, Uri quickly unfolded Zeideh's pristine white sheets, and laid them on the *shtender*. He recognized immediately that the script was written with the same gold pen that he and Yirmiyahu had used in their learning. He glanced at the pen on his desk, at Zeideh's own handwriting that lay before him, and he felt Zeideh's presence powerfully, as though he was watching him.

He began reading.

> *My beloved grandson, Uri!*
>
> *If you have carried out my wishes, then you are reading this at dawn, and soon the sun will burst forth to a fresh day. This is the time when Hashem's mercy is greatest, when the day is still pure and innocent! That is why I wanted you read these few words now.*

How much I loved you, Uri, how I was proud of you! You have no idea! Your learning, your idealism, your kind neshamah! May every blessing of Hashem descend upon you and your family!

Uri! Now I must explain why I did what I did, and ask forgiveness if you suffered because of it.

Uri, believe me! The money I bequeathed on you, Deep Blue and all its revenues, which must be worth a huge fortune now — you would have received it whether you fulfilled my wishes to learn all Shas or not! But if you are reading this letter, it means you kept your loyalty to me! You are reading this only if you completed all of the Talmud for the tikkun of my soul, and there is hope that my neshamah will yet rise to its true Heavenly place.

So, I beg your forgiveness. I made you struggle for eight years. Why? I so much loved you, Uri — so why did I not just give you the money, and let you enjoy? Because that would have meant that you were eating nahama d'chisufa, bread of humiliation, enjoying wealth that you did nothing to earn — except for an accident of birth.

But since you are reading this letter, baruch Hashem, it means that you learned day and night, year after year, when you were tired and when you were awake, when you felt good and when you were sick. You learned out of love of Torah — and out of loyalty.

Now this is a fortune that you have earned!

Your bread is a bread of kavod, bread earned by the sweat of your brow! It is bread from Hashem's table — not mine.

And now, Uri, the hardest part!

I must explain to you why I made you endure another of your Zeideh's whims.

Uri, I will tell it the way it is... If you will be angry with me for the rest of your years, I am sorry, but I will now reveal to you the truth!

Uri, I knew your name! I did! I do!

Your name is Uri.

But I called you Eerie! Do you know why?

Because, Eerie, I wasn't speaking to you!

You are Uri – but I was speaking to Eerie, my city! When I stared into your pure, pure, blue eyes, I did not see you, but I saw the blue skies of Yerushalayim! I saw a holy spark of intense yearning for Eretz Yisrael, for the holy city, for the Mikdash! You have a nitzotz of Yerushalayim burning in your soul, Eerie!

When I called "Eerie, Eerie," I was not calling to you! I was calling out to the holiness of Yerushalayim that shone in your eyes! But, perhaps, I missed the mark? Perhaps the beam in your eye came not from you, but from your children? Perhaps I saw the spark of Yirmiyahu in you, longing for Zion!

Meanwhile, you suffered mockery from that name, Eerie. I beg you to forgive me... But Uri, Uri, where are you now? Are you dwelling on the mountaintops of Judea, are you learning Torah in the forested valleys of the Galil? Uri, Uri, are you longing, yearning for the Mikdash with all your heart?

Uri laid down the letter. His eyes grew misty. Oh, Zeideh! He dried his eyes across his sleeve. He looked out the window, and he saw that the clouds were blowing away. The downpour had ended, and the first pink streaks of dawn broke forth. The cardinal stirred and ruffled its wings to dry them. The little bird began chirping.

Uri lifted the letter:

> *And so, my beloved Uri, this letter comes to end. You now go your way, and I – to my portion in the Next World. But who knows where that will be?*
>
> *When my soul stands before the Heavenly Court and they say to me: "Eliyahu ben Elazar! You are not yet worthy of Gan Eden, nor do you deserve Gehinnom! You did not complete your mission in life, and you must go back and mend your soul – how do you wish to go back?"*
>
> *I shall answer: "O Heavenly Judges! Please, let me return as a little songbird! I shall perch on every branch and bough and sing praises to Hashem! I shall sing of His infinite greatness and His kindness, and I shall sing of Zion and Jerusalem and Mashiach!"*
>
> *So, Uri, this is our goodbye! Please don't forget me, please say Tehillim for me – please listen for my joyous song!*
>
> *Shalom, dear Uri!*
> *Shalom, dear Eerie!*
>
> *Zeideh Elijah*

Uri laid the letter on his *shtender*. Outside, the clouds had dispersed, and bright sunlight illuminated the heavens. The little cardinal waved its wings, lifted its head, and began whistling joyously.

Morning had come!

Uri watched the bird closely, expecting it to fly off. But the bird just hopped back and forth nervously, like a *mispallel* waiting for *shacharis* to begin.

"Are you waiting for me?" Uri asked softly.

Uri took the *Tehillim* from his desk and laid it back on the *shtender* over Zeideh's letter.

"Come, little bird," he said, "we will daven together!"

He turned to chapter eighty-four, gazed up into the pure skies, and began:

"*Mah yedidos mishkenosecha, Hashem Tzevakos!*

"How beloved are Your dwelling places, O Hashem of Legions!"

"Tweet, tweet, tweet," sang the bird.

"*Nichsefah v'gam kalsah nafshi l'chatzros Hashem,*

"*Libi u'vesari yeranenu el Keil chai!*

"My soul yearns, it pines, for the courtyards of Hashem; my heart and my flesh pray fervently to the Living G-d!"

"Chirp! Chirp! Chirp!" answered the cardinal joyously.

"*Gam tzipor matzah bayis, u'dror kein lah asher shasah efrocheha es mizbechosecha, Hashem Tzevakos, malki veilokei!*

"Even the bird finds its home, and the free bird her nest where she laid her young... Oh, to be at Your altars, Hashem, Master of Legions, my King and my G-d!"

The bird stretched its little wings high and sang Uri's words with all its heart, with all its soul, with all its Lilliputian might — so strongly that Uri feared it might harm itself.

He stepped to the window and approached the little cardinal, who still stood at the ledge, whistling and chirping.

"*Tzipor,*" he whispered, "it is time for you to fly home! You have achieved your *tikkun*! You are complete! You are complete!"

Uri clapped his hands and commanded:

"Little bird, fly home!"

In a flash, the cardinal flapped its wings and sped off eastward. Uri followed its flight until it disappeared behind the next house. He returned to his *shtender* and closed his *Tehillim*. He walked to the bookshelf, and reached for Zeideh's Gemara *Berachos*.

Uri laid the magnificent volume on his *shtender* and opened to *daf beis*. He closed his eyes, slowly began swaying, and whispered:

"Oh, fly to Yerushalayim, little bird, for I shall soon meet you there!

You will fly on crimson wings, and I shall soar on crimson words of fire!"

He leaned over the Gemara, pressed Zeideh's pen against the page and, in a voice that cleaved shafts of fire, he cried out for the whole world to hear:

"*Mei'eimasai!*"